THE NABATEAN SECRET

JC RYAN

BOOKS

By JC Ryan

Carter Devereux Mystery Thriller Series

Nothing New Under The Sun

The Wolves Of Freydis

The Alboran Codex

The Nabatean Secret

The Labyrinth of Minos

Vinci Books

vinci-books.com

Published by Vinci Books Ltd in 2025

1

Copyright © JC Ryan 2017

The author has asserted their moral right to be identified as the author of this work in accordance with the Copyright, Designs and Patents Act 1988. This work is a work of fiction. Names, characters, places and incidents are the product of the author's imagination or are used fictitiously. Any resemblance to actual persons, living or dead, places and incidents is entirely coincidental.

All rights reserved. No part of this publication may be copied, reproduced, distributed, stored in any retrieval system, or transmitted in any form or by any means, including photocopying, recording, or other electronic or mechanical methods, nor used as a source for any form of machine learning including AI datasets, without the prior written permission of the publisher.

The publisher and the author have made every effort to obtain permissions for any third party material used in this book and to comply with copyright law. Any queries in this respect should be brought to the attention of the publisher and any omissions will be corrected in future editions.

A CIP catalogue record for this book is available from the British Library.

Paperback ISBN: 9781036703301

Printed and bound in Great Britain by Clays Ltd, Elcograf S.p.A.

Prologue

US Army Garrison Patch Barracks, near Stuttgart, Germany, 2 a.m., January 11

Sentries at the Main Gate of Patch Barracks had turned away the last of the local Fasching revelers an hour or so before, laughingly joking with them that the Barracks were too quiet for their parties. A few soldiers, somewhat worse for wear after joining the locals for the opening night of Germany's "Fifth Season", straggled in around midnight. They were cheerfully waved through the gate by the envious guards, who had pulled duty that night and didn't get to celebrate.

Since then, the night had been still, only the night sounds typical of the region breaking the silence. The cell and radio tower behind the thick trees was lit by an eerie glow from the remains of the Fasching bonfire a few miles away. It would be six long hours until sunrise and their relief.

The peace of the night lulled them to silence.

Behind them, an eerie blue-white blinding flash bloomed.

No sooner had it lit the night sky than the first sentry opened his mouth to ask, "What was that?"

But the words never left his lips—before he'd even formed them, his lips, along with the rest of him, vanished. Had his mate not been meeting the same fate at the same time, he would have been shocked to see his comrade in arms evaporate into nihility.

Every living being, structure, and object within an 800-yard radius of the epicenter disappeared as if he, she, or it had never been there.

No one in the circumference of the blast zone survived to describe the beauty of the majestic, but fatal, blue-white flash. A few souls, lucky enough to be farther away, saw glimpses of it through the surrounding trees.

No one knew what it was.

The next person to arrive at the Main Gate of Patch Barracks found, much to his drunken confusion, nothing.

No gate, no trees, no cell tower. No barracks. No buildings. No guards.

Only emptiness.

Not finding the Main Gate where he was sure it must be, the soldier sat down on the ground. Alcohol and rationality have never been good stablemates.

His inebriated brain could not handle the duel, and mercifully, he passed out. He never heard the screams of pain and horror from the injured survivors far enough from the epicenter and fortunate enough to escape obliteration.

Later, first responders approached with caution, finding the drunk soldier passed out where the gate should have been and the void beyond, which had always been occupied by buildings.

They moved into the base to search for survivors. They found few, most of them critically injured and out of their minds with shock and confusion.

Everyone capable of speaking asked the rescuers the question the rescuers had wanted to ask the survivors: What happened?

Chapter One

DAMN YOU, CARTER DEVEREUX!

18 Months Previously; 24 Hours After the Attack on Freydís

Graziella Marie Nabati paced the room, the very picture of an avenging angel. Most men would have quailed at her countenance, though she was coldly beautiful—like an iceberg. The man in the room with her was safe, however. Her son, Mathieu Nabati, was as angry as she, and in any case was only a hologram.

Graziella was in her mountain hideout high in the Andes in Peru, where she took up residence when the existence of the Council of the Covenant of Nabatea was discovered by the CIA. Her luxurious, high-tech lodging was close to the Incan citadel, Machu Picchu, where she felt as at home as she'd felt in her house above the ancient catacombs of Paris.

Mathieu, in contrast, was in his own hideout in a remote area of the Ural Mountains in the western part of Russia. His dwelling boasted the latest in quantum computing and communications equipment possible. Only his mother knew where he was and how to reach him.

"What is our situation?" Graziella managed to whisper instead of growl.

"Unfortunately, *maman*," he answered, "it was another miserable failure. Nine of the sixteen operatives are dead, and the rest have been captured, amongst them one wounded. They are in CIA custody and have been transferred to America.

"I have just learned they are trying to make a deal. No extradition to Russia in exchange for their cooperation. In other words, they are singing like the proverbial canaries, and they are beyond our reach. Only our care in putting several layers of go-betweens in place has kept us safe so far. But soon someone will peel away those layers.

"As you know, the leader of the task force is aware of who hired him. Once he gives up the Director, we are exposed. If he has not done so already."

"You know what to do," she stated. It never needed to be spelled out between them. As the primary guardians of the secrecy of the Council of the Covenant of Nabatea, they were of one mind. That secrecy was paramount. In its service, everyone except them was expendable.

"Of course. I'll see to it immediately."

Graziella nodded graciously. She trusted her son implicitly and with good reason. The last layer of go-between was one of the Council, but all councilors understood their position.

Peter Nikolaev, the Director of the Federal Security Service (FSB) of Russia, was about to suffer a fatal incident.

Nikolaev was a fit and vital man of fifty-seven years, as well as an important government official. His death would cause repercussions, no matter how it occurred. However, a violent death, even an auto accident, would raise more questions than a natural one. Mathieu set his mind to arrange the perfect assassination.

His first task was to locate Nikolaev.

After discreet inquiries, he learned that the Director had taken a holiday and was currently skiing the forty miles of groomed slopes located within the Rosa Khutar ski resort, site of the XXII Winter Olympics.

Mathieu, an expert skier, immediately recognized the opportunity to take care of the matter himself, which would avoid involving yet another person who would then have to be eliminated in an escalating series of incidents.

He notified his mother that he would be taking a small ski-holiday and that everything would be fine by the time he returned.

Twelve hours later, he inconspicuously followed Nikolaev as he made his way to one of the high-speed chairlifts and headed for the Ozernaya slope.

Once more, Nikolaev was making it easy for Mathieu.

Ozernaya was a perfect slope for speedy carving. Nikolaev exited the lift and prepared for his run. Mathieu was a few chairs behind him. When he got off the lift, rather than carving the slope like Nikolaev, he made his run in a straight line, easily overtaking his target. With no one to witness it and ignoring Nikolaev's indignant shout when they approached a line of trees at a speed of close to seventy miles an hour, Mathieu shouldered him ever so slightly—enough to steer Nikolaev straight into the trees lining the run. There was no time and no room for Nikolaev to counteract—the collision with one of the trees ended Nikolaev's life abruptly.

Travelling at thirty-three feet per second, Mathieu was almost ten yards away by the time Nikolaev met with the tree. He had no reason to check that Nikolaev was indeed dead. Even if he had survived the collision, he wouldn't survive for long in the extreme temperature. Other skiers would overrun his tracks and obscure the reason for Nikolaev's accident.

It was the perfect crime.

Mathieu was on his way back to his hideout by the time Nikolaev's body was discovered. When he arrived and contacted his mother, he found her watching news coverage of the "tragedy."

Tears streamed down her face for the loss of another noble Nabatean from their bloodline.

"Well done, my son." She sighed. "Our secret has been sealed again."

"Thank you, *maman*. I believe our immediate problem has been solved."

"True, but we have another, and it will not be so easily dismissed," Graziella said. "Our operatives were captured with the four devices we gave them to defeat the electronic defenses of that accursed Freydís. It won't be long before US security forces have reverse-engineered it, and then our advantage is gone."

"One problem at a time, *maman*. I agree, it is a setback, but there is little or nothing we can do about it. At least it can't expose the identities of the rest of the Councilors."

She nodded slowly. It was a relief.

Nevertheless, *Damn you, Carter Devereux!*

Chapter Two

IN IT FOR LIFE

In an undisclosed location, the captured Spetsnaz operatives from the Freydís raid were being interrogated. Tales of rendition and enhanced interrogation techniques frightened them, though no such methods were being used—neither sanctioned by President Samuel Houston Grant's administration.

Nevertheless, they refused to give up information, trying to negotiate terms to keep them out of the hands of the Russian government.

Indeed, the interrogators and the captives had reached the point of playing penny-ante poker together while the captives' request for asylum was considered.

Among other things, urgent messages were flying through secure channels regarding the Devereuxs' and the Canadian government's willingness to drop trespassing, reckless endangerment, and other, more serious, charges.

Only if so could the US offer protection to the Spetsnaz operatives in the form of the promise they'd be held in American prisons.

Every last man of them agreed an American prison was a cakewalk compared to what they'd face in Russia. Or rather, not *face*. There, the likelihood was a bullet in the back of the head. An American prison sentence could even come with the possibility of parole and being free men someday.

Even then, the request would also have to clear the highest levels of government.

However, interrogators convinced the operatives that before any consideration whatsoever could move forward, their case could be strengthened by a practical demonstration of their willingness to cooperate. One such gesture would be for them to demonstrate how the strange devices that defeated Freydís's electronic surveillance worked.

CIA technicians were on standby to immediately reverse engineer the devices. Then they'd upgrade every vulnerable technology.

Eager to demonstrate their sincerity, the Spetsnaz operatives were just as eager to demonstrate the devices as the technicians were to receive the information.

Before the outcome of the asylum request had even been determined, the most important answer the Spetsnaz squad leader could give, who gave them their orders, had been rendered moot. Peter Nikolaev was dead, and with him the chain of information that could lead to the Nabateans and their group.

The Secretary of the Treasury of the United States, Jason Sullivan, took a secure call from Peru a week after the death of his fellow Councilor.

"Jason, I trust you are well," purred Graziella.

Sweat started to pearl on his forehead as he fought to control his voice. A personal call from the chairwoman of the Council of the Covenant of Nabatea was a rarity—used only in cases of extreme importance.

"Certainly, Graziella. Never better." It was a lie he hoped he could pull off. "To what do I owe the pleasure? Have you and the rest of the Council decided on my request to relinquish my office?"

"Yes, we have. That's the reason for my call. I wanted to tell you in person, the request is denied."

Sullivan swallowed to clear his throat of the sudden dryness. Graziella's voice sounded as if it originated from the Arctic. The words "tell you in person" had a much deeper meaning—it was a warning, not a courtesy.

"But..." he began. Mopping his forehead with a previously pristine linen handkerchief, Sullivan stopped himself just in time. It wouldn't do to voice his suspicion that Peter Nikolaev's death wasn't a simple accident, nor that he feared the same fate if the captured Spetsnaz squad's information led to his exposure.

Speaking smoothly, as if no "but" was on the table, Graziella continued. "You are our most valuable asset inside the US government. You *will* uphold your oath."

She might as well have added the missing parts of that sentence— "or you will be eliminated", and the second part, "no one is irreplaceable."

"Of course," he replied obediently. Every councilor knew that once they took the oath, there was no turning back. They were "in it" for life. Breaking the oath meant life would become very short.

"Good." Graziella disconnected without further niceties.

Jason Sullivan sat abruptly in his favorite chair. The

phrase "stuck between a rock and a hard place" had never been more appropriate than now.

Chapter Three

A MOST UNUSUAL NIGHT

Washington D.C., January 10, 8:00 p.m.

Kelly White had a moment's reflection that she was on a most unusual date before the man in question flashed her a smile that promised a most unusual night to come.

Russell McCormick, Assistant Director of the Counterintelligence Division of the FBI, handsome, a young-looking fifty-year-old, and thank God divorced, was a most unusual man. In fact, something could actually come of this, their third date in two weeks. Russell was apparently unintimidated by her reputation.

Kelly knew she was not unattractive. At forty-five, she was fit but still curvy. At five feet ten inches, she looked average men in the eye, and most who got close enough to know her feared her. Her career as one of the top Counterintelligence Special Agents in the US Army Intelligence and Security Command, INSCOM, was part of the problem. A no-nonsense, professional, married-to-my-job kind of woman, her demeanor overcame the attraction most men felt, often on the first date.

That's if it even got to a first date.

Kelly's ambition was to be the first woman in charge of INSCOM. She hoped when it happened it would compensate her for the sacrifice of a romantic relationship and family. But now that Russell was in the picture, maybe she could have both.

Later, she'd wonder if the thought itself jinxed her.

No sooner had the pleasant thoughts crossed her mind than two CI agents she didn't know flanked her and ushered her away without a word of explanation. She could only cast a glance behind her and give an apologetic shrug at her date. His mouth open in an unspoken, almost painful-looking protest, he stared after her.

Her boss, Terrance Ham, met her on the tarmac beside a Gulfstream G280 whose engines were already warming up. An aide handed her a small bag, remarking, "Your clothing, ma'am."

"Terry, what's this?" she asked. The same question had received no response from the CI agents who transported her there. But Ham answered.

"It's all on this flash drive. Your team members are already aboard. You were the last we tracked down. We're already behind schedule, so get your briefing from the information on the drive and then brief your team. I'll get back to you with more details as soon as I have any.

"Oh, by the way, you're on your way to Germany. Good luck."

With that, he turned away, and Kelly squared her shoulders. She had made a name for herself as a Counterintelligence Special Agent and was tenacious when working on an assignment. She was good at her job and got results.

I can handle this.

Counterintelligence Special Agents, aka CI's, were trained to conduct undercover counterintelligence activities to assess, counteract, take advantage of, and neutralize adversarial threats to the United States Army and US Department of Defense.

Kelly, like the rest of her team, carried a badge and a gun, confirming her status as a federal law enforcement officer. She had arrest powers and jurisdiction in the investigation of national security crimes, including treason, spying, espionage, sedition, subversion, sabotage, and international terrorism.

A brief discussion of their destination revealed the current assignment to be one of the latter, or so she assumed. How else could an entire Army base disappear into thin air? Unbelievable. If she hadn't been on a plane bound for Stuttgart, she'd have considered it a hoax.

Chapter Four

AN INTERESTING ASSIGNMENT

Each of Kelly's seven team members had a different story about what they were doing when they were hustled away on this mission. For the first hour or so of the flight, while they were waiting for Kelly to study the brief, they lightheartedly exchanged those stories. One or two had tales a bit too embarrassing to let out all the details but enough to generate a few rounds of raucous laughter and razzing.

Kelly had ignored the party atmosphere, but the expression on her face eventually caught the attention of her team members. Now they had gone quiet and were staring at her, waiting for her to tell them what was going on.

She became aware of the silence, looked up, and found them all gazing at her. She schooled her face to professional neutrality and cleared her throat.

"Okay, here it is. Please save your questions. There was an incident at Patch Barracks, USAG Stuttgart, Germany, at about 1 a.m. Zulu. Some kind of explosion. First reports are it's ugly, hundreds of people dead, buildings turned into rubble, and all electronics rendered inoperable, fried. We're to get the details on site.

"Soldiers from the Panzer Kaserne, Kelley Barracks, Robinson Barracks, and Stuttgart Army Airfield were called in to cordon the place off and keep it locked down—no media is allowed near the place.

"Casualties were medevaced to Landstuhl Regional Medical Center in Landstuhl, Rhineland-Palatinate, Germany. It's the largest military hospital outside the United States. During the Iraq and Afghanistan wars, it served as the nearest treatment center for wounded soldiers coming from the frontlines. It also serves US military personnel stationed in the European Union as well as their family members."

She shrugged. "As much as I would like to tell you more than that, I can't. There *is* nothing more. All I have here is history and background about the base and German traditions. You're welcome to copy it over to your laptops and read it. I hope Terrance will have more information for us before we land." She held her secured satellite phone up.

Shocked into solemn silence, each team member produced a thumb drive and handed it to her. Within a few minutes, the cabin was quiet again, everyone reading.

A lot of questions and "what ifs" were running through Kelly's mind. *Incident or accident? Deliberate? Terrorist attack?*

Patch Barracks was home to units critical to national security—US European Command (EUCOM), the Department of Defense Unified Combatant Command for Europe and Northern Asia, Special Operations Command, Europe (SOCEUR), which commands US Special Operations Forces units in Europe, Defense Information Systems Agency, and NSA/CSS Representative Europe office (NCEUR).

A terrorist strike against Patch Barracks would not just be a statement. It would seriously hurt US Military operations in Europe and harm their European special operations command and information systems.

Furthermore, it would send a message to the US—*we can attack you anywhere, even your military installations.*

That didn't even take into account the tragedy of the lives lost. Kelly brought her racing thoughts under control. *Don't borrow trouble. Wait until you have the facts, all the facts, and nothing but the facts.*

It was a long flight to Stuttgart. Eight hours. To occupy her mind with something other than useless conjecture, more out of frustration about the lack of information than interest, she re-opened the flash drive and selected one of the background files, named *Germany's Fifth Season*.

Fasching? Is that how it's pronounced? Jeez, they let off steam for four months? That's a lot of steam. Right up until Lent. Hmmm. Kelly read the first few paragraphs and then paused to think. *Silly season—all sorts of "foolish" events.* The incident took place on January 11, just four days after the official start of this Fasching season—*that would be the ideal time for an attack. Foolish indeed—an attack on an American military installation.*

She silently catalogued the list of such attacks. *Thirteen attacks on US embassies and sixty deaths during the presidency of George W. Bush alone. Another nine during Barack Obama's presidency, including Benghazi, Libya, in total causing thirty-nine more deaths.*

A favorite pastime for terrorists, it seems.

Except this one was not an embassy or consulate. It was a military base. *Well, there's precedent there, too. Yes, there have been horrific attacks.* Ft. Dix, Ft. Hood, and the Washington, D.C., naval yard sprang to her mind.

Stop thinking about it, she commanded herself. *No lone*

gunman here, and none of those ever wiped out an entire base, buildings and all.

It was futile to guess. She'd know soon enough.

She closed her eyes, intending to sleep. Within seconds, her satellite phone rang.

"Terrance. What do you have?" The man on the other end of the phone, despite being her commanding officer, was also a good friend. Her use of his formal first name rather than the shortened "Terry" she usually called him would alert him to her stress. Too late now, though. The word was already out of her mouth.

"Kelly, are you okay?"

"I'm fine. Anxious to be on the ground and get to the bottom of this." She winced again at her clipped tone. *Chill. He's going to pull you off the mission if you don't get yourself under control.*

"About that. I have a bit more, and you aren't going to like it. Preliminary intel says it wasn't a normal explosion. Not like one caused by military or commercial explosives, that is."

"So, we can rule out accidental?" she interjected.

"I'd say so. This was something weird. It flattened a large part of the most important buildings on the base. So far, the body count is three-hundred and fifty, with scores more injured.

"But here's the thing. It fried every electronic device within a two-mile radius."

"EMP, electromagnetic pulse?"

"Likely. But of unknown origin. That's up to you and your team to determine. Investigators already on scene report they can't get much that's useful out of the survivors. They all say they saw a bright, blue-white light—one blinding flash.

"Some are describing it as alien, as in extraterrestrial, except it didn't come from the sky—it originated from the ground level upwards. Then the explosion and the noise when the buildings collapsed. And then people started screaming."

Kelly listened without interruption, though she jerked in surprise and snorted when her very practical boss said "extraterrestrial." She expected to hear more, so when he stopped, she didn't immediately answer. After several seconds, he asked if she was still on the line.

"Oh, yes, I am. Did you say extraterrestrial?" She fought to keep the skepticism out of her voice and failed to keep it low. Some of her nearby team members looked up in surprise. She shook her head at them.

"Just an expression, Kelly. That's what the eyewitnesses are saying."

"Should be an interesting assignment," she said dryly. "Hopefully not in the Chinese sense of the word."

He chuckled. "Let's hope not"

"We'll do our best, Terry."

"You're the best there is, Kelly. I have full confidence you'll have the answer in record time. I'll keep you posted. On site, everyone has orders to report to you. You'll keep me informed."

"Of course, I will."

With that, Ham broke the connection, and Kelly was left to explain what she'd learned to the others.

Chapter Five

RUMINATING IN A SPA

Mykonos Island, Greece, January 11

Mackenzie was relaxing with her mother in a luxury spa attached to the hotel where they were staying on the idyllic Mykonos Island in Greece. It was one of several stops on their leisurely European tour. The men had taken the children on an excursion, but Mackenzie had pleaded exhaustion, and like the devoted husband he was, Carter had arranged the mother-daughter day, complete with spa, massage, manicure, and all.

So much had happened since she and Carter had returned from their first Alboran expedition. The translation of the plates of the Codex they'd retrieved on that expedition were the highest priority, followed closely by the debriefings they were subjected to, which delayed their return to Freydís.

At first, Carter had been required to travel to D.C. far more often than he wanted—often weekly or even more. Tired of the constant disruptions to the translation work and family life, he arranged to go just once a month, for five days at a time.

He was also required to travel to the Alboran site on a regular basis, where a properly equipped and staffed research ship was located, with a Navy destroyer patrolling nearby.

Mackenzie wanted to accompany him on the Alboran site trips, to visit with her beloved dolphins and introduce her children to the fascinating creatures. It was also convenient for them to take short breaks in Europe, traveling to Switzerland, France, Italy—everywhere they could enjoy the rich European history and educate the children. Mackenzie hadn't seen much of Europe previously, and Carter loved to show her his favorite cultural sights.

They both liked to visit the Alboran site, but it was an arduous journey every time, requiring they get to a major city, either Quebec City or Montreal, or an international airport in the US. From there, they'd take a commercial or military flight to Spain or Casablanca, and then to the site by boat or ship.

After the third trip in as many months to the Alboran site, Carter determined there must be a better way.

His answer was a Dassault Falcon 7X, which set him back a cool $50 million. But what was the use of having money if he couldn't spend it to make their lives easier?

Mackenzie and Carter loved the jet. It was large enough, roomy enough, fast enough, and luxurious enough to make the transatlantic crossings in comfort. Flying from Freydís to Casablanca now took less than six hours. Freydís to D.C. was now a little over an hour.

The 7X had a lower than average landing speed, which Carter explained meant they could land at hundreds of airports where the conditions wouldn't allow landings for other aircraft in its class. Best of all, with seating for up to sixteen passengers, it could accommodate the entire family and several friends if they wanted. She had to agree with Carter's philosophy about his inheritance.

Of course, having to use a hired pilot cramped Carter's style and had the potential to compromise urgent or secret missions. He soon corrected that issue by upgrading his pilot's license to get rated on his beloved 7X.

Mackenzie's thoughts turned to the library which they had retrieved from the Alboran site. It had taken weeks to scan the plates, now known as the A-Codex to differentiate them from the Egyptian plates, similarly termed the E-Codex. More translators had to be vetted and hired.

Samantha, the CIA computer expert, had been permanently co-opted to them at her own request. Rick's loss was a serious blow, not only to the project but to his friends. They all missed him—Samantha most of all.

At some stage during Mackenzie's reverie, her thoughts also turned to her respirocyte research project. She and Liu had made a significant breakthrough a few months before Carter's search for the ancient nukes took center stage. Her research had to take a backseat, but now she and Liu could get back into it.

James and Irene, who had hired her specifically to find useful medical technologies used in ancient times, encouraged and supported her to get her project going again. To this end, Sam updated the translation algorithms and AI to extract respirocyte specific information from both codices.

The DARPA scientists, Dr. Cate Nelson and Dr. Scott Watson, whom she had met shortly after she had joined A-Echelon a few years ago, had also been enquiring about her progress. They were quite excited when she gave them an update a few months ago and were hinting at the possibilities of a joint project.

She and Carter agreed, now that their lives had returned to normal again, to allocate some of Liu's time to her project when they were back on Freydís. She was looking forward to it.

She couldn't help but ponder her and Carter's concerns about the growing number of people who had access to the Codices. Sean, Dylan, James, and Irene agreed, even though most of those who had access only had limited access pertaining to their area of specialization and only after proper vetting.

Leading scientists, including some from friendly countries, had been given access to the preapproved sections covering engineering, medicine, electronics, nuclear physics, quantum mechanics, astrophysics, anthropology, archaeology, and more.

Naturally, the National Security Council were also informed and were, in fact, the final point of approval for anyone who wanted access.

Even though all possible precautions had been taken to avoid leaks, it was impossible to control every word out of everyone's mouths. There were also the peripheral people—assistants, spouses, and potentially even sleeper agents to consider.

They all knew the aphorisms about secrets—to keep your own secrets is wisdom; but to expect others to keep them is folly. And three may keep a secret, if two of them are dead.

No wonder she was exhausted.

Chapter Six

HOW TO NEUTRALIZE A NUKE

Before they could prioritize the order in which the A-Codex was studied, they knew the plates would have to be scanned in their entirety then translated. It was a mammoth task, since there was at least thirty times more information involved than in the E-Codex.

It also required more computing power. Their own highly sophisticated computers weren't up to the task, so Carter had a couple of supercomputers brought in at his own expense and optimized for parallel processing. Then the coding geniuses were put to work to improve and optimize the algorithms as well so one wouldn't be waiting on the other. Once the latency problems were conquered, the translation went much faster.

At times, it boggled Mackenzie's mind that so much money was at her husband's disposal. She still hadn't grasped the extent of his holdings, and truth be told, she got the impression neither did Carter have a complete grasp of his net worth. It was something that just didn't bother him.

With the increased concerns about the ever-growing

number of rogue nations and even terrorist groups trying to build nuclear weapons, President Grant had been breathing down their necks to produce the answer the Giants had found to neutralize nukes.

Carter understood the urgency, and he didn't want to wait for the painfully slow process of securing government funding. Maybe he'd be reimbursed, maybe not. It didn't matter.

As soon as the nuclear physics sections were translated, Carter flew to Los Alamos to present the material directly to the LANL scientists charged with discovering how the Giants had disarmed those ancient nukes.

They'd all agreed that with the use of neutrino beams it was possible to accomplish it—in theory. In practice, no one had the slightest inkling how.

Years ago, a team of Japanese scientists had postulated that a super-powered neutrino generator could be used to instantly destroy nuclear weapons anywhere on the planet. If such a generator was ever built, it could be used to obliterate the nuclear arsenal of an enemy by firing a beam of neutrinos straight through the Earth.

Neutrinos are basic particles with no electric charge and virtually no mass, produced in the nuclear reactions within stars. They pass through the Earth in their thousands every day, and as they pass through ordinary matter, they break up atomic nuclei.

The theory was the scattering of uranium or plutonium nuclei by the neutrinos would destabilize a nuclear bomb, causing the weapon to melt down, preventing the triggering of the chain reaction needed for it to fully ignite.

They speculated that the extremely high-energy neutrino beam hitting a nuclear bomb would fizzle the explosion down from what the full explosion would have been. But they were not sure by how much. The fact was there would still be an explosion.

Further realities were the generator would have to be more than a hundred times more powerful than any existing particle accelerator on the planet, six hundred miles wide, require fifty gigawatts of power, and cost in the region of $100 billion to construct.

Scientists across the world were saying, "...the maths and physics seem to be right. But it is really quite futuristic."

But the Giants knew, and it turned out to be relatively simple.

Simple, at least, if one's mind could make the leap and accept that the Giants had flying machines so many millennia ago. And they had the means to seek out the devices and fire neutrino beams at them with pinpoint precision. Not to mention the capability of producing those beams in a device twice the size of a large suitcase but with hundreds of times the power of a modern-day particle accelerator like the one at CERN, thanks to their mastery of the quantum physics concept of Zero Point Energy.

Clearly, there was much to learn in the Codex, and Carter had left the scientists eagerly perusing the material.

However, not before unsettling them with his sobering observation that for every piece of knowledge gained to advance science for the good of humanity, there was someone who was willing to exploit it for the opposite purpose. It sobered the scientists as it had sobered Mackenzie months before.

Perhaps their predecessors in the twentieth century had entertained the same thoughts when they developed the first nuclear weapon. Was this the right thing to do? General Eisenhower had certainly objected to the use of nuclear weapons back in the day. And his president had overruled him.

Now President Grant desperately wanted this technology as he wanted to put the nuclear genie which was let out then back in its lamp.

Over the months leading up to the meeting at Los Alamos, Carter often reflected on the conversation he and Mackenzie had that night after they had loaded the last of the ancient nukes onto the Navy vessel in the Alboran Sea, which would transport it to the US.

Carter used the opportunity to give them the summarized version of that conversation, which was, "If you manage to build the technology to neutralize nukes, you'll have a new problem to deal with."

When they looked at him probingly, he explained, "Just think how happy will the world's nuclear powers be when they find out their nukes have been turned into useless toys. And that we're back to the 1945 to 1949 era, when the US was the only nuclear power on the planet."

The scientists realized whatever they discovered, one thing was certain; it had to be kept more secret than the strange goings-on at Area 51!

After Carter's visit, it had taken them about eight months to figure out how the Giants did it and would take another twelve before they could develop the technology to achieve it themselves.

Chapter Seven

PROGRESS WAS HAMPERED BY ONE MAN

Among their many secrets, one of the most closely guarded, which the Nabateans had been able to keep for millennia, was that among people of their bloodline, there were many who demonstrated exceptional brilliance in one or two areas while being severely challenged in every other aspect.

In centuries past, the Nabateans were forced to hide these individuals from grisly fates when society still viewed them with superstition, accusing them of sorcery and persecuting them. Only in modern times had scientists made some progress in analyzing the phenomenon. However, it still wasn't well understood. Now-termed "savant syndrome" had gained prominence through popular culture and movies such as *Rain Man, Phenomenon,* and *A Beautiful Mind*.

The Nabateans understood long before modern times, however, that these members of their bloodline were to be protected, valued, and used. They considered them a gift, a blessing bestowed on them from their ancestors, and treated them as deities. Significant numbers of their bloodline were blessed in this way at birth, demonstrating exceptional skill in music, art, mathematics, science, and many other disciplines.

From the moment the Council was formed in the distant reaches of time, they recognized the need for special care and treatment of their savants. Despite their special brilliance, such children were difficult for families to raise, especially in early times, when they were the targets of hatred and discrimination. Thus, the Council established special accommodations and developed programs to provide them with everything they needed to practice their skills.

As time passed, the Council learned more and more from those who ran their savant program and the associated schools. Only over the last half-century or so did the rest of the world start to develop a better understanding of savants.

However, by then, the Nabateans were lightyears ahead of them, having already been exploiting their gifted members for millennia, with great effect. This program was what had given them the significant technological advantages they had over the rest of the world.

Highly-qualified scientists of specialized studies were recruited to think tanks where they were given free rein. "Think outside the box. Dream. Let your imagination run wild. No restraints," were the words used at those dream-time sessions, as they called it, to get the scientists to play "what-if" without having to worry about derision by peers and superiors.

And the ideas from these groups were fed to the savants, no matter how farfetched. Many were germinated between the pages of science fiction. Others required solutions to problems that scientists in the rest of the world were working to solve as well. When the savants came up with the answers, instead of publishing them, the Nabateans kept them secret. Their scientists gained more than the prestige of a Nobel prize. They gained unlimited power and wealth for their people—the Nabateans.

In a modern world, it is difficult to maintain a secret of this magnitude for long. By now, the savant labs were known as special needs centers, and outsiders knew them as places where people on the autism spectrum especially were treated with the latest methods. The Nabateans operated their centers on a by-invitation basis, and each application went through an extensive vetting process before the child would be accepted.

Occasionally, a child not of the bloodline would be admitted so no one could ever trace the admissions policy to the bloodline. Such children would inevitably "wash out" of the program before they reached the stage where they would be put to work. Only savants of the Nabatean bloodline remained to work on the technologies that the Council of the Covenant of Nabatea had at their command.

Among the many astounding proficiencies were mathematical algorithms that could predict weather patterns and the behaviors of stock markets with breathtaking accuracy.

By studying hundreds of thousands of the strangest possible correlations over many decades, they found profound patterns, tantamount to insider information, except they had the information before the insiders had it. They exploited this to build their wealth with shrewdness and unobtrusiveness. It was impossible for anyone, other than Mathieu Nabati and one other on the Council, to ever uncover the vast wealth of the Nabateans and the power they could wield over the world's financial markets.

If they wanted to, they could collapse the world economy within twenty-four hours.

Other advantages included the ability to predict election

results, the outbreak of war, or acts of terrorism. Not only could they do so with astonishing accuracy, they could with equal precision predict the outcomes. Pollsters, had they known of it, would have sold their own mothers for the technology.

A secret that explained the extraordinarily long lives of the Council members lay in their medical advances. While the scientists themselves, the doctors, and even the savants enjoyed the same benefits, ordinary Nabateans, like the rest of the world, knew nothing of it. They kept their ability to extend lives to the human maximum, an average of one hundred twenty years, strictly to themselves.

They used some of their medical knowledge to infiltrate and control most of the pharmaceutical industry. However, certain discoveries, such as the cure for the common cold, all autoimmune disorders, dementia, and cancer were all withheld from the world, to be used by them when the time was right to restore the kingdom of Nabatea.

Had the world known that the means to relieve the atrocious suffering from so many "incurable" diseases existed, but were kept secret by a small group of people for the sole purpose of world domination, the Nabateans would have been wiped out in a blink of the eye.

Advances in energy technology gave them another domain of unfair advantage. Their plan for world domination included at some point collapsing other energy source markets to replace them with their own. Meanwhile, some of their secret facilities enjoyed free energy sources. They found ways to tap into the magnetosphere and were on the verge of cracking the unlimited energy potential of Zero Point Gravity. Nuclear fusion, the subject of great controversy among the physicists working to crack the technique, was already theirs, as was the ability to generate vast quantities of energy with microbial fuel cells.

Not to be outdone by such marvels, their computer scientists had supplied them with the best computer technology on the planet. The Holy Grail of computer technology, quantum computing, was not only routine for them. The savants had solved the problem of what to do with it. And it involved the optimization of when and how to roll out all the other technological advantages to give the Nabateans what they'd always desired. Total world domination.

About a decade ago, the Council ordered an acceleration of one of their neuroscience programs. Their advances in neuroscience had given them two advantages. First, their savants were now able to understand their own uniqueness. Second, even though it didn't cure their autism, it did mean they could give the answer to acquired savant syndrome.

While the autistic savants were born with the seeds of their abilities programmed into their DNA, people with the much rarer condition known as acquired savant syndrome were made that way by an outside event.

Modern-day scientists know that acquired savant syndrome is caused by trauma in the brain—either a head injury or disease that causes neurological disturbance, such as a brain tumor, but they still didn't know how it happens.

On the other hand, the Nabateans' savants had given their scientists the ability to replicate what happens and how it happens.

They were now able to produce savants on demand! It was a thrilling breakthrough for *them*—and highly unethical for the rest of the world.

But the world didn't know.

In much the same way as quantum theory postulates

that an object can exist in two states at the same time, the Nabatean savants now had the ability to be both normal and savant at the same time.

It was this plan of world domination that Graziella, Mathieu, and the rest of the Council were committed to following. However, to their frustration, of late, their progress was hampered by one man—Carter Devereux.

Chapter Eight

YOUR TASK IS DONE HERE

When Kelly and her team finally arrived in Germany, they had all managed more or less four hours of uneasy sleep. They suspected it was probably going to be the last they had for a while.

Kelly was briefed by the senior investigator on site.

"Was it nuclear?" she asked, reflecting her earlier question to Terrance Ham about an EMP.

"No, we don't think so. We haven't detected any radiation. But you need to know the media is going nuts and speculating the same thing. Can I take it that you and your team are going to take on the media duties from now?"

"I'll speak to my superior officer and get back to you. But if there's no radiation, we need to determine what else it might have been. I have two forensic experts with me, so that will be their first task. Can you take me to the epicenter?"

"No need," he said, pointing to an area where no buildings, trees, or anything else could be seen. "The weird thing is there's no hole in the ground. But you'll see that for yourself. If you'll excuse me, I need to let *my* superior know you're here."

Kelly nodded and quickly dispatched her team according to their specialties, sending some to interview witnesses and others to analyze residue, blast pattern, how the buildings were destroyed, and any other evidence they could collect.

It started almost immediately and became nauseating over the course of their two-week investigation—the incessant harassment by media, foreign governments, and their own command. What the hell happened there?

To dispel the speculation and thriving conspiracy theories about a mini-nuke, along with the frank disbelief when they said it wasn't, Kelly was allowed to invite nuclear scientists from four countries to conduct tests. The scientists, shocked when they saw Kelly's crew combing the ruins sans protective gear, were finally convinced when their own tests revealed no radiation.

However, they couldn't answer the next question. If not a nuke, then what?

There was no residue indicating chemical or conventional explosives, either.

If not for the magnitude of the destruction, Kelly might have advocated trying to sweep it under the rug and deny there'd even been a blast. However, there was no way to hide three-hundred and fifty deaths, nor to prevent Russian and Chinese satellites from photographing the devastated area and publishing the photos.

The world demanded an explanation. The headache had turned into a migraine.

The fact that Kelly and her crew, and by extension, the US government, couldn't explain it would leave everyone from the President of the United States on down to the lowliest military PR flak with egg all over their faces.

No explanation was not an option.

The German government, the European Union, NATO, everyone demanded answers.

It's a well-known phenomenon that the most ridiculous tale will be believed by everyone provided it is repeated often enough. The professional spinners within the US government went to work and came up with something everyone could at least understand.

It was a meteorite strike, like the one that hit Russia at almost the same time of year in 2013—but smaller.

On the surface, it was logical. At least now there was an explanation. All they had to do was repeat it until everyone stopped asking.

Closer examination, however, showed the meteorite explanation had a few critical holes, unlike the epicenter of the explosion at Patch Barracks. That didn't matter much, though. The explanation pacified the public, and that's what was important for the politicians.

Kelly and her crew had a different role to play in this drama, and making politicians and the public happy was not it—they had to find the true source of the explosion and the perpetrators.

None of the eyewitnesses saw or heard anything coming from the sky. In fact, that was the one thing they were consistent about, the weird blinding flash of blue-white light preceding the explosion rose from the ground up to the sky—not the other way around.

There was no impact crater. The devastation was circular, so it hadn't been caused by a near-miss.

Kelly and her team remained perplexed and had to call for reinforcements in the form of nuclear physicists from the

US when one of her crew mentioned the possibility of a fusion explosion.

When she spoke to her first choice of expert, a leading researcher from Princeton University, he offended her before she'd finished explaining what she wanted.

"No one has the ability to explode a pure fusion bomb," he sneered. "You're mistaken in your premise."

It took all of Kelly's patience to rein in her temper. "Give me a little credit, Dr. Wilson. I understand the difference between fission and fusion. And I'm not saying the latter is definitely what we're faced with. I'm only asking you to come and take a look, because we haven't been able to come up with a more plausible explanation. There's no radiation. None."

"That indeed sounds like a puzzle we'd enjoy solving for you," he answered, heavy on the sarcastic tone. "But I'm afraid my own research is at a critical point. You'll have to wait several weeks."

By then, Kelly had realized she'd have to drop her own bomb to get what she required. "I don't think you understand your position, Dr. Wilson. Your research is funded by the US government. I'm telling you *your* government requires *your* expertise *now*, not in several weeks. If you don't want your funding to dry up in a hurry, you and whoever else you need will be on a plane to Stuttgart in twelve hours or less. I'll see you tomorrow."

With that, she disconnected, confident he'd comply.

It was hours later when her own impatient internet research turned up a possible connection. It was well-known that German scientists at the Max Planck Institute were amongst the world leaders in the research of hydrogen fusion technology. Could one of them have been behind the blast?

None of Kelly's team had the expertise to determine if it had been, but they all agreed that no one on earth had the technology to detonate a fusion bomb in so contained an area. Even if they did, there would have been some radiation, that much they knew.

Two days later, the nuclear physicists were equally baffled.

After their tests, Kelly asked Dr. Wilson, "Well, do you have an explanation?"

He lowered his glasses to the tip of his nose, looked over the rims at Kelly, held his hand up, and made a series of mindboggling scientific statements as he counted down on his fingers,

"One, a massive amount of energy must have been released."

You could have fooled me.

"Two, by an unknown, and three, inexplicable source."

No shit, Sherlock!

Kelly took a deep breath. "That's it? Your conclusion?" Kelly asked with a strained voice.

Wilson nodded and raised his glasses back to the normal position.

Disgusted, Kelly kicked at a stray piece of concrete. "That's worse than nothing. I would've felt better if you blamed aliens."

A thoughtful look stole over his countenance. "Well..."

"Do NOT go there! If I hear the word extraterrestrial come out of your mouth, I'll have you stripped of your PhD." She grinned. "So, what's your best guess, really?"

The scientist, who hadn't appreciated the joke, answered stiffly, "It was a meteorite."

"Yeah, I can see that now. One of those that come from beneath, not above. It leaves no crater, sort of levels and cleans up after itself. How could I be so stupid?" Kelly muttered under her breath. "Thank you for coming, Dr. Strangelove. I think your task is done here."

The humorless Dr. Wilson cast her a look of confusion after being called Dr. Strangelove, apparently not a big movie fan.

On the afternoon of January 26, two weeks after their arrival in Stuttgart, Kelly called her crew together. "Have we discovered anything new in the last five days?" Receiving a negative answer, she told them to pack up. "We're going home. Be ready to leave in two hours."

Carter and Mackenzie, on holiday with their family in Europe, had been following the news about the explosion since it broke.

When the meteorite story was presented, both felt that it was a bit too fanciful for their liking. But the thought that this was connected to their own work never entered their minds.

Chapter Nine

ANOTHER ROADBLOCK

January 27

Kelly reported to Terrance Ham's office before even going home to freshen up.

"Terry, this is driving me crazy. No one can tell us what caused that blast. And without knowing that, we have no clues as to *who* caused it. I need some help."

"Anything you need, Kelly. We've managed to deflect media attention, but the security crisis remains. This could happen again. Tell me what kind of help you want, and I'll see to it."

"We need physicists to look at this. I think this is a case for DARPA's scientists," she said. Her morose expression said it all, but Terrance clarified.

"You want me to have the most senior officer in this Army tell the President of the United States that it's true what they say about Army Intelligence—it's an oxymoron? And we need DARPA to bail us out?"

"Well, when you put it that way—" she began.

"I take your point, and I don't see any help for it, either. Give me a couple of days to make it happen. For now, go home and rest; you look like you need it. I'll call you when you're to meet with them."

Grateful he hadn't belabored the point that DARPA was an independent agency, or berated her for her failure, Kelly did as commanded and went home.

Meanwhile, the request went up the chain of command, meeting with resistance but ultimate acquiescence at each step. At last, Terrance received a call from *his* superior, Brigadier General Jonas Fleming.

"OK, two of the eggheads from DARPA will be at your disposal tomorrow. It better be worth it."

Terrance gulped. He hoped his own head wasn't on the chopping block along with Kelly's.

On January 29th, at 10:00 a.m., Kelly met with Dr. Marco Ramos and Dr. Charles Dyer to hand over her team's evidence, including all test results, photos, and transcripts of eyewitness and survivor interviews.

She was slightly amused when she saw them—almost carbon copies of the physicists she'd met in Germany, right down to their short-sleeved shirts and pocket protectors. Less amusing was the concern that they'd be of equal use as the previous physicists—that is, none.

Nevertheless, she liked them. They seemed somehow more human, or at least more personable, than the university researchers. They charmed her by calling her "ma'am" and then hastening to explain they didn't know how to address a female military officer. After watching them turn red as they inserted their feet further and further into their mouths, she smiled to let them off the hook.

"You may call me Kelly, but only as long as you can

solve my problem, gentlemen. I don't need to tell you this is of the highest national security concern."

"Yes, ma'am," they answered in unison.

She spent half an hour explaining to them what her problem was and left them to study the evidence she gave them.

Unbeknownst to Kelly, Drs. Ramos and Dyer were two of the three DARPA people to have access to the Alboran Codex containing detailed information about quantum physics concepts.

Therefore, they already knew the ancient giants who'd left the codex, known as the A-Codex, had understood subjects that today were being studied only as theory, not applied science. The Giants had known about and used Zero Point Gravity, antimatter, and other technologies that DARPA was eager to incorporate into their own body of knowledge.

Ramos and Dyer immediately had a couple of ideas, not involving nuclear reactions, about the origin of the strange blast. And after making an in-depth study of the evidence, they reached a preliminary conclusion.

Frustratingly, it was one they couldn't share with Kelly White. Neither she nor her team had the necessary Q Clearance, though all had top-secret clearance.

Once again, communications went through channels, and Kelly again found herself in Terrance Ham's office. This time he had a quizzical expression.

"Please, sit down, Kelly."

Wondering if she was in trouble, Kelly complied. "What's this about, Terry?"

"Damned if I understand it. Evidently, before your DARPA friends can report to you, you have to get Q Clearance."

Kelly tilted her head and wrinkled her forehead. "What? Why?"

"Dunno. And I don't get to know. But you've got to get it, because that's the only way we don't get cut out of this investigation."

"I'll certainly go and get it. I'm mystified, though. You sure you don't know anything at all about why?"

"Nope. Go see the man, and once you know, please edify me."

Kelly's steps were slow as she reported to the security officer. *If this is so sensitive Terrance doesn't even understand it and doesn't know why I need Q Clearance, how am I supposed to keep him in the loop?*

At the same time, her excitement grew. *If it was above top-secret and I got it, would it help my career?* Surely that would give her an advantage over any rival for her ultimate goal, to head Army Intelligence. Remembering Terry's remark of three days before, she harrumphed. *Oxymoron, indeed. I'll show them!*

She was told what Q Clearance meant—the type of clearance that would definitely enhance her résumé—but at the same time it scared her.

Q-type clearance was a Department of Energy (DOE) security clearance required for access to top-secret, Secret Restricted Data, and DOE "security" areas, the highest-risk sensitivity levels in the country. People with these clearances held exceptional accountability because of the potential to cause grave and immeasurable damage to the national security of the United States. It was required for anyone with access to CNWDI (Critical Nuclear Weapon Design Information) or "SIN-widee".

Listening to the security officer's explanation, she had to shake off a few shivers running down her spine.

After turning over every detail of her life, the lives of her parents, siblings, and friends, and signing stacks of documents authorizing them to investigate anything and everything about her, Kelly was told to wait. Another roadblock and more frustration, though she couldn't have known that even pressure from the President couldn't move the process any faster.

The only bright spot during the next two weeks of waiting turned out to be the new guy in her life. Assistant Director, Counterintelligence Division, FBI Russell McCormick was both braver than previous beaus and more patient. Despite her leaving him before they'd even ordered on their last date, he wanted another!

Chapter Ten

LET'S INFORM THE PRESIDENT

First week of February

While waiting for Kelly's clearance to go through, the Director of DARPA, Taylor Rice, determined that Drs. Ramos and Dyer's suspicions were too explosive, no pun intended, to wait. He made an appointment with his friend, Bill Griffin, Director of the CIA, to talk about what his employees thought caused the explosion.

They met in Bill's office. Rice began with a classic line.

"Houston, we have a problem."

"Oh, shit," Bill muttered.

"We think that explosion at Patch Barracks was an antimatter bomb."

"You're not serious!"

"Dead serious."

"But no one has the means to build an antimatter bomb," Bill protested.

"The European Organization for Nuclear Research, known as CERN, in Switzerland has produced antimatter.

According to them, it's time consuming and prohibitively expensive. After all these years, by their own admission, they have produced barely enough to power a light bulb for a few minutes. So, they have the technology to produce and stockpile antimatter. What we don't know is, are they lying about how much they have, and have they built a bomb? I think the answer to both questions are no."

"So, if you and your scientists think it was an antimatter bomb, and let's assume CERN is not involved, how do you explain this?" Bill asked.

"Only one other possibility we can think of, Bill. The Alboran Codex…"

"What do you mean?"

"Well, we have been studying the parts of the A-Codex about the Giant's knowledge of antimatter. We're just beginning to get our heads around some of those concepts. In other words, we haven't even started producing antimatter yet—"

"Wait a minute," Bill interrupted. "Are you saying somehow the information in the Codex has leaked out… and…"

"Yes, Bill, I am. If it's an antimatter bomb, then as far as I am concerned, we're looking at the following possibilities; One, CERN has manufactured more of the stuff than they are admitting, and they developed the bomb or someone stole their antimatter and developed the bomb.

"Two, someone got hold of the A-Codex information and used it to make antimatter and the bomb."

"Who… who would leak the information, and who has the capability to make a bomb once they have the information? As far as I understand, it's not like you could cook this up in your kitchen. You need sophisticated equipment and a lot of people with white coats, thick glasses, and a lot of brains. Yes?"

Rice nodded. "Well, many countries—the UK, France, Germany, Russia, China, etcetera—have the brainpower and equipment to do it, *if* they have the A-Codex information."

"Taylor, I sincerely hope you're wrong. I don't even *want* to think what a mess it will be," Bill whispered.

Rice chuckled. "I'm with you on that, Bill. As a scientist, it's not often I have a desire to be wrong. The problem is, the evidence, which we have studied, supports no other hypothesis. My scientists will have to visit the site and do their own tests."

Bill went quiet for a while and then said, "Let me get James Rhodes and Irene O' Connell, the Director and Deputy Director of A-Echelon, in here right now."

The two of them went in search of coffee while they waited for James and Irene to arrive.

Within minutes after joining the meeting, James and Irene were staring at Bill and Taylor in shock and awe.

"Let's assume CERN is out of the picture for now," James started. "That leaves us with the A-Codex, and as far as I can see, there are two ways the information could have leaked out—from DARPA's side or from Carter Devereux's side."

Everyone agreed.

"So," Bill mused, "who did it?"

"We can only speculate about that, Bill," Irene replied. "That's up to Kelly White and her investigative team."

"Agreed," Rice said. "She's a top-notch CI in Army

Intelligence, but she doesn't have Q Clearance, so we can't tell her what we think yet.

"I'd like your help in informing the President. He probably already knows something's up, because we asked his Chief of Staff to have him help fast-track that process."

"Agreed," Bill said. "We need to inform the President right away." He excused himself to have his assistant make the appointment then returned to find the others discussing the Devereuxs.

"They're on holiday," Irene explained. "They were onsite in the Alboran Sea for about two weeks, and now their children, Mackenzie's folks, and her brother have joined them for a four-week vacation in Europe. They'll be back by mid-March."

"I'd stake my life that none of them is the source of the leak," James added. "We'd better confirm the theory before we involve them."

Irene nodded. "Let them enjoy their holiday. Until we have solid ground to stand on, let's keep them out of it."

"I feel the same about Drs. Ramos and Dyer. They would not have done it. Be that as it may, let's inform the President, and I'll get a team ready to travel to Germany to investigate as soon as Kelly has Q Clearance and is in a position to authorize their trip. And as soon as Kelly White has her clearance, we'll read her in. Agreed?"

Everyone nodded, and Bill said, "Agreed." With that, the meeting was over.

All that remained to be done for the moment was to inform the President—not something he was looking forward to.

Chapter Eleven

WHAT NOW?

Kelly was on pins and needles. Two weeks was too long a wait for the critical Q Clearance. Another attack could come at any moment and catch the US with its figurative pants down. And that was exactly the way she put it while appealing to everyone she could think of to hurry up the process.

The President agreed. He was also pulling strings, and his Chief of Staff, Scott Eadie, had taken to ducking out of the room any time the President lost his temper about the bureaucratic red tape. He'd explained three times why Grant couldn't accomplish the task simply by issuing an executive order, and the last time he'd tried to explain, his boss had practically bitten his head off.

In the end, it was Kelly's connection to Russell McCormick that did the trick. With his help and schmoozing behind the scenes, Kelly and two of her team members got their clearances in record time—thirteen instead of fourteen days.

In the last week of February, Kelly and her two team

members finally had the opportunity to sit down with James and Irene and get the gist of what was such a big secret.

The initial briefing was an abbreviated version, but even so she almost believed she'd been gas-lighted.

James explained there was much, much more to the story, but he and Irene had learned that dumping it all onto unsuspecting first timers always left them catatonic. He was only slightly kidding.

It just sounded too fantastic—like conspiracy theory, aliens, Area 51—the realm of total nut cases. For a mind as logical and educated as hers, the idea that ancient civilizations had been more advanced than her own was indigestible.

It took James and Irene a few days to get her and her team over the hump and get them to the *okay-let's-see-about-that* stage. During that time, revelations about ancient giants, talking dolphins, and ancient nukes, among others, left them thunderstruck time and time again.

In the evenings, Kelly took the opportunity to talk to Russell about what she'd learned that day. Since he also had Q Clearance, she had no fear of sharing national secrets.

For the first couple of days, she treated it as a huge joke, referring to the briefings by James and Irene as her "daily cocktail of absurdity juice." However, to her surprise, Russell didn't see much humor in it—he took it all seriously. He constantly asked "what-if-it-is-true" type questions, reminding her that as an investigator it's critical to keep an open mind and not discard anything until it can be disproved.

In fact, he turned out to be a big help, discussing and thinking through the evidence and giving her ideas for further investigation. It was almost as if he was as excited about the case as she, even though the FBI wasn't involved.

It wasn't their jurisdiction, since the attack had taken place on foreign soil and on a US Army base.

When Kelly and her two team members had heard all they needed to know about the A-Codex and complementary information, it was time for a briefing by the DARPA scientists.

There, they encountered another level of astonishing facts. They learned of the depth of knowledge recorded on the plates Carter had discovered, including the applied technologies the Giants had put to use. Quantum physics concepts, Zero Point Gravity, and antimatter among them.

"And that's only a tiny fraction of the information stored on those plates," Dyer noted.

Ramos and Dyer, now in their element and able to talk freely, eagerly brought Kelly up to speed.

"So, these concepts weren't new to us. That's why we could understand what the Giants had to say almost immediately. But for us, it had all just been theory before. And in fact, to most scientists, it still is. Practical application is still out of their reach, but these records have put us way ahead of anyone else, as far as we know," Ramos said.

Dyer continued. "One thing DARPA knew more about than anyone else already is antimatter. We've been researching it on behalf of the Air Force since the end of World War Two."

Kelly held up her hand. "Wait a minute. You mean we already have the antimatter bomb? You know for sure that's what caused the blast at Patch Barracks?"

Ramos shook his head as Dyer answered, "No, no. An antimatter bomb is still theory for us. As far as our knowledge stretches, there are a few insurmountable problems to produce such a bomb and explode it."

Now it was Kelly's turn to shake her head. *If insurmount-*

able, why do these brainboxes think the Patch Barracks explosion was due to antimatter? "Go on."

Ramos took over again. "The first two issues are size and transportability. Have you ever seen the reproduction of the Hiroshima and Nagasaki bombs at Los Alamos?"

Kelly shook her head.

"Well, the smaller of the two, Little Boy, was about ten feet long and not as big around as my waist, and it weighed a total of about two hundred eighty pounds. It produced an explosion equivalent to about fifteen kilotons of TNT and devastated the city of Hiroshima, killing over sixty-six thousand people instantly.

"Now, consider the size of the blast at Patch Barracks. Much smaller, yes?

"Okay. Well, in theory, it would take only a fraction of a gram of antimatter to do it. I'll spare you the formula, but suffice it to say that a gram of antimatter reacting with a gram of matter would release the same energy as a forty-three kiloton TNT explosion."

Kelly's eyes widened and her jaw dropped. "I take it one gram of antimatter isn't very large in volume. Someone could carry it concealed in their pocket, say?"

Ramos and Dyer laughed. Ramos said, "Yes, but I wouldn't recommend it!"

Dyer explained, "That's one of the first of the insurmountable problems. Antimatter and matter react as soon as they come into contact, and that causes the explosion. In essence, they annihilate each other, releasing enormous quantities of energy. So, containing the antimatter is an issue.

"To keep it safe and prevent it from annihilating, you have to keep the antimatter away from matter. So, our modern-day methods are to place the antimatter in a specifically designed magnetic container, almost like a bottle, called a Minimum Magnetic Field Trap. The MMFT is fitted with magnets, which keep the anti-atoms, or antimatter, in suspension, away from the walls of the trap, and thus prevent them from annihilating.

"As you can imagine, that setup is delicate. It can't be easily moved around without the risk of obliteration. I would definitely not want to be the one to carry it around in *my* pocket."

Kelly thought about it for a moment, mentally scratching her head.

"The next insurmountable is, it's unbelievably expensive to produce. Millions of dollars for a few atoms. A gram would cost many hundreds of billions and would take centuries to collect."

Kelly frowned in frustration. "So far, you've only told me why it *can't* be antimatter that caused that blast. Yet, you still think it was. I'm perplexed."

"Well, that's the thing. It's the only theory that explains the evidence."

"Great. Round holes and square pegs," Kelly muttered. "So, how do we prove this theory, and who would have the means to do it?"

"The Giants knew how to overcome all these problems. But it's going to take us another six months or so to even start testing their method of producing antimatter. We've no idea how long it will take to get to the bomb-making stage.

"As for proving the theory, we'll have to go to Germany to gather more information."

Kelly sighed. It sounded like a dead end, but it was her only lead. "Thank you, gentlemen. You've been most helpful. I'll get back to you about the visit to Germany."

She stood, and her two team members, who had

listened without comment during the entire meeting, stood with her. After handshakes all around, the team exited DARPA headquarters.

"What now?" one of them asked.

"I'll meet with Terrance and ask him to set up a meeting with Bill Griffin for me. I'll call you when I know."

After meeting with Bill Griffin, Kelly was told to stand down again until he had checked with the other security organizations—some fourteen that she knew about, and potentially others so dark the old saying "If I tell you I'd have to kill you" actually applied.

Chapter Twelve

WHAT'S LEFT IS ZERO

She got the travel authorization for the two DARPA scientists to visit Patch Barracks, and they left the next morning. Two days later, she got the message from Taylor Rice—Drs. Ramos and Dyer confirmed it was an antimatter explosion. They had no idea how it could have happened.

Shortly after, Bill Griffin called her to his office. The long and short of his inquiries were none of the other agencies were working on an antimatter bomb or knew of any country in the world capable of building one, and none of them knew anything about the A-Codex.

Bill's conclusions were, "We have the mother of all security leaks. A national security crisis of colossal proportions. *Someone* has gained access to the A-Codex information and used it to construct an antimatter bomb. That 'someone' must have brilliant scientists, sophisticated facilities, and unlimited funds.

"Kelly, you can imagine what governments might want to embarrass the US with a stunt like this and who might

The Nabatean Secret

want to let us know through an act of terrorism. The usual suspects, of course. Russia, China, North Korea, not to mention a number of Middle Eastern countries.

"What you don't know, and is more top-secret, need-to-know information, is there's an organization out there committed to a goal of world domination. Let me tell you about the people who call themselves the Council of the Covenant of Nabatea…"

Kelly listened without comment for a few minutes, and then pulled out her smartphone and began to take notes as Bill read her in on the Nabateans.

He concluded with, "I'd bet my bottom dollar they were in on it somehow. If not to instigate it, then to fund it. Find them, or someone connected to them, and you'll have gone a long way toward finding specifically who did it."

Kelly agreed.

The fact that the foremost security organizations in the world didn't know, and neither wanted to guess who that "someone" was, nor admit that they could even exist, was terrifying. And now that "someone", who obviously had a gripe with the US, had extremely dangerous information—*and, in fact, they had the means to apply it.*

A large antimatter bomb would make the Hiroshima bomb look like a single firecracker on the Fourth of July.

When Drs. Ramos and Dyer returned from Germany, Kelly met with them to get all the details and got even more bad news. The antimatter bomb at Patch Barracks could have been the size of a woman's lipstick or smaller. It could have been delivered by a single person, and it could have been remotely detonated.

"Great. Just great." Kelly imagined her career going up in a puff of dust like what she imagined happened when this antimatter stuff collided with matter—annihilation. Ramos had given her a striking analogy. "When matter and antimatter meet each other, it's like adding plus-one and minus-one. What's left is zero."

Zero was just about what Kelly had in the way of leads. But she did have an approach. It didn't make sense that any of the governments Bill had mentioned or the creepy Nabateans had all of a sudden stumbled upon the answer to antimatter energy. The most likely source was the A-Codex.

But how had *that* gotten into the hands of the bad guys?

Clearly, it had been placed there by a leak. The one and probably only way they had left to go about the investigation of *who* was to examine the individuals in the information chain from the source—Carter Devereux's translation team—to the hands of whoever might be working on it. That meant DARPA, and she couldn't disregard the people with access to the CIA vault where all translated data was kept.

Only the President, Bill Griffin, Irene O'Connell, and James Rhodes had access to the vault. *To suspect, let alone investigate any one of them would be… I don't want to even think about it.*

However, somewhere in that chain they'd no doubt find the person or persons who had both opportunity and motive. That the investigation had to be discreet to avoid alerting the perpetrators went without saying.

The task was enormous. There were too many people who had knowledge of the A- and E-Codices. While not everyone knew all the details, most of them had a good idea of what information was covered in the Codices.

The leak could be anywhere.

Chapter Thirteen

MORE THAN ONCE TOO OFTEN

Mathieu Nabati had been besieged by the Carter Devereux problem. His *Maman* was not pleased he hadn't been able to solve the problem permanently, which was not a safe position to be in. He had no doubt he was somewhat protected from her wrath, being her only child. But bulletproof? No, probably not. So, this damned Carter Devereux and those associated with him had to be eliminated once and for all. But how?

Mathieu was still licking his wounds from the catastrophic failure of his last plan—the attack on Freydís.

Attacking it again would be fruitless. The place was now a fortress. They might as well plan to attack the White House, for Freydís was now equally well-protected, with at least two geostatic satellites permanently stationed above it and equipped with the latest technology. Solar-powered drones crisscrossed the skies above the ranch twenty-four seven.

Those "eyes in the sky" would detect any unexpected

human movement, day and night. They were so sensitive they could detect a heat signature that differed from the ambient temperature, even during the summer when the temperature rose above that of the normal human body. If he didn't know better, Mathieu would have thought one of the Nabateans' own scientists had been involved in the development of those satellites and drones.

No, another attack on Freydís was out of the question.

Maman's sources who were privy to the information gathered from the surviving members of their unsuccessful attack—the traitors! —reported the captives were telling their interrogators tales of wild wolves guarding Freydís.

Mathieu had his reservations. No one had ever heard of wild wolves protecting humans—discounting the Roman myth of Romulus and Remus.

Nevertheless, the tough-as-nails Spetsnaz troops had been spooked by something. They reportedly could only speculate about the numbers of the devilish beasts and couldn't even begin to explain the mystical connection between the animals and the humans they protected. It was unfathomable that his pawns could be so duped, but the informant assured them the captives could not be shaken in their stories.

Furthermore, he'd been told every person on Freydís was now equipped with a tracking device, which they carried with them always. And since the attack, there were more guards and electronic surveillance, in addition to the satellites, than ever before.

It seemed the only option to attack Freydís would be from a remote location. A missile, launched from another country. For a moment, Mathieu entertained the mental image of the place wiped off the face of the earth by a hell-fire missile, leaving nothing but a scorched swath of useless dirt. However, that would defeat the purpose, of course. Such an attack might rid him of the Devereux pestilence, but it would also destroy the information the Council of the Covenant of Nabatea sought, not to mention starting World War Three.

In the end, in frustration, he had to admit an attack was off the table and decided not to even suggest it to *Maman*.

Instead, with the approval of the rest of the Council, he'd found a way to neutralize Devereux, and the first step of the plan—the explosion at Patch Barracks—had been a rousing success.

The essence of the new plan was to discredit Devereux, and with him everyone around him, from the Black Ops agency, A-Echelon, that recruited him and his wife right on up to the current President of the United States. Not only would that neutralize Devereux, but it could also serve to put a new administration in place that might not know about them.

Mathieu, had he been the type to chortle, would have done so over the ammunition all these idiots had given him. But as it were, he was Swiss, and they were not known to be very humoristic people.

President Grant had stepped on the wrong side of the law when he authorized that raid into Saudi Arabia, not to mention when he'd allowed the CIA to venture into illegal territory with his full knowledge. There'd be no plausible deniability for him when Mathieu was finished with him.

And Carter Devereux was a thief! He'd stolen the library of the Giants from the City of Lights in Egypt. Mathieu would have done so himself, of course, but that didn't absolve Devereux of the crime. Even his wife was larcenous. She'd in effect stolen the Sirralnnudam from that library in Armenia. Between the two of them, they'd gotten in the way of the Council's plans more than once too often.

Oh, yes. Destroying their reputation and those of their friends was going to be a lot of fun.

Chapter Fourteen

A CRIMINAL OF THE WORST SORT

February 28

As if the events unfolding under cover of national security secrecy weren't enough to worry about, President Samuel Houston Grant had another issue on his hands. In his final year in office, his task was to help his party remain in power. Any controversy could derail the campaign, as his Chief of Staff constantly reminded him.

Tensions were high as the media dug for any tidbit that could be parlayed into a firestorm, since *their* task was to gain attention from the public and feed the ever-growing demand for news, news, news. Even if they had to manufacture it. The more sensational they could spin it the better.

In this atmosphere, journalist Howard Crane at the Washington Post received a hand-delivered letter from an anonymous source. The source claimed he had a story that would shake the US and the world.

It was the stuff of cloak and daggers, and Crane was old enough to remember the fame and fortune that came to

Bob Woodward and Carl Bernstein after their publication of material supplied to them by "Deep Throat", leading to the Watergate scandal.

This letter Crane held in his hand could easily have been a hoax. On the other hand, it could also easily be his route to a Pulitzer. Without telling anyone where he was going, he followed instructions in the letter to meet with the source.

Late in the evening, in a dark corner of a parking garage near the same Watergate office complex that was the center of the political scandal, Crane's source provided him with a flash drive.

The mysterious source called himself Shadow, and it was an apt description. Bundled in dark clothing including a ski mask, the figure was obscured by the bulk of a coat, and Crane couldn't even tell if it was a man or a woman because of the voice distortion device "he" wore. Crane decided to think of Shadow as a man— for his own convenience and to stop the headache the speculation about the person's gender gave him.

He also decided if the information was real, he didn't want co-workers reading about it over his shoulder and perhaps scooping him. If it wasn't real, he didn't want to be the one who got burned for releasing it. Therefore, he took the flash drive home and disconnected his laptop from the internet before opening the files.

What he learned was explosive stuff. Black ops against American citizens? Supposedly sanctioned by the President? A man named Dwayne Miller had purportedly been abducted, held in custody illegally, and forced to testify against the directors of his company, Competitive Response Solutions. Nate Gordon, a director of Competitive

Response Solutions, also abducted and shot in the knee to make him talk.

Worst of all, a conspiracy of major proportions. Supposedly, the late Vice President, George Robertson, had been assaulted by an unidentified ex-Special Forces operative, *in the presence of the President*, in the Situation Room.

The story the VP had suffered a stroke, but his family had been restrained from seeing him, and a persistent rumor he'd died of a gunshot wound rather than a stroke.

This bore more investigation. It was screaming for answers.

Howard Crane was no fan of Sam Grant. Hadn't voted for him, and probably wouldn't vote for anyone in his party —ever.

But he was a patriot, and this was stuff that could bring down a government. He also had a well-placed contact. Though he wasn't certain she felt the same about him, he had a crush on the White House press secretary. At least he was friends with her. If he could persuade her to privately funnel questions about these allegations to the President himself, he would be satisfied that when he broke the story, he'd have given the man a chance to answer them. It was worth a shot.

And it was the honorable and patriotic way.

It didn't hurt his feelings any that he'd also get a chance to spend time alone with Daniella. In his eyes, she was the perfect woman. Slightly above average height for a female, she was, nevertheless, enough shorter than his six feet two inches to make him feel manly when standing next to her, even when she was wearing those ridiculous four-inch heels women seemed to favor these days. He guessed she must be about five six, maybe five seven. Her thick, shoulder-length, chestnut hair looked just right to run his fingers through, usually styled in loose waves. Her deep blue eyes were startling against her flawless tan.

Crane shook. Mooning over her beauty wasn't going to solve his dilemma.

His next move was to contact the subject of his attraction, White House Press Secretary Daniella Stewart, and invite her to dinner. He hinted he had some information she'd *definitely* want to know about.

She met him at the best steak house he could afford, and they exchanged pleasantries while waiting for their meals to arrive. Crane could tell Daniella was impatient to hear about the information he had, but he couldn't mention the nature of it in a public place, even at a whisper.

After the server left them alone with their food, Crane took a small bundle of papers from his inside pocket and handed it across the table to Daniella. He felt a bit of apprehension. He'd tried to write his questions in non-confrontational language, but the likelihood of his ever being able to date Daniella after this was slim to none if she read them.

"Daniella, what's in these papers is controversial, and for the President's eyes only. I'd have asked for one-on-one time with him, but I thought it best if you show him this first. Would you deliver them to him?"

Daniella looked down at the folded bundle, which wasn't sealed. "For his eyes only, but you didn't seal them?"

Howard nodded. "I trust you." It was a ploy, to be sure. But he'd bet a fortune nothing would make her look at the questions now. "One more thing, Daniella. The story is time-sensitive. If he chooses not to answer me within ten days, I'm going to have to run with it. Will you tell him that?"

Daniella's tone turned frosty along with her expression. "That sounds like a threat, Howard."

"No. It's just a fact, nothing more."

"And if the President takes it as a threat?"

"I can't control how he'll react. But I'll guarantee this. If I have to break this story without his side of it, there'll be hell to pay. Believe me. You don't have to tell him that. If there's any truth in the allegations, he'll know it as soon as he sees the questions."

He watched her tuck the papers into her purse.

With his last statement, he'd opened the possibility she'd look at the documents after all. He couldn't be concerned about his love life or lack thereof, though, not when the President of the United States might be a criminal of the worst sort.

Chapter Fifteen

TEN MORE DAYS

March 1

President Grant re-read the questions his press secretary had passed him with dismay and then handed them to his chief of staff. He wandered over to the windows to look out at the White House Rose Garden, the stalks of the rose bushes just beginning to turn green in anticipation of spring.

He wondered if he'd be there by the time the roses bloomed.

Behind him, Scott Eadie, Chief of Staff, first turned pallid and then exploded. "What the hell! Where'd this come from?"

Sam half turned. "Keep reading. He signed it."

When Scott finished reading, he looked up and found the President looking at him. "I know Howard Crane," Grant said. "He asks the toughest questions during my press conferences. I know he's not a supporter, but I'll give him this. He had the integrity to approach me first and not trumpet it out in the media first."

"But how could he have gotten this?" Scott whispered. "He must have a source inside the White House—close to you, Mr. President."

"Scott, you know our enemy. For God's sake, they even had George Robertson under their thumb. Does it surprise you that they would have someone else? A high-ranking someone, who's kept a low profile?"

"Mr. President, this is a fiasco. There's no way out that doesn't end with you in jail *and* the party out of office."

"I knew I was carrying the risk of exposure when I made my decisions. I'm satisfied I did the right thing, and if I go down because of it, so be it," the President replied.

"But Mr. President—"

Scott didn't get any further. "I think we need Bill, James, and Irene in here for a powwow immediately."

"I'll get hold of them right away, sir."

Half an hour later, a breathless Irene arrived on the heels of Bill and James and apologized. "Sorry! I was—"

"It's all right," the President interrupted. "I know you have a life. I'm sorry to have disturbed it." He waved Irene into a seat and gestured for Scott to explain.

"Earlier this evening, Daniella Stewart brought us this list of questions," he began, waving the papers. "Very disturbing questions, I have to say. And the message from the journalist who handed her the list is he is going to publish the story in ten days. If we provide answers, he will publish those as well."

With that, he began to read the questions, interrupted periodically by exclamations of enragement from Bill, James, and Irene.

When he came to the end of the last question, he looked up at them and said, "We have to formulate a response, or a plan, or some way out…," he trailed off. Abruptly, he sat down. "What a clusterfuck."

"Scott," chided the President gently.

"Apologies, Mr. President, Irene. But I feel that's exactly what it is," Scott replied.

Bill spoke up. "Scott's right; it's a titanic Charlie Foxtrot. But right now, we've got to consider our options."

"Blackmail or threaten Howard Crane," the chief of staff suggested.

"No, that I won't do," Grant said firmly. "We have enough trouble as it is. We can't and won't use illegal means to silence Crane. Anyway, even if we could silence him, *his* source would just go to someone else.

"We can't go after his source, even if the information was obtained illegally—unfortunately, journalists are protected by law against having to reveal their sources."

"Not to mention, that would just bring more attention to the whole pile of shit," Scott moaned. At an admonishing glance from the President, he amended it to, "whole pile of crap."

"Scott, no matter what we call it, the reality we have to face is that everything is true. That is what happened," Grant reminded him.

"What if we offer him a deal? Prior notice of breaking news events in return for not breaking *this* story?" Irene offered.

"Wouldn't work," Bill said. "*This* one will get him a Pulitzer. I doubt there'd be anything we could offer that would stop him. What could be better than this, from his perspective? He will bring the President and his party down in one fell swoop—he will be a hero.

The Nabatean Secret

"The point we're missing is this is not about Howard Crane. This is about the force behind him. That force is out to destroy the President, his party, and everyone who was involved with this.

"If Crane doesn't publish it, someone else will. You can bet your sweet a... sorry, you can bet your life on it."

They sat glumly, trying to come up with a better solution.

"I know," said James. "Issue an Executive Privilege Order classifying all the information as top-secret. That way, we can threaten him with jail if he publishes."

"Two problems with that," Grant answered. "First, criminal behavior by the President can't be top-secret, even if much of this subject matter really is. That would lead to a situation where a felonious President can't be brought to justice. All I have to do to turn us into a dictatorship after that is to appear on TV on horseback without my shirt.

"In Russia and a few other countries, maybe. In America, no chance."

"And the second thing?" James asked.

The chief of staff answered for Grant. "Let's say he does. Then the journalist publishes a story that says, 'I have information about criminal behavior by the President, but I can't print it because he classified it.' How's that going to go over in an election year? It would hand the election to the other party, that's what."

"We could tell Crane the truth and appeal to his patriotism," Irene suggested. The others just stared at her in disbelief. "What?" she asked.

"The whole truth is a dangerous thing in the hands of an ambitious journalist," the President answered. "And besides, this journalist is of the opposite political persuasion. As much as I'd like to think an appeal to his patriotism would work, I can't trust that it will. But some of it's going to have to come out. We'll have to sanitize some of it for the sake of national security, of course."

"Sam! Doing that means you'll probably go to jail!" Bill exclaimed.

"I don't see any alternative. Maybe I could pardon myself and anyone else involved," Grant quipped. "Or the new president could do it. Maybe I should start wooing the other side."

Scott Eadie grinned. "Nah, your new Veep owes you for his office. He'll take your seat, and he'd pardon you right away. Which is lucky, because the newly-elected President won't take office for ten months or so. That's a long stretch in the slammer, and if this comes out, like you said, the new President's likely to be of the opposite political persuasion anyway."

James brought them back to business. "Mr. President, I recall our conversation over breakfast one morning shortly after the raid on the Saudi facility outside Mecca. The three of us" —James pointed to Bill, Irene, and himself— "made you a promise then we would stand by you if this situation ever arose.

"I'm prepared to take the fall. The rest of you stay out of it. You can pardon me on your last day in office. I need a bit of a break in any event."

President Grant was on his feet. He had turned his back on them and was looking out the window. What they couldn't see was he was fighting back tears. After a long silence, he turned slowly and spoke softly, "James, I appreciate that more than you will ever know.

"But that's not going to happen. I'm prepared to face the music. I wouldn't run away from the consequences of the decisions I made in good faith and the best interest of my country when I had to.

"If I must go to jail, then so be it—I'm prepared to accept that. What I won't do is let anyone who works for me take the blame. I'll also not reveal top-secret information that could endanger the US just to save my own skin. I did what I did at the time because it was in the interest of national security, and it was the right thing to do.

"And in the interest of national security, I can't and won't give any top-secret information to the press, or the courts, or a Congressional Oversight Committee, even though it could save me from prosecution."

Irene snapped her fingers. "That's it! We need to buy time!"

Grant didn't know what extra time might do for him, but it couldn't hurt.

So, he called in Daniella and handed her the papers. "Your friend has presented us with a dilemma. This story touches on national security. We need more than ten days to answer.

"If you agree to help, it could put you in a bad position, so think carefully before you agree.

"First, read the documents, ask what you want to know, and then decide if you want to help. You've got no obligation to help. You have my word, your position on my staff is secure."

Daniella paled as she read the papers. She looked up at him to find him gazing at her with an open expression.

"Mr. President... is this... ah... is it...?" she stammered.

"Yes, Daniella, it's true, and I want to warn you there is probably a lot more to come," he answered without hesitation.

She'd admired the man, helped him get elected to office,

and served as his spokeswoman since before he became president. She trusted him. He was an honorable man, and she respected him as much as she respected her own father.

"Yes, I'll help. And yes, I know I don't have to and that I might end up in a bad position, as you've put it, Mr. President. But I have no hesitations."

"Thank you, Daniella. Please keep me posted."

At a different restaurant, this time one of her choosing, Daniella let her expression soften and leaned forward to plead her case with Howard. His gaze was on her low-cut blouse, so she believed the battle half-won.

"Howard, the recipient of your letter sends his thanks that you were considerate enough to go to him before publishing your story. And I thank you for coming to *me* with your questions.

"I've been asked to tell you there's much more to the story than meets the eye, and most of it touches on national security. More time is needed to prepare the answers—it is critical to have more time."

Howard's eyes lifted to look into hers. Worried that she was losing him, she slowly put out a soft hand, covered his with hers, and lowered her voice. "*I* need more time, Howard." She looked at him with pleading blue eyes. "I'm authorized to give you prior notice of breaking news events, if you'll hold off. Just for a while," she added.

Crane looked away, and she thought she'd overplayed her hand.

But then he turned his hand face up and grasped hers. "Ten more days," he said. Almost apologetically, he added, "That's really it. If I don't break the story in the time I was given by my source, I'll lose it to another reporter. You understand, don't you? If you lose me, you'll have to practice your charms on someone else, who might not feel the same about you as I do." He smiled.

"Perfectly," she breathed. He gulped as she leaned over the table to kiss his cheek. "Thank you, Howie."

Chapter Sixteen

A HAND-DELIVERED PACKAGE

Kelly leaned back into the arms of Russell McCormick and sighed. The more she tried to untangle the Gordian knot of the source of the information leak, the more people she found who could have been that source.

How could such a crucial secret have become so widespread?

"What is it, Kell?" Russell asked.

"I can't get my head around it. This is the most open top-secret, Q Clearance, eyes-only information I've ever heard of."

"Never mind all that. Let's work through it. How does the information get disseminated again?" Russell knew the answer, but asking the question served to focus Kelly. Together, they could trace the path the information took from there.

"Okay. The original plates are at Carter Devereux's ranch in Canada. Freydís. They've got a team of techs and translators working on it, about ten people. The contents of the plates are fed through a computer translation algorithm, and then humans check to make sure it makes sense, editing as required.

"After that, the translations, in digital form, are placed on mass storage devices, which are locked inside a steel box. So, the first place for a leak is among the people working on Freydís.

"The box can only be opened by the retinal scan of a handful of authorized people, including Devereux, Bill Griffin, James Rhodes, Irene O'Connell, and the President. Unless those individuals are involved, there's no way for the leak to happen during transport.

"The box is transported by plane to D.C., where either Rhodes or O'Connell pick it up in person and transport it to CIA headquarters, and Griffin personally locks it in a secure vault. Again, unlikely for the leak to happen in that part of the chain, unless those people are involved.

"However, the antimatter information, specifically, was given to three people at DARPA, who all work with the information and know where it came from. So, that puts them on the suspect list as well.

"Right now, everyone is a suspect, and the people I've named, the team at Freydís, and the DARPA people are in the top tier of suspects.

"I've got to consider that the second tier could be involved as well. That's the pilots and crew of the transport plane."

"Don't waste too much time on them," Russell said. "Despite what they show us in the movies, there is no way to defeat the retinal scans."

"Right, makes sense. It still drives me crazy that I can dig into the background and setup surveillance on most of them, but just to keep up appearances, we can't touch *some* of the suspects. I'm forced to start at the one end and work my way through everyone in the hope I'll eventually get to them through the process of elimination."

Russell hesitated. Was she saying what he thought she meant? "And those are?"

"Griffin, Rhodes, O'Connell, and God forbid, the President."

Russell whistled. "Wow, you don't pull your punches, do you? So, what if it comes down to those four? What will you do?"

"Let's just hope it doesn't. But for now, I don't trust anyone. Everyone in that chain is a suspect. They all have opportunity. I may need to find motive before I can go after any of them, but if I do, I'm going in with blazing guns. I *will* get to the bottom of it.

"Nobody kills three-hundred and fifty servicemen and gets away with it on my watch."

True to her word, Kelly ordered intensive surveillance on everyone but the four VIPs. Her team bugged their homes, their phones, their cars, computers—everything.

To her relief, the meteorite story and repetition thereof worked well enough as media speculation about the blast died down as other news took over the headlines. That gave her leeway to do her job properly. But nearly two weeks passed without a breakthrough. It was beginning to look like she'd have to make herself very unpopular, not to mention potentially damage her career, by expanding her investigation to the four VIPs.

Fortunately, before she could start on that, in the second week of March, a hand-delivered package from an anonymous sender reached her. In it were highly disturbing allegations. At first, she considered tossing it—anonymous tips could be dangerous. But then she thought a second time. Ignoring it could be just as dangerous.

She decided to follow up on some of the allegations to see if they could be verified.

Chapter Seventeen

DON'T FORCE MY HAND

March 9

Howard Crane paced as he waited for Shadow to arrive. He'd known when he gave Daniella another ten days for the President to come up with answers that he was pushing the limits. Yesterday, just two days shy of his deadline, Shadow had contacted him and demanded another meeting. Now Howard feared he was about to lose his award-winning story.

He nearly jumped out of his skin when Shadow appeared silently behind him. They were now face-to-face, or rather face-to-mask, in the dim light of the parking garage.

"Shit! Don't do that!" he exclaimed. Shadow just shrugged.

"My employers are unhappy with you, my friend," said the computerized voice from behind the ski mask. "They want me to give you a message." He reached into his pocket.

Crane tensed and the hair in his neck stood on end. Was the "message" a bullet at point-blank range? He sighed quietly when Shadow instead pulled another flash drive from his pocket.

"More details," Shadow stated. "If you don't publish this and the previous information within five days, we'll find someone who will. There are plenty of other journalists who'd be happy to bring this President and his cronies down."

Crane reached for the drive only to have Shadow pull it back. "Do we understand each other?" It was a threat not a question.

Crane nodded and tried to conceal the gulp he swallowed.

"We do. Please, give me a day or two to digest this new information and write the story. But you must realize, my publisher *will* make me substantiate everything. I can't do it in five; I need a week."

"This hits the headlines in five days, or you're out," Shadow hissed.

Crane started to wonder if "you're out" might have a different meaning than what it sounded like. Nevertheless, it was the best he was going to get, so he nodded his assent. "You'll see it." He held his hand out again for the flash drive. It was almost as if Shadow was reluctant to put it into the waiting hand.

"See that we do."

Howard didn't wait to get home to look at the information. He plugged the flash drive into his laptop right there in the parking garage and skimmed the information. What he found angered him.

There was more detail about the raid into Saudi Arabia, an ally—one of a very few in the Middle East.

Why hadn't he asked the Saudis to take care of the raid? It hinted of a lack of trust that would shake the alliance and jeopardize the major source of oil for the US.

People had lost their lives—the horror of beheading or even just being jailed in a Saudi prison. The President had authorized the raid but only told the Security Council after that fact.

Even more disturbing, Howard now learned of the existence of yet another black ops agency. A-Echelon it was called, and it was funded off the books out of the black ops budget. The director of A-Echelon reported to the director of the CIA and the President only. No wonder they could spend their time unhindered by any other form of oversight while engaged in the most ridiculous endeavors, which only a conspiracy nut would believe. And on the unsuspecting tax payers' money.

The controversial billionaire Carter Devereux, also part of the ridiculous A-Echelon, committing acts of antiquities theft from Egypt. Bringing his illegally-obtained booty to the US and making the President himself an accessory after the fact, not to mention Bill Griffin and two people Howard hadn't heard of. James Rhodes and Irene O'Connell, Director and Deputy Director of this A-Echelon circus.

And finally, Carter Devereux's wife, Mackenzie. Even she had gotten into the act, illegally copying a priceless historic document from an Armenian library and smuggling it into the US, with the full knowledge and consent of the President and the other three.

There were few details, but just the bare bones of the stories were explosive—enough to send the media and public into hysteria.

He couldn't see how the President would excuse these

allegations, but he certainly looked forward to the entertaining song and dance he'd no doubt get.

It would make a great story, *definitely* Pulitzer material. Maybe a bestselling book and a few movie deals in the years to come.

Howard Crane, play this right and it's your ticket to early retirement.

Despite the late hour, Howard called Daniella. "Time's up. I need those answers now."

"You said—"

"I know, I said ten days. But the situation has changed, and in any case, you've had nine."

"Howard," she pled, "I can't go to the President with this tonight. It's late."

"Tomorrow morning without fail, Daniella. Please don't force my hand. You still have the opportunity to respond, but I can't move the deadline."

Howard disconnected the call. His dreamt-of relationship with Daniella was dead in the water, and his career would be, too, if he didn't comply with Shadow's demands. If his editor ever learned he'd sat on the story *this* long, he might as well resign right now anyway.

Chapter Eighteen

DAMN STRAIGHT

As Daniella lowered the phone, she realized this couldn't wait until morning. She had no choice but to wake the President and present him with Howard's ultimatum. She sighed. The President would be mad, of course, but he'd forgive her when he heard what Howard had told her. She'd known when she took the job as press secretary it meant she'd have no life for at least four years, which had turned out to be eight.

But she hadn't known it would be this hard.

Just after midnight, she joined President Grant, Bill, James, and Irene in the Oval office, along with Scott Eadie. Wordlessly, she handed over the typed pages Howard had given her earlier that evening. They contained the story Crane would run, with or without the President's comments.

The President read it aloud.

This time, Bill offered to take the fall. James and Irene backed him up, offering to share the blame as well, if the

President would just allow them to do so. And once more, President Grant declined.

"Do you remember the sign President Truman kept on his desk? In his farewell address to this country as he left office, Truman made a statement that every President would do well to remember. He said when a decision is before you, the decision has to be made. You can't pass the buck to someone else. The buck stops here."

Catching and holding the gaze of each of his visitors in turn, he paused long enough to let it sink in.

"The buck stops with me. It's my *job*, and I'll *do* my job. *Your* job is to help me decide the path of least damage to the country. Your advice I'll gladly accept. Sacrificing yourself for me, never."

After deliberating more options, they concluded that something would have to be forfeited—the hungry beasts had to be fed something.

Bill had done a thorough background check on Howard Crane after the first meeting and was satisfied the man was truly a patriot. The President agreed and pointed out Crane's choice of how to handle the situation with such devastating information at hand attested to his devotion to his country.

They had no doubt someone was pulling Crane's strings. The question was whether he knew that was the case or if the potential of fame mesmerized him. The only way to know was to meet with him and find out which was prompting him.

They'd moved Heaven and earth to ensure it was safe to bring Crane into the fold before his deadline passed. At eleven that Saturday morning, Daniella called him. "You're invited to a private briefing. You'll be provided with all the answers and then some. I hope you're ready for it."

Since the last call with Daniella, Howard had convinced himself President Grant would stonewall him and deny everything—trying to make him look like an idiot. Therefore, he'd spent the morning checking facts and drafting the beginning of the story. This invitation was a surprising turn of events and caught him off guard, but he was eager to get the rest of the story, so he agreed.

"I'll text you an address," Daniella said. "It's going to be a long meeting. Come prepared to spend the night." She disconnected before he could reply.

Howard spent all of two minutes considering whether he was being lured into a trap and might disappear. However, he managed to put it down to irrational paranoia born from watching too many thriller movies. He threw a change of clothes and his dopp kit into an overnight bag and waited for Daniella's text message.

An hour later, he found himself in the company of the Director of the CIA, along with Daniella and the two he'd read about but didn't know, James Rhodes and Irene O'Connell.

They were in what he presumed was a safe house in Bethesda, Maryland. Daniella introduced him to each of the others, who invited him to call them by their first names.

He remained skeptical. *Flagrant attempts to soften me up... the actions of people in trouble, needing a favor from me. We'll have to see about that.*

"We're going to be here a while," Bill said. "Let's have lunch before we get started."

Without much choice, Howard agreed. The atmosphere was strained. Looking at the table with the lunch, the thought of drug- or, worse, poison-laced food crossed his mind. The thoughts vanished when he saw his hosts digging into the soup and sandwiches—he began to relax. These were just normal people, not the monsters he'd allowed his brain to imagine.

He remained on his guard, with his bullshit-meter activated. Guest or no guest, he didn't intend to let them get away with any.

After lunch, they moved to the family room, which had been outfitted as a conference room, with a whiteboard hung on the wall, a retractable screen, and video setup. There were comfortable chairs around a conference table. Bill began by explaining the roles James and Irene served in A-Echelon after reciting their qualifications. Then he turned the meeting over to James.

Over the next few hours, they briefed him on everything, starting with a quick overview of the truth about human history. Then the discoveries made by Carter Devereux, which supported the mind-bending age of human civilization.

By the time, James got to the discovery of the fifty thousand-year-old City of Lights in the Egyptian desert, Crane was shaking his head with incredulity.

James paused and looked at him. "I know, Howard." James smiled. "Irene and I have gone through this a few times over the years. And so far, we have never had anyone who could get their heads around it right from the start.

"But the good news is once we gave them the full picture, there has been no one who didn't believe us. So please put up with us."

"I'm still listening," Howard replied curtly.

James continued and told him about the plates now known as the E-Codex, and why Carter had appropriated them, the sinister organization known as the Council of the Covenant of Nabatea, who saw themselves as the principals of the Nabateans and their evil intensions.

He continued and told him about the ancient nukes, the search for them, the Alboran Sea expedition, the discovery of the A-Codex, and the important role Carter played in all of it.

He ended the report with an emphasis on how those discoveries had saved the world—so far.

The briefing paused once for dinner and carried on into the early hours of Sunday morning before they agreed to get a few hours' sleep.

Howard welcomed the break. He wouldn't sleep—he knew that. He struggled with a sense of having stepped unwittingly through the looking glass.

He'd always dealt in facts, and though he wasn't above manipulating them for maximum effect, he'd never manufactured news.

But this... What do you call this, Howard? Do you want to risk your career, go out there and dish this up as fact?

His beleaguered mind was trying to make sense of it all.

His logical mind was saying, *there is no way this could be real.*

To which, the little inner voice was saying, *but then the four of them have missed their calling—they should have been actors. No one can make up all this stuff, let alone present it with so much conviction if it was bogus.*

The little voice kept on asking, *what if it's true?*

If so, this would be a nightmare of immeasurable and unthinkable proportions.

By sunrise, he'd made his decision to make his hosts cut to the chase. Though he'd slept very little, he made his way to the kitchen in hope of finding coffee. As he approached, the aroma of bacon lured him in. He found the others up already and sitting around the table, waiting for him.

Irene handed him a cup of coffee and gestured to the table. "Have a seat. Dig in. Bill made breakfast. It's not often that the Director of the CIA makes us breakfast."

He accepted the invitation eagerly. He ate one slice of bacon, took a sip of coffee, and looked at Bill, the most senior of his hosts. "What do you expect of me?"

Bill replied without hesitation. "Howard, like it or not, I did a background check on you before this meeting. And although we have different political views, I know you love your country as much as any one of us does. That's why we've shared with you the most secret and most damaging information possible.

"We're appealing to your sense of patriotism to make the right decision.

"And take note, I'm not asking for preferential treatment for any of us. None of us, including the President, are worried about the damage the revelation of this information will do to our names, fame, and reputation. Rather, we are deeply troubled about the damage the disclosure of the information can cause—not only to the US but the rest of the world."

Howard stared at him with what he could only hope was a neutral expression in order to hide his true feelings, which were swinging like a pendulum between belief and disbelief.

He exhaled. "I'm not sure how to respond to that. I'm still struggling to believe what you've told me. Even if I do, how can I stop this from going public? You know I have a sword over my head—if I don't publish, he will find someone else who will. In other words, if I… we… want to keep some control I *have* to publish something."

Bill was encouraged by Howard's response. It seemed as

if he was finally beginning to come to grips with the gravity of the situation. "Before we discuss that, I want to give you one more bit of information, Howard. Just to illustrate the magnitude of the issue.

"You are familiar with the meteor strike at Patch Barracks in Stuttgart, Germany, two months ago?"

Howard nodded. "Yes, absolutely. I followed it closely, right from the beginning."

"Howard, here's the nightmare. That was not a meteor strike. It was an antimatter bomb."

Howard's eyes shot wide. "Bullshit! You're not going to peddle that crap to me—I'm not buying." Crane's face was ashen. This revelation on top of everything else he had heard was threatening to be too much for him to stomach.

Bill looked at Irene, the best technical mind among them. "Irene, will you please step Howard through the details?"

Irene nodded. In laymen's terms, she explained about the enormous amount of energy released when matter and antimatter collided. She then delved into the research that had been done across the globe before she broke the news about the findings of the DARPA scientists. She concluded with the current investigation into the explosion and the theory that the information was leaked out of the A-Codex into the hands of the evildoers.

Howard needed more coffee. If it wasn't so early, he would have asked for something much stronger. While sipping at the java, he stared at each of the four faces in turn.

Then it struck him. *I'm being used by Shadow and whoever he is working for to further their agenda!*

Then the realization came like a lightning strike. *What these people told me is true! The one that has been deceived is me!*

"Bastards!" he exclaimed to the consternation of Bill and the others, thinking they had pushed Howard too far.

Bill started, "Howard—"

Howard saw their expressions and interjected, "No, not you, Bill, or anyone else in this room. I'm referring to my contact and whoever he's working for. I have been set up—used, deceived. I'm pissed.

"Let's work out what has to be done to bring them down." Howard was shaking with shock and rage.

Bill smiled. "Phew, Howard. For a moment back there, you had us worried."

"I'm convinced my contact's source could be none other than these Nabateans you told me about, if he isn't one of them himself." He snorted. "I should have smelled the rat and known it was a setup."

Bill started nodding, and Daniella said, "We know. That's why you're here, Howard. We'd like to shape how it comes out, if you agree."

"Damn straight, I agree. What's your plan?"

As the afternoon wore on, the five of them strategized, with the first decision being to finally inform Carter and Mackenzie of what was going on, before the A-Echelon story would break. Irene informed the others the Devereuxs were about to return home from their European holiday. It wouldn't do to have them walk into a media circus unaware.

Chapter Nineteen

WHAT NOW?

March 14

Howard's first assignment was to meet again with Shadow. As expected, Shadow had been paranoid about security. He led Howard on a tour of the city, sending him to the Lincoln Memorial, where he was contacted by a kid on a bike, who handed him a note saying to go to Georgetown, and so on for two hours. Howard assumed Shadow was nearby, trying to spot anyone following. But finally, they met up, ironically in the same parking garage where they had their first meeting. Howard was exasperated, but he contained his annoyance for the sake of appearances.

"Why hasn't the story appeared yet?" Shadow demanded, more aggressive than ever.

Howard held both hands out, making a calming motion, pressing down on the air with his palms. "I told you my editor would make me verify. I've just managed to get a lead on this A-Echelon group. You were right; it's a Mickey Mouse outfit, just wasting the taxpayers' money chasing down conspiracy theories. God knows how they got this Carter Devereux clown, or how he stumbled on his so-called *discoveries*."

Shadow chopped the air, cutting Howard off. "Get to the point," he snapped. "You wanted to meet. Why?"

"I just wanted to let you know how I'm going to spin it," Howard said. "Since A-Echelon is where all this started, I'm going to expose them first. They'll get investigated, and in the process, they'll open it up to everything else.

"It will look completely natural. That way you and I won't be exposed. No one will know that we know as much as we do. It will all come out in the course of the investigation. And we can steer the investigation from the backseat by asking the right questions."

"I don't care about that," Shadow muttered.

"You should. Trust me, it's best. We don't want the attention on us, we want it on A-Echelon and their antics."

"Do it your way, then. Just do it, and do it now. We're tired of waiting."

Howard grinned. "Just make sure you get your copy of the Washington Post tomorrow."

When Howard reported back to Daniella, he told her the publication of the story would only buy them time, not absolution. They had to brace themselves for the hurricane of shit about to hit them. No matter how he shaped it, some very important people, including the President, were going to find themselves in the middle of it.

Over coffee at an out-of-the-way café, he gazed at her pretty face with regret. But when she looked up at him, he was surprised to find a hint of the same emotion clouding her blue eyes.

That look from her made him think, *maybe, just maybe, there is hope after all.*

Later, Daniella briefed the others. "The odd thing is," Irene observed, "there's not been any mention of Sean and Dylan, of Executive Advantage. Could it be the Nabateans know nothing of EA? Or are they saving it for another bombshell later?"

On the thirteenth of March, late afternoon, Carter, Mackenzie, and their entourage arrived back home on Freydís, relaxed from their extended vacation but happy to be home. It wasn't to last. No sooner had they unpacked than an encrypted message arrived from James.

Something was going down in D.C., and they needed to get there *tout de suite*.

As Carter read the message to Mackenzie in their bedroom, they stared at each other.

What now?

Chapter Twenty

CLICK OF THE DOOR BEING LOCKED

March 15

Kelly White continued to have her team surveil everyone in the information chain from Freydís to the CIA vault. She didn't have any results of the surveillance to share with anyone, not even Terrance Ham. To her frustration, there was nothing of value to report, except that everyone in that information chain continued to be a suspect. In her reports to her boss, she only said she was spreading her nets wider and investigating everything.

However, when she got the anonymous package, Kelly began quietly investigating the allegations contained within. She didn't report it to her boss. She was unwilling to get him or anyone else worked up about a potential hoax. She was even careful with what she shared with her own team.

It was early morning on the fifteenth of March when Carter and Mackenzie boarded the Dassault Falcon 7X for their trip to D.C.

The Ides of March. Mackenzie couldn't shake the

ominous feeling when she thought about this day in history —when Julius Caesar was assassinated by the Roman senate in 44 BC. To travel on this day of all days was giving her an uncharacteristic superstitious dread.

Carter dismissed her fears, saying it was likely some administrative detail that couldn't be done remotely, and everything would be fine.

Mackenzie opened her laptop when Carter gave the okay and checked the news. The moment she saw the first headline, she blanched. "Carter, this looks like trouble."

Carter glanced at his lovely wife and noticed her shock. "What is it, Mackie?" he asked with concern.

"This."

She read him the headline. "*Secret Government Agency Uncovered: Aliens Among Us?*" The story went on to expose the existence of A-Echelon, lampooning their missions, and attacking the logic of having an agency take such matters seriously. Screaming about the waste of vast sums of taxpayers' money on the preposterous notions that some ancient relics posed a threat to our modern civilization.

Worse, it named James, Irene, Carter, and her as perpetrating a hoax to cover up archaeological indiscretions—hers and Carter's thefts of ancient artifacts.

"Carter, I think this is why they want us in D.C. What are we going to do? Could we be in some kind of trouble?"

"I don't think so, but we'll know soon enough, Mackie. I'm sure we'll be able to sort it out fairly soon."

Mackenzie kept on reading and searching for more information about the story for most of the flight.

Trouble was waiting in the form of Kelly White when they landed in D.C. at nine a.m. Mackenzie's heart sank as two people who were clearly security agents met them and their two EA bodyguards just outside customs.

"Professor and Doctor Devereux, I am special agent Kelly White of the United States Army Counterintelligence..." Though dressed in formal business attire rather than uniforms, the badges they produced confirmed who they were. INSCOM - U.S. Army Intelligence and Security Command.

Army! Why don't they have uniforms? Mackenzie had no reason to know that INSCOM staff seldom dressed in uniforms and certainly not while in D.C.

Before they could ask any questions, CI White explained she was investigating the incident at Patch Barracks, and she had reason to believe they might be able to help in her investigation.

Mackenzie risked a quick glance full of confusion at her husband. She was not reassured when she saw he was just as confused. *What could we possibly help with?* She was calmed a little when Carter answered in an untroubled tone.

"Of course, we'll be happy to help as much as possible." He didn't voice his questions. The public area of Dulles International was not the place to discuss top-secret information. He took Mackenzie's elbow and guided her in step with the two agents.

It sounded as if they wouldn't be long. Their meeting with James and Irene wasn't until noon. A short detour to Army Counterintelligence offices in Ft. Belvoir, Virginia, just a forty-minute drive, shouldn't make them late.

Carter's first hint that all was not as it seemed should have been when, instead of taking the on-ramp toward Reston, the driver looped around then headed north toward Sterling.

As they pulled up to a modest home on the outskirts of Sterling, a suburb of D.C. with modest enough prices to attract many government employees, Carter thought *safe house. Why a safe house?* Nothing he saw when they entered changed his mind. Two obvious security guards were stationed in the foyer, where Carter, Mackenzie, and the two EA bodyguards were asked to sign in and leave their belongings.

Carter gave an unobtrusive hand signal to the bodyguards when one of them appeared disgruntled at being asked to leave his cell phone, weapons, and personal tracking device. Calmly, Carter complied, and the others followed suit.

Once they'd all turned over everything they had, *except our freaking wedding rings—they certainly are security conscious,* the Devereuxs were ushered into the dining room and asked to have a seat at the table. Their bodyguards were instructed to have a seat on the chairs outside the room.

"May we offer you something to eat or drink?" Kelly asked in a friendly tone.

"No, thank you," Carter replied, equally politely. "Mackenzie, do you want anything?" She shook her head, gazing steadily at Kelly, who, with her team, were seated with their backs to the wall across the table from them.

"In that case, let's get started," Kelly said. She picked up a copy of that morning's Washington Post, with the headline screaming in large font about the A-Echelon scandal. She smiled as she pointed to it.

"Your names appear several times in this story," she

stated, still smiling. "I suppose that's because you, Professor Devereux, are sure to draw attention, since you and your discoveries are so famous."

Carter shrugged and grinned but didn't say anything.

When Kelly got no response from Carter she looked questioningly at Mackenzie.

Mackenzie smiled as well. "I'm sorry, but the activities of our agency are top-secret and compartmentalized. Even if you have the proper clearances, we still can't talk about any of it without authorization from the directors, or the President."

Kelly broadened her smile. "Not to worry. I was just curious. I don't want information about your missions or assignments. I hope this meeting won't distract you from carrying on your excellent work.

"In fact, we," she indicated herself and the team members with her, "have top-secret and Q Clearance. We've already had very interesting conversations with James Rhodes and Irene O' Connell as well as two DARPA scientists. They told us all about your work at A-Echelon and about quantum physics, Zero Point Gravity, antimatter, and some other mindboggling subjects.

"To think this all dated back to more than fifty thousand years ago. Well, I'll just have to repeat myself. Mindboggling."

Though he could feel Mackenzie's glance turning to him, he kept his face impassive. Kelly White was on a fishing expedition for something. He didn't know what, but he didn't intend to bite.

Mackenzie was taking her cues from him and didn't respond either.

Finally, seeming to realize she wasn't going to get them

involved with this approach, Kelly switched tactics and showed her hand.

"You see, Professor and Doctor Devereux, we have reason to believe the incident at Patch Barracks was an antimatter bomb explosion. We have checked with the CIA and every other security organization in the US, and there is no one they know of who has the knowhow to develop such a bomb.

"In fact, none of them, except DARPA, has been working on that technology, and as far as we could establish, no one in the world has been working on it—until now. That's to say, until the information out of the Alboran Sea Codex has been made available to them—DARPA *and* someone else. "

Carter's senses started to tingle. He had a bad feeling about what was coming next, but he didn't dare communicate his apprehension to his wife.

Kelly continued, confirming his intuition. "This leads us to only one conclusion. There must have been a leak of the information coming out of your ancient libraries to someone who has used it to build an antimatter bomb and use it against the US armed forces at Patch Barracks. That *someone* killed almost four hundred people, injured close to six hundred, and destroyed almost the entire base."

Mackenzie let out a small cry and clapped her hand over her mouth. Carter, too, was in shock. He shook his head to clear his mind of the racing thoughts.

Kelly was now on a roll and jumped to something else. "Tell me about your trips to the Alboran Sea and every visit you've made to Europe since your discovery of the underwater city in the Alboran Sea, Professor Devereux."

Carter's mind was racing at lightspeed to explore the meaning of the question. *Is she trying to pin the leak on us? What does she have that would lead her to that conclusion?* His instinctive response was to show no fear.

"I suggest before we go any further with this, we ask the Director of A-Echelon, James Rhodes, and the Deputy Director, Irene O'Connell, to join us."

The only indication he'd fazed her was the momentary blush of anger that faded as quickly as it came. "In due time, Professor, in due time." Her demeanor suddenly changed. She leaned forward over the table, and her eyes were stark. "No need to call them yet. I first want you and Doctor Devereux to answer a few more questions, which I am sure the two of them won't be able to answer."

Ignoring Carter for the moment, Kelly focused on Mackenzie. "Doctor Devereux, please tell me about your trips to Europe, and why you went there three times in the past eighteen months."

"I'm wondering why it is of any importance to you, but to satisfy your curiosity," Mackenzie said in a steady voice, "I haven't seen much of Europe before, and we were using the opportunity, while we were in the region visiting the site in the Alboran Sea."

"On all three occasions, you went to Switzerland. Correct?"

The penny dropped for Carter. All along, he'd known something wasn't right, and now he knew what it was. He started playing with his wedding ring, suddenly relieved they *hadn't* taken that from him. It was his signal to Mackenzie that they were in danger, and she should be careful.

He wished they had mental telepathy with each other. But his Mackie was smart and calm. They'd been set up, probably by their sworn enemies, the Nabateans. Was Kelly White one of the bad guys, or did she genuinely believe he and Mackenzie had crossed over to the dark side? That they'd even dream of betraying their country? And for what? What could...

It doesn't matter. Either way, we're screwed. Probably suspected of treason.

By the time Carter reached his conclusion, Mackenzie had noticed his signal and acknowledged his warning by rubbing her left eye, as if something was irritating it. A sense of relief flooded him. A small comfort, that she had remembered the signal they set up, even though they'd never had reason to use it before. He could only hope she remembered the rest of the drill as he began his part.

He made a quick but discreet assessment of who was in the room, where everyone was sitting, and their body language. He made a mental note of whether they were carrying a weapon and where, whether they were relaxed or tense, alert or lulled by the exchange.

What he saw convinced him that if he couldn't persuade Kelly to summon James and Irene, he and Mackenzie were in deep trouble.

He had to do something to take Kelly's attention off Mackenzie. So, he went on the offensive. "Yes, we went to Switzerland on every one of those trips—Mackenzie and I love the country. Have you ever been there?"

Kelly shook her head and opened her mouth to respond, but before she could say anything, Carter said, "You're missing out on something very beautiful.

"But I now have a question for you. Why is it I get the feeling you're not entirely honest and forthcoming with us, Special Agent White? Why am I getting the impression you have something up your sleeve you want to surprise us with? My suggestion is you stop beating around the bush and lay it all on the table."

As he'd hoped, the ploy worked. He got under Kelly's

skin, and she turned her focus on him, which allowed Mackenzie to casually look around and make her own assessment of their surroundings to use if it became necessary to get out of there.

Kelly stuck her chin out. "Okay, here we go then. On your first trip to Switzerland, you opened a numbered bank account and deposited twenty-five million dollars. A week later, thirty million dollars more, and every few weeks, more deposits were made; from Russia, Iran, and Saudi Arabia. You bought a fifty-million-dollar jet soon after opening the account. There is close to two hundred fifty million dollars in the account right now."

As Carter opened his mouth to deny it, she overrode him. "Don't bother to deny it. I have the account statements here, with all your personal details when you opened the account. I even have a video clip of you at the bank when you opened the account.

"You see, Professor and Doctor Devereux, contrary to popular belief, we do get the cooperation of the Swiss bankers in certain cases. Especially when there are requests from one of the US security agencies suspecting money laundering and transactions related to the security of the US and its allies.

"In cases like that, they gladly break their code of secrecy."

Carter didn't blink. He looked her straight in the eyes. She was lying or misguided. But which?

He'd never opened a Swiss bank account nor ever set foot in a Swiss bank, for that matter.

The video clip claim was a puzzle. Either she had one, or she didn't. If she did, how? It had to be fake. A body double? Someone made up to look like him? He knew security videos in most stores and gas stations in the US were of low quality and easily fooled. But a Swiss bank would certainly have the best there was.

Carter managed to suppress the anger. He knew Kelly, one of her team members, or someone else who might be able to see them on camera could misinterpret anger as an admission of guilt.

Mackenzie was less successful. Her redhead's complexion betrayed her as she first went red and then white, though she pressed her lips together to keep from expressing her wrath. Maybe only Carter knew her well enough to know what the change in her eye color meant. The gold sparks that usually sparkled in her green eyes had turned to a fiery color that meant someone was about to get hurt. He'd even swear her hair was on fire. He closed his eyes in a brief entreaty to the Almighty. *Please don't let her try to strangle the bitch.*

"No response, Professor?" Kelly smirked.

"Oh, sorry, I thought you told me not to deny it because you had all the proof. Please continue." To start defending himself and Mackenzie at this point would only make them look guilty. So far, no crime had been implied. It wasn't illegal to open a Swiss bank account, and the numbers she'd thrown at him like accusations of something nefarious were well within his wealth. He had no reason to respond to a vague implication of wrongdoing.

Kelly slapped the table. Carter observed with interest the difference between a frustrated brunette and his own angry redhead. Mackenzie's skin would always betray her emotion. The other woman resorted to dramatic gestures. Now she flung both hands into the air and raised her voice.

"Deposits were made to your account from three countries that interest me very much. Russia. Iran. Saudi Arabia. You are aware, I assume, that America, *your country*, has imposed sanctions and trade embargos on the first two. And why would you have dealings with anyone in the country where your wife was kept in custody for almost a year?"

She flung a folder full of documents proving the deposits on the table in front of him. "*Now* do you have any comments?"

Mackenzie was steaming but remained quiet.

He glanced at the documents and then met Kelly's gaze. He still had no need to respond, and his determination not to had already given him information about Kelly's agenda, though not what was driving it.

She'd exaggerated the restrictions on doing business with Russia and Iran. There was no outright embargo. Her knowledge of Mackenzie's ordeal meant she had far-reaching access to top-secret information. But unless she had other fake documents "proving" an actual crime, they'd do better to gather all the information they could before responding or making their move.

What that move should be remained unclear. He'd like to stand up, take Mackenzie's hand, and walk out without any trouble. But he already suspected that idea was hopelessly naïve. Everything that had happened since they sat down in this room indicated the CI had made up her mind and was now trying to entrap them into saying something incriminating.

He regarded her impassively, his poker face intact despite her insinuations. His mind, however, was furiously busy. He was now convinced beyond the shadow of a doubt the interview was being recorded, though he hadn't spotted the devices.

He squeezed Mackenzie's arm, both to comfort her and to signal her to remain silent and let him deal with the questions. She was angry enough to explode, and whatever came out of her mouth when that happened would be used against them.

So far, he believed Kelly didn't have enough to justify an arrest but was instead poking around, hoping something would jump out. He still didn't have a firm conclusion about her role—whether *she* had manufactured this false evidence herself or had been duped by it. Either way, if he or Mackenzie became aggressive, it could force Kelly's hand. They'd be taken into custody, and then they'd be well and truly screwed.

Once upon a time, due process required a warrant for arrest, and a warrant required the authorities convincing a judge there was probable cause. Arraignment and a formal charge had to follow in a timely manner, or the suspect had to be released unless a judge ordered incarceration until trial.

However, since 2012, suspected terrorists could be detained indefinitely without trial. The National Defense Authorization Act of 2014 extended the law, and it remained in effect in direct opposition to the principle of "innocent until proven guilty." Carter suspected it was a thinly disguised permit to badger confessions out of suspected terrorists. Though he agreed with the principle that terrorists could not be allowed their freedom even if there wasn't enough evidence to convict them, it bothered him that the innocent people of America couldn't be protected without such draconian and potentially unfair tactics. Now law enforcement was also judge and jury, and it went against his sense of fair play.

In fact, the current situation was a case in point. If Kelly suspected them of an act of terrorism, as she was implying, then she could detain them indefinitely without trial. She'd get away with it, too. No one knew where they were. They

The Nabatean Secret

could effectively disappear, and though James and Irene would certainly look for them, it was entirely possible they wouldn't find a thing. Even if they were found, there would be nothing that anyone could do to free them, as long as the suspicions against them remained.

Carter's only defense was to remain calm and keep Mackenzie calm as well. He could see it was getting to Kelly. She was probably used to dealing with suspects who were more nervous and in awe of her. Not to mention *actually* guilty.

As the tension drained from Mackenzie's arm under his hand, he recognized his unspoken message had been received. He smiled at her, gave her arm a pat, and withdrew his hand.

Even when Kelly's questions became more and more accusatory, Mackenzie remained cool as the proverbial cucumber. If they hadn't been in such peril, he'd have been a bit disappointed. Mackenzie didn't lose her temper often, but when she did, the fireworks were exciting to watch.

He brought his attention back to Kelly, aware that only by staying hyperalert could he and Mackenzie navigate the perilous waters, infested with mines planted by her.

Kelly kept on firing barrages of questions at them like a battery of howitzers.

"What were you selling to these people?"

"Nothing. We've never sold anything to anyone in those countries, never traded in anything with anybody there. In fact, we're not traders at all."

"Professor, you must acknowledge you removed that library from the ancient city of the Giants in Egypt—outright antiquities theft. Admit you are unethical at best and nothing but a common thief at worst."

"No comment. You should take that up with James

Rhodes and Irene O'Connell. I repeat my request that you bring them here."

"Not going to happen," she said, and then fired a question at Mackenzie, "Doctor Devereux, you're no better than your husband. You illegally made a copy of that ancient text in that Armenian library. A text, I might add, that has since disappeared. What did you have to do with its disappearance, and what excuse do you have for violating the stipulation that no copies could be made?"

Mackenzie repeated Carter's answer to the letter. "No comment. You should take that up with James Rhodes and Irene O'Connell. I repeat our request that you bring them here."

"Tell me about your time in captivity in Saudi Arabia. What did you do there? Who kept you prisoner, and what did they do to you? What were you working on?"

"No comment. You should take that up with James Rhodes and Irene O'Connell. I repeat our request that you bring them here. For this question, we may also need the President of the United States and the Director of the CIA."

Unable to shake Mackenzie again, and recognizing she'd lost the advantage of Mackenzie's fit of temper, she turned back to Carter.

"How did you know where your wife was being held? Where and how did you get that information? Why did it take you so long to set her and your son and daughter free?"

The last question almost brought Carter out of his chair. It was a low blow. Intellectually, he knew the preparations that took ten days felt like an eternity to him at the time but were necessary to get all the information and prepare for the mission. That's what made the raid successful. However, waiting had strained his control to the breaking point, and he still felt overwhelming guilt that Mackenzie had given birth to their daughter without him while under lock and key.

He needed to do something about this before he lost it. Summoning all the calm he could muster, he held up his hand, stopping Kelly mid-sentence. "Okay, this has gone far enough. We have answered your questions, and there is nothing we can do about the fact that you don't like the answers. Now, I insist you bring James and Irene here immediately or take us to them. My wife and I will not answer more questions until that happens."

Kelly struck a sarcastic pose. "Oh, you scare me, Professor Devereux. I'll bring them in *if and when* I deem it necessary. Anyone else you want? Didn't you also mention the Director of the CIA? And let me see... oh yes... the *President of the United States*? Do you take me for an idiot? You think you can just throw their names around, and I'll believe you have a personal relationship with them? Preposterous."

Carter smiled, but with no warmth. *I have already decided a while ago that you are an idiot. All we have been trying to do for the last hour or so is to determine how big an idiot you are.*

Aloud, he said, "Your opinion notwithstanding, we will no longer engage with you in this outrageously ridiculous conversation. Your accusations and insinuations are baseless, offensive, and rude. If you have such a good case against us, why don't you explain it to the people we work for? Or do you have some sinister reason why you are afraid to let them hear what you have to say? Either bring in James Rhodes and Irene O'Connell, or we're out of here, unless you charge us with something."

Kelly returned his cold smile. "I don't think you understand your situation, Professor Devereux. It would be in your best interests to cooperate. You know as well as I do that I can invoke the powers granted to me by the NDAA. And I will, if you don't cooperate. I have a lot more information and a lot more questions. Even if the Director of the CIA or the President himself came here, as ridiculous as that notion is, they couldn't save you from answering for your crimes."

Something in her smug expression stopped Carter from what he was about to say—that he and Mackenzie had been working directly with and for the President and Bill. And that one phone call would put her skinny ass in a sling. His mind flashed to the headlines Mackenzie had shown him earlier that morning. Despite his best intentions not to react, he felt his pupils dilating as he made the connection.

We're not the only ones in trouble here. She's right; Bill, the President, James, and Irene probably can't save us—they're going to be too busy saving themselves.

To his relief, Kelly stood, and her team members jumped to their feet a few seconds later. "I'll let you think about *that* for a while."

The distinctive *click* of the door being locked signaled her intentions.

Chapter Twenty-One

DETAINED SOMEWHERE ELSE?

Both James and Irene had been dealing with phone calls all morning. They'd agreed to the A-Echelon story breaking knowing full well this would be the consequence, but it was still stressful. They'd been on edge and paranoid ever since Howard Crane's questions to the President had drawn them into this swamp. Trying to drain it while they were up to their asses in alligators was proving to be more than they'd bargained for. All either could say to the media was, "The matter is under investigation. I can't comment at this time."

That was all very well for the media. The media knew that line—it meant they'll have to wait. And while they waited, they could speculate. The members of Congress and other high-ranking officials, however, weren't so easily put off and left James's and Irene's ears ringing with threats when they wouldn't say more.

Neither had much time to think about not hearing from Carter and Mackenzie early in the morning, even though they usually called when they landed. It wasn't until almost noon when there was a break in the phone calls long enough to check in with each other that they both realized neither had heard from the Devereuxs.

Usually, either Carter or Mackenzie would call as soon as they landed. Then they'd check into their hotel and make their way to the A-Echelon offices. Irene tried to suggest they were probably napping or something, since they hadn't had time to rest from their European vacation before being dragged to Washington by a mysterious summons.

James shook his head. "It's past noon. We had a firm appointment. And they would've seen the headlines and known the shit has hit the fan. Something's wrong."

Irene nodded. "You're right. I'll call." She dialed Mackenzie's number first, and when it went straight to voicemail, she tried Carter's. "Their phones are off."

"Try the bodyguards," James suggested. He was already picking up his desk phone to call the hotel and see if they'd checked in. After a ridiculous song and dance wherein the desk clerk said he couldn't give out information about guests and James lost his temper and threatened to have the clerk arrested for interfering in a government investigation, he got his answer. They had not checked in.

Then Irene told James the bodyguards' phones had gone to voicemail as well. Shaken, she fumbled the number and had to start over as she called the executive terminal at Dulles to determine whether they'd ever even landed there. In a moment, she reported to James.

"They did land. They and their bodyguards went through customs with no problems just before nine a.m. What could have happened to them?"

"There are still their GPS trackers. Check their location now."

Irene made the call to Operations and put the phone on speaker so James could hear the answer for himself. They learned the trackers had been switched off. Major alarm bells went off.

"No, they haven't," he said to the Operations tech. "They can't be. There's no on/off switch on this model. The only way to make them go silent is to take out the battery or destroy the device."

"Maybe it died?" the tech suggested.

"All four of them at the same time? Give me their last location." He took down the address, a private residence on the outskirts of D.C., and disconnected without another word.

"Get hold of Sean. I don't like them being off the grid this way. I'm afraid something's seriously wrong."

Carter stood and pulled Mackenzie up on her feet and held her in his arms. She pulled his head down and whispered softly in his ear. "Carter, we have to get out of here."

He buried his head in her hair and whispered. "Yes. But be careful what you say. I am sure we're being watched and recorded."

Outside, the EA bodyguards went on alert when they saw Kelly lock the door. They stood as she turned around and faced them.

"Ma'am, what's going on? Why did you lock that door?"

"It's none of your concern. I know you work for A-Echelon. Maybe you don't know yet, but your Mickey Mouse organization has been outed as being part of the CIA. I have authorization from the Director of the CIA and your boss, James Rhodes, to question the Devereuxs," she lied with complete confidence.

The bodyguards hadn't just fallen off a turnip truck.

They sensed something was wrong, but without their weapons they had no way to challenge the Army Counterintelligence agents. They also didn't know if it was time for a show of force. They looked at each other and tacitly agreed it was probably best to wait and see what happened.

The walls and door weren't soundproofed. Carter and Mackenzie could hear most of what Kelly told their bodyguards, and neither believed it for a minute. Mackenzie flashed him a questioning look, and he shook his head. There was no way James and Irene would do this to them.

Was there? What had happened in the last few weeks while they were out of the loop?

Carter would have given a significant portion of his considerable wealth to have a half-hour conversation with either James or Irene right about now.

There were more questions than he could think of, but no answers at all.

Continuing to hold Mackenzie as if comforting her, he glanced around the room, looking for the least likely place for a hidden camera. He turned until he could whisper to her without, he hoped, a spy lens being able to see his lips move. Risking also that his words couldn't be picked up by the most sensitive of listening devices any security organization could deploy, he rapidly gave her his conclusions.

"It's obvious Special Agent White, and we have to assume her superiors, have made up their minds we're guilty of something. She's going to use every trick in the book to pressure us into admitting wrongdoing. The fact that she's refusing to call in James and Irene can mean several things. Either she doesn't want to spoil a good story with the facts, which means she is in cahoots with the bad guys. Or James and Irene are in trouble up to their necks, too. Or... I am almost scared to say this; James and Irene have indeed agreed to this."

"Well, all of those scenarios require that we escape," Mackenzie said. "We can't let her arrest us and lock us up until..."

"Agreed. Here is my plan," Carter said. He went on to explain what they'd do.

She agreed.

"Okay, let's go through the so-called evidence she left here. Maybe we'll be able to piece together a theory," Carter said. He gave her a last squeeze and then let her go so they could both sit down and look through the documents.

Damned if they didn't look absolutely authentic.

Mackenzie leaned over and said, barely audibly, "If I didn't know for a fact these are false, I'd swear in court they were authentic. Who has the technical ability to do this to us? Who has the means to produce all this false evidence to set us up, and why?"

Carter rolled his eyes at her. "Who do you think? The Nabateans, of course. They have virtually unlimited resources, as we know by now. Why they'd choose this particular method, we'll soon find out. My guess is this time they're not just after the two of us. This will have wide repercussions, from us right up to the President. They must have a plant, or more likely several, very high in the government."

"You don't think...?" Mackenzie started. Then she put her hand over her mouth, and Carter could see from her widened eyes that she'd had a very disturbing thought. He'd already dismissed the same thought. They couldn't both have been so blind as to misjudge James and Irene.

Carter shook his head. "I don't. I seriously doubt that

James or Irene has anything to do with it. Nor do I think Bill or the President is involved. In fact, I think they may be in as much trouble as we are. Put it out of your mind."

He couldn't help but harbor some concern, though. It was now noon-thirty, and they'd missed their meeting with James and Irene. Would that signal the two of them that something was amiss with him and Mackenzie? Or were they being detained somewhere else?

He had no doubt if Kelly White had her way, he and Mackenzie weren't going to see the light of day anytime soon. Most likely, the next time they saw her, she'd be invoking the provisions of the National Defense Authorization Act.

Chapter Twenty-Two

MORE TO THIS THAN MEETS THE EYE

Sean Walker was on his way to A-Echelon headquarters to discuss the morning's headlines when he got a call from Irene O'Connell.

"Sean, where are you?"

"On my way to see you, about fifteen minutes out."

"Good. Make it ten. We've got problems."

Sean stepped on the accelerator, pushing the speed limits all the way to A-Echelon. He arrived about ten minutes and thirty seconds after taking the call and sprinted to James's office, where he found James and Irene waiting for him with their eyes on their watches.

Irene would normally have made a joke. The fact that she didn't alarmed him more than anything else.

He listened without interruption as Irene rapidly filled him in on their concerns about Carter and Mackenzie. She handed him a slip of paper with the address of their last GPS location.

"On it," he said. Ten minutes later, he and three of his men rendezvoused and he jumped into their SUV. While one of the men drove, Sean opened his laptop so he and the other two could check satellite views of the house online. Balancing the need to determine Carter and Mackenzie's situation against public safety, they were relieved to learn the house backed a vacant lot. Though there were houses on both sides of the one where they hoped Carter and Mackenzie still were, the lot behind had several trees and bushes but no building.

At 1:10 by Sean's wristwatch, they drove past the front of the house at the GPS coordinates. Two government SUVs bearing the insignia of INSCOM were parked in the driveway. Baffled, Sean directed the driver to turn the next corner and stop. A quick discussion with his men convinced him there was something strange about this situation.

INSCOM? What were those guys doing with Carter and Mackenzie? This might be one of those times when all was not as it seemed.

He concurred with the assessment that there was no way to reach the house by stealth. It was the middle of the day. They were wearing civilian clothes, and the weather was cool, so they were wearing jackets that would conceal their weapons. But if they approached openly and it went sideways, they'd have lost the element of surprise.

It might be best to storm the house simultaneously from front and back, and apologize later if that was warranted. Either way, the situation was dicey. They'd have to be careful. And hope no one started shooting, especially with Carter and Mackenzie potentially in the crossfire.

While Sean and his team were discussing their approach, Kelly and hers unlocked the door to the room where Carter and Mackenzie were being held. They ignored the questions of the EA bodyguards, who by now were highly suspicious and getting a bit agitated.

Kelly and her two team members took their seats as before. All three agents faced Carter and Mackenzie, who had their backs to the door. As the agents sat in unison, all three bent forward slightly to pull their chairs closer to the table. It was the unguarded moment Carter and Mackenzie anticipated.

Carter shoved the table with every ounce of his strength. The sudden move caught the INSCOM team by surprise. The edge of the table caught the three of them in their stomachs, doubling them over the table and knocking the breath out of them. Inertia aided the Devereuxs as they slammed the agents' heads down on the table.

Mackenzie had claimed Kelly, who had infuriated her earlier. She used both hands to smash Kelly's forehead into the table and stun her. Carter used one hand on each of the other agents, putting a bit more effort into the shove he gave the male agent, to make sure he was out of the fight immediately.

It was over almost before it began, with the male agent unconscious and the two females dazed. Carter and Mackenzie worked like the team they were to quickly disarm the others. Mackenzie got two guns in her hand and pressed one into each female's forehead. She hissed, "Be quiet and don't move."

Carter relieved the male agent of his gun, located some linen napkins in a drawer in the china cabinet, and used them to gag the three agents. He assumed the guards in the foyer would be able to see them on video—they had to move quickly. He took Kelly's keys and unlocked the door, his finger already on his lips to silence his bodyguards.

Mackenzie handed Carter her weapons, and he gave one to each of the EA guards then signaled them to come in.

Finding the INSCOM agents stunned and gagged, the EA guards finished the job of neutralizing them by securing their hands with cable ties. Now their only barrier to escape were the two remaining INSCOM agents out in the foyer.

Carter sent a silent prayer of thanks for the carpeting throughout the house. One of the EA guards burst through the door into the foyer to catch one INSCOM agent reading on his mobile phone and the other watching TV. Before they could react, he'd moved out of the doorframe to give his partner room to join him.

He shouted, "Don't move! Put your hands in the air. Now!"

One of the INSCOM agents shot his hands into the air as directed. The other was stupid and went for his gun. The second EA guard, who'd just burst through the door, fired about two feet above the agent's head, and shouted, "Next one's between your eyes! Don't be an idiot. Hands up, now!"

Carter threw each INSCOM agent off his chair and told them to stay on the ground, on their stomachs, hands behind their heads. One EA bodyguard covered them while the other efficiently immobilized them with cable ties and stuffed their mouths with paper found on the desk.

Mackenzie walked in with her hands full of mobile phones and briefcases she'd liberated from Kelly and company. She'd also gathered the files they'd left behind and shoved them into the briefcases. While she, Carter, and one of the bodyguards located their belongings—their weapons, phones, GPS trackers, and incidentally the keys to the SUVs

—from the security desk, the other found the landline into the house and ripped it out.

Their last precaution was to look through the window and make sure there were no more INSCOM personnel or neighbors who might have heard the shot outside. Seeing no one, they rushed out.

Sean and his partner had given the other two EA operatives a few minutes to get in place in the back of the house. When they clicked their throat mics to signal they were ready, Sean got out of the car and headed for the house, followed closely by his sidekick. They'd made it almost to the corner when they heard a gunshot. Both pulled their weapons and dashed for the front of the house.

Carter, Mackenzie! We're coming. A prayer came close on the heels of his first thought. *Please don't let the neighbors be home.* As Sean sprinted, he keyed his mic. "Gunshot! We're ten seconds out. Hit that back door, but be careful!"

Then all his concentration was taken by the need to stay on his feet as he leapt through the landscaping and took cover behind a thick shrub. He motioned his partner to take cover as well.

He flinched when the front door burst open but was under control again as he leveled his weapon at the emerging figures. As soon as he got a clear view of the first one, he lowered his weapon and spoke into his throat mic to the team approaching the backdoor. "Stand down."

The first figure, whom he recognized as one of his EA men, had cleared the door, and now the second came through, both cautiously assessing the surrounding area with guns at the ready.

Following them, Carter, gun leveled and ready, and finally Mackenzie, carrying what looked like an entire office worth of briefcases. They were headed for one of the INSCOM SUVs in the driveway.

Sean called out but didn't leave his cover. With what must have been some excitement inside, he didn't want to become collateral damage from a trigger-happy member of his own team.

The four stopped and looked around cautiously. Sean called out again.

"Carter! It's Sean." Only when the three men lowered their weapons did he stand and wave them over. "Let's go!"

Carter threw the keys to the INSCOM vehicles into the shrubs. A ride with Sean was better than a charge of grand theft auto on top of everything else they were already facing. When they got into the vehicle with Sean, he did wish they'd brought one of the bigger cars. Eight people stuffed into a seven-passenger SUV wasn't his idea of comfort.

For Carter's group, however, it still beat the room where they'd been held for the past several hours, and the company was also much friendlier.

"What happened?" Sean asked.

Because the members of Sean's rescue team weren't all read in on the top-secret information, Carter and Mackenzie had to keep their answers vague. However, what they gave Sean was enough to help him formulate a plan.

He dropped his men, including Carter and Mackenzie's bodyguards, on a street corner and told them to get a taxi or Uber ride to EA headquarters, and he'd be in touch.

Then he drove Carter and Mackenzie to Bethesda, to one of the EA safe houses. As they drove, the two of them told him the rest—in detail.

Sean agreed there was plenty to concern them all.

In turn, he told them about his day—how he tried to reach James and Irene as soon as he saw the headlines but was unable to get through. How he got a call from Irene while on the way to A-Echelon headquarters, and how he'd found them with the help of their GPS trackers' last known coordinates. And he joked about how he'd almost had an embarrassing accident when he heard the gunshot.

"You and that INSCOM guy both," Carter bantered.

The three of them laughed with the abandon of people who'd been in mortal danger and escaped.

"There's more to this than meets the eye," Sean said after he'd stopped laughing.

"Tell us something we don't know," Carter responded. He took Mackenzie's hand and squeezed.

Chapter Twenty-Three

WHERE THEY STOOD ON THE MATTER

At the A-Echelon safe house, Carter and Mackenzie handed Sean the documents they'd been given to prove their guilt—of what, they weren't quite sure.

Although, they were pretty sure it would include treason, among other things. The three of them talked at length about how this false evidence could be connected to the A-Echelon scandal in the press.

None of them believed the timing of their detention and those headlines had been a coincidence. A-Echelon had been compromised, somehow, and there was no knowing who was involved, but the Nabateans were definitely high on their list of suspects.

Sean, Carter, and Mackenzie would have staked their lives that James and Irene had no idea about this. They were probably in the same or similar trouble to Carter and Mackenzie's. Therefore, Sean couldn't just walk in and ask to see them. By now, the INSCOM agents would have been found or at least missed. Carter and Mackenzie's escape was bound to be the next big news story, and Sean could be put under surveillance if he were spotted.

Their phones were no good to contact James and Irene, either. The ones they had with them weren't encrypted, and even if they had been, the leak at A-Echelon might have compromised the decryption algorithm.

Their only chance was to get a coded message to the directors to meet Sean and make one hundred percent certain they weren't followed or under surveillance themselves.

Sean left Carter and Mackenzie resting while he went out to make his arrangements. An hour later, Irene out of the blue got a delivery of her favorite treat, a Starbucks mocha latte, which she didn't order. *How thoughtful of James.* When she handed the delivery boy a tip, he exchanged it with near-professional sleight of hand for a note she only noticed in her hand when she picked up the cup of coffee. *How the hell?*

When she read the note, Irene went straight to James. "Sean's got them," she whispered. "Don't say anything. Meet me outside."

Irene was waiting just outside the front doors of the office building where A-Echelon had its headquarters.

When James came walking out, she said in a low voice, "James, don't turn around. Look up and down the block." As he followed her directions, she explained, "We need to meet Sean at the elevator on the third level in the parking garage at Tyson's Corner Center. He wants us to arrive separately and make sure no one follows. Seven p.m." She knew he understood when he gave a decisive nod and strode away from her toward a Metro station.

She returned to her office and worked until five, telling anyone who asked she hadn't seen James in a while and didn't know where he went. At five, she left, retrieved her car, and drove to Tyson's Corner, thirteen miles from downtown D.C. She found a parking spot on the third level of the mall and made her way to the elevator, where she saw James loitering but didn't speak to him. In a moment, a black SUV with tinted windows pulled up. It was identical to thousands of such vehicles in the D.C. area, but when the driver shoved the door open, she saw it was Sean. She got in, and James got into the back seat behind her.

"What the hell is happening?" Sean asked, his expression reflecting the intensity in his tone.

"We should have warned you," James said. Irene echoed his apology. The two of them filled him in on the Shadow and Howard Crane situation. "We brought Carter and Mackenzie to D.C. to let them know there was trouble. I guess we underestimated how fast it would come down."

"You think?" Sean said. He was furious, but it wouldn't help to blame the messengers. "Let me tell you what happened when they got off their plane this morning." He brought them up to speed on the INSCOM angle and told them what Carter and Mackenzie had been reluctant to say. "There's only one explanation for the way Special Agent White treated them and the direction of her investigation. They're suspected of treason."

"Oh, my God," Irene exclaimed. "Kelly—" She bit off whatever she was going to say. James picked it up.

"We've met Kelly White. In the past several weeks, we've given her a lot of information about A-Echelon and our activities. Also about Carter's role and his and Mackenzie's comings and goings. I never got the impression she suspected them of anything. Did you, Irene?"

"No."

James went on. "There's no way Carter and Mackenzie

have committed treason. I'm certain of that. What's their assessment?"

Sean explained. "They've been framed, no doubt about that. Special Agent White has either been duped or is part of the conspiracy. The evidence against them has been very cleverly manufactured. Whoever is doing this to them has impressive resources."

"Where are they now?" Irene asked.

"With all due respect, it may be better for you not to know. Suffice it to say, they escaped from Special Agent White, and they're safe right now. But they're fugitives from the law. To clear their names, they'll eventually have to give themselves up. However, before they can do that, we'll have to gather the evidence to show that they are not guilty."

James agreed. "They probably did the right thing to escape. It might have been a very long time before we found them if Kelly White had managed to invoke NDDA. What worries me is her failure to inform us of her suspicions."

"She told them she had your full cooperation, and you didn't need to be there. In fact, she said that she had your authorization to question them," Sean said.

James had on what Irene called his Thunder-god look. It meant everyone better get out of his way. "Bitch!" he hissed. "She'll hear from me the moment I see her again."

Irene suddenly sat up straight. "James, could this have anything to do with our meeting being cancelled?"

They'd had a meeting scheduled with the President to assess the reactions of the media, the public, and Congress to the A-Echelon story and to plan their response. Daniella had called them just before Irene got Sean's message to let them know the meeting was cancelled. She couldn't give them a new time or, in fact, a reason for the cancellation and had only said she'd be in touch.

Considering the revelations about Carter and Mackenzie's day, it took on a new and worrying meaning.

It felt like quicksand was about to swallow them. James's temper didn't improve when Sean added that Kelly White had repeatedly refused Carter's and Mackenzie's requests for him and Irene to be brought into the interrogation to vouch for them and explain.

"Who is this woman? Her methodology is as suspect as her motivation. For God's sake, she's got top-secret and Q Clearance, how the—" James didn't get further.

"Is she acting on her own, either out of a misguided passion to bring a pair of suspected traitors to justice or because she'd been duped? Or is she one of the bad guys?" Irene asked.

"Perhaps working for the Nabateans?" James added.

"I don't know whether this is oversight or a trap," Sean said, "but you guys haven't mentioned EA's name coming up in any of this."

"No, you're right. It hasn't," said Irene. "But neither did any hint of Carter and Mackenzie being suspected of treason. I don't know what to think."

"Until we know differently, then, we may be the only ones who can help. We can get messages through, and we can provide protection," Sean suggested.

"I appreciate that, Sean," James said. "It's part of the plan that will soon be suspended from our duties pending the investigations that will follow. We won't have the ability to directly talk to anyone, including Bill and especially the President. When we made that plan, we didn't know Carter and Mackenzie would be caught up in anything like this. If INSCOM, or God forbid, the FBI get to Bill or the President and make a case against them, the whole house of cards could come tumbling down."

"I understand."

"I'm sure you do, but just to be certain we're all on the same page," James said, "if the President or Bill can be convinced by this false evidence that the Devereuxs are traitors, it will be bad not only for them but for us. We hired them, and we were supposed to be supervising them. Furthermore, we hired *you*. And if whoever manufactured that evidence wants to bring us all down, we'll all go down together."

More discussion followed, with the pros and cons leading them to one dead end after another. There was no clear direction except to wait and see and meanwhile do what they could to try to understand what was going on.

For now, Carter and Mackenzie would remain hidden. The three of them didn't know who they could trust, and while they wanted to trust the President and Bill, it might depend on who had whispered what into their ears by now.

They all knew the drill. No communication by electronic means of any kind. Encoded, hand-delivered messages through anonymous go-betweens like the Starbucks delivery boy would be their only form of communication.

Meanwhile, Sean would get in touch with Dylan and bring him to D.C. to be briefed before being sent back to Freydís to batten down the hatches there.

James and Irene would try to get a meeting with the President or Bill to determine whether they knew about the allegations against the Devereuxs and where they stood on the matter.

Chapter Twenty-Four

BETWEEN A ROCK AND A HARD PLACE

The INSCOM safe house guards managed to free themselves first. The landline was down, and there were no cell phones left in the house, so they freed the others and then one of them went for help—on foot.

Once communications had been reestablished, Kelly reported to Terrance Ham, and he in turn reported to his supervisor. At Kelly's urging, Terrance persuaded his ranking officer to reach out to the FBI for help. At an emergency meeting in the Pentagon, the Director of the FBI agreed to issue an APB for Carter and Mackenzie Devereux. With a little prompting, he also assigned Russell McCormick to work with Kelly. Their directive was to work fast. This was a crisis impacting National Security, and they had the go-ahead to pull out all the stops.

McCormick convinced Kelly the package she'd received from an anonymous tipster was legitimate. Otherwise, why would the Devereuxs escape rather than stick around to sort things out? Kelly bought it, hook, line, and sinker. At Russell's urging, she took it to the Director of the FBI to try to convince him that the President and the Director of the CIA were part of it and should at least be suspected of *some* wrongdoing. And the "it" in question was that the A-Echelon story was only the tip of the iceberg.

FBI Director Alec Burnett fumbled for his nitroglycerin tablets. This was why he took them. News like this could, no-kidding, cause him to have a coronary. He needed to retire. But before he did, he was going to kill that INSCOM bimbo with his bare hands. And possibly send Russell McCormick to a post in BFE Idaho. Why in tarnation had they sat on this info?

He perused the documents. Proof that this Carter Devereux had accepted foreign payments for God-knows-what, but it looked like they'd transferred highly sensitive, deadly technology to someone who wanted to destroy the US. Swiss bank records, video clips, emails, and freaking NSA recordings of phone calls. He wasn't supposed to know about those, though it was common knowledge. It was illegal, for Heaven's sake. Was he going to have to arrest his counterpart at NSA? Not to mention the freaking *President of the United States*? Did he even have the authority to arrest the President? Probably not. Then he remembered, the Sergeant at Arms of the United States Senate was the only person with authority to arrest a sitting president.

What the hell am I thinking? He popped another nitro tablet and then had Kelly White and Russell McCormick summoned to his office and unloaded on them everything he'd felt when he studied the information.

Kelly was taken aback that she was under fire. "Director Burnett, I couldn't just hand this over to someone and risk that it wasn't legitimate. I did my duty. I apprehended the suspects and proceeded to interrogate them to verify these allegations. Before I could, they attacked me and my team and escaped. I considered that to be verification of their guilt and brought it directly and immediately to you through appropriate channels."

Director Burnett had to admit she had him there. It still put him between a red-hot rock and a granite-like hard place. The President and the Director of the CIA would not be easy to take on. He wasn't even sure how it could be done. The President, of course, would have to be impeached before he could be investigated. But that would involve giving every member of Congress sensitive, top-secret, and Q-Clearance information, regardless of their clearances.

What a nightmare!

And what if they were in the dark about what the Devereuxs were up to? If the President and Bill Griffin were innocent, the damage to them and the country from the accusations alone was unthinkable. He wanted desperately to believe that none of the people mentioned were guilty. There was no love lost between him and Bill Griffin, but the animosity between them was not bigger than the interests of the country.

In the end, he determined that the only course of action was to personally confront them with the information and judge for himself based on their reactions. He could believe their involvement with A-Echelon and its activities. He knew more about some of that hocus-pocus, science fiction stuff than the average citizen, and even agreed that some of it should be investigated. But actively betraying their country and selling information to the enemy? He couldn't even believe that of Bill Griffin, much less the President. Not until he had concrete evidence.

As he picked up his phone to schedule a meeting with them, he comforted himself by reasoning that if they hadn't been specifically named in the letter, which they hadn't, then they probably weren't involved. If someone wanted to bring down a government, the President or the Director of the CIA would be much bigger fish to land than the two scientists, Carter and Mackenzie Devereux.

Chapter Twenty-Five

TWO SOURCES OF THE INFORMATION LEAKS

Neither Carter nor Mackenzie were inclined to sit on their thumbs and let others solve their problems. If they couldn't leave the safe house, at least they could try to make sense of the information they'd been blindsided with that morning. They resumed their interrupted perusal of the evidence Special Agent White had handed them and added what they found in White's and her teams' briefcases.

Following a method Mackenzie suggested, they spread everything out on the dining table. They first sorted the true information from what they knew to be false. Someone had gone to a great deal of trouble to manufacture it.

Along with what they'd already seen was quite a bit more, White had not shown them yet—most of it more bogus information.

And then there was the true stuff. Disturbingly accurate, and on the surface of it damning, information about A-Echelon activities. They supposed that James and Irene must have cooperated fully with the investigation. Whether that meant those two were also involved in the entrapment... they didn't want to believe it. A happier explanation would be they'd been duped by Special Agent White. Her modus operandi earlier in the day, when she "asked a few questions" was ample demonstration of her capability to deceive.

How was it possible to produce such a perfect face of Carter on video and match his voice so flawlessly? Mackenzie could have sworn it would even match on a digital voice analyzer.

"Mackie, this was done so professionally it would convince anyone—even our best friends. Unless technical specialists can expose this hoax, we're in the worst trouble conceivable."

Mackenzie stared at him. "I'm sure the CIA has the technical knowhow to repudiate this. Let's hear what Sean can do to help when he gets back."

Digging through all the pockets and compartments of the briefcase for more hidden evidence, Mackenzie found a pen-sized digital recorder. Could White have been using this to record their interrogation? She tried to turn it on, but the battery was dead. In another compartment, she discovered the charger and set it up to charge while they continued to go through the evidence.

Now that they knew the extent of the information, both true and false, Mackenzie's method required they reorganize it, putting like with like to form an idea of what the bad guys were trying to accomplish with it. The immediate connection confirmed their instinctive suspicion that the Nabateans were behind it all. Mathieu Nabati, the Swiss banker, had the means to fabricate the false evidence concerning Carter opening the Swiss account.

"It's their revenge, right?"

Carter nodded slowly. "When Perrin Durand handed over Xavier Algosaibi's laptop and flash drive to the CIA, we seriously disrupted their organization. They came to within a hairsbreadth of total exposure."

Carter was referring to the shadowy Council of the Covenant of Nabatea, and specifically to Nabati and his mother, Graziella Marie Nabati, head of the Council of twelve and the only members whose names they'd discovered. Mother and son had vanished when they were compromised by the information retrieved from the laptop and flash drive.

"That attack on Freydís was their first attempt at revenge," Carter continued. "The Chinese interference in our Alboran Sea expedition was the second. This is their third attempt, and it's going to be ferocious. They'll throw everything they have at us."

"It scares me to think they have the technological capability to create, assemble, and somehow insert all this fake evidence into the record. I don't even want to begin to think about the levels to which they have infiltrated our government or any other government in the world," Mackenzie replied. Her famous temper was about to go on full display again; the gold flecks in her eyes were sparking flame-colored.

Carter had the fleeting thought that if he put Mackie up against Mathieu Nabati when she was in *this* mood, the Nabatean wouldn't know what had hit him. It caused him to smile fleetingly. But there was serious business afoot, and his amusement didn't last long.

"We'll have a better idea what to do about it when Sean gets back. I can't believe James and Irene would buy into this, but I'd give my fortune to know whether they're aware of it. On the other hand, if they saw the same evidence you and I saw over the last few hours, no one could blame them if they believed us guilty. And I can't even imagine what the President and Bill Griffin think. They don't know us like James and Irene do," Carter remarked.

"You can't think—" Mackenzie began. Tears formed in her eyes as she considered what it would mean if they'd lost the trust of their two friends as well as the President and the Director of the CIA.

The children. When will I see my children again?

Carter recognized the moment when her temper gave way to doubt. He put his arm around her. "We'll know soon enough. And once we know, we'll make a plan, whatever we face. We'll get through this, Mackie. We will."

Mackenzie nodded, remembering her months of captivity in that hellhole in Saudi Arabia. She almost gave way to despair again, but then she remembered her vow never to give up fighting this evil force until it was utterly destroyed.

She gave Carter a tremulous smile and patted his cheek. "I know, love."

They were still speculating about how that video of Carter in the Swiss bank and the telephone conversations he supposedly had with his Russian, Iranian, and Saudi clients could have been composed when Sean returned.

It was after midnight.

"Glad you're up. Let me brief you—"

"Before you start," Carter interrupted, "Mackenzie and I want to look you in the eye and tell you we aren't traitors. We didn't do this—whatever they're accusing us of. Whatever 'evidence' they produce, we're not traitors."

Sean stopped, momentarily nonplussed. "Did you think I ever, for one minute, doubted you? What do you take me for? It's not worth talking about."

"Sean, I—we—are grateful for that. But first you'll have to look at the 'evidence' on that table," Mackenzie pointed to the table where she and Carter had sorted the information into categories.

An hour later, Sean looked at them in turn and said, "One thing is as clear as daylight. These people are on the warpath, and they have the means and resolve to cause immense damage. But this hasn't changed my mind about your innocence."

Mackenzie rushed over and hugged him.

"Thank you." Carter nodded.

Sean said, "Okay, now we have that settled, let me tell you about the meeting with James and Irene."

He gave them a quick summary of what James and Irene had told him.

By then, the recorder pen had finished recharging, so they played the recording of their interrogation.

As they listened, Carter closed his eyes to visualize the evidence as a Venn diagram—his own method of organizing information. He'd bet anything that where the circles intersected, they'd find the source of the leak. But no matter how he mentally placed the evidence, nothing intersected.

Suddenly, he had it. His eyes flew open, and he sat up straight, startling Mackenzie and Sean.

"There are *two* sources of information leaks. The first, concerning the activities of A-Echelon operations over the past few years, has the President, Bill, James, Irene, and us in the crosshairs.

"The second has to do with the technical information about the antimatter bomb coming out of the A-Codex, which has placed only Mackenzie and me in the crosshairs so far."

Mackenzie and Sean waited for him to pull it together for them.

"Don't you see? The first type of information isn't in the Codex, while the second is. The first type could only have come from someone who had access to what James, Irene, the President, and Bill know. I'd swear on the lives of my kids that none of them leaked it. Even so, just think about it. They aren't the only ones who have the information. Besides the three of us and Dylan, who I'd also swear didn't leak it, the National Security Council, in part or in whole, and the Chief of Staff know about A-Echelon and its activities. It's got to be coming out of there."

None of them were naïve enough to believe it couldn't happen. They'd already flushed out one Nabatean plant, the former Vice President. It didn't require a stretch of the imagination to know that the Nabateans' ability to infiltrate the hallways of power to the Vice-Presidential level would make the penetration of the National Security Council a walk in the park.

Sean and Mackenzie, accustomed to Carter's eidetic memory, were not surprised when he began to name each of the dozen or more members from memory, along with their titles. In addition to the statutory members—the Secretaries of State, Defense, and Energy; the Chairman of the Joint Chiefs of Staff; and the Director of National Drug Control Policy—there were plenty more who were non-statutory but always invited, as well as some who were invited to meetings pertaining to their responsibilities.

One or more of them had to be the leak. Most likely this informant, Shadow, was either one of them or was being fed information by one of them.

Mackenzie was the first to regain her power of speech after Carter had shocked them to the core. How could it have happened again? They thought they'd flushed out the rat when the late Vice President's cover was blown. Now they had too many suspects to get a handle on. "How are we going to figure out who it is when we can't even leave this house?"

"We'll use EA, of course," Carter replied "And we'll start with those who are regarded as the most important members, because they're probably privy to more of the secret information than the others. If it isn't one of them, we'll work our way down through the ranks.

"Sean, we need to turn the lives of the Secretaries of Defense, State, and Treasury, and the Attorney General inside out. Covertly," Carter added.

Sean rolled his eyes.

Mackenzie said, "Carter, you said there were two sources of the leaks."

"Yeah. The technological information coming out of the A-Codex. That's a different story altogether. A superficial look at our process of keeping the translations secure shows it's impenetrable, and the only way it could leak is through one or more of the people handling that information.

"Obviously, Kelly White came to the same conclusion, especially after she got the nice video of me, the recording of my telephone calls, and banking information. Given that 'evidence'," Carter made air quotes, "I don't blame her for pointing at me. Although I would have appreciated it if she'd made a bit more of an effort to substantiate her so-called evidence."

Mackenzie seized on "superficial" as the operative word. "What made you say, 'superficial look at our process', Carter? We designed it to be impenetrable. Isn't it?"

Sean turned a curious look on Carter as well. "Yeah, isn't it?"

"Well, I don't know enough about computers to express an expert opinion or give you a technical explanation of how it could be exploited. But I do know the Nabateans have quantum computing technology. And I've been told with that technology, any encryption, no matter how sophisticated, can be broken in seconds. A few minutes at the most."

"But Carter, that means they'd have to get their hands on the mass storage devices, plug them into a quantum computer somehow, break the encryption, and copy the data, all without being detected," Mackenzie protested.

They all knew the rest of it. Retinal scans were required to open the boxes in which the storage devices were transported. Once in the vaults at CIA headquarters, only the President, Bill, James, or Irene could open them.

Speaking her thoughts aloud, Mackenzie said, "And we know none of them did it... or should we have second thoughts?"

"No. Not at all. I'm still adamant none of them did it," Carter said.

"So, let's assume that no one in the translation team and no one on the CIA side nor the President is involved. What other possibilities are there?" Mackenzie asked.

"Again, it's out of my league to explain, but they obviously have technology we don't," Carter said. "I mean, look at that video clip of me doing something I never did, in a place I've never been, or having a telephone conversation I've never participated in!

"What if they have the technology to access the data off

the devices even when they aren't connected to a computer? What if they can do it remotely, without having to open the boxes or the vault doors? In other words, doing it without leaving a trace."

"If you hear hoofbeats," Sean muttered.

"I know. Assume it's a horse, not a zebra. Do you have a better explanation?" Carter demanded.

Sean had to admit he didn't. But he added that he couldn't see how it was possible, either.

While they were talking, Mackenzie had been thinking about it. "I guess it's not too farfetched. I know that even when a computer is switched off, it still has its CMOS battery running. That's for the clock, right? What else could it be running? I've always wondered how a computer hard drive 'remembers' its information when it's unplugged."

"Well, there you go," Carter agreed. "I don't know much about it, either. Maybe it's different now, but I remember as far back as 1985, this guy named Wim van Eck proved you could read side-band electromagnetic radiation emissions coming off all sorts of electronic devices. He called it phreaking."

"Freaking what?" Mackenzie asked, laughing. "Like, freaking crazy? Freaking amazing?"

"P-H-R-E-A-K," Carter corrected. "I don't know why he called it that, but it was called phreaking eavesdropping. Capturing those emissions and replicating the data they represented. He also proved you could compromise election voting machines with it."

Sean chuckled. "I think we're all too tired to think straight. You guys have had an especially long day. Tomorrow, oh wait, it's already tomorrow. So, later today, I'll make some discreet inquiries with the IT specialists at the CIA to see what they say about this. I'll also pull an EA team together to help me investigate those NSC people."

"I could use some sleep," Mackenzie admitted.

"Good. In a few hours, Dylan will be here for a briefing. He'll carry any messages or instructions back to Freydís for you. After that, we'll move you to a different safe house, and we'll continue to move you every few days until we get a handle on all this."

Chapter Twenty-Six

A STAB THROUGH THE HEART

Though James and Irene didn't know it when they met with Sean, they'd already been outflanked by FBI Director Alec Burnett, and a crony of his, Brigadier General Jonas Fleming, the current head of INSCOM. General Fleming had been the last step in the conduit for Burnett's briefing and had made Ham and White available for Burnett's ass-chewing. The least he could do now was support his old friend in his scheme to assess the President's degree of guilt. The old "what did you know and when did you know it" was paramount in his mind as the two were led into the Oval Office.

Burnett nodded to his CIA counterpart, Bill Griffin, who returned the nod stiffly. Trailing Burnett and Fleming were Kelly White and Russell McCormick.

"Mr. President, Bill. I've asked Special Agent White to present information she has discovered with the help of Assistant Director Russell McCormick from my office. I think you'll find it a serious matter."

Burnett and Fleming observed the President and Bill Griffin closely as Kelly handed over one damning piece of evidence after another. They were looking for subtle signs of prior knowledge or any other indication of guilt.

Kelly began with the letter and package of evidence she'd received from the anonymous source, explaining that she'd corroborated the evidence before taking it to her supervisor in the division. The President and Bill recognized the A-Echelon information as an exact replica of the information Howard Crane had brought to them. Before they could say they'd already seen it, she started presenting the information about Carter and Mackenzie—that was new. Their blood ran cold when they watched a video clip on her laptop of Carter Devereux in the lobby of a Swiss bank whose name could clearly be seen on the walls in the video.

Kelly followed that up with a running narrative of Carter's suspicious activities as she presented the proof—deposit records and more.

Grant and Griffin didn't want to believe it. Independently, they flashed on the notion that whoever was out to destroy them hadn't bet on just one horse. Howard Crane had either withheld or hadn't been given the evidence they were seeing now.

What was this game, and who was playing it?

Kelly had planted a seed of doubt. She watered it by playing NSA recordings of phone conversations between Carter and two other men, one Russian, one Iranian.

When it came to the evidence of leaks from the A-Codex data and Kelly's report that the Patch Barracks explosion had been a direct result, they both exhibited shock and disappointment.

For Bill and the President, it was damning evidence that persuaded them the Devereuxs had gone rogue and sold secret technology to enemies of the US.

Kelly put the lid on the coffin when she gave her final

piece of evidence. The Devereuxs had overpowered her and her team and escaped earlier that day, even before she'd accused them of any wrongdoing. For her, it was an admission of guilt.

Bill couldn't believe he'd been such a fool. If the Devereuxs had been innocent of these allegations, why didn't they call for James, Irene, or even him to be there during the interview? That they chose instead to escape and go on the run was evidence they *were* guilty. He could see from the President's expression that he was equally disturbed.

Kelly had fallen silent to wait for a response from the President. She'd neglected to mention the directors of A-Echelon, or the fact that Carter and Mackenzie had repeatedly asked for them to be present. In fact, she hadn't mentioned it to anyone in the chain of command. It was irrelevant. She was one hundred percent sure of her conclusions.

She'd soon have them in custody and get their confessions, and then it wouldn't matter that she'd cut a few corners. She was almost never wrong when she got a hunch, and in this case, it was much more than a hunch. Just look at all the evidence. A conviction was certain. Another feather in her cap in her bid to advance in her career.

At last, the President, bearing an expression of hurt and disappointment, dismissed them with a solemn voice and the statement that he'd have orders for them at seven a.m. the next morning.

He signaled for Bill to hang back as the others left. When they were all gone, he turned to Bill, troubled.

"What do you make of this, Bill? How could Devereux have pulled the wool over our eyes for so long? And for God's sake, why?"

Bill answered, frowning, "You've got me. Usually it's a case of money, but the man's already got more money than most small countries. I don't know what could be motivating him. It's inconceivable to me that I could have been such a poor judge of character."

"Don't beat yourself up, Bill. He fooled me as well. And, I assume, James and Irene."

Bill looked up, stricken. "Can we trust *them*? They've been close to the Devereuxs, visited them at home. They hired them and managed them. Could they be in on it?"

The President considered the question. "You're right, they could be, and then we've got four people, and maybe more, in a conspiracy to destroy the country of their birth. What could possibly motivate Rhodes and O'Connell?"

"Money. They aren't wealthy like Carter. James is only a year away from retirement. The money could come in handy. Irene has a family. It's crazy, but not impossible." Bill fell silent. The reason he'd given was a thin one, considering the stakes. But money had a habit of turning good people bad in the blink of an eye.

It was a stab through the heart.

After a moment of silent reflection, the President called in his Chief of Staff, Scott Eadie. "Scott, forgive me. If I'd known what we were about to see, I'd have had you here in the first place. We," he added, indicating Bill and himself, "have just received some very disturbing news that impacts the plans we made with Howard Crane."

He spent a few minutes summarizing the evidence against the Devereuxs and the doubts he and Bill had about James and Irene.

Scott stopped making exclamations of dismay, and his expression became grimmer and grimmer with his teeth tightly clenched and his lips pressed tightly together as the President spoke.

"Your thoughts?" Grant asked.

"I think a couple of the Congressional oversight committees are going to have a field day with this," Scott responded.

"You think we must put this before them?"

Scott nodded vigorously. "*Oh*, yeah. House Intelligence and Homeland Security, for sure. Maybe others. If you don't take it to them, they'll slaughter you when it all comes out, once these clowns are caught and put on trial.

"But it's not all bad. The Devereuxs make perfect scapegoats if we can spin it right. It helps they're guilty of treason. We apprehend and incarcerate them, it takes the attention off you."

The President lifted his chin, which had fallen to his chest with Eadie's cynical statement. "We don't know they're guilty yet."

"With all due respect, Mr. President, if it walks like a duck… This gets everyone out of this mess, except Rhodes and O'Connell. And they were out anyway, in our previous plan," Eadie said.

It wasn't lost on the President that Eadie was satisfied, if not actually happy, that the solution to their political problems had been handed to them on a silver platter. But Eadie was paid to be an advocate for the President, and more so for the office of the Presidency, in all matters. And he was a spin-master extraordinaire—he could pull it off. He couldn't be blamed for his attitude.

Grant's own heart was heavy, however. He would never understand treason, no matter what the traitor's reason. The Devereuxs' treason was not just against their country, it was also personal—it was as painful as the loss of a loved one.

Chapter Twenty-Seven

THE MORNING AFTER

March 16

If he had slept at all, Sean would have regretted his late night. But when his session with the Devereuxs had broken up, it was already past three a.m., and Dylan was due just a couple of hours later. Sleep was overrated, anyway.

He made a couple of phone calls to people, who helpfully pointed out the time of day, and then headed for the airport where Dylan arrived on schedule at five thirty a.m. They went straight to the safe house.

Carter and Mackenzie hadn't slept much, either. Both were showing signs of stress, but they put on cheerful faces to greet Dylan. Carter was frying bacon, and Mackenzie offered the newcomers coffee.

After accepting, Dylan sat at the kitchen table and said, "Okay, Sean's given me some of it. You guys are in trouble, and I get the feeling I'm going to be cut out of the fun part. Rushing in like your knight in shining armor and all. What's the scoop?"

Mackenzie smiled at his whimsy. "Aw. Poor Dylan."

Carter, now frying eggs while Mackenzie manned the toaster, turned and gestured with the spatula. "It may not be fun, but you're the guardian of the castle, man. We wouldn't trust our privacy, not to mention the kids, to anyone else. We've talked about it, and we don't see a path that brings us out the other side without a lot of media attention."

Dylan rearranged his face to wipe the grin off it. "It's true then. Sean told me you're being targeted as *traitors*?"

Carter nodded silently.

"Just letting you know, I know you're not traitors," Dylan said. "What's the plan?"

He kept his mouth shut and his ears open as they filled him in on what they would do to clear their names and what they needed him to do at home, including the messages to their children, family, translation staff, and the EA people at Camp Tala.

Finally, Mackenzie said, "Try to keep the kids from knowing we're in trouble. Just tell them Mommy and Daddy love them, and something's come up at work, but we'll be back as soon as we can."

"You can bet on that, Mackenzie. I promise you, we'll take such good care of them they won't even miss you!"

President Grant was up at his usual time, five a.m., to meet with Scott Eadie and other advisors. At precisely seven a.m., his staff informed him Alec Burnett and his entourage were there for their meeting.

He stood to meet them as they were ushered in and remained standing. "Gentlemen, Special Agent White, this won't take long. Based on your evidence, you are to arrest

Carter and Mackenzie Devereux immediately. It's paramount that you keep it under wraps so we don't have the media all over the manhunt, but use every other tool at your disposal, including the full cooperation of all security agencies. Refer anyone who resists cooperating to my office, and I'll deal with them. I want these traitors brought in yesterday. Do you understand?"

Burnett resisted a powerful urge to snap off a salute. Instead, he answered crisply, "Yes, Mr. President."

General Fleming *did* salute.

"That's all. Keep me informed."

Less than half an hour later, James Rhodes and Irene O'Connell arrived for their rescheduled meeting with the President. Both were bewildered by the cold expressions on the faces of the President and Bill Griffin. James tried to shake off a bad feeling as he held out his hand to shake Bill's, but Bill made no move to take it.

"Sit down." The President's utterance sounded more like an order than an invitation. James and Irene sat.

"Listen very carefully, because I'm only going to say this once. You'll do well to follow orders without question."

James and Irene shared a quick glance with a *what's this about?* look on their faces.

"You are to close A-Echelon operations within the hour. Bill will help redeploy staff to Langley and elsewhere. You will not answer questions from your staff. You're both suspended, with pay for now. When you're done clearing out your offices, go home and be quiet.

"By 'quiet', I mean you are not to talk to the press, and you are not to contact Carter or Mackenzie Devereux. If you know where they are, you will turn that information over to the FBI immediately or face charges of impeding an FBI investigation. Your *only* communication will be with the investigators, or when the time comes, to testify before Congressional oversight committees.

"Do I make myself clear?"

James and Irene both started to ask questions at once, but the President made the universal signal to stop talking by swiping a flat hand across his neck. "No questions. If you don't follow these orders, your pay will be suspended and your pensions will be in danger. Is *that* clear?"

James and Irene were gob smacked.

Irene nodded miserably, a tear escaped and rolled down her cheek.

James made one more effort, getting out the question, "Why?" before Bill repeated the President's gesture.

However, the President relented just a bit. "Your employees and friends, Carter and Mackenzie Devereux, have gone rogue. Their security leaks have put me and this country in an untenable position.

"As of this morning, they are public enemies, numbers one and two."

Irene, still too intimidated to speak, widened her eyes and shook her head violently. *This is NOT happening.*

James said, "But—" and was promptly interrupted by Bill.

"Give it up, James. There's irrefutable evidence. Now get out, and do as you were ordered."

With no opportunity to tell the President or Bill they were acting on false information, James and Irene left. They were both in need of a strong drink, but considering the hour of day, they made do with a quick stop for a Starbucks takeaway with a double shot of espresso. They'd arrived in separate cars, but Irene left hers in the parking garage and got in with James.

"James, how could this be happening? What happened to make them refuse to at least consider the possibility this could be a setup? Not even giving us a chance to speak," she said. "And is it only me, or are they now suspecting us of some transgression?"

"It certainly looks like that, Irene," James replied. "It would have been nice to get the opportunity to tell them what we have learned.

"I'm afraid our fears came true—Kelly White got to them and pumped their heads full of crap.

"They're playing right into Shadow's hands."

"What do you mean?" Irene asked.

"This is all an elaborate scheme of the Nabateans—I'm sure of that—to eventually get their hands on those codices.

"In the process, they'll take revenge for our part in their past failures and destroy us all."

"It's clear we've lost the support of the President and the CIA," Irene said. "I have a feeling A-Echelon is going to become the proverbial albatross around our necks."

"No, we won't have to wear a damn bird around our necks for punishment," James retorted. "There won't be enough left of us after the President throws us under the bus."

"It's mind-numbing to see how quickly trust and loyalty can become casualties in D.C.," Irene murmured.

"Hey, I hear that! To think, I offered to take the fall for the President when it was him under threat. But it's a lot different to take the fall and still have his support as opposed to taking the fall when you're all but accused of treason and then get stabbed in the back. What a difference a day can make in this place."

Irene brightened. "You know what? He didn't tell us not to talk to Sean. Thank goodness Sean wouldn't tell us where Carter and Mackenzie were. And thank goodness, we still have a way to get a message to them. Our best hope is to help them clear their names, whatever the risk."

"You're right. Let's get a message through to Sean ASAP. Set up a meeting for right after we close our offices."

After James and Irene left, Bill excused himself to President Grant. "With your permission, sir, I need to secure the Codices at the Devereux ranch. May I be excused?"

"By all means. Of course," Grant agreed. "Keep me informed of your progress."

Bill hurried to his own office, where he summoned a senior agent. "Get a team together and requisition a cargo plane and crew. You're going to Canada. What do you know about Carter Devereux and his ranch, Freydís?"

"That's where they've got all kinds of hush-hush research going on, isn't it? It's A-Echelon territory. Why not send them after it?"

"Look, I don't have time to give you the song and dance. A-Echelon is being shut down as we speak, and the Devereuxs are fugitives. Just get there, retrieve everything that belongs to the US government, including personnel, and get back here ASAP. I'll deal with the Canadians."

"Yes, sir. You'll fill me in when I get back?"

"It's need-to-know. If I can, I will."

Chapter Twenty-Eight

A STANDUP ARGUMENT

By nine a.m., Sean had taken Dylan back to the airport and dropped him off already when he received a call from Bill Griffin's office. He was to report immediately to Bill.

Uh oh. This could get dicey. Sean confirmed and said he'd be there as soon as possible.

Twenty minutes later, he arrived and found Bill in a foul mood.

"Sit down." Bill's order echoed the President's to James and Irene an hour and a half before. Since then, he'd been working at top speed to contain the disaster he could see overtaking the country in the wake of the Devereuxs' presumed leak, and his demeanor as well as his desk showed it.

Sean took in the disarray in the office and Bill's obvious distress. This wouldn't be a good time to give the man any flak. He sat down, wary.

"I assume you've seen the headlines yesterday and this morning. You need to know it's just the tip of the iceberg. There's no way to soften this, Sean. Carter and Mackenzie have betrayed us." Seeing Sean was about to respond, he held up his hand.

"Wait. I'm not finished. There's more trouble brewing, I'm afraid. So far, Executive Advantage hasn't been mentioned, but we can't assume anything from that. Maybe they don't know yet, and maybe they're just holding back to feed the story out over time, to keep it in the public eye. You know these media types—they're like sharks drawn to blood.

"Anyway, it's just a matter of time before you and EA get drawn into this whole mess. I don't need to tell you what would happen to the part of your funding and resources that come from foreign countries if they lose confidence in the US government."

Once again, Sean tried to respond, but Bill overrode him.

"What we're going to do is get Executive Advantage just as far removed from A-Echelon as possible. You've got three days to get your people off Devereux's property and back home. You need to call them immediately, because I'm sending a mop-up team to retrieve the Codices. Your people are not to interfere with them in any way. Got it?"

Sean waited a beat, first to be sure Bill was done, and second to control his own temper. He hesitated until he saw Bill visibly calm down. Maybe Bill had expected an argument from him. Well, he wasn't going to disappoint.

In a conversational tone, Sean started slowly. "You know, Bill, I'm surprised at how little it took for you and the President to turn against two of the most patriotic people I've ever had the privilege to know." Seeing Bill's temper rise again, Sean held *his* hand up.

"No. You've had your say. Now you're going to listen to me. There is no way on God's green earth that Carter and

Mackenzie would or could ever turn against this country. I'm prepared to stake my life on that. I've worked closely with them, closer than any of the rest of you, for the past several years now. I *know* them. They wouldn't do it. End of story."

Bill had risen to his feet when Sean challenged him, and by the time Sean paused, both were standing, nose to nose like fighters trying to intimidate their opponent.

If it became physical, Bill wouldn't last more than ten seconds. He knew it but stood his ground; he had a point to make—he was not going to allow Sean to intimidate him into sitting down again.

Sean saw the realization in Bill's eyes and seized the advantage.

"I know what's going on, despite your elaborate effort to withhold the details. I've seen the information Kelly White has probably used to poison your mind and probably the President's. Did she rub your noses in it? What's more, are you sure she told you everything?

"I know everything about the allegations against Carter and Mackenzie, and everything about the allegations against A-Echelon. I've seen the evidence, and let me tell you, it's the biggest pile of hogwash I've seen in my life."

Sean's fists were clenched, his face red, and the tendons in his neck stood out.

Equally furious, Bill shouted, "How the hell? Have you been in contact with them? When? Where are they? I want them in custody immediately! You'd better not be harboring fugitives, Walker."

Sean ignored his questions and the implied threat.

"Bill," Sean's voice turned soft and measured, "please sit down in your chair, before I knock you into it. And then shut your yap and listen to me."

Bill's eyes shot wide. He had never seen Sean like that—but he had heard about it. Slowly he took a step back and sank into his chair. This was not the time to try and pull rank.

Sean continued in the same tone, "I know you're all under a lot of pressure from this media leak, and I guess your heads are on the chopping block. But you're acting as if you've already lost your head and your brain with it. I don't believe you'd throw two innocent people to the dogs if you didn't believe the evidence, so I'm not going to insult you by accusing you of pointing the finger at Carter and Mackenzie to save yourself.

"But haven't you considered this could all be a fabrication? It's a frame-up by the Nabateans, or someone like them. Have you given that any thought at all?"

Bill deflated a bit but was still angry. "I don't *want* to believe it of them. But how can there be any doubt? You've seen the video, you said. Have you heard the audio files?"

"Have *you* had them forensically analyzed?" Sean shot back. "Good Lord, Bill, you of all people should know not to believe everything you see and hear. And where did Kelly White get the information? Did you verify with the Swiss bank that they gave it to her? How'd she get the NSA sound files? Did you even stop to ask her those questions, or is your head so far up your ass your brain is numb?"

Sean was too worked up to think about protocol. When he'd think about it later, he'd reflect that probably no one had talked to Bill like that since his first teenage indiscretion. Maybe his dad had.

Bill had no trouble remembering protocol. He turned red in the face, ready to go ballistic, but he was man enough to admit they were valid questions. And he didn't have good answers. In the heat of the moment, and with the President as angry as he'd been, Bill just hadn't been thinking straight. He *hadn't* asked those questions—just blindly trusted that INSCOM and the FBI would have done their jobs properly. Why he'd think that, when the age-old rivalry between his department and the Feebs meant that each assumed the other were idiots, he couldn't say.

"Let's assume for a moment that you're right. That Kelly and the FBI bought a bunch of bull crap they can't verify. If that were the case, why would Carter and Mackenzie have assaulted and tied up Kelly and her team? Why run if they were innocent? They had to have known that would make them look guilty. Why didn't they call in James and Irene? Shit, why didn't they call me? Or ask Kelly to call the President?"

Sean smiled. He'd been through this before, with James and Irene. "Bill, do me a favor. Tell me exactly what Kelly told you and the President. Don't leave anything out, because I suspect she left out a few vital pieces of information."

For the next half-hour, Bill went through Kelly's presentation. He started by telling Sean the Director of the FBI and Russell McCormick, Assistant Director Counterintelligence Division FBI, and the head of INSCOM were at the meeting the night before at the White House. He then went through the allegations one by one in the order Kelly had presented them and the supporting evidence she had.

When Bill got to the end, Sean asked, "Did Kelly ever mention that Carter and Mackenzie repeatedly asked for James and Irene to be brought in? Did she say at some stage they even mentioned you and the President?"

Bill dropped his jaw a fraction of an inch and then tightened his features. "No, she did not."

Sean pulled out the pen recorder and held it up for Bill

to see. At Bill's nod of agreement, he turned on the recorder and fast-forwarded it a bit at a time until he came to the first of the places where Carter refused to answer Kelly without James and Irene present. Then he let it run. As Bill heard the Devereuxs repeatedly ask for their directors, he slumped further into his chair.

When Sean turned off the recording, Bill said, "Oh, my God. We played right into their hands! This Kelly White has misled us. Why? Who did this, and how?"

"That's not important right now. First, let's mitigate any damage already caused and prevent any more."

After some discussion, Bill agreed to change the orders of the mop-up team he was sending to Freydís. He would give the team leader amended instructions to leave the E-Codex there and allow the translation to continue normally. For now, he and Sean agreed, it was best to remove and secure the A-Codex along with any related information, at least until Carter and Mackenzie were proved innocent.

Next, Bill would send a couple of computer forensic experts to Freydís with the mop-up team. They'd be tasked with doing a complete audit on the servers and any networked devices to determine if someone could have been copying information.

Because Sean had already given Dylan instructions to prevent any interference from outsiders, he would send one of his own men, David Longley, with the mop-up team. He'd take Dylan a written message updating him on the new orders. Those would include David taking over command of Camp Tala, which they obviously wouldn't shut down now. EA would remain on Freydís for protection and to continue their training missions.

Dylan, in turn, would return to D.C. to help Sean sort out the mess.

The most important, and most challenging, thing would be to keep everyone, including Kelly White, Russell McCormick, and their agencies, in the dark about what was going on.

Even the President couldn't know.

Bill was sticking his neck out a mile by keeping it from the Commander in Chief, but they needed to play the game now. The culprits could very well be among them, and it could expose the President to danger if he let on.

It couldn't be hidden for long. Bill could hold off for no more than seventy-two hours, and that's how long Sean had to get a forensic analysis of the videos, sound files, and everything else Carter and Mackenzie had snatched from Kelly and company when they escaped.

It was a monumental task for such a short time. Bill agreed to make CIA forensic experts available to Sean, but even with their talent, it would be uncertain they could complete it before the deadline.

It went without saying that Sean wouldn't give Bill any information about the whereabouts of the Devereuxs or their plans while they worked to clear themselves from suspicion. In fact, they tacitly avoided the subject so Bill wouldn't have to arrest Sean for obstruction of justice. He only hoped he wouldn't be the one under arrest when the seventy-two hours were up.

Chapter Twenty-Nine

WE'VE GOT HIM THIS TIME

March 16

As the media storm intensified throughout the day, with political commentators now joining to report on the melee in both houses of Congress, the Council of the Covenant of Nabatea held their own virtual meeting to celebrate. Each in their separate eyrie, they toasted their impending victory with the finest champagne. Everyone except Graziella.

They all believed it was only a matter of days before they'd see arch-enemy Carter Devereux arrested, the President overwhelmed by scandal, rendered powerless or impeached, and the hated CIA devoid of power, under threat of elimination.

Congress was already in utter chaos as well, which left a void. As the old saying went, while the cat's away, the mice will play. The Nabateans could now rapidly advance their agenda without fear of interference.

Graziella, however, was more temperate than the rest of them. She cautioned, "It is true our enemies are under fire, and even better, they are shooting at each other. However, I needn't remind you they have slipped through our traps before. We haven't won until Carter Devereux and his wife are in jail, President Grant and his administration ousted, and the heads of the CIA and especially A-Echelon dismissed and charged with crimes."

"But what could go wrong, Graziella?" one of them asked as he lowered his champagne glass.

"That is what we are here to discuss," she answered in her cool, measured way. "To identify and analyze the risks. What can go wrong, and what can we do to mitigate or avoid it?"

Mathieu, remembering—with apprehension—previous failures, spoke first. "One or more of our agents could be caught and made to talk. I'm speaking of our plants within the US government and elsewhere, as well as operatives charged with retrieving the Codices and other projects. I believe this is a low risk in most cases, because we've structured our dealings with them in such a way they don't know who we are, or that we are behind them."

Graziella responded, "Yes, that's a risk. Depending on who gets caught, it is as you say, probably with little to no chance of exposing the Council but with high chances of derailing our plans to destroy our enemies.

"Who are the most vulnerable of our operatives?"

"Right now, it's Russell McCormick, Assistant Director of the Counterintelligence Division of the FBI," Mathieu responded.

He smiled smugly as several of the councilors gasped. "Yes, my friends. It is a coup, no? I have put one of their watchdogs to work for us. And he has done an impressive job—almost singlehandedly causing the current pandemonium in the media and political arenas.

"He has also managed to become the lover of the chief investigator of the Patch Barracks explosion, Kelly White. With his romantic influence over her and the information we have carefully fed him, he was able to subtly influence her to go after Carter Devereux and his wife as the main suspects of her investigation."

The Councilors applauded Mathieu's canniness.

"That's all well and good," said the new councilor who had replaced Peter Nikolaev, the Director of the Federal Security Service (FSB) of Russia after his fatal *accident* eighteen months ago. "But it sounds like McCormick knows a lot. Maybe too much for our good, no?"

The new councilor, Igor Ustinov, was a publicity-shy former security agent, held no political office, yet he was the Russian President's closest lieutenant, secretly known as the "de facto deputy", more influential than the Prime Minister. Western media often speculated that he was Russia's second-most powerful person. Forbes magazine regularly had him on their list of the top 100 richest people in the world, but no one knew the extent of this oil tycoon's real wealth and influence.

Mathieu responded, "McCormick has a lot of information, but we gave it to him through many go-betweens, so he does not know the source. He knows he is of Nabatean origin, and supposedly he doesn't know of the existence of this Council. But make no mistake, McCormick is not stupid. He must know by now that he was serving some powerful secret organization or other—"

"How did you persuade him to work for us?" the member from China asked.

"Well, as you know, we keep track of the members of the bloodline, and when we see someone with potential, we promote them and help them reach their full potential.

"McCormick came to our attention soon after he was recruited by the FBI. Since then, we have been instrumental in his rise to the top—opening doors at the right time, whispering in the right ears at the right time…

"As we do with everyone in whom we are interested, we also kept a very thorough record on him—his private life included.

"So, to secure his cooperation, we used a combination of tactics, admittedly some of them were to remind him of a few detrimental indiscretions in his past."

Ustinov spoke again. "If his cover is blown and it's discovered that he is Shadow, he will lose his job and, in all likelihood, be arrested. No doubt he'll then become useless to us. I suggest we keep a vigilant watch on him and prevent his arrest."

He didn't have to explain what that meant. Every councilor knew all too well that the Council's secrecy ranked higher than the life of anyone.

The Councilors all nodded in silence.

Mathieu continued. "If he is *not* discovered, he is in an excellent position to rise to the very top in his agency.

"However, although I have to concede that I judge the risk of his discovery to be somewhat higher than I'd like, he doesn't know enough about us to jeopardize this council. Also, his mission has already been carried out. The damage to our enemies cannot be undone now, even if he is discovered as the source of the information."

"Are there any other operatives posing risk to us?" the member from London asked, knowing full well there was a compelling reason why Jason Sullivan was not invited to the meeting.

"I'm surprised you don't remember, especially since he

is not present for this meeting. I'm referring, of course, to Jason Sullivan," Mathieu replied.

"But... He is one of us!" Several members of the council blurted similar protests at once, causing Graziella to raise her hands for quiet.

"There are two issues. The first is I have had conversations with him wherein he requested to resign his post as Secretary of the Treasury. I reminded him that was not possible, but I fear his commitment to his duty is wavering. That alone would be grounds for considering replacing him on the council."

She paused as she let her statement sink in. She didn't have to explain what she meant by "replacing him on the council"—members were replaced upon death only. When Graziella was satisfied they understood, she went on.

"The second issue is he is the source of much of the information we've gleaned about Carter Devereux and his discoveries. His seat on the National Security Council has given us a virtual seat on the same. It's only a matter of time before one of the Devereuxs or their handlers realize the leak of their secrets has come from there. And from that realization, it will not take much longer before they investigate each member of that body.

"The third is he knows everything about this Council.

"I don't need to tell you the consequences if they interrogate one of our own council members with extreme measures."

A long silence descended as everyone ruminated on the implications of Graziella's words.

"May I give my opinion?" Mathieu asked carefully when he was sure his mother was finished speaking.

"Please do." She nodded slightly.

"Sullivan is still of use to us. Right now, the Devereuxs

are fugitives under suspicion. Their escape has all but sealed their fate. The government officials, up to and including the President, are angry and confused as to the source of the leaks.

"Therefore, I suggest that until they start pointing fingers at the National Security Council, we leave Sullivan in place. We can still get good mileage out of him."

Graziella put it to a vote, and Sullivan was granted a stay of execution—for the time being.

"While we are on the topic, we might as well discuss one of our longstanding risks," Graziella announced after they'd voted on Sullivan's temporary reprieve.

"We still have not had a lead on our original library. Since it disappeared around 106 AD, we have been searching for it, and never more thoroughly than in recent years. I probably don't have to tell you what a disaster it will be if that library is discovered by anyone other than us."

Historians had been speculating for ages about the absence of written records of Nabatean history. They'd just accepted that none existed because the Nabateans never wrote anything down. That was the easiest way out but, of course, ignored the fact that the Nabateans, during their heyday, were the most literate and advanced group of people of the era.

The Council knew different. The written record did exist. That knowledge and a few other bits and pieces of information were passed on to the successive generations of their leadership through the millennia. What was lost over time was how, when, and where that information was concealed.

The Nabateans had preserved some of their myths, legends, secrets, and what was believed to be accurate information through oral tradition. Among their secrets was that gigantism was over-represented in their bloodline, leading the council to the conclusion that they were descendants of the Giants. Those very Giants whose libraries Carter Devereux had flagrantly stolen.

Another secret was that some of them lived to a very old age—beyond the presumed maximum human age of 120. Graziella had a particular reason to keep this secret. She had just passed her one-hundred fiftieth birthday, though everyone presumed she was at most fifty-five, and a very beautiful fifty-five to be sure. Mathieu was one of the beneficiaries of his mother's secrets—celebrating his ninety-fifth birthday a week before this meeting, but officially he was only in his mid- to late thirties.

Their savants were yet another of those secrets.

But the true prize was the location of their library. It had been front and center on Graziella's mind since they'd lost the E- and A- Codices to that damned Carter Devereux.

May he rot in the worst level of hell.

"We all know Carter Devereux has a habit of finding artifacts no one believes exist to be found in the first place. If, by some miracle, Devereux escapes the ambush we've laid for him this time, it will be imperative to kill him immediately.

"No more indirect actions and elaborate schemes. We hire assassins and get rid of him.

"I can only imagine the calamity if he finds our library before we do…"

"I'm almost sure we've got him this time," Mathieu said with confidence.

Chapter Thirty

WHAT KELLY WHITE WAS SUPPOSED TO DO

March 16, about 11:00 a.m.

"Have we covered everything?" Sean asked.

Bill looked at his watch. "Affirmative. The seventy-two hours started fifteen minutes ago. Get your ass in gear and sort this out, Walker. If anyone can do it, it's you and Dylan. Make it happen."

Sean snapped off a mock salute with a grin, turned on his heel, and made a show of racing out of the office. Bill shook his head. He knew Sean took it seriously, all right. But it was obvious that some of Carter's humoristic streak had rubbed off on him.

Sean hated to do it to them with no notice, but with the no-electronic-communications rule in place, he'd get to the safe house where Carter and Mackenzie waited without prior warning that they had to move again. This time, he wanted them farther outside the boundaries of the District. It'd be less convenient for him to get to them but more secure.

He took them to Severna Park, a bedroom community to the south of, and more closely associated with, Baltimore. It was only about an hour away from Washington.

To his relief, Carter and Mackenzie had already packed the evidence into two of the briefcases and were calmly waiting for him—as if they expected the relocation.

Mackenzie asked if there would be an opportunity to purchase some clothes and other necessities.

Sean smiled. "If you write your sizes down, I promise I won't look at them, and I'll get someone to do some shopping on your behalf."

"Thanks, Sean. You're such a gentleman. No wonder Samantha's got the hots for you," Mackenzie teased.

Sean laughed. "Nothing of a romantic nature will ever escape your notice. Will it?"

"You've got that one nailed buddy." Carter chuckled. "But you must admit, there's been plenty to notice lately."

Sean pretended to look innocent. "I have no idea what you mean, *buddy*."

Mackenzie broke in with a wide smile. "Your excursions with the lady in question haven't gone unnoticed. Horseback rides, long walks in the woods..."

Carter got a mischievous expression and added, "Calves' eyes at each other and deep sighs."

"All right, you two. So, I'm attracted to her. What's wrong with that? She's smart, witty, easy on the eyes—"

"Don't forget that killer smile," Carter added.

Mackenzie smacked him on the shoulder with the back of her hand.

"Well, it is," Carter defended himself.

As they drove through a maze of backroads toward the Chesapeake Bay, Sean filled them in on the conversation he and Bill had that morning. He didn't tell them about the tone of the conversation or the near physical encounter.

"It's hard to believe the President and Bill were so quick to condemn us," Carter said, his voice heavy with disappointment. "But I guess I can see what pressure they were under, now that we know how it all went down."

"I'm worried about James and Irene," Mackenzie said.

Sean replied, "Me, too, but they're not in imminent danger of arrest. I'll let them know about the latest developments as soon as I can."

The safe house in Severna Park was a typical suburban three-and-two, with eat-in kitchen and small living room, furnished as it had been in the 1970s when it was new. Not very different from her parents' house in Boston, where Mackenzie grew up.

Sean had set up his laptop and portable printer on the dining table. Carter and Mackenzie helped him word the letters his deputy, David Longley, would carry to Freydís the next morning. The first was official orders David would hand to Dylan. Dylan was to hand over the reins to David and get back to D.C. immediately for an updated briefing and to help Sean with the investigation.

A second letter was to Mackenzie's parents. It would assure them, and they were to pass on the assurances to the rest of the family and staff, that Carter and Mackenzie were safe. It asked them to cooperate fully with the CIA team, try not to worry, and as much as possible, relax and wait. It urged them not to believe anything they saw in the media, and that all their friends in D.C. were working to resolve the issues.

Sean then explained to Carter and Mackenzie that he

would need some recordings, pictures, and videos of the two of them for the CIA forensics team. He asked each of them to speak normally, read from a book, and perform other actions. He recorded their voices and made some video clips on the equipment handed to him by one of the forensics experts before he left CIA headquarters.

"Why are you doing all this?" Mackenzie asked.

"Voice and facial recognition," Sean replied unhelpfully. "I don't know how the technology works, but the geeks told me this is what they need to do their analysis."

"In other words, exactly what Kelly White was supposed to do before jumping on the bandwagon and accusing us of treason," Carter mumbled.

"Yep." Sean nodded.

Telling Mackenzie, he'd bring the personal necessities when he came back, he put the briefcases with all the evidence back in his SUV and headed for Langley to see the forensic experts.

When he'd gone, Mackenzie explored the bedrooms until she found a loose robe, which would do to wear until Sean brought what she asked for.

She was dying for a long, hot shower, and Carter could use one, too. She wrinkled her nose as she kissed him before disappearing into the bathroom. He got the hint.

Chapter Thirty-One

THE LIBRARY OF THE NABATEANS

March 16, Afternoon

Wearing her borrowed robe, Mackenzie poked around the kitchen for something they could eat while Carter took his shower. She had to laugh despite their circumstances when he appeared wearing a pair of pants that were far too large and a Henley that might as well have been a tent.

"I'm guessing the last guy they had here was a bit portlier than me," he said, joining in her amusement.

"At least you smell a lot better," she replied. "We have tuna or tuna. What do you want for lunch?"

"Do we have any tuna?"

By two p.m., they'd had enough of going in circles about what they could do to prove their innocence. They'd aired and considered every possibility. Every single option hinged on one starting point—the forensic analysis of Kelly White's "evidence" had to exonerate them before they could do anything else. They could only hope the CIA's technology was sophisticated enough to achieve that.

Without electronic communication devices, and with nothing but soap operas and political drivel on TV, not to mention having to watch their names and faces splashed on all but the kids' channels, there wasn't much to do besides talking and waiting.

For the two of them, used to being part of the action, the sad reality was they had to take a passive role, stay out of sight, and wait for others to do the work for them.

The irony wasn't lost on them. They were now responsible for proving their innocence in a country where people were considered innocent until proven guilty. The age of the internet with no measures of control over what people said and no system that held people accountable for what they said had turned the tables on that notion. Now everyone believed anything they saw, and anyone accused of anything was guilty until proven innocent—and sometimes remained guilty even after proven guiltless.

They might as well have been in Saudi Arabia or some other dictatorship.

When they'd talked that concept to death, Mackenzie said, "I wish there were a way to turn the tables on them."

"On whom, Mackie?"

"The Nabateans. You and I both know beyond a reasonable doubt it's them behind this."

Carter fell silent. *Mackie, you beauty!* A quirk of his eidetic memory was to throw related images to his mind just when he needed an idea, and Mackenzie's whim had triggered it.

The Nabatean library! He'd read about it on the Algosaibi's laptop after Perrin Durand turned it over. It had been in the back of his mind as something to search for ever since, but he had to put it on the back burner then.

His mind was now working overtime. If they could dig that library up, it could give them an advantage over the

Nabateans. Their superior resources might be neutralized if the library contained some secret that revealed a vulnerability or even gave them a clue to help them track the modern descendants. At the very least it could be such an embarrassment to them, if someone else found it, they might just overreact and blow their own cover.

Carter sighed. There was nothing they could do in their present circumstances, and where and how to start looking for it was the first obstacle. But if Sean's plan worked, and he could get them out of their current predicament, finding that library was his next target.

He told Mackenzie what he was thinking. "It's frustrating, though, having to just sit here and wait."

"We don't have to just sit here, though. We can work on a plan and be ready to implement it as soon as Sean gets back with good news. Let's brainstorm it," Mackenzie said. As far as she knew, it would just be mental exercise, but it beat watching Judge Judy or Dr. Phil on TV. And she knew from experience how to stimulate Carter's mind—it always produced positive results.

"If there's one thing I know would seriously worry the Nabateans, it's that their written record, if it exists, hasn't been discovered yet. I believe it does exist and that it contains at least one secret—but I would bet on many—they want to keep hidden for some reason."

Mackenzie encouraged him, though she now remembered having heard it before. "Why do you believe that, Carter?"

"Because, in a time when everyone loved to write things down about themselves—on clay tablets, papyrus scrolls, and temple walls in ancient graffiti— the Nabateans, the most educated bunch of their time, wrote nothing down.

"I find that improbable.

"The answer is more likely to be found in the fact that the Nabateans specialized in the covert, and they hid that information from the Romans—anything that could give them an advantage or that would make them vulnerable if known."

"Just like they're doing now," Mackenzie remarked.

"Exactly. The current Council of the Covenant of Nabatea must be desperately worried that someone will find it. I'm thinking they haven't yet, or they wouldn't be so eager to get their hands on the older knowledge—the Codices.

"It must be embarrassing for them. After nineteen hundred years, they still haven't found it. Somehow, the location wasn't passed on, or it got lost, and they have no idea where to look for it."

"We're in danger of the same thing happening to us," Mackenzie said.

"How do you mean?"

"No one writes anything down anymore. Not on paper, which has a limited lifespan in any case, and certainly not on clay tablets, and walls, and copperplates. Everything is stored on computers, and these days in the Cloud. If a calamity hits us and wipes us out, in two thousand years' time, someone will dig up our civilization and find a bunch of plastic, wires, and electronic garbage, but no written record."

Carter stared at her. Could that have been it? The modern Nabateans had been on his heels for every discovery of ancient knowledge. Had they really left a permanent written record, or did they have access to more ancient technology, something to store their information electronically?

A nomadic civilization probably wouldn't have stored it

on clay tablets and scrolls. That would have been too difficult to transport and even more difficult to hide from their own people so thoroughly it wouldn't have been found after all this time.

The most pressing question—what was in that library? He could only speculate, and hope, it was significant enough to be used as leverage against the Nabateans.

Maybe so significant it could destroy them.

Chapter Thirty-Two

AS LONG AS IT FITS

Sean met Bill at Langley and was escorted to the forensic labs. Bill gathered everyone who would be involved into a small conference room, where he had Sean introduce the problem and the evidence. Once he'd described what he wanted, the experts assured him it would be a relatively easy task to do what he was asking.

The lab supervisor summarized, "You'd be surprised at how near perfection voices, videos, and images can be engineered. But our technology is sophisticated enough to pick up voice tampering. Videos and images are even easier. We don't have to work through enormous databases, just compare the sets of recordings. We'll be able to give you answers soon enough—with ninety-five percent accuracy."

Sean handed over the equipment.

If the lab techs were curious about how Sean got recordings of wanted fugitives, they didn't voice it.

"Ninety-five percent?" Sean asked

"I say ninety-five percent accuracy because we couldn't record this in a properly setup studio."

"Close enough for reasonable doubt," Bill interjected. "If you can get to within ninety-five percent certainty, I'll wring the other five percent out of Kelly White's neck if I have to."

The lab techs didn't ask who Kelly White was either.

"Give us a few hours."

With time to kill, Sean picked up a CIA make-up specialist he'd dated in the past. That was until he found out she was old enough to be his mother. She'd gotten quite a laugh at his expense, but they were good friends now. She was happy to help him out. They made a stop at a Wal-Mart on the way back to the safe house.

Sean handed her the note with Mackenzie's sizes and laughed. "Greta, just one favor, please. Make sure you emphasize the fact that I haven't looked at the inside of that note when you hand the clothes to the woman for whom you are buying."

"Sean, are you in some kind of lady trouble I should know about?"

"No, nothing of the kind. You'll understand when you see her. She's married, and she's got red hair." Sean winked.

"Aha, I see. Sean Walker finally found someone that scares him."

"Yeah, well... let's just leave it at that." Sean chuckled.

When they arrived at the house in Severna Park, Sean burst out laughing at Carter's attire. He knew better than to tease the redhead, and besides, she looked as beautiful as ever in her robe.

Two hours later, Carter and Mackenzie were different people. Neither their family nor their friends would have recognized them without hearing them speak. Thanks to the latex film Greta used and showed the Devereuxs how to use, neither would most facial recognition software. It wouldn't stand up to close scrutiny, nor to the sophisticated techniques of the NSA, CIA, and other security agencies. But they'd be able to get around without having to worry about traffic cameras and other low-tech surveillance.

Getting into the spirit of the makeover, Carter made various suggestions about how he could affect a limp and therefore enhance the disguise. Greta took the time to instruct him on why his suggestion was good but only to a degree.

"How good an actor are you?" Greta asked. "It's true that people's gait is as unique as their fingerprints. But be careful. An exaggerated limp will draw more attention to you. The key to hiding in plain sight is to be invisible, in the sense that you don't stand out in any way. A limp that changes in severity will also draw attention. I wouldn't do it if I were you."

Carter looked at his stunning redhead and frowned. "How the heck are you going to make *her* invisible? She turns every man's head when we go out."

Mackenzie took a playful swipe at him. "Silly."

"No, I'm not just giving you a compliment. I'm serious."

Greta shook her head. "First, we have to do something with her hair."

"You're not going to color it!" Carter exclaimed with mock horror. "That's what knocked me off my feet the first time I saw her. I'm a sucker for red hair!"

"Let me just set the record straight. You were the one who remained standing after that collision. I'm the one who got knocked off my feet—literally." Mackenzie grinned.

"No. We're going to give her a weave that will look natural and mute the color with gray. We'll actually have to do the same with yours. Then, I think for Mackenzie, we're going to have to give her something that will make people look away."

Greta rummaged in her bag and came out with a realistic-looking silicon burn scar. She first applied a layer of latex film to Mackenzie's face and neck and plucked at it as it dried to form the wrinkles that would foil the newest skin texture recognition software. She then applied the silicon scar to Mackenzie's neck and over her jawline to just under her left eye and blurred the edges with heavy foundation.

"There. People tend to look away quickly when they see something like this. Children won't, though. They're likely to ask in a loud voice what happened to you. It also won't fool skin texture recognition in an ideal way. The software will recognize it's makeup—it just won't be able to see underneath.

"That's why you'll wear these prosthetics in your mouths whenever you go out, to help change the shape of your faces." She handed them silicon pads to wear between their teeth and gums. "This also won't work for long. If I had more time, I could make it impossible, but this is the best I can do in the time we have."

"I'll do my best to stay away from children," Mackenzie quipped with heavy sarcasm and a lisp caused by the pads in her mouth. "Especially my own. It would scare them to death."

"Probably not, unless you let them watch horror movies," Greta said. "Children are curious but accepting."

Sean spoke up. "We hope this will be unnecessary, but this will mean you're prepared if we have to run. By the way, we bought you some clothes and er—"

"Underwear," Greta supplied. "Serviceable, but not fashionable, I'm afraid."

"As long as it fits," Mackenzie sighed.

"Oh, I almost forgot," Greta, who had caught on with their jibing, said with a feigned serious face, "Sean never looked at that note with your sizes."

"With friends like Greta, I don't need enemies," Sean growled.

Chapter Thirty-Three

THE RESULT OF THE ANALYSIS

March 16, evening

Sean dropped Greta off at her home on the way back to Langley and regretfully declined her invitation to stay and have dinner. "They're in trouble, Greta. I've got to get the evidence to clear them ASAP."

"I understand. Are you certain of their innocence?"

"As certain as I am of my own," he returned.

"That's good enough for me," she answered. Patting him on the cheek, she breathed, "If only I were twenty years younger."

Sean was still grinning about Greta's unambiguous flirtation when he drove away. But he wouldn't tell Sam about it. She *might* think it was funny, but there was no reason to risk that she wouldn't.

Bill met him at the gates and escorted him back to the lab, where the forensic experts were waiting to brief them both on their findings. They'd barely walked in the door when the team leader met them with a strong handshake.

"You were right. Those recordings at the bank and the phone conversations are fake."

"No doubt?"

"Under oath, as a scientist, I'd have to say about ninety-five percent certainty. Off the record? One hundred percent. It was a damn good fake, but that wasn't Carter Devereux."

He went over it all with them, showed them the anomalies on the film, and the differences in the voiceprint images. "If you're already convinced of the subject's guilt, your brain can easily play tricks on you and ignore the obvious. But anyone with an open mind will see—it's not the same guy."

"Okay, thanks. And good work!" Bill said. He took possession of the records and directed the experts to forget they'd seen anything unless and until they were called to testify at a trial.

Although he looked happy, his mind was in turmoil, chastising himself. *I've been an idiot. I've allowed my judgment to be clouded—played right into the hands of the enemy. And in the process, I've almost destroyed the lives of two very good people.*

To Sean, he said, "We need to put our heads together."

After a hurried dinner at a chain restaurant, they met in Bill's office to go over the evidence.

Bill asked Sean, "Are you thinking what I'm thinking?"

"Nabateans," Sean answered.

"Not a doubt. Mathieu Nabati could fake those banking records with one hand tied behind his back. Between his contacts in the Swiss banking system and their advanced technology, it would be child's play."

"But the phone conversations. It says here" —Sean pointed to the analysis the forensics experts had given them — "these are almost certainly NSA recordings, but they've been modified. How did the Nabateans get such deep access to NSA records?"

"Their quantum computers. Remember, that's exactly what it said in those documents on Algosaibi's laptop and flash drive. They can break into any computer network on the planet. No encryption can stop them."

"Shit! Bill, can you imagine what information these people have. And it is as easy as that; the NSA collect it for them, and they copy it. Information about... well... everyone and everything... secret, private, you name it... politicians, leaders, terrorists across the globe. These guys have access to more information than our own government."

"Horrifying, isn't it? But let's park that for a moment. There's no question the Nabateans have the technology to manufacture this evidence. Our key to their back door may be Kelly White and how she got her hands on it," Bill said.

"Yeah. The Devereuxs and I have asked that same question a thousand times in the last two days. And what's her stake in it? Is she just an unsuspecting pawn of the Nabateans, or is she in on it?"

"We need to take a closer look at her to figure that out," Bill responded.

"Carter had an idea, which I think is worth investigating," Sean said, snapping his fingers as he remembered. "He pointed out we've got two sets of leaked information.

"The most damning, to *them*, the Devereuxs, is the false evidence right here. We're all morally certain that came from the Nabateans.

"The most damaging to *us*, CIA, A-Echelon, and the President, is the stuff that's true. The information that came out of the A-Codex itself, and..." He hesitated to say it.

"Spit it out, Sean, before I wring your neck," Bill growled.

"...the National Security Council," Sean finished. He waited for the explosion.

"Son of a bitch!" Bill yelled as the realization struck him like a flash of lightning. "We've got a traitor in the NSC!"

"That's what Carter thinks, and he makes a convincing argument. He still wants to know if there's any way to read information from the mass storage devices without taking them out of the metal boxes. In fact, we need to close off all speculation that someone could have taken the info from your vaults or that there's a mole on Freydís," Sean said.

"The team on its way to Freydís first thing in the morning will look at the possibility of a leak from that quarters. But I'm not waiting for them. Who knows what damage can be done in the meantime? I'm going to dig up every secret of every member of the NSC since they were old enough to walk and talk. We'll find the traitor."

"Wait, Bill. That could destroy your career. Wait for the analysis of the storage devices, please!"

"If this SNAFU doesn't take me down before then, I'm out of a job next January anyway. Politicians have the luxury of plausible deniability. I get judged by what I was supposed to know and what I did about it."

Sean shook his head. "It's domestic, Bill. Not your purview."

"The Nabateans aren't domestic. The sons of bitches are global. I'm sick of these assholes, and I'm going to take them down—with me. Like Samson, in the book of Judges in the Bible. He ripped the pillars of the temple out, which collapsed the building and killed all the damn Philistines with him."

Before Sean could argue further, Bill summoned the IT

forensics experts to the lab. While they waited, he sent Sean to the office anteroom and called in several of his top operators and ordered deep, and highly illegal, surveillance on every member of the National Security Council.

Sean watched the operators emerging one after the other from Bill's office with dubious expressions.

When that was done, Sean accompanied Bill back to the forensics lab where they briefed the IT experts. Bill told them who he was sending to Freydís and what they were to investigate.

"Have I left any base uncovered?" he asked, glaring at the experts.

The team lead, accustomed to Bill's leadership style, was the only one to answer. "No, sir. They should be able to give you the answers."

As they left, Bill said to Sean, "I can't believe this shit happened on my watch. Whatever we find out, I'm going to tender my resignation to President Grant."

"Get your head out of your ass, Bill," Sean admonished. "You'll first have to help us get Carter and Mackenzie off the hook. They're counting on us. That'll only be the first battle in the war. After that we need to sort these Nabateans out. Only when that's done can you resign—if you still want to."

"Yeah, and if I'm still alive and free to do so," Bill added.

Chapter Thirty-Four

THE FREYDÍS MOP-UP

March 17, early morning

Dylan was awakened by the insistent buzz of his secured satellite phone on his nightstand. He came alert immediately and snatched up the offending device to view the time. 4:20 a.m. What the hell?

Swiping the screen to answer, he jerked the phone to his ear. "This better be good."

"Dylan, it's David Longley. I'm on approach to your airfield with orders. Meet me there in ten minutes."

"What the hell, Longley? I have no notice of orders. It's going to take me longer than ten minutes. You'll be met by my men."

Dylan punched the End Call icon with rather more force than required.

"Who was that?" Liu asked with a very sleepy voice.

"David Longley. He's about to land at the airfield and wants to meet me."

Liu was fully awake now sitting up. "Is there trouble, Dylan?"

"I don't know, Liu. But don't worry. If it was serious, Sean would have let me know. Why don't you go back to sleep? I'll go and find out what's going on and let you know."

"Mmm... good idea." Liu yawned and slipped back under the blankets.

He turned on his bedside lamp and reached for his pants. He took the time to get a cup of coffee. Wonderful inventions, these one-cup instant brewers.

At 4:40 a.m., Dylan sauntered across the tarmac after parking his electric cart. Four of his men with weapons pointed down but at the ready, accompanied by five wolves, surrounded a plane, an Alenia C-27J Spartan of the United States Special Operations Command, with David Longley and six men and two women standing outside. He expected their feathers to be ruffled, but they were standing very still and not arguing with his men. The fact that Longley and company didn't have their hands up in the air or were on their faces on the ground gave Dylan the idea that the exchanges so far had been reasonably friendly.

Maybe part of the reason for the visitors' calm behavior was the fact that Mackenzie's wolves were part of the welcoming committee.

When he was within range, David Longley stretched out his hand. "Dylan. Good to see you, man." He sounded relieved.

Dylan ignored the hand. "What's this about?"

"Like I said, orders. It's all in the letter. Basically, you're to turn Freydís over to me and get to D.C. Sean needs you there."

Dylan gave him a level stare. He looked at the others, who hadn't spoken, and pointed at them with his chin. "Who are they?"

"Dylan, just read the letter, okay?" David held it out.

Dylan took it but didn't open it. "Wait here."

He went back to his cart, located his satellite phone, and called Sean, well aware it was a breach of their agreement not to use electronic communications.

When Sean answered, Dylan asked, "Do you know who this is?"

"Yes. Keep it brief."

"Package arrived. What do you want me to do with it?"

Sean took his turn to look at the time on his bedside clock. *The mop-up team must be on Freydís.* He replied, "Instructions included."

"You want me to open the package?"

"Yes. Follow instructions."

Now Dylan knew the orders were legitimate. Miffed that Sean hadn't given him earlier warning that someone was coming, he answered in a word. "Roger." He disconnected the call and opened the letter.

As he read it, he wished he'd taken the opportunity to lace his coffee with something stronger. He was indeed to hand over the EA operations to David, which wasn't as easy as it sounded. His men didn't know David that well. He was a former Delta Force operator. A crippling knee injury, requiring a knee replacement, forced him to work behind a desk. He was the head of EA's administrative and logistics unit.

Dylan could only hope it would be a smooth transition.

It also wasn't going to be easy for the staff to accept the next order, but he recognized it had to be done. He and

David together would explain that part. He sighed. No time like the present, despite the early hour. He went back and stuck out his hand toward David. "Sorry about that. Had to be sure."

David nodded and accepted the proffered handshake. "No worries. Shall we get started?"

"Might as well." Dylan started with the four who were still guarding the forensics team. "Stand down. These folks are here to make sure there aren't any unfriendlies lurking among us.

"David here is going to take over my duties for a while so I can go help Sean keep Carter and Mackenzie safe. You guys get back to camp and round up the men so I can introduce them to their new commander. While you do that, I'm going to get things started with the translation staff."

He turned to David. "That okay with you?" His question signaled his men it was real, and they headed back for camp at a trot, the wolves in tow. Dylan watched them go.

"This is a tight unit. Well-trained, highly capable. They won't give you any trouble. When I get back, they better be just as tight as they are now."

David grinned. "Gotcha. Just hope those wolves will accept me as well."

"They will, as long as you treat their handlers and them well." Dylan grinned.

With that, Dylan signaled to David and his entourage to follow him.

David joined him at the lead. "We got here a little early, didn't we?"

Dylan nodded. "You did. I guess it makes sense. No one up yet, you get the advantage of surprise. But they're going to be worried because this early means bad news."

"Maybe not all bad," David said. "We expect to be able to clear them all. That's what Sean was willing to bet on."

"Let's hope so," Dylan said, rolling his eyes. "If you find a rat, it's going to be bad."

Together, they entered the dormitory and gently woke the residents—the translation team. Then they went to Carter and Mackenzie's home and woke Mackenzie's parents, who had moved over from their own place to take care of the children while Carter and Mackenzie were away. Dylan asked them to call Ray Anderson, Mackenzie's brother, and everyone else, including Liu, to meet them in the conference room at the translation center. Mackenzie's mother, Mary, started to object she needed to stay with the children.

"We'll take them with us," interrupted Mackenzie's dad, Steven, who could see it was important to comply. "Don't worry; they won't even wake up."

He was right about Beth, who slept soundly on his shoulder on the way to the translation center. Liam was a different story. He was already awake and dressed when they went to his bedroom. His grandfather shushed him when he started to ask what adventure was beginning now. "Don't wake Beth," he admonished. Liam made a show of closing his mouth and followed eagerly.

Dylan and David strode ahead a little way. "Are Carter and Mackenzie all right?" Dylan asked when he was sure Liam couldn't hear them.

"As safe as they can be. You're supposed to read the letters from them, one to the staff and one to the family." He pulled the letters from his pocket and handed them over. A small hand slipped into Dylan's other hand as he reached for the letters.

"This is about Mom and Dad, isn't it, Dylan?" Liam asked. The tyke was too smart for his own good.

"I think so, sport. But David here says they're okay. Can you be brave and help your little sister?"

"Dad says when he's away, I'm the man of the family. I'll take care of Beth," Liam answered.

Just like his dad. He's going to be as good a man as Carter someday. Dylan squeezed the boy's hand.

As they passed the dormitory, one of Dylan's men poked his head out the front door. "Breakfast will be ready in half an hour. Coffee's on now."

"Good thought. Bring in the coffee when it's ready. Thanks for thinking of it," David replied.

When they'd all assembled in the conference room, Dylan introduced David. "Folks, this is David Longley. He's going to be the camp commander while I go to Washington to attend to some business. I hope you'll all welcome him and give him all the courtesy and cooperation you would give me.

"I'm sure you're wondering why you've been rousted at this time of the morning, and before I explain, let me assure you coffee is on the way." He paused as a weak cheer went up from the group.

"I'm sure you've seen some of the news coming out of D.C. in the past couple of days. I have a letter from Carter and Mackenzie, and I'd like to read it to you." He smiled at Liam, who'd left his side and gone to sit with his grandparents and sister.

"First, let me assure you, they're okay." He paused again as the audible sigh of relief interrupted him. Then he started reading:

"Dear Family and Staff,

> *We want you to know first and foremost that we have done nothing wrong. Please ignore any news that says otherwise.*
>
> *Our friends in Washington, D.C., are working to clear up this misunderstanding. The people who will ask you to give them full access to your work and personal computers, cell phones, and more are doing so at our request. Please give them full cooperation.*
>
> *They will also be removing the A-Codex plates and all material concerning them for safekeeping.*
>
> *That's all we can say for now. Please try not to worry. We'll explain everything as soon as we can."*

The buzz of conversation that started with the words "personal computers" was a dull roar by the time Dylan finished reading the letter. He held his hands up for quiet and noted with relief his men were circulating with trays of Styrofoam cups full of coffee.

"Is there anyone who doesn't understand the request for full cooperation?" He looked around at the audience, watching for apprehension on any face. All he saw was confusion.

"All right. I'm told breakfast will be ready in the dormitory shortly. Let's head over there and get out of the way of these good folks." As the staff filed out, he asked the forensics experts if they needed anything else right then.

"No. We'll need access to the personal devices, but we'll start here. Thanks for keeping them calm."

"It would have helped if I could tell them more. But Liam, Carter and Mackenzie's son, was paying close attention, so I didn't want to speculate."

"For the record, there's no way the information can be copied without leaving a trail. If there's a breach, we'll find it."

Dylan nodded and left. *If someone here leaked sensitive info... a traitor... wait, let me not even go there.*

Before he served his own breakfast from the buffet spread, he circulated among the translation staff, Liu by his side, reassuring them Carter and Mackenzie really were safe, the forensics people would surely clear them of any wrongdoing, and the translation effort would likely continue soon.

The staff, in turn, kept their voices down as they talked to each other. They'd do their part and cooperate, even though they were worried sick about Carter and Mackenzie. A few flicked their eyes over to the family group, where Liam was helping his grandparents persuade Beth to eat something. They'd also conceal their worry from the little boy who was far too young to shoulder such a burden.

By evening, there wasn't an electronic device of any description on Freydís that hadn't been thoroughly vetted. The forensics team had confiscated every single one, assisted by the EA men searching every nook and cranny for hidden ones—there were none. Their diagnostics showed there were no breaches whatsoever from Freydís.

By six p.m., they'd left with Dylan accompanying them and the A-Codex plates secured. They'd assured everyone no one there was suspected of treason and they could all get back to work when they were ready.

To any observers, life on Freydís would go on as usual. The EA people would continue their training, and the translations would continue, albeit only on the E-Codex. The "milk" plane would come and go as always.

Dylan spent some time whispering in Liam's ear that he was going to see Liam's parents. Did he want to send them any message? In response, Liam put his arms around Dylan's neck and came near to choking the life out of him.

"Give them that hug. It's from Beth, too," the little boy said. His young voice wavered, but he didn't sob.

Dylan nodded and solemnly shook Liam's hand. "I'll give it to them, soldier, and tell them it's from Beth, too."

His last task before the plane lifted off the tarmac was to call Sean on the satellite phone again.

"On the way. No bogeys."

"Thank God. See you soon."

Chapter Thirty-Five

THE GOLD FIELDS OF A-ECHELON

March 17, 7:00 p.m.

The clock was ticking on Bill's seventy-two-hour deadline—thirty-one of those precious hours had already passed. Sean had accomplished a major breakthrough when he, with the help of the CIA forensics experts, established that the evidence against Carter was all a sham. Both he and Bill were now convinced the source of the leak had to be in the National Security Council.

Bill had already met with President Grant once to address the A-Echelon story, and he'd have another meeting in a few hours. Grant wanted a daily consultation with him to agree how to best deal with the questions flooding in from both houses of Congress, foreign countries, and his own Press Secretary, who was besieged by journalists and social media alike.

Bill knew he was going to face some serious retribution from the President, but it was premature to alert him about the covert mission with Sean.

First, they still needed to determine Kelly White's role and decide what to do about it. More importantly, they had to determine which of the National Security Council members was the traitor and how the translation material from the A-Codex got leaked in such detail that the bad guys could use the science to build an antimatter bomb.

In addition, Carter and Mackenzie had to stay hidden and out of reach of Kelly White and the FBI for a few more days.

Bill's team of special operators investigating, highly illegally, the members of the National Security Council were under orders to report every eight hours at a minimum, and if they found anything suspect, to report immediately.

Sean's urging him to leave it to the FBI fell on deaf ears.

"That's like setting the fox to watch the hens, Sean, and you know it. I'll take the consequences."

Just short of twenty-four hours from his first orders, Bill had the first report on Kelly White. Its contents caused him to raise his eyebrows. From the Oval Office meeting, a few days before, he already knew McCormick was assigned to the case. However, the fact that McCormick and White were sharing a bed was startling. Maybe a conflict of interest? Bill smelled collusion, and his olfactory sense was usually quite accurate.

He ordered the team who'd discovered this little gem to dig further, and for them it was almost too easy. Hunters seldom expect to become the hunted. Neither Kelly nor Russell practiced good field craft—why should they? They weren't spooks. They were investigators. Consequently, their own security was slipshod.

The media, both traditional and internet based, hadn't been silent during this time. It couldn't have come at a worse time in the ebbs and tides of political news. An election year always brought a carnival atmosphere to the news, and this election year was no different.

In the rush to make a name for themselves, journalists, bloggers, and political pundits seized upon any story with the slimmest potential to cause controversy. Actors and musicians, artists and writers, indeed, anyone with a soapbox and a handful of followers felt duty-bound to regale those followers with their opinions, no matter how uninformed or misinformed.

Nothing was sacred. The private lives of the candidates, their spouses, and families were put under the spotlight. A tiny transgression became a nugget of gold, to be weighed, swapped, and put up for public view. In the already bloody political arena, easy access to social media and the millions addicted to it, believing that anything in writing must be true, every tidbit sparked a free-for-all feeding frenzy—it was like sharks tasting blood in the water.

The journalists, real and self-proclaimed, couldn't believe their luck when the A-Echelon story broke. To have a story like this to investigate, speculate, report, and twist to their liking in the midst of all the political shenanigans already in progress was like the discovery of gold leading to the California Gold Rush.

This was the Gold Rush of journalism, and they descended upon the gold fields of A-Echelon like the forty-niners of old. All of them hoping A-Echelon would produce the mother lode.

Chapter Thirty-Six

WE'LL TALK ABOUT YOUR FUTURE AFTER

March 17, late evening

"Put us to work, Bill."

Sean and Dylan reported to Bill the moment Dylan was wheels-down in Washington. They found him in his office, and to their relief, James and Irene were also there. Carter and Mackenzie were still in hiding in Severna Park—it was decided they would remain out of sight for a while longer.

"By some miracle, not even a whisper of Executive Advantage has hit the news. We'd like to keep it that way. We'll have more freedom of movement without the damn journalists and paparazzi on our heels at every turn," Sean continued.

"Agreed," Bill said, nodding. He then brought Sean and Dylan up to speed. "James, Irene, and I were just discussing what we've discovered about Kelly White. You're not going to believe it."

As he revealed the cozy relationship Ms. White had with a top FBI official, Sean gave a low whistle. "We *really* need to know whether she's just a pawn or in it up to her neck as a willing participant."

"I'm going to get hold of General Jonas Fleming and ask him if he's aware of this," Bill said, looking at Sean. "I'll brief him tonight, but I want you and Dylan to be there when Fleming questions his agent. I can't go with you because then I'll have to explain to the President what I was doing there. We're not ready for that yet.

"INSCOM is independent of the other security agencies, but Jonas owes me a favor. I'll make sure he cooperates."

"Just say when," Sean acknowledged.

"Yesterday," Bill snapped, as he picked up his phone to make the late-night appointment.

March 18, early morning

Kelly White received the summons to General Fleming's office first thing the next morning. Expecting to be praised for her breakthrough in the Patch Barracks case, she was puzzled when she arrived to find two men she didn't know also in the general's office.

Fleming invited her to sit down, but his tone immediately alerted her that praise wasn't going to be forthcoming.

Her eyes flicked to the two strangers, who continued to stand until she seated herself and then took seats across the room from her and slightly closer to Fleming's desk.

Something in the demeanor and the eyes of the two men gave her pause—*special forces maybe?* A tickle between her shoulder blades forewarned her to something wrong.

Fleming introduced Sean and Dylan, omitting their

surnames and affiliation. Kelly's trouble antenna went up a little further. Then the one called Sean began to speak.

"Special Agent White, we have some questions for you."

She turned to Fleming, a question in her eyes.

"Please cooperate with these gentlemen, Kelly. Your career is on the line here."

Now thoroughly spooked, she turned back to Sean. "Go ahead."

"I believe you are sleeping with Russell McCormick, Assistant Director for Counterintelligence of the FBI. Is that correct?" Sean wasn't known for his exemplary diplomatic skills.

Kelly felt affronted by the invasion of her privacy but was nervous enough by now to know she was in some kind of trouble. Despite her apprehension, she saw no reason to deny it. "Yes. What of it?"

"Where, when, and how did you meet him?" Sean fired.

She felt the anger rising. No one had spoken to her in that manner for a very long time. She was about to let out a profanity, which would have had something to do with sex and travel, when her better judgment prevailed.

"I... Let me think. I guess I met him in December? Yes, that's it, at a Christmas party. Probably sometime in mid-December. Why?" The small frown between Kelly's eyebrows deepened. *Where is this going?*

"And you began dating him immediately?" Dylan took up the tag-team questioning.

"Yes. Please! What is this about? Oh, Lord. Please don't tell me he's married."

Sean took over again. "I wish it were that simple. No, not that we know of. Let's move on. When did you start discussing your investigation of the Patch Barracks case with McCormick? Before or after you got Q Clearance."

Kelly hesitated for just a moment too long. "Only after I got Q Clearance. He has the same clearance."

Sean knew she was lying. But it didn't matter much. "Q Clearance and top-secret clearances are compartmentalized. You know that?"

Kelly felt cold shivers running down her spine. She nodded silently.

"So, you understand what compartmentalized means, yet you spoke to him about the case. Why?"

"I... well... he had the same clearance, and he's also counterintelligence. I... I... all this strange information... It was just too overwhelming, mindboggling... I needed someone to help me process all the information—I trust him."

"And not your team," Dylan stated.

"No, I trust... But later on, Russell was also assigned by the Director of the FBI to help me investigate. We thought we could help each other."

"Yes, less than three days ago," Sean retorted.

Kelly suddenly felt as if she'd forgotten to put on her clothes. She resisted an urge to cross her arms defensively over her chest and decided the best defense is to attack.

"You aren't answering *my* questions. Am I suspected of some wrongdoing I'm unaware of? Is Russell? I won't answer any more questions until you answer mine."

General Fleming cleared his throat. "Kelly, I think you'd be better off cooperating with these gentlemen."

Dylan, unfazed by her aggression, took over. "Where did you get your evidence against the Devereuxs?"

Kelly froze. *Oh, no. The parcel. The letter. Could they have been bogus?* "I... I received a package... anonymously," she said slowly.

"The evidence... Russell helped me look at it, and—"

"Show us the results of the forensic verifications you ran on the evidence," Sean demanded. He was sure she had none. He wanted to see if Kelly was going to lie about it.

"Russell... I... we... no, I didn't." Kelly's face drained of all blood. She looked as if she had seen a ghost.

"No, you didn't what?" Sean snapped.

"Do any forensic analysis... I'm... we've... ah..."

General Fleming was shaking his head and growled something, which sounded a lot like *stupid bitch* as he fixed Kelly with a flaming glower.

"Agent White" —Dylan had a murderous expression on his face— "let me just get this straight. You received a package with information from an anonymous source, right?"

She nodded.

"You looked at it with your boyfriend, McCormick, and decided there was no need to verify it, right?"

"Well, we... ah... I... thought..." She shook her head. "Yes, that's correct. I'm—"

Sean interrupted in a soft and measured voice. "I did your job for you, White. My forensic experts say the documents, video, and audio files, the whole fuckin' lot of it is fake—fabricated."

General Fleming contemplated for a fleeting second reprimanding Sean for his language, but let it pass. He felt like ripping Kelly White's throat out. His breathing had become burdened.

Of the four people in the room, it was only Dylan who knew what was about to happen when Sean started speaking like that. He'd better take over here, quickly. Kelly had to be kept alive to help them unravel this mess.

"Agent White," Dylan started in as soft and gentle a

tone as he could muster, "during your interview with the Devereuxs, did they ask for anyone else to be present?"

There was no more blood to drain out of her face. Kelly started to feel dizzy. She had no idea what these guys knew or not. It seemed like they knew it all. Including her brazen miscarriage of justice when she repeatedly refused the Devereuxs' requests to have Irene, James, Bill, and the President present. She started shaking her head.

Sean pulled Kelly's pen recorder out of his pocket and held it up without saying a word.

She immediately recognized it and changed the shaking of her head into a nodding motion. Her voice was an almost inaudible whisper when she spoke. "Yes, they did."

Dylan said, "For the benefit of General Fleming here, who hasn't had the opportunity to listen to the recording of your interview yet, would you want me to play it for him, or will you save us time and tell him?"

Kelly didn't answer. She just stared at each of them in turn.

"Kelly?" the general prompted.

If she had been wondering about it before, now she was absolutely sure—she was going to be court-martialed. "I'm not prepared to answer any more questions. I want a lawyer."

General Fleming, surprisingly calm, took the receiver of his phone off the hook and held it out to her. "Go for it. Call him right now and tell him to get his ass over here post haste—we are dealing with a matter of national security. There's no time to waste."

Kelly started to reach for the phone, but her hand started shaking uncontrollably. She pulled her hand back and leaned back in her chair.

General Fleming kept the phone extended to her and,

in total silence, held her gaze for what felt like a very long minute or two, before he spoke. "So, you want to lawyer up or not?"

She shook her head. "What do you expect of me?" she asked quietly. "I've made a grave mistake... Is there... anything... What can I do to remedy it?"

Fleming looked at Sean and Dylan inquisitively.

Dylan spoke first. "For now, we" —he pointed to Sean and himself— "have no interest in pushing for disciplinary measures against you. But make no mistake, as far as I'm concerned, you deserve it. General Fleming can decide about that."

"We've got one concern and one only—national security," Sean said. "In that regard, if you were serious about redressing your wrongs, you'll have to work with us to prevent another disaster like the one at Patch Barracks.

"You've seen the devastation there. And the DARPA scientists told you, *that* explosion was just a little warning of what the bad guys really have in store for us.

"So, what's it going to be?"

"I'll work with you... I want to apologize for—"

"Save that for later," Sean interrupted. "You'll get ample opportunity to apologize to the people you maltreated, offended, and misinformed. For now, we need you to start answering our questions again."

"I'll answer any questions you have." She sounded relieved.

"Russell McCormick," Dylan started. "We want you to tell us everything about him—and best would be if you could persuade yourself that you have no romantic feelings for him.

"Start from the moment you met up until now—leave nothing out—no detail is irrelevant."

Kelly felt like one who had received a presidential pardon from death row. She took a deep breath and dove into the details of her history with Russell, without reservation—embarrassing and private moments included.

Every now and then, one of the men would interrupt her to clarify certain matters.

And as she unwrapped the story for them, her brain, for the first time since she met the man, reigned over her emotions.

Like a kaleidoscope, memories of Russell's face as he surreptitiously, over time, persuaded her of the Devereuxs' guilt overwhelmed her.

Tears began rolling down her flaming cheeks as she realized how he'd manipulated her. She'd *slept* with the son of a bitch. This was worse than if he'd been married. Much, much worse—*he didn't only betray my trust, he used me and destroyed me.*

It all tumbled into place. From the "accidental" meeting at the Christmas party to the "convenient" timing of the package, just when she'd thought her investigation was at a dead end. It had arrived the day after she confessed to Russell she had no more leads.

Russell's gentle persuasion to convince her the evidence was above reproach and she had to make an arrest before the affluent culprits could use their money and connections to get away. Even saying she'd get all the glory—and a promotion.

Castration's too good for him.

Her savage thought surprised her, but once she got over the surprise, she agreed with her subconscious.

The more she talked, the more she became aware of the terrible injustice she'd done to the Devereuxs, to her team, to her President, her country—all of it to satiate her self-serving ambitions.

Humiliated beyond words, she stopped talking and broke into heart-rending sobs. After a few moments, she became aware of the discomfort of the men in the room.

She pulled herself together and whispered, "I think I know where that package came from."

Sean took a deep breath and let it out in a huff, echoed by Dylan.

General Fleming's scowl told Kelly all she needed to know—her career was over.

"What can I do to help?" she pleaded.

"It won't be easy," Sean cautioned.

"I know that. I'll have to—" She wrinkled her nose in disgust as she realized she'd have to maintain the relationship—even in bed. The idea filled her with nausea. But she'd do it. Give the bastard enough rope to hang himself. That's if she didn't hang him herself before that—which would be a pleasure.

"We'll get back to you with specifics," Sean said. "We'll have to bring the FBI Director into the picture and get his cooperation.

"For now, you should behave as if nothing's wrong," he added, confirming her assumption.

"Why don't we just arrest the son of a bitch?" Fleming asked.

"Shocking as it may be that a traitor could get that high in the FBI, we don't think he's the top," Sean explained. "We need to watch him and see if he'll lead us to whoever he's working for."

General Fleming turned his gaze to Kelly. "I'm going to defer my decision about your indiscretions, White. You've been given an opportunity for redemption. From this moment, it's in your hands and your hands only. Are we clear Special Agent White?"

"Yes, sir. I thank you, and I promise, you will not regret it," she said as she wiped the tears from her face. "When this is over, I'll hand in my resignation."

"I'm not asking for that, White. You go and do your job, and we'll talk about your future after."

Chapter Thirty-Seven

AN UNRESERVED APOLOGY

March 19, the day of the deadline

Bill dressed carefully for his day, which would determine whether he'd leave Washington in disgrace or be thanked by his old friend, President Samuel Houston Grant, for acting outside his authority and investigating people he shouldn't. That the goal sanctified the methods notwithstanding, Bill was breaking the law.

With the support of his opposite numbers in the FBI and INSCOM, though, he might get away with it—*if* Grant didn't take his head off for concealing it from him.

A few hours later, he stood tall in the Oval Office, flanked by his fellow agency heads from the FBI and INSCOM, and confessed what he'd been up to. As he'd expected, Grant was more than a little unimpressed.

"You did *what*?" Grant exploded. "And you two! You stood by... no! You *aided and abetted* while the Director of the CIA committed a felony? I should fire the lot of you! What were you thinking?

"No one will believe I didn't condone it... not to mention didn't even *know* it! What's worse, it will hand the other party the election. I could kill you with my bare hands! I've got a good mind to call the Secret Service agents in here and have you shot." The President was shaking with anger.

While ranting, Grant was pacing in a furious circle around the three penitents. None of them dared say a word in self-defense. Only when he spluttered to a stop, unable to find any more expletives to employ, did Bill venture a word of explanation.

"Please, Mr. President. Jonas and Alec didn't know I was doing it until it was done. If you must have a scapegoat, fire me. But before you do, I'd like to explain."

Grant looked at him expectantly but didn't give him the satisfaction of an answer. Bill took Grant's silence as an invitation to continue.

"Everything I did was necessary to keep up appearances. You have a viper very high in your inner circle, and any open accusation or investigation would have warned whoever it is.

"Before you ask, we don't yet know who it is, but we've narrowed it down to the National Security Council."

Grant made an involuntary noise, sounding as if he was about to throw up.

"May I brief you on what we've done so far, the current theory, and what we plan to do to catch this asshole?"

Scott Eadie walked in just about the time Bill got the last phrase out. "What asshole?" The President's glare at Bill was broken as he greeted his chief of staff.

"Scott, these *idiots* have for the past twenty minutes been making my day. They've got the balls to walk in here and tell me how they've trampled all over Federal law because they think we have a traitor in the NSC. Rather than have them arrested, they'd like me to turn them loose to break more laws and find out who it is."

"Sounds like a plan," drawled Eadie. "I mean, Mr. President, what on earth can possibly go wrong? We're in so much shit already, it's only the depth that can vary now."

The President threw his arms in the air. "Oh, my God. Another joker in our midst!"

Bill ventured his first small smile of the day. If Scott was on their side, they had a chance.

"All right," Grant sighed. "Sit down and tell me this cockamamie scheme. And you'd better hope you're right. One push of this button here" —he pointed to the intercom on his desk— "and the Secret Service will walk through that door, and I'll order them to arrest you and ship you to Guantanamo Bay."

Bill knew he was on safer ground when he caught Grant's slight wink at him. There was one thing about Grant's famous temper. It ran white-hot but burned out fast. He didn't think that would be the case for the traitor among the NSC members, though. *He or she* was likely to go down hard. But they had to catch the bastard first.

Bill took a deep breath. This was going to be complex. "First, I need to tell you that from the beginning, Dylan and Sean were convinced of the Devereuxs' innocence. Sean persuaded me that the evidence needed to be forensically analyzed. I used CIA resources to do so and discovered it was all fake.

"Once the Devereuxs were cleared, Jonas, Sean, and Dylan confronted Special Agent White and got her admission that she hadn't bothered to verify it for herself. She didn't give us the full story in that briefing the other night, and McCormick backed her up because they were sleeping together."

At that, the President rolled his eyes. "Spare me the details."

"Right. Well, without going into detail, we suspect McCormick is a plant, and White is now cooperating with us to trap him. But before we spring the trap, we'd like to see if he can lead us to whoever *he's* working for. And that leads us to our theory.

"Actually, Carter came up with it. There are actually two sources of the leaks. We don't yet have a theory about how the translations could have fallen into the hands of people with the means to put it to use. But we believe the Patch Barracks explosion came about because of that leak."

Grant nodded wearily. It was a lot to take in. "And the other source?"

"The information about A-Echelon could only have come from someone who knew about them—someone who has a reason to want to embarrass your administration. We've narrowed it down to the NSC. We agree with Carter's theory." He waved his hand to include General Fleming, Alec Burnett, and himself.

"We still don't have a handle on who it is. Everyone is a suspect, and therefore, it *has* to be business as usual.

"We can't let any of them know we've cleared the Devereuxs. INSCOM and the FBI will continue to search for them, but Kelly White is now on board with their innocence. We're certain Russell McCormick used her to frame them.

"She'll keep us informed if either agency is getting close, and we'll move Carter and Mackenzie in time to keep them from being apprehended.

"James and Irene will continue to keep a low profile,

and I'll brief them daily on our progress. However, they'll be responsible for keeping the press and especially Congress off our backs. They'll use delaying tactics, and both will develop extreme forgetfulness."

"What about that ranch of Carter's?" Grant asked. "Did you eliminate anyone there as a source of the leaks?"

"We did, sir. A CIA forensics team went over every electronic device on the place with a fine-tooth comb. We're certain no one copied data from the servers or the plates."

"That means I owe the Devereuxs an unreserved apology," the President noted.

"Yes, sir. Not only you; all of us do."

"The briefings with the National Security Council are the only source we can think of where someone could have picked up so much and such accurate information about A-Echelon operations as we have seen so far.

Chapter Thirty-Eight

BATTEN DOWN THE HATCHES

March 21 to 22

Sean received word from Bill it was now safe to bring the Devereuxs back to a more convenient location. He explained the manhunt for them was now a ruse to keep the Nabateans from suspecting their plot had been discovered. However, they must still exercise care, because the FBI agents under Russell McCormick's control were still searching for them in earnest. They needed to let it stay that way until they were ready to confront McCormick.

The first meeting in the new location was a bit stiff, as Sean and Dylan brought Kelly White with them. Fortunately, they had the foresight to give the Devereuxs forewarning about that. They were convinced that if they didn't and just turned up there with Kelly, she would have been in mortal danger, especially from Mackenzie, who was becoming more and more like a grizzly mother with a sore tooth with every passing day she couldn't talk to her children.

However, Kelly started apologizing profusely, sincerely, and nonstop as soon as she stepped in the door.

Mackenzie recognized Kelly's genuine regret and deep embarrassment, and forgave her immediately. Carter, knowing his redhead didn't forgive easily when her family's health and safety were concerned, put aside his reservations and accepted the apologies as well.

With that out of the way, they sat down and worked through their next steps.

Discovering who had the means to obtain the translations was paramount. It was the full translations and nothing less that would have made the Patch Barracks attack possible.

Sean reminded Carter, Mackenzie, and Kelly of what he and Dylan had already learned. The computer and hacking experts at Langley had cleared the translation staff and everyone else at Freydís and were in the process of doing the same within the CIA, where the vaults containing the translations resided.

However, there were two theoretical possibilities for how it could have happened in transit.

The experts hadn't been aware of existing technology that could do it, but the Van Eck phreaking theory could, *maybe, sort of, possibly* been adapted and perfected. In which case, the pilot and crew of the "milk" plane could potentially be involved. Or one or more persons might have rigged the plane with technical equipment that could read the mass storage devices.

Everybody knew, now that Kelly had been read in on them, that "person or persons unknown" meant the Nabateans.

"What can we do to help discover which?" Mackenzie asked.

"Nothing. The experts are working on it. I mean, if either of you has a brilliant idea in the night, let us know. Meanwhile, it's just for your information to let you know where we are," Sean answered.

"It's so frustrating to be out of the action," Carter lamented, putting his arm around Mackenzie, who nodded.

"Frustrating maybe, but being *in* the action is nerve-wracking, especially when we get to play it one way for the media and the damned Nabateans, and another way for real."

Sean's statement went double for the President and his staff. Between the media and Congress, it was approaching civil war with the President in the middle. With nothing but stalling tactics coming out of the A-Echelon offices, speculation and accusations were spreading like a brush fire.

The opposition party had been handed a golden opportunity to discredit the President and thereby steal the election. They were the most vocal publicly, and it was becoming harder and harder to ignore them.

James and Irene knew to stand fast and not defend themselves.

Scott Eadie had a harder time not lashing back at those who would denigrate the President.

Sam Grant was somewhat insulated from the clamor, but he couldn't set foot outside the White House without being beset by screaming journalists with microphones. He was a virtual hostage to the issue.

Supporters of the President spouted unreserved support, but they had no real information to back it up and were therefore on shaky ground. No one liked being in that position. The result was that members of the party, both in public office and private contact with the President or his Chief of Staff, were demanding answers.

Answers that neither could or would give.

Scott's health was taking a beating, as he was responsible for the political stock of the President as well as running interference between the man and those who would take his time and energy.

Party leadership wanted to know what the President was doing to redeem himself so they could count on his support for whichever party candidate won the right to run for next term. The convention was right around the corner.

The loudest of all were the conspiracy theorists. They were having a field day. Previously relegated to late-night TV or supermarket yellow journalism, they now had the internet to thank for their platform. They made full use of it, leveraging social media to spout their theories, some even going so far as to manufacture news stories. Not since the assassination of JFK had they had such rich material.

Even the lunatic fringe, as Theodore Roosevelt termed them, got into the act. Because A-Echelon was tasked with investigating unusual subjects, everyone with a theory about Area 51, time travel, star gates, remote viewing, mind reading, shape shifting, or that humans were actually creatures of an alien race had something to say about what A-Echelon was really all about. Each of them claimed to know the truth.

It was all a circus, with James, Irene, and the President standing in the main ring and refusing to comment. When the noise became overwhelming, the President held a tightly controlled press conference. He read his statement to a carefully selected group of journalists, including Howard Crane, who'd started it all.

"Ladies and gentlemen, please hold your questions. I have a statement.

"It has not escaped the attention of my office that there have been charges levelled against one of our security agencies. As your President, I give you my word that these charges are under investigation and have been under investigation since they were first brought to our attention.

"In the interest of national security as well as world peace and stability, certain aspects of the investigation will not be made public now or in the future. However, the decision about what will and will not be made public rests in the hands of the National Security Council and not me.

"Should the investigation reveal wrongdoing by me or any of my appointees, I will bear the consequences, whatever they may be. I assure you, the orders to the investigators are to leave no stone unturned, no secret unexplored, and no person untouched by reason of his or her office.'"

Grant looked out at the sea of faces. "That's all. Thank you."

As the roar went up, each journalist shouting his or her questions, the President turned and left the podium. Scott Eadie stepped forward and spoke unnecessarily into the microphone. "No questions."

Watching in their offices as the press conference was aired, James and Irene turned to each other. James spoke first.

"Batten down the hatches. They'll come after us."

Irene smiled. "And we'll be ready for them. I've practiced my 'no comment' until I can say it in my sleep. Let's just hope the others get to the bottom of this quickly."

Chapter Thirty-Nine

NOTHING OF USE HERE

March 23

Packing up for yet another move, Mackenzie confessed she was tired of living on the run. "I'd like to hang my clothes up for a change, not live out of the suitcase."

"I thought you hated those clothes," Carter said, looking at the drab, distressed jeans and gray T-shirt Mackie had on today. Honestly, he hated them, too. And he hated the weave that turned her flaming hair down to a low simmer. His Mackie had many fine features to be in love with, but that hair was the kicker. For a moment, he considered what it would be like when it began to naturally fade and turn gray. *Nah, she'll dye it back to its natural color. She likes being a redhead as much as I like teasing her about it.* A moment later, he admitted to himself that he'd love her if her hair was pink with purple polka-dots, and a muted redhead was better than no redhead at all. He'd still have her temper to love.

"Don't get me wrong, Carter. I'm grateful to have them.

They just aren't very flattering." She glanced at herself in the warped mirror, noting with interest that it made her look pregnant. Or maybe it was the shapeless T-shirt that did that.

"Well, at least we aren't on the run for real. It's like hide and seek, but with secret clearance not to be arrested." Carter grinned and caught his wife in his arms for a moment. He kissed her until she relaxed and then licked the end of her nose.

"Ew! Carter!"

Carter laughed. "Come on, our chariot awaits us."

No more than twenty minutes after the Devereuxs left in Sean's SUV, Kelly White, Russell McCormick, and an FBI SWAT team arrived at the safe house and entered after an authoritative knock at the door.

"Clear! Clear!" rang through the house as the SWAT team did their usual.

"No one's here," the team leader reported to McCormick.

"Damn. We missed them," he said to Kelly. To the team leader, he ordered, "See if you can find out how long ago they left."

"Or if they were here in the first place," Kelly added. McCormick shot her an irritated glance. Lately, she'd seemed distant.

"I'm confident they were here. We have an eyewitness," McCormick snapped. "They're clever. They move around constantly, but the noose is tightening."

Kelly worried for half a second and then decided

Russell was being his normal, arrogant self. She didn't answer.

"Coffeemaker is still warm. I'd say we missed them by minutes," the team lead reported ten minutes later. "I'm no expert, but we've got fingerprints. The lab geeks will be able to say if they belong to the suspects, sir."

"Wrap it up here, but keep looking. They can't have gone far."

A few miles away, in a different subdivision in a different bedroom community outside the Beltway, Carter was explaining about his idea of finding the library of the Nabateans.

"I don't know," Dylan mused. "Would it be much good?"

Sean elaborated, "I thought civilization *de*volved after the Giants. Why would you risk money and your life to go after something from modern times?"

Mackenzie laughed at the notion of a mere century after the birth of Christ being "modern" times.

Dylan had more to say. "I'd rather put our efforts into finding the Nabateans and taking them out to Freydís for a bit of wolf-enhanced interrogation."

"Well, of course, that would be the ideal outcome. But I still think there's merit in looking for their library," Carter said.

"I've got to admit, you have made some astonishing discoveries in unexpected places," Sean answered. "Maybe it's a good idea, later, but a bit dangerous at the moment—"

"What we want to do is figure out where the library

might be from the information available," Mackenzie said. "Carter will go looking for it after we're allowed to move around freely again."

"Oh, why didn't you say so?" Dylan asked. "We can get you the full file we have on them. Will that help?"

"It's a start."

After they were settled in their new "home away from home" as Carter called it, Sean brought them a stack of boxes. "Sorry for the low tech. Still not safe to have you making queries about them on the internet."

"No problem," Carter and Mackenzie chorused.

"I love the smell of paper and ink. It's almost as good as the smell of papyrus." Carter grinned.

They dove into the work and read quickly through everything the CIA researchers could find on the Nabateans. It was a mix of old information and the new data from Algosaibi's laptop and flash drive. Unfortunately, there was nothing Carter didn't already know.

"Nothing of use here," he said, disappointed.

"It was a good refresher, though," Mackenzie remarked. Carter was the one with the eidetic memory. She needed to see most things more than once to fix them in her mind.

"We need more," Carter mumbled.

"What about the Smithsonian? It's a treasure trove of undiscovered information," Mackenzie said, remembering it was there she'd found her first serious lead to the ancient respirocytes. That had led her to Armenia and the Sirralnnudam. Maybe a similar discovery could lead them to the ancient library of the Nabateans. *Heck, maybe the whole library is in there. It could certainly be hiding in that dusty warren.*

Carter startled her by swooping in and giving her a bear hug. "What would I do without you, Mackie?" he asked rhetorically. "You've done it again!"

The request was an unusual one and not easy to accommodate. Sean and Dylan couldn't make it happen on their own, but they asked Bill to pull strings, and he finally found one that rang the bell.

Chapter Forty

A BOX OF CHOCOLATES

March 23 to 24

Sean and Dylan had been busy. In addition to setting up Carter and Mackenzie inside the Smithsonian, they'd made a clandestine raid on the hangar where the specially-outfitted plane that flew back and forth from Freydís was kept.

Dubbed the "milk" plane for the ruse it had first used to disguise its missions, the plane belonged to the CIA now, and a CIA pilot and crew were assigned to it. But Bill trusted no one, now that a top FBI official had been implicated. He'd put surveillance on the pilot and crew, and now a team of engineers who knew nothing of the missions were to accompany Sean and Dylan on a thorough inspection of the aircraft.

Specs in hand, they went over it with care. Behind one of the walls, they found a device that wasn't accounted for in the specs. About the size of a one-pound box of chocolates, it was wired into the craft's electrical system. It could have been simply a modification the original designers weren't aware of, but the engineers didn't know what it did or how it worked. Only that it wasn't on the specs and therefore of suspicious origin.

After discussion with Sean and Dylan, they decided not to touch it. For all they knew, it could belong to the bad guys and could be rigged to send a warning to them if anyone interfered with it. Or worse, blow up in their faces.

Instead, they planted a few modifications of their own. From the cockpit to the tail, they planted microscopic bugs. The tiniest and most sophisticated available. If the pilot or the crew were involved in the leak and talked about it, they'd know. If they even came within a yard of the device, they'd know.

For her part, Kelly White had also been busy. At night, after Russell had gone to sleep, she padded through his apartment barefoot, planting bugs of her own. She even managed to drop a couple in his car.

Keeping up the appearance of the relationship was a strain, and she sometimes caught him looking at her in a curious or speculative way. If he asked her whether something was wrong, she'd always plead exhaustion and the strain of the case. It was imperative that he not suspect her.

By now, she knew the Nabateans' reputation for ruthlessness. Not only was learning who the NSC leak on the line. Her life could be forfeited as well.

Twenty-four hours after the request found its mark, Carter and Mackenzie were ushered into their next "home away from home". Mackenzie couldn't help but wonder who or what had last used the bed they were given, tucked away in a locked and windowless section in a sub-basement of the Smithsonian. Countless scenes from old black and white movies full of reanimated mummies and other horrors flashed through her memory until she noticed Carter's eyes were sparkling.

"What are you so happy about?" she asked a little peevishly.

"Who's going to find us here? Literally one person in the world knows exactly where we are. She'll bring us food, drink, other necessities, and *anything we ask for* that the Smithsonian has for us to research. I could stay here for years and not run out of material to study. What more could I want?"

Mackenzie didn't lack for a list. "Sunshine, fresh air, our kids—"

"Mackie, relax, it's just for a few days."

"Remind me how this person that we've never seen and who has never seen us is supposed to see to our needs," Mackenzie said, knowing she'd never be able to explain to Carter about her unnamed and formless fears. She just didn't like dark, underground places. Never had, but especially so since she'd been held in Saudi Arabia.

"We have a computer here," Carter said, showing it to her. "It isn't connected to the internet, nor to the Smithsonian's network. It communicates directly on a similar computer with the deputy director of the museum, who knows someone is here but not who. She will personally see to it our requests are met. She's set guards outside the doors to this area in case someone wanders into out-of-bounds areas. They think they're guarding a priceless artifact."

"You mean like a mummy?" Mackenzie asked. She was beginning to grin. Maybe it wouldn't be so bad after all.

Chapter Forty-One

IN SEARCH OF THE SECRET LIBRARY

March 24 to 26

It soon became apparent to Carter and Mackenzie just why their lair had been carved out of a corner of this particular sub-sub-basement under the original Smithsonian castle. In addition to the alcove where their bed, small refrigerator, and microwave had been placed, just a few steps away was another with a couple of desks.

Extension cords with power strips attached to the ends snaked through the area, providing them with the power outlets that hadn't been included when the edifice was completed in 1855. Nor in later improvements, which at some point had included overhead electric lights and a bathroom down the hall that must have dated from the 1930s.

For Carter, accustomed to conditions on archaeological digs, it was the height of luxury. For Mackenzie, a little better than camping out, but without the charm of the campfire.

What fascinated them both, however, was room after room of ancient tomes, and thankfully, card catalogs to help them locate anything useful. Carter observed the card catalogs probably hadn't been digitized and added to the electronic records of the museum. He based that on the amount of dust covering the books and catalog cabinets alike.

Even better, this section appeared to contain examples of everything ever written on ancient Arabic and Middle Eastern history. Surely, if any ideas about the location of the mythical Nabatean library existed, they'd be found here.

Mackenzie, having more recent experience with old-school search methods like card catalogs, suggested they divide and conquer. Each small room contained hundreds of books—they'd better narrow down the search quickly. Carter agreed, and that was why he was alone when he found the room with early archaeologists' best guesses about the Nabatean tribe.

"Mackie! I've got it!" he shouted. Dust scattered from the card catalog where he'd found an entire section about the Nabateans.

From somewhere nearby, Mackenzie's muffled reply sounded something like, "I'm coming." But it was several minutes before she arrived, looking flushed and with a smudge of dirt on her nose.

Carter's hands were full of books by the time she arrived. "Look! We aren't the first to be curious about the Nabateans. Help me skim through these books!"

Mackenzie helped carry the first batch of books back to the office alcove, where they each took a desk and a chair and carefully opened the old books. For the next several hours, they compared what they were seeing in the books, and Mackenzie took notes on her laptop as they endeavored to understand the ancient history of the obscure tribe.

The Nabateans had been nomadic, like most of the tribes in the area. Through the ages, they'd developed the reputation of being excellent traders and navigators on the sea of the desert. Presumably that had made them wealthy in their day. Each treatise mentioned the curious lack of written records, though Carter said it made sense.

Written records and a nomadic lifestyle didn't really go together, especially in a time before the use of papyrus was widespread. Clay tablets and metal plates would be cumbersome.

"Was it really before papyrus?" Mackenzie asked.

"According to these books, it could have been. The Nabateans themselves couldn't name the origins of their tribe. Several modern tribes, in the sense of any time after Christ, claim they're the descendants."

"What about their city? Petra? Could it be there?" Mackenzie asked.

"You'd think so," Carter answered. "But archaeologists have been all over the ruins like ants. I'd think it would have been discovered if it were there. Traditional lines of thought among archaeologists aren't going to get us anywhere. I'm wondering if we're on the wrong track altogether."

"What about coming at it from the other end? Who are these people today? Not the group of megalomaniacs we're dealing with now, but the people as a whole?"

"That's another dead end, I'm afraid," Carter said. "You can see by the accounts of these guys we're reading that no one knows what happened to them after 106 AD, when the region was taken over by Rome. One says they were poor, backward, and despised by the other tribes. I suppose eventually they were absorbed."

"But then who are the Council of the Covenant of Nabatea? Is that just a name they gave themselves?

Wouldn't the surname Nabati indicate they were members of the tribe?"

Carter couldn't fault Mackenzie's reasoning, but there simply wasn't enough to go on for a definitive answer. Maybe Graziella and Mathieu Nabati could tell them, but they weren't available to ask. And it was doubtful they'd give a straight answer anyway. He shrugged. "I just don't know."

Mackenzie wasn't ready to give up. She'd seen Carter make intuitive leaps again and again, and she knew that he'd make a connection in that magic brain of his, if she could think of the right prompts.

"Carter, you said what happened after 106 AD, when the region was taken over by Rome. What did happen? How did they take over?"

"Well, that's interesting. There's no record of a Roman military campaign into what's now Jordan at that time. And yet, the region, and Petra itself, was absorbed into the Roman Empire. The region was called Arabia Petraea, and Petra was its capital, under Roman rule. It seems to have continued to flourish."

"How could that have happened?" Mackenzie wondered. "If the Romans moved in, where did the Nabateans go? Carter, why don't we try to imagine what might have happened to them?"

"Imagine? Mackie, that's not the way archaeology is done. Nor the way you work. It isn't scientific method."

"Actually, it kind of is. You think about a problem, postulate a solution, and then test it. Obviously, we can't test it right now, but we might as well lay the groundwork."

Carter sighed. *Mackie isn't going to let this go until I try it. Redheads are so stubborn!* "Okay. Look, here's a guy who has a theory that sounds like a good starting point. He thinks maybe the wealthy Nabateans became Romanized."

"Meaning?"

"Meaning they took Roman and Greek names, which were popular at the time, and continued business as usual. They were excellent traders, and it says over here in this book they were talented engineers. What's the most valuable substance in the desert?"

"Food?" ventured Mackenzie.

"Close enough. Water. They had the means to collect and store water from the flash floods that carved the valley in the first place. They'd sell it to merchants on the trade routes. No one could get through that part of the desert without stopping at Petra. It was like a gas station in the Australian Outback, you know those with a sign that says, no gas for the next four hundred miles!"

"Okay, so what did that mean for them after 106 AD?" Mackenzie was encouraged. She could almost see the wheels spinning in Carter's brain.

"They'd have wealth to squirrel away, and maybe they'd want to keep secrets. But to have the privileges they were accustomed to, they'd need to be Roman citizens. I'll bet they were absorbed into Roman culture, lock, stock, and barrel."

"So, what happened to their secrets?"

"Could have been one or more of several things. They'd save what they considered important, of course. That would be anything that gave them a commercial advantage. Maybe religion, but less likely. To act like Roman citizens, they'd have to adopt Roman gods."

"Regardless of how important records were stored, where would they have put them?" Mackenzie asked.

"That's the million-dollar question, isn't it?" Carter returned. "We're getting ahead of ourselves. What they didn't consider important, they'd have destroyed. A secretive tribe, determined to keep the advantage for themselves? They wouldn't have wanted anything to fall into the hands of their enemies, or their so-called friends, the people who assimilated them."

"The Romans?"

"You bet. Imagine you're a proud, wealthy member of a society where you're top dog. You've got it made. And then along comes a superior military force. If you fight and lose, you'll lose your wealth and prestige as well. If you concede but negotiate an equally prestigious place for yourself in the new society, how do you feel about your new friends?" Carter watched Mackenzie's eyes widen, and he knew exactly what was coming when she answered.

"I'd stab them in their sleep," she whispered. "Figuratively."

"Exactly. What if they did write everything down, but then when the Romans came, they committed what was important to memory and then destroyed the written record?"

Mackenzie objected. "Then this exercise is futile. It either never existed, or it was destroyed except for oral tradition."

"I don't think so. Think about the Nabateans we know today. Wealthy beyond measure and possessing technology even the United States doesn't have. How'd they get in that position if they didn't start out with an advantage? Somewhere, the seeds of that advantage are recorded."

Mackenzie suddenly jumped out of her chair, her eyes sparkling. "Carter! They might have plates somewhere, just like the E- and A-Codices! Same era—prehistory. All their knowledge in nanodots, and only a few with the knowledge to read them!"

Carter laughed. "I wish. Then it would just be a matter

of searching for them, knowing what we're looking for would be different—something that earlier archaeologists might have missed. But slow down a bit. The Nabateans were thousands of years after the Giants. As we've discovered, human beings have forgotten a much, much bigger part of their history than what is known to them today."

"Okay, keep thinking. The Romans didn't just walk up to the door like neighbors and say, 'we're taking over now.' The leaders of the Nabateans had to have seen it coming. They'd have had time to prepare. What if they *did* know how to read their ancient records. What would they have done then?"

Carter considered Mackenzie's question. He had what Mackenzie always described as his "thousand-yard or thousand-*year* stare", as his eyes focused on nothing while his brain went into overdrive. After a few minutes, he almost whispered.

"They'd have entrusted it to a few people to hide. And then, because two may keep a secret if one of them is dead, they'd have killed the ones who concealed it."

"And then?" Mackenzie prompted him in a quiet voice.

"And then, the ones who were privileged to know the location used the knowledge to their advantage—maybe plotting to take over the Roman empire and then the world. The location was passed from father to son until one day the last person with the knowledge of the location died or was killed before he passed it on." He spoke those last words in an almost inaudible whisper.

Mackenzie could see his mind was working on something. She remained silent, just staring at him, waiting for more. Sitting next to him, she could see he was staring at images on his laptop.

He clicked back and forth between a few screens and

started mumbling. A smile broke across Mackenzie's face. She has seen that act a few times before—a major unveiling was in the cards.

Carter's mumbling became a bit louder. Mackenzie remained as quiet as a mouse while her smile stretched wider. Then she could make out some of what he was saying. "…seen this… come on… where… see it?"

Suddenly he was out of the reverie. He looked at her and started smiling. "I'm getting old… I—"

"Not on your life, Carter Devereux! Your brain is as sharp as the day I met you. And as for the rest of you—" She stopped talking and started grinning. "No need to expand on that. Now, tell me what have you discovered on your trip into the other dimension in the last fifteen or so minutes?"

He pulled her closer to him and kissed her. He always did that when he came back from the other dimension—she had no idea which dimension it was—but she knew that's where he often got answers to the most challenging of questions.

When they came up for a breath, he turned to his computer and pointed to an image on the screen. "That image on the rock face you see in the picture there is on a rock just outside Petra. I've seen it with my own eyes when I was there." He paused.

Mackenzie leaned forward to have a better look. It was faint; she had to strain her eyes before she could make out the unmistakable images of five dolphins in the form of a pentagon.

"That's weird, is it not? Petra is a long way from the sea. I know the Nabateans did a lot of trading and owned some port cities, but dolphins in Petra, in the middle of the desert? What could be the significance of it?"

"I don't know. I thought you might be able to tell me." Carter struggled to keep a straight face.

Mackenzie was surprised at that. She was so sure he had the answer. She looked at his face and realized he was having her on. She jumped up and threw him off his chair onto the floor and sat on his chest.

By now, Carter was roaring with laughter.

"Okay," she said, "now you have two seconds to tell me, or I punch you in the throat—just like you taught me to do with bad guys."

Carter finally got his laughing under control and said, "Seriously, Mackie, I don't know what it means, but I have seen that same image somewhere else—"

"Where?" she demanded. "You better tell me, or you're going to regret it." She clenched her fist and waved it in front of his face, laughing.

"Matera!" Carter yelled.

"Where's that?"

"In the Basilicata region." At Mackenzie's puzzled look, Carter started laughing again. "Mackie, Matera is a city in the Basilicata region of Southern Italy. The Ionian Sea is to the south, not too far, and the Adriatic Sea is about equidistant to the west. "

"Well, I guess we're going to Matera then?"

"Just as soon as you get off me." Carter chuckled.

Chapter Forty-Two

CONGRESSIONAL OVERSIGHT

Mackenzie looked at her useless cell phone for the tenth time. It was so tempting to call the kids. She didn't dare even turn the thing on. It had been more than two weeks since she'd been home, hugged her kids, talked to her mother, or saw her beloved wolves.

They'd left the Smithsonian after a few days of work, convinced there were no more insights to be gained. And they still hadn't been able to stay anywhere long enough to make hanging her clothes up worthwhile. They moved to a different safe house every day or two.

Even though they'd been cleared of all suspicion by anyone who counted, to keep the bad guys in the dark, they couldn't appear in public and had to stay "on the run." For as long as it would take to find the real source of the leaks, no one else could know they'd been cleared.

It was understandable.

Mackenzie couldn't help but be homesick anyway.

The story of A-Echelon's existence and secret funding hadn't fallen into a vacuum. No story about government, good or bad, went without notice in the nation's capital. Senators and Congressmen arrived in their offices to find the story among their news brief clippings or had seen it online or on TV before they even left their homes.

From the beginning, Congress had wanted in on the A-Echelon circus. In an election year, it was fodder for political gain, and the politicians just couldn't help themselves. They wanted—no, *craved*—the political mileage they thought they could get out of airing the scandal in public.

Every lawmaker and lobbyist in the city jockeyed for position as public opinion swayed this way and that. The media, of course, had taken the position that the existence of such a department was an enormous and scandalous waste of taxpayer money. The political side of the aisle most often associated with the media trumpeted that line as their own.

On the other side of the aisle, the opposite stance was taken on principle. Whatever *those* guys said couldn't be taken seriously. Some lawmakers were savvy enough to remember and trot out the seldom-remembered Stargate Project, wherein the Defense Intelligence Agency and others investigated the potential for psychic phenomena in military and domestic intelligence applications from 1979 through 1991. To the dismay of the naysayers, it had been primarily their party that funded such projects.

Though no specific crime was alleged, the scandal was shaping up to be the defining moment of the Presidential race, and the only opinion everyone had in common was it should be investigated by one of the Congressional oversight committees and the findings published as quickly as possible.

Never mind that both the President and the Director of the CIA claimed national security was at risk. Both sides of the Congressional aisles believed they stood the most to gain from dissecting the whole mess in public. Their insistence was fed by the media and the new game in town, social media. The people demanded answers, and Congress was eager to get them for their constituents.

Back and forth the arguments went. President Grant and Bill Griffin stood between Congress and their targets, James Rhodes and Irene O'Connell, pressing for closed-door hearings. But Congress, with the weight of the people behind them, prevailed. The hearings would be open, broadcast live on CNN and numerous online feeds.

Both parties figuratively rubbed their hands in satisfaction. The folks at home would see how hard they were working and vote accordingly. It was perfect! No cost for the exposure, no need to stump at home this early in their campaigns. This was going to be good!

There are those who are eager to testify before such a committee. James and Irene weren't among them. Originally meant to be part of the checks and balances among the three branches of government, the establishment of the oversight committees purported to make Congress the watchdog of the people—their constituents—against excesses of the Executive branch and federal agencies.

However, human nature exerted influence. John Dalberg-Acton, who said, "Power tends to corrupt, and absolute power corrupts absolutely," might have warned the earliest lawmakers it was coming. Unfortunately, he wasn't born until decades after the longest-standing committees, Finance, Foreign Relations, and Judiciary, were established.

Over the years, the system had been turned into a political playball to serve partisan interests and certain individuals' kingdom-building ambitions. Advocates for every conceivable committee with even a miniscule claim of interest had been arguing, with each other and on the Senate and House floors, that their committee should be the one to investigate. The most opinionated of them all, and possibly the most powerful, Senator Michelle Davis, was tired of the debate and ready to take matters into her own hands.

Davis, the senior senator from California, chaired the Senate Intelligence Committee. She was a fifth-term veteran political gladiator, and commonly known among her cowed colleagues as a real ballbuster. Davis shared an intense dislike of the CIA and its James Bond license-to-kill and do-whatever-it-takes ways with many of her colleagues. She wanted to rein them in, get those loose cannons under control, put a leash on them, and tie them to a pole, only to be let loose when the Senate said so.

She rushed down the hall to her office, struggling not to shout at and shoulder everyone out of her way, with only moderate success. Reaching the privacy of her office, she kicked off her thousand-dollar, black, leather, Christian Louboutin pumps, opened the top drawer of her desk, grabbed a pack of cigarettes and lighter, and lit one up. No one who knew what was good for them would point out the universal No Smoking regulations to *her*. Least of all her staff.

She put her feet on the desk, and with the first puff of smoke, she mumbled, "Bunch of retards…"

For the past three hours, she'd had to use every bit of restraint she could command with colleagues debating and reasoning which committee should be investigating the A-Echelon debacle. For three full hours, they'd been squabbling. *It must be the Foreign Relations Committee; Why not Judi-*

ciary? Intel and Armed Services; What about Homeland Security? One stupid question and argument after another nonstop for one hundred and eighty minutes.

What a colossal waste of time!

"Idiots," she snarled through the cloud of smoke drifting to the opening of the ventilation duct in the ceiling above her. "Homeland Security… John Macnab… you must be shitting me. The Intelligence Committee, *my* committee, should have this. We're the only ones with the brains to handle it. There's a *reason* it's called the Intelligence Committee. Homeland Security should be second on the list, maybe—a distant second. But it ain't over, Johnny boy. I'm going to pull the rug from under your feet."

This was going to be the biggest scandal D.C. had seen since Watergate. A scandal for the history books—and the end of the CIA's free rein. She'd been cautioning presidents and senators about the CIA for years, but no one had listened. Now they would have to admit she was right all along.

She stubbed the cigarette out in an ashtray, put the latter away in a locked drawer of her desk, and picked up the phone to call in a few overdue favors, make a few promises, and utter a few carefully veiled threats.

Chapter Forty-Three

GOTCHA, YOU BASTARD!

April 6

It had been about two weeks since the newly-formed team of Sean, Dylan, and Kelly White had planted bugs in the "milk" plane and in Russell McCormick's apartment and car, and to Dylan's frustration, nothing had come of it.

The pilot and crew never approached the "chocolate box"; there was no chatter in the plane about anything more important than the last basketball game.

The bugs in McCormick's apartment and especially those in his car produced more interesting insights into his personality, but nothing regarding the leaks. Dylan got a laugh out of playing the best parts for Kelly and watching her kick the walls and furniture because she couldn't kick the son of a bitch she was still pretending to care for.

She could now see the narcissistic tendencies she'd been blind to before. The bugs were sensitive enough to pick up the scrape of his razor as he shaved in the mornings. The slap of his hands on his face to apply the aftershave she'd come to hate, and then his smug voice.

"Well, *hellooo*, ladykiller! Go get 'em, tiger."

The first time she'd heard it, she'd mimed sticking her finger down her throat, which made Dylan laugh until he cried. The second, third, and fourth times were just too much. "Okay, Dylan, I get the point. Don't do it to me anymore—I know I was an idiot."

Dylan grinned. "How about this one, then? He's in the car."

He clicked on the sound file, and to Kelly's disgust, Russell's voice again came through loud and clear, singing, "I'm Too Sexy."

"He really thinks he's God's gift to women," she remarked.

Dylan just nodded. He didn't want to rub salt in her wounds.

"One has to wonder how he got past the psych testing when the FBI hired him." Kelly had her chin grasped between her thumb and forefinger.

Dylan shrugged. "Some are born that way and some become that way."

April 12

A week later, Dylan had enough data to start spotting patterns in McCormick's movements. He was studying the GPS tracking log for anything obvious.

McCormick kept a reliable schedule. Morning: to work, either from his place or Kelly's, and then back again, with side trips on the way back to locations that turned out to be restaurants. Kelly confirmed that on those nights, they'd gone out to dinner, and she'd been with him for almost every minute. Unless he was exchanging information with someone in the restrooms, those places were a bust for clandestine activity.

Sometimes he'd go from work, to his place, and then to Kelly's, then back to his place, and to work the next morning. Other times, he'd go from Kelly's to work in the morning. *Must have spent the night those times.* Dylan knew Kelly was sensitive about that and saw no need to ask her about it.

He'd just about given up on finding anything interesting when he spotted an anomaly. The day before, Russell had driven somewhere else in the afternoon. Dylan pulled up a map and overlaid McCormick's route on it. He'd taken a drive out into the countryside, or what passed for countryside in this crowded area near Washington, D.C. Outside the Beltway and across the Potomac.

As Dylan zoomed in on the map, it looked more and more familiar. *Of course! Hyde Field.* The Devereuxs used that airport for their travels, and the "milk" plane was hangered there, too. Coincidence? Dylan didn't believe in them.

And wait. There was another trip in that direction, too. When?

Feverishly, Dylan went over the records again. Last Wednesday. Yesterday was a Wednesday. But he didn't take the same route. Not the same road, not the same time. Not a pattern. He followed the hunch, though. There it was—another trip on the first Wednesday after the bugs were planted. Not the same road or time, again, but all three trips traveled the roads around Hyde Field.

When it clicked into place, Dylan slapped his forehead. Why had it taken even a minute to see the connection? The "milk" plane made its runs on Wednesdays, usually arriving at Freydís around ten a.m. and back to Virginia before three p.m. It couldn't be a coincidence.

Gotcha, you bastard!

"Sean, come have a look at this!" he yelled.

Sean agreed it couldn't be coincidence, which by the way, he didn't believe in, either. But what could McCormick do from the distances he was keeping? He never got closer than five miles from the landing strip in any direction. There were no stops at all, not even one long enough to retrieve something from a dead-drop.

It was Sean who got the brainwave. "Let's bring in some computer geeks. I want to know if there's any way to transmit data during a drive-by? How far away can someone be from a hot-spot and still receive a private transmission? And how long would it take to retrieve the data from one of those mass storage devices?"

They questioned the egg-heads carefully, not revealing the size or even the existence of the mass storage device. All theoretical, right?

And the experts came through with the right answers.

Well, it depended on the device. With a cell phone, maybe thirty yards. But with different protocols and the right equipment, it could be up to hundreds of miles. Yes, high-speed transmission was possible.

What if the receiver of the data was moving? Could it get a signal and reliably download data without corruption at five to ten miles?

Sure, easily, and you wouldn't even need a big router on the sending end to pick it up on your laptop.

After dismissing the technical consultants, who preferred that term to what Sean had been calling them, Sean and Dylan shared a high-five.

Bingo! They had the means. Now they just needed the method.

Russell drove near the jetport every Wednesday after the "milk" plane returned from Freydís, somehow activated the transmission from the "chocolate box" remotely, and downloaded the data from the mass storage device. The "chocolate box" must be programmed to retrieve the data from the storage device, probably during the flight, and transmit it when McCormick turned up.

Now they had to determine what he did with it. Probably kept it stored on his laptop until he could offload it to his handler, either by transmitting it securely, in the same way he got it, or maybe he copied it to another storage device and handed it off via dead drop.

Whatever method he used, the receiver of that data was the next link in the chain to the leak—maybe even the main culprit. Therefore, the next thing to investigate was what McCormick did with the data.

Kelly was most familiar with his routine while at work or with her, and she knew she'd never seen a laptop at his home. He had one at work, but it would have been extremely risky to use it for clandestine activities. Government laptops, even for the lowliest employees, had encryption built-in, safeguards against pirated software that would prevent a user from adding anything to the hard drive, and were subject to random recalls for the IT departments to make changes. It was therefore highly unlikely he'd use it, or even be able to use it, to download data from the "chocolate box".

"What about phones?" Dylan asked.

"Two smartphones, one for work, and it has the same problems the laptop would. Plus, it's like mine, it's a couple of generations behind the times, and I doubt it would have the storage capacity. His personal smartphone is the best bet," Kelly replied.

"Do you know the password?"

"It's a Z-pattern he traces around dots on the screen. Yeah, I think I could duplicate it."

Sean said, "Then you'll have to check it. We'll get the geeks to give you a scanning app. Assuming you can get hold of the cell phone long enough to do it."

"I think I can. Dinner, wine, bed," she said, lifting a corner of her lip as she said *bed*. "And to be sure he stays asleep after all that, a nightcap with some liquid Benadryl."

The plan worked flawlessly, except for the fact that there was nothing suspicious in McCormick's phone, Kelly reported.

"Maybe it was hidden so well the scan couldn't detect it?" Dylan suggested.

"The IT guys told me it would have seen a blank area that it couldn't read. It just wasn't there."

All three were silent for a few minutes as they thought about how someone would retrieve the information from the "chocolate box" on the plane without the help of the crew.

Kelly spoke first. "What about the maintenance crew?"

"We've dug up every secret, connected associates, and specks of DNA the crew and maintenance crew might have back to their great-great-great-grandfathers. They're clean," Sean said. It was only a slight exaggeration.

Dylan snapped his fingers. "Of course! We've been stupid. It's another 'chocolate box'. We've got to get a better name for the damn thing."

Sean took up the idea. "You mean, Russell has one, too."

"No doubt about it. And there's probably another one he transmits to after he grabs the data."

"Let's not get ahead of ourselves," Sean cautioned. "It's a good theory, but we need to verify it. Kelly, can you get McCormick to spend the night at your place again?"

"Sure. But why?" she asked.

"You'll let us into the parking garage, and while he's with you, Dylan and I will tinker with his car a bit. Just go with whatever happens."

"Okay," Kelly said, drawing out the syllables. "Are you guys going to take his car apart right there? My neighbors might get suspicious."

"Nope. In the morning, it won't start. Offer to call a mechanic, and we'll take it from there. You can give him a ride to work."

Kelly grinned broadly. "Okay, I've got it."

Sean and Dylan waited where Kelly told them to, in an alcove opposite the elevator in her building's parking garage. Wearing all black and with their faces blackened, no one could see them in the shadow. Sean's cell phone buzzed a few minutes after they saw her car pull into its designated slot and Russell's follow and park in a guest slot. There was just one word in the text from her: *go*.

They slipped between parked cars until they came to Russell's. After a quick look around, Dylan slipped underneath the car, applied a clamp to the soft fuel line, and crawled back out.

"You sure that will work?" Sean asked.

"Yeah. Where I put it, the car will start and then die. After that, it will just act like it's going to start, but it won't be getting any fuel," Dylan answered. "I did it to a guy that pissed me off in high school."

"Good man. Remind me not to make you mad."

The next morning, Sean got a call from Kelly. "A1 Mechanics? Hi. You guys helped me out when my car wouldn't start a few months back. I have a friend who's got the same problem. Can you pick up his car and take it to your shop for a checkup?"

Russell was happy she was making the arrangements with her mechanic; he had no mechanical skills. Kelly took him to work.

Shortly after they had left, Dylan met the CIA techs at the parking garage and pointed out the correct car. They towed the car away, and for the next few hours, they took the car apart and put it back together again, finding nothing but the "chocolate box" Dylan had suspected.

The box was hidden behind the side panel of the driver's side door, and again the techs didn't want to interfere with it in case doing so would alert Russell or someone else. They told Dylan that unless they could take it out and analyze it, all they could say was it was identical to the one in the plane as far as they could tell.

It was a good guess the thing was both a receiver and a transmitter, as they'd speculated about the one in the plane. Frustrating as it was not to be permitted to take it apart and figure it out, they simply couldn't risk it. It could be rigged to blow up if someone interfered with it, or it could alert the very people Executive Advantage and the CIA were trying to trap.

It seemed the only way they were going to get to the bottom of it would be to interrogate McCormick. And that was going to be a political hot potato.

Chapter Forty-Four

PLANNING A KIDNAPPING

April 13

A debate among Dylan, Kelly, and Sean was raging. Dylan was all for kidnapping Russell McCormick and beating information out of him. Kelly thought the kidnapping was a good idea but wasn't sure beating Russell would be productive. Sean agreed with the abduction, but wasn't sure Bill would condone it.

Sean asked them to wait while he had a quick meeting with Bill. Half an hour later, Bill walked into the coffee shop where Sean had asked to meet him, and the two strolled out one after the other, as if by coincidence, with takeaway coffee in their hands.

"We've identified another of those black boxes like in the plane," Sean said, not looking at Bill, who was by now walking in tandem but looking across the street.

"Where?" Bill glanced at the sidewalk as he spoke.

"In Russell McCormick's car. We need to question him but without alerting his handler."

"That bastard! You want me to set it up with Alec Burnett?"

"No. We want you to run interference if there's any fallout after we kidnap him," Sean said. Though Bill still wasn't looking at him, he made a wry face.

"You're not serious!" Now Bill did look at Sean, but Sean was examining the crowd around them in the reflection of the windows they were passing.

"We may have to get rough."

"You'd better be damned sure he's involved," Bill muttered.

"Oh, we're sure. There's no question."

"Then you have my full support," Bill said firmly.

Ten minutes later, Sean gave the go-ahead for the kidnapping, and the rest of the conversation involved planning it.

Kelly had just one day to set up the trap. Her first move was to invite Russell for a weekend getaway. "I haven't been myself lately," she explained over dinner. "I think I need a break, and I'd love to have you join me. We could do something on the Outer Banks. I don't want to go far."

"Sounds like fun," Russell said. He gave a slight leer as he asked if she'd be taking a bikini.

"I'm sure I will be," Kelly responded, smiling, a smile that didn't meet her eyes. Russell didn't even notice. "I'll make a reservation. This is my treat for a change."

The next morning, she gave Sean and Dylan the address of the beach cottage she'd rented. "Will this be secluded enough?"

"It will do for the snatch. We'll take him to one of our safe houses not far from there," Sean answered.

"How many safe houses do you have?" Kelly asked. She'd already learned of several in the D.C. area where she and Russell had done fruitless raids to capture the Devereuxs.

"I'd tell you, but then," Dylan said, smirking. "You know what I'll have to do then…"

"I'd better go and pack. We're driving down there tonight. When will you do your thing?"

Sean answered, "I think it's better you don't know. Just relax and know we'll be there. That way you won't get nervous just before the time comes and be honestly surprised when we do."

"Oh, smart," Kelly responded.

Chapter Forty-Five

TELL US WHY

April 14

Even though she'd agreed to be in the dark about when the kidnapping would take place, Kelly sincerely hoped it would be before she had to go to bed with McCormick again. Admittedly, she was partly to blame for the situation she found herself in, but she felt she'd endured the unwanted relationship long enough. After tonight it would be over. Nevertheless, she'd do what she had to if it would bring him down, along with whoever he was working for.

When the door of the cottage burst open just as she was pouring the wine for the dinner she'd cooked, her first thought was *Thank God!* Her second was an irritated *They could have waited another hour so we could eat this.*

"What the hell?" Russell shouted, as Sean, Dylan, and a couple of their men grabbed him.

"Mr. McCormick, you're coming with us."

Russell continued to struggle and shout as they cuffed his hands behind his back and frog-marched him out the front door. Kelly noticed with even more irritation he hadn't even once expressed concern about her. She followed the others and watched as Russell was stuffed into the back of one of two identical black SUVs.

She got into the second, and the two cars set out on the reverse route from the one she and Russell had taken from Washington, but somewhere near Grandy, North Carolina, they turned off the highway and made their way to an isolated farmhouse inland.

As soon as she got out of the car, Kelly could hear Russell shouting. She peered through the darkness to see he had a bag of some kind over his head. Looking around her, she was amused to see what Russell couldn't. No amount of shouting was going to reach the ears of any human being. Not a speck of artificial light showed in any direction.

Dylan and his man muscled Russell into the house, and light bloomed through the windows. Sean, his man, and Kelly followed. Sean handed the two operatives a couple of brown bags, apologizing for the simple fare, and sent them outside to keep watch. He turned to Kelly.

"I'm sorry you didn't get to eat," he said, handing her another brown bag. "I'm sure *your* dinner would have been better than this."

"Oh, I don't know. The food maybe. But the company is probably better right here," she answered.

Russell jerked when she spoke. He still had the bag over his head. "Kelly? They got you, too?"

Kelly sent Dylan a questioning look. At his nod, she walked over and snatched the bag off Russell's head. He blinked a couple of times and then frowned at her. "Kelly, what is this?"

"Why, Russell, I took you to be smarter than that. Based on the fact that you've been handcuffed and taken somewhere you didn't intend to go, I'd say you've been kidnapped. My friends here" —she pointed at Sean and Dylan in turn— "have some questions for you. Apparently, you've done some things that annoyed the crap out of them. I'd advise you to answer them." She leaned forward and whispered, "The big one over there," she thumbed to Dylan, "would like nothing better than to beat the answers out of you."

Sean raised his eyebrows and gestured for everyone to take a seat. Russell remained standing. "You'll pay for this. Do you guys have any idea who I am? Did that bitch tell you? I can have you put away for the rest of your lives and then some. Your families will never know what happened to you."

Dylan slowly unfolded from the chair he'd taken and walked up to Russell, standing nose to nose. "That's no way to refer to a lady. Sit. Down." He accompanied his clipped words with a poke in Russell's chest, powerful enough to shove him into the chair.

Kelly wasn't surprised when Russell continued to be defiant, lifting his chin and signaling his hatred of Dylan with a fiery gaze. She'd known he was arrogant from almost the first moment she met him. She gave a small shake of her head as she thought about how she'd admired that about him at first.

"That's right, Kelly. Your boyfriends have the advantage of me now, but it will go even worse for them if they want to play rough. Tell them who I am."

"They know who you are, Russell. The issue is they know who you *really* are, I mean other than what you do for a day job. You might as well cooperate."

"Stupid bitch. You've been following my lead since we

met. If I'm in trouble, so are you. You've been the perfect patsy."

Kelly snarled, but waved Dylan down when he would have taught Russell some manners.

Russell seized the advantage to get in more digs. "I knew everything about you—more than your mother even knew—right down to your sizes, the color of your panties, before I even met you. Your favorite music, color, chocolates, boyfriends. Oh, and now I even know that none of your boyfriends ever gave you as good a time in bed as I did!"

That was the last straw for Kelly, who stood up, took two long strides, and slapped him. "You're delusional. You're the worst lay I ever had, asshole."

"Kelly, that's enough," warned Sean. "McCormick, we know you've been stealing data—"

Ignoring him, Russell stared at Kelly. "I know your teammates at INSCOM call you Ice Queen. You'd be the last woman any of them approached after one too many drinks. In fact, it would take more than a few too many for any man who didn't have an agenda to take you to bed at all."

Kelly, who had remained standing after slapping him, screeched and went for him with both hands. Dylan jumped up and held her back.

"Kelly, take it easy. We need him alive." He was having a hard time not laughing but knew his head would be next on the chopping block if he did. His amusement stemmed from the fact that Kelly hadn't wanted to beat the information out of McCormick, but she was now ready to murder him over a few taunts. "You can kill him later," he added, keeping his face as straight as he could.

"Kelly, please sit down," Sean said firmly. "Russell, I swear I'll turn her loose if you don't start talking. And if you try to lie, I'll turn Dylan loose. And if you make one more derogatory remark about Miss White, *I'll* shoot you in the kneecap. Do I make myself clear?"

Sean's outburst took Russell's attention off Kelly, who was visibly shaking. Dylan saw Russell had pushed Sean's buttons, too. If Russell knew what was good for him, he would calm down immediately. He made a small noise and got Sean's attention, then gave a slight shake of his head.

"Okay, Casanova," Dylan said. "Let me see if I understand you correctly. So, you did this brilliant job of setting Kelly up. Mind telling us why? Let me rephrase that. Tell us why."

Russell recognized his braggadocio had given them information he didn't intend to give, and now he had to bluff it out. "To steer the investigation in a certain direction," he said, lifting his chin again.

"You mean, like framing and accusing innocent people of treason," Dylan stated in a cold tone dripping with anger.

McCormick didn't answer. Dylan asked the same questions in several different ways, trying to trip McCormick up, but got no answers. Dylan decided to change tactics. He opened a briefcase that was lying on the table.

"What about your share in this?" he asked, showing McCormick several photos of the devastation at Patch Barracks.

Russell glanced at them and then up at Dylan. He shrugged. Dylan clenched his fists, resisting a powerful urge to punch McCormick in his smug face. Instead, he selected a few more photos, close-ups of the wounded and maimed bodies. He kept hammering. "How about this? Or this?"

For every pair of photos Dylan thrust in his face with

both hands, Russell shook his head. "I don't know anything about that. I had nothing to do with it."

Dylan chose more and more heartrending photos—small children crying, parents and wives touching the flag-draped coffins of the victims, and sobbing men and women with missing limbs or in hospital beds covered in bandages. Over the course of half an hour or more, he shoved photos in McCormick's face and yelled, "What was your part in this?"

When Russell started shaking and denying any complicity in the explosion more and more desperately, Dylan knew he had his prey where he wanted him, ready to break. Suddenly, he softened his voice and asked a different question.

"Why do you drive out to Prince Georges County every Wednesday?"

Russell had been staring at the floor, unable to meet the eyes of his accuser. Now his head came up. "What?"

Patiently, Dylan rephrased his question. "Why do you drive out toward Hyde Field every Wednesday?"

"How the hell would you know that?" Russell burst out, oblivious to the fact he'd just admitted his secret.

"Vee haf our vays," Dylan taunted, faking a German accent. "Never mind how. Why do you do it?"

Russell slumped. They had him on the trips to Hyde Field. How, he didn't know, but if they knew that, then they likely knew other stuff. Now it was a matter of his own survival. "I'm just supposed to. Every Wednesday. I don't know why. If I can't do it during the day after a certain time, then I must do it at night. And if I can't do that, I just wait for the next Wednesday."

"Tell us why."

"I don't *know* why. That's just my orders."

Dylan, Sean, and Kelly exchanged looks. The bastard was lying, but they were making progress. Every small admission was a crack in his façade. Dylan raised one eyebrow. Sean nodded. It was time to bring out the big gun.

"Tell us about the Nabateans."

Russell's reaction to the word was an admission. He flinched so hard he almost went over backward in his chair. Barely recovering, he let his chair settle for a moment and then carefully smoothed all expression from his face.

"I only heard about them from Kelly."

Kelly jerked in surprise. Dylan glanced at Sean.

Sean slowly stood up. McCormick cowered. He'd watched Sean and his reactions while Dylan had been questioning him. No question Sean was the one with the short fuse, and it looked like he'd run out of time. *If that dude's taking over, I'm SOL.*

"W-wait. Okay, m-my father. All right? My father is into genealogy. He told me about them. Said we were descendants, but I can't remember exactly how. It never interested me that much."

Dylan wasn't through asking him specific questions. "Have you heard of the Council of the Covenant of Nabatea?"

"Yes, Kelly told me about them. She got it from James Rhodes and Irene O'Connell of A-Echelon."

"Tell us about Shadow," Dylan demanded.

Russell shrugged. "Don't know anything about shadows. No idea what you're talking about."

"Stop playing games, Russell!" Kelly shouted. "I told you I got an anonymous package from someone called Shadow. Now, tell us what you know about Shadow."

With Dylan asking more and more pointed questions,

and Kelly or Sean throwing in an occasional jab, they slowly dragged the truth out of McCormick. Yes, he was Shadow. He was the one feeding Howard Crane, and he'd had the package delivered to Kelly when Crane dragged his feet on the story.

And that was the admission they needed for the payoff. Dylan took a deep breath, glanced at the other two, and asked the million-dollar question. "Who recruited you, when, and how?"

McCormick turned white. "You don't know what you're asking me."

"Sure, we do," Dylan said. "Who recruited you, when, and how? It's easy—give us a name, tell us when, and how. Just open your mouth and start speaking."

Russell looked around and summoned the last of his arrogance. "For all the good it will do you, I was contacted by a man about three or four years after I joined the FBI, and he convinced me it would be in my best interest to do as I was told.

"For about twenty-five years, I've done just that. Never saw the guy again, but now and then I'd get written messages about tasks I should perform, or information I should get and leave at dead drops. I knew the consequences if I refused. So, I didn't refuse. But if you think I know who they are, you're dead wrong." He set his jaw and stared at Sean.

Dylan took the information in stride. It was a story as old as history itself. But a piece was missing. "We need to know what this man had over you. Twenty-five years is a long time for a secret to remain so dangerous. The quicker you tell us, the quicker we can move on and see if we can help you out of the shit you've created for yourself."

McCormick had recovered his composure in telling his

story. "No, I think it's the other way around. Maybe *you've* created more shit for yourself than you can handle. Shit man, I'm an FBI agent! Do you know what—"

Sean had heard enough and interjected. "You really don't know in how much shit you are, do you? Mr. FBI Agent."

He proceeded to relate the story of Durand and his killing, the Algosaibi children's deaths at the hands of the Council, and more. Things Russell should have known or suspected but never thought about.

Sean wasn't above embroidering the facts when Russell stuck out that annoying, arrogant chin. And he kept it up until he played his final hand, only after seeing the doubt creep into Russell's eyes.

"You know, we had Durand in protective custody when he was killed. We're good, McCormick, we're damned good —and they still managed to find and kill him. Do you think we'll even *try* to protect you if you don't tell the truth?"

Russell tried one last, desperate ploy. "If you can't protect me anyway, why should I tell you anything?"

"Well, I didn't say we couldn't protect you. We've learned a few things. But right now, seeing that you have given us nothing, it doesn't look too promising for you, McCormick. All we have to do is have Kelly arrest you."

Russell looked over at Kelly, who was nodding enthusiastically, with a big smile on her face.

Sean went on, "Then we contact the media. The headline reads '*New discovery about the A-Echelon case – Russell McCormick, the Assistant Director Counterintelligence Division FBI head offices in D.C. found to be involved in illegal activities.*'"

"It'll never stick. I'll accuse her of framing me."

"Hypocrisy in full bloom, I see." Sean smirked. "You

had no problem framing other people. But that doesn't matter. The Nabateans will terminate you in less than twenty-four hours. You'd be dead before you can be brought before a judge to ask for bail. That's how they operate. That's what happened to Durand and Algosaibi's children. And that's probably what happened to Peter Nikolaev, the Director of the Federal Security Service (FSB) of Russia, who ordered the attack on Freydís. He died before he could be arrested and questioned."

"But I'm valuable to them," Russell tried.

"Well, in that case, let's find out just how valuable you are to them. Shall we?

"Kelly arrests you, and we make sure the Nabateans get to know about it via the media. Then we set our watches and see what happens.

"Shall we put a wager on it?" Sean looked at Dylan and Kelly. "What's your bet?"

"Eighteen hours, max," Dylan replied.

"Maybe he'll get to twenty-three, although, as far as I'm concerned, the quicker the better," Kelly ventured.

Russell's eyes were darting back and forth between the three while they were speaking as if he wasn't there.

Dylan and Kelly were looking at Sean to tell them what his bet would be. "If they can kill people in US protective custody and the Director of the Federal Security Service (FSB) of Russia before his men could give him up... I reckon twenty hours at the most," Sean said and turned to McCormick. "So, Russell what's your bet?"

Everyone fell silent to let McCormick reflect for a moment. When the silence had stretched to an uncomfortable two minutes, Dylan took it as Russell's tacit agreement to answer the questions and resumed.

"So, where were we? Oh, yes. You wanted to tell us about the power this mystery man wields over you."

McCormick sputtered. "It's not like that. I benefit from this arrangement. I told you, money flows into my bank account. I get tips on cases and solve them. That gets me commendations and promotions. That's why I'm where I am, career-wise, now. Why would I throw all that away?"

Dylan crossed his arms. "Are you kidding me? What part of you'll be killed within twenty-four hours do you not understand? What do they have on you?"

McCormick was defeated, and he knew it. Damned if he told them, dead if he didn't. He was hungry, physically and emotionally exhausted, and confused about how he'd gotten to this point.

Sean pulled his pistol and pointed it at McCormick's right knee.

"Stop! I'll tell you," Russell blubbered. A spot of wetness appeared on the front of his trousers. "I… Oh, God, this is so embarrassing. A couple of years after I joined the FBI, I was undercover, about to bust this child pornography ring. It was the kid or me, I swear."

"What do you mean?" Kelly asked, her voice like ice.

"I molested this kid, okay?"

Kelly went ballistic. She lunged for McCormick with both hands outstretched. Russell used his feet to scramble backward, chair and all, but it went over backward with him. He kept scrambling and managed to turn himself, chair and all, on his side.

Once again, Dylan had to hold Kelly back. When she

went still, he let her go but stayed alert. She didn't go after McCormick again, though. Instead she left the room.

McCormick tried to justify himself. "He was already a child prostitute, right? They suspected me. If I hadn't, they'd have killed me. I thought no one would know, but then not long afterward, this guy showed up and showed me a video. If I hadn't done as he asked, I'd have gone to prison. Help me up, okay?"

Dylan clenched his fists, as did Sean. Neither made a move to help Russell right himself. The two of them were still trying to control their impulse to beat him senseless when Kelly flew back into the room with a large butcher knife. This time, Dylan had only a split second to decide what to do. Tackling her might cause her to stab herself, and grabbing her around the waist like he'd done twice before might get his arm slashed or worse.

"Stop!" Dylan's shout made Kelly hesitate and turn toward him, butcher knife still dangerous in her upraised hand. "Think what you're doing."

"I know exactly what I'm doing," Kelly answered, her voice shaking slightly. "I'm going to make sure he can't ever do that again."

Dylan put out his hand to stop her, and she slashed at it with the knife. "Tell me I'm wrong," she snarled.

Sean used his most commanding tone to say, "Give the knife to Dylan. Now."

Kelly turned a wild expression on Sean. "No. I'm going to Bobbittize him. He's done enough damage with that thing."

Dylan was approaching her stealthily as Sean engaged her attention, but Russell screamed, "No!" when she uttered the threat, and she whirled toward him. The wet spot near his crotch was now prominent.

Dylan was within arm's reach. He snatched the knife out of her hand, receiving a cut to his palm in the process.

"Dylan! I'm sorry... I didn't... Oh, God!" Kelly gasped.

"You need to calm down, girl. Or we'll have to truss you up like McCormick. Capisce?" Dylan said. "Can I trust you not to lose it again so I can go take care of this blood?" He held up his injured hand to demonstrate that blood was dripping from it freely.

Kelly hung her head. With tears in her eyes, she said, "Yes. I'm sorry, Dylan."

He winked at her as he walked out of the room, heading for the kitchen.

The crisis averted, Sean walked over and hauled Russell and his chair upright again. "Next time, we don't stop her. You've got a choice right now. You start cooperating or—"

Sean's grim, veiled threat was the final straw for McCormick. "Okay! Okay! I'll talk, but I want a deal."

"You're in no position to make deals," Kelly spat.

Sean quelled her with a look.

Russell's jaw clenched. "What do you want me to say?"

"The truth, the whole truth, and nothing but the truth about those trips to the airport. No more bullshit. Or we give Kelly back the knife."

Kelly gave a faint smile. She didn't think she could go through with it now that the heat of her burst of temper was gone. But the smile looked a bit evil, and it did the trick.

"Okay, but keep that crazy bitch away from me! I told you, I'm supposed to drive around that place. I drive around until I hear five short beeps. That means I'm done. I don't know what it does, or what happens afterward."

"I told you no more bullshit. You know what it does." Sean gestured toward Kelly.

"*Okay*, yeah. They told me it's a data download. But I

swear I don't know anything about what happens next. I go back to work, or home, Kelly's, wherever. And the next week I do it again."

"Who's your contact?" Sean asked, growing impatient and showing it in his sharp tone.

"I don't know. I mean, I don't have one."

Dylan walked back in with a dishtowel wrapped around his injured hand. "Don't have what?"

"He claims he doesn't have a contact to hand the data to," Sean said, looking steadily at Russell.

Dylan gave Russell a hard stare. "Do you want me to go back in there and get that knife? If Kelly can't follow through, I sure as hell will."

Russell's desperate glance at Sean finally convinced him. "So, you're telling us that you never see anyone retrieve the data from that device?"

"What device?" Russell asked.

"Shit!" Dylan yelled, finally understanding. He hit the doorframe with his injured hand and yelled out again.

Sean and Kelly turned to look at Dylan. He motioned with his head for them to follow him. They got up and followed him to the bedroom farthest from the living room where Russell remained handcuffed and tied to his chair. "We're going to have to keep him active to try to trap them," Dylan said. "They're too well-organized."

"It's a risk," Sean said. "If they suspect he's talked to us, he's dead inside twenty-four hours. And he might just be stupid enough to try and do something about our little chat with him tonight."

"Those are risks we have to take. Can't be avoided. Let's go give him the choice."

Back in the room with McCormick, Sean made the offer. "You can work with us, or you get arrested tonight."

"Oh, no. You already told me I'd be dead in forty-eight hours if they get wind I've talked. Like that Durand guy," Russell said.

"Twenty-four hours," Sean corrected him. "We can try to protect you, and we're pretty good at what we do, now that we know what we're up against. No guarantees, though. The only thing that's going to keep you alive for long is bringing down the Council. Could be four weeks of survival with our help, could be longer. Either way, it's better than a guaranteed death in twenty-four hours, right?"

It didn't take Russell long to agree. "What do I need to do?"

Sean deferred to Dylan, who explained, "To stay alive to a healthy old age, you're going to have to help us bring down the Nabateans. Specifically, the Council. You must carry on as if nothing is different, and we'll give you instructions as they come up. No one can know you spoke to anyone but Kelly this weekend. We'll take you back to the cottage tonight, and you two will have the nice weekend you planned. Then we'll be in touch."

Kelly had heard enough. "I object," she said. "I can't keep up this charade any longer. If I have to be alone with the scumbag one more time, he *is* going to lose his family jewels."

Russell was almost as vehement. "You can't leave me alone with her! I'd rather take my chances with the Nabateans."

"Hold on," Sean said. "Kelly, may we see you in the other room again?"

Back in the bedroom, Sean spoke intensely. "May I remind you of your complicity in this case? And your boss's words? As I recall, General Fleming used words to the effect of, '*...defer my decision about your indiscretions. ...an opportunity for redemption. ...it is in your hands and your hands only...*.'"

"You're asking me to—"

"You don't have to be intimate with him. But you *do* have to keep up appearances. Or would you rather we told Fleming you won't cooperate? Or worse, let the Nabateans explode another antimatter bomb, this time vaporizing D.C.?"

"I hate you, Sean Walker."

"I'll get over it." Sean grinned. "And if it helps us nail those Nabateans' scalps to the wall, you're welcome to keep on hating me."

Once again, they trooped into the room with McCormick. Kelly's eyes were squinted almost shut when she spoke to Russell. "All right. I'll do what they say. You're safe as long as you don't get within ten feet of me. Just know I'll be carrying this" —she held up the knife she'd snagged off the kitchen counter as they passed through— "always. One false move and I swear I'll cut it off and feed it to a dog."

Russell summoned one last word of defiance. "I wouldn't touch you if I was wearing a hazmat suit. You're poison."

Kelly smiled her evil smile again. *Just give me one excuse, and you'll be singing soprano.* She said nothing.

"Okay, that's enough. Let's get down to business. We've got to get you two back to the cottage before daybreak. McCormick, do you know when the black box was installed in your car?" Sean was all business now.

"Roughly," he said, implicitly admitting he'd been lying before, "about sixteen months ago. I got a message to leave my car at home and take a taxi to work. The message said to leave everything alone. I assume it's in the panel next to the driver's seat, because that's where the beeps come from. But I've never looked. They told me they'd know immediately if I did."

Sean and Dylan kept silent. They'd already had a look, and while they didn't touch the box, they knew it hadn't sent a message to anyone. If it had, McCormick wouldn't be sitting with them now. He'd be fish food at the bottom of the Potomac, probably. The same went for the discovery of the box on the plane.

"How do you communicate with your handler?"

"I've *told* you. I don't! He communicates with me. He gives me instructions. I carry them out. I have no way to get in touch with him."

In a way, that was a good thing, Sean reflected. McCormick couldn't let them know he'd been compromised. Not that he would, since he had a healthy regard for his own skin. But it didn't hurt to have the extra guarantee. On the other hand, it posed a problem. The trail had reached a dead end.

Dylan was watching McCormick closely when the thought crossed his mind. "Kelly said she met you before all this mess broke, December last year. How did you know she'd be assigned to the case?"

McCormick made a disgusted sound in his throat. "I didn't. They told me to talk her up. I did as I was told. I don't know anything else."

Sean, Dylan, and Kelly exchanged looks. *Someone* had known she'd be assigned to the case before there even was a case. "Who assigned you to the case, Kelly?"

"My immediate supervisor. But I'm sure he's clean."

"No one is clean until we've run the background checks. Someone above you in INSCOM is dirty, that's for sure.

They made sure you'd be assigned, because they already had their hooks in you. You just didn't know it yet."

Kelly wanted to utter a string of curses that would smoke the air, but she had only herself to blame. Instead, she said quietly, "Then we need to find out who."

Sean replied, "Yes, we have to, but definitely not now. Asking questions like that will raise suspicions."

Kelly nodded assent.

Chapter Forty-Six

THE FIRST HEARING

April 18

The political jockeying was finished—at least that's what it looked like. William (Bill) Griffin, Director of the CIA, James Rhodes as Director of A-Echelon Division of the CIA, and Irene O'Connell the Deputy Director of A-Echelon, plus Carter and Mackenzie Devereux had been summoned to appear before the Homeland Security Committee to answer questions about the activities of A-Echelon.

Carter and Mackenzie would shortly be held in contempt of Congress for failure to appear, but their employers were hopeful that could be sorted out later.

James was appalled as he turned the corner of the hallway leading to the Homeland Security Committee's meeting room and saw the crowd. The room and the hallway were teeming with politicians and their staffers. The place looked like the cotton candy stall at a school carnival.

He shrugged. *Why am I surprised? This is probably the only entertainment this group of overpaid, partisan pen-pushers will get for the duration of their tenures in servitude to their powerful political masters.*

Irene was already seated in the first row of chairs behind the witness table, facing the semi-circle podium where their twenty-seven confronters would take up their seats shortly.

He sat down next to her, looked around the room, and took a deep breath as he tried to pacify the rage building up inside him. This meeting was supposed to be held behind closed doors. Nothing said here today was supposed to reach the ears of anyone other than the members of this committee and the people called to testify before it.

Nothing of the top-secret information was supposed to be shared with the staffers crowding the room, but that was not going to be. They would hear it, too, and they would be coming and going, gofers for their bosses including those who weren't on the committee, relaying messages between them and the sitting members.

The hearing might as well have been open to the public and the media. It would have saved them the trouble of getting the information secondhand.

"The circus has arrived in town," James said under his breath to Irene. "Twenty-seven politicians and their entourage of staffers, numbering probably forty, will know all about us before the sun goes down today. Security leaks on steroids."

"I wish I could disagree with you, Jim. But you're right, this is the end of A-Echelon's secrecy. All we can do is to skirt around the real facts as much as we can without being charged with perjury or obstruction of justice."

"It's demoralizing to think that they have no idea what they are doing. These self-serving boneheads are doing this for political windfall, while hiding behind the façade of serving the best interests of the American people."

"That's our job, James," Irene said thoughtfully.

James looked at her, frowning. "What do you mean?"

"It's our job to look out for the American people, James. These clowns won't. It's as you said—they know not what they're doing."

A few minutes later, Bill Griffin arrived and took a seat next to James. The committee members, surrounded by their staffers, started drifting into the room and took their seats.

Another few minutes passed before Senator John Macnab, the chairman of the committee, and two more senators arrived at almost the same time. Shortly after, Bill Griffin's boss, Sebastian Birch, the Director of National Intelligence, also arrived and took a seat next to Bill.

Bill leaned over to James and whispered, "At least they had the decency to honor us with a full house."

"I wouldn't have been satisfied with anything less," James quipped.

The latecomers struggled to get to their seats, as every few feet they were stopped by staffers and colleagues who had some final messages and questions.

Finally, after another ten minutes of chaos, everyone had a seat, and the chairman gaveled the hearing to order, after which he launched into a series of procedural matters and motions, taking up another fifteen minutes. By the time Senator Macnab was ready and looked at the DNI, Bill, James, and Irene, the hearing was more than an hour behind schedule.

No wonder nothing gets done in this place. James looked at his watch. *If any of us had been late, they would have held us in contempt. But maybe those rules ain't for them.*

Macnab called James to the witness table first. James stood, raised his right hand, and took the oath before he sat down.

Macnab theatrically took off his glasses and cleared his throat, making sure he had everyone's attention. "Director Rhodes, there has been a lot of discussion amongst the senate members about which would be the appropriate committee to hear this matter. There had been several arguments to have it heard by one of the other committees…" He paused for effect, replaced his glasses and looked down at his notes. "Be that as it may—"

He didn't get any further.

Senator Michelle Davis's voice was forceful. "I would like to place on record my strongest possible objection about the appropriateness of bringing a matter, which so clearly is within the ambit of the *Intelligence* Committee, before the Homeland Security Committee.

"A-Echelon is a subsidiary of the CIA, Central *Intelligence* Agency, part of the U.S. *Intelligence* Community. The CIA reports to the Director of National *Intelligence*.

"The CIA is tasked with gathering, processing, and analyzing *intelligence* from around the world. Its focus is on overseas *intelligence* gathering, with only limited, if any, domestic jurisdiction."

She paused for effect. "Will the members please note the number of times the word *'intelligence'* appears in those names and the fact that neither the word *'Homeland'* nor *'Security'* is ever mentioned?

"Mr. Chairman, this is not the committee that should conduct this hearing; it should be *my* committee, the Intelligence Committee."

While Davis was talking, Macnab's face had turned red. It was clear he did not expect this. His eyes darted across the committee members, taking note of their body language, and realized he had been outmaneuvered. He immediately knew if he would put it to the vote, he would lose—not only the vote, but also face.

"Your objection is noted, Senator Davis. I'm not going to debate the matter as part of this hearing. I'm calling an hour recess so committee members can reach agreement before we proceed." Macnab didn't wait for anyone to agree or object. He gathered his effects and stormed out of the room with the rest of the members trailing out behind him like a bunch of sheep.

James turned around in his chair and looked at Bill and the others. He could see that Bill and Irene were struggling not to explode in raucous laughter. The DNI had a stern expression on his face.

"What now?" James asked.

The DNI grinned. "Now we wait, again. Macnab doesn't have enough support from his committee. Otherwise he would have put it to a vote and continued. My guess is this will be referred to Davis's Intelligence Committee."

"May God have mercy on us, because she won't," Bill said. "She hates my guts and everything related to the CIA. She's been looking for an opportunity to bring us down since long before my time. Finally, she's going to have her moment of glory."

The DNI nodded. "That might be so, but this little squabble of theirs has bought us another week or two. Let's use it for more preparation. You can never be too ready for these hearings."

Two hours instead of one hour later, the meeting was reconvened, only to let the witnesses know it has been agreed to refer the matter to Senator Michelle Davis's Committee, and they would be notified of the date.

Irene shook her head ever so slightly. *It would be interesting to know how many careers have been ruined, heads knocked, butts kissed, and palms greased the past two hours to reach that "agreement".*

Chapter Forty-Seven

JAILED OR WORSE

Mathieu Nabati paced in his luxurious hideaway in the Ural Mountains in western Russia. The Devereux project was going much too slowly, thanks to the ponderous American political system. The moronic Congressional committee had held one meeting that ended in chaos. The journalist, Howard Crane, had been a disappointment, and the joint INSCOM-FBI investigation had come to a standstill for some inexplicable reason.

Carter Devereux and his meddlesome wife should have been in jail by now, CIA director, Bill Griffin, fired, along with his henchmen, James Rhodes and Irene O'Connell. The President of the United States should have resigned by now.

It was time to shake things up. He picked up the phone.

The next morning, headlines in all the major news outlets revealed shocking news.

Journalist Howard Crane Diagnosed with Aggressive Brain Cancer.

After breaking the A-Echelon story, Howard had become something of a celebrity, appearing on morning talk shows, Meet the Press, Face the Nation, and even The Howard Stern Show. The news of his sudden terminal illness shocked and saddened the nation.

It also shocked Howard, who'd had no such diagnosis. He called each major outlet to deny the story, telling them it was a sick joke. Those who eschewed fake news apologized and promised to run a retraction. He didn't bother with the others, knowing it would be a waste of time.

He called Daniella to quote Mark Twain with a twist. "News of my imminent death has been greatly exaggerated."

Daniella laughed through tears and invited him to dinner. Over the meal in her apartment, he told her it had to be a sick joke. "No one could tell me exactly where it came from," he added.

"Why would someone do that?" she asked, pouring him another glass of wine.

"No clue. But let's not allow it to spoil the evening. We've got better things to do than worry about a stupid prank." Howard moved closer to Daniella, who tilted her head back for a lingering kiss. They'd been dating for a while—since he'd agreed to help manage the allegations in the package he'd received, in fact. At first, it had been coffee, or a working lunch. Lately they'd become more serious.

The next afternoon, Daniella opened an email and received another shock. She was still reading it when her phone began to ring. It was Scott Eadie.

"Did you get the email?" he asked, sounding out of breath.

"Yes. I've just opened it. I don't understand. Is this another sick joke?" she asked. She read aloud, skimming through the awful words. "... *time is up. Can't go through the cancer... choosing out.* Scott, what does this mean?"

"Crane was found dead in his apartment fifteen minutes ago. Cops called me because he also left a note, addressed to the President. It said, *'President Grant, I get the last laugh. Spin this.'* He sent that email to dozens of people, too. Most of whom are bombarding this office with angry calls, demanding answers."

Daniella made a small cry when she heard "found dead." But with Scott's last sentence, though tears were running uncontrolled down her face, she asked, "What? Why your office?"

"You didn't get to this part: *'Before I go, everyone should know I received this information a few weeks ago, and the President threatened me if I reported any of it. He's kept me quiet until now, but I no longer have anything to lose. Up yours, Grant.'* He goes on to expose everything he agreed to keep quiet."

Daniella couldn't believe it. "There's some mistake."

"I don't know how you can call a guy with his brains blown all over his bed a mistake. The gun was in his hand. Homicide detectives have ruled out foul play. This was a suicide."

"Scott, I don't believe that. I don't care what the cops say. I saw Howard last night. He was upset about that stupid prank over his health, but he wasn't suicidal. The cancer story was a hoax. He was upbeat, and he was in a great mood when he left this—" She stopped.

"This what? Oh, hell, Daniella, were you sleeping with him?"

"None of your business. But mark my words, this wasn't a suicide," she sobbed. Daniella hung up and then locked her office door. She wept for what could have been fifteen minutes before pulling herself together. There'd be fallout. She needed to do her job.

Daniella arrived in the Oval Office to find she was late. The President, Scott Eadie, the Secretaries of State, Homeland Security, and the Treasury, the Attorney General, and the heads of both the CIA and the FBI were there already, all shouting to be heard.

The President spotted her as she walked in. She wondered if he'd been briefed about her near-slip of the tongue and if he noticed her red-rimmed eyes. He put her apprehension to rest as he crossed over to her, took her hand, and spoke quietly, for her ears only. "I'm so sorry, Daniella. Would you like to delegate this to your staff?"

"No, Mr. President. In fact, I insist on handling it. There's something very wrong here, and I want to be in the loop when you get to the bottom of it. Meanwhile, what can I do to help?"

"I'm afraid there isn't much. Everything we wanted to keep under wraps—the mission into Saudi Arabia, the questionable tactics used against Dwayne Miller, Nate Gordon, and the late Vice President—they've all escaped Pandora's Box. And like the pestilence from the myth, we can't put them back in again." Grant took a deep breath. "I've heard the word impeachment more than once today already. I think about the best you can do is announce we have no comment today."

"Mr. President, I strongly suggest you reconsider. With

all due respect, that sounds like an admission that it's all true."

"Daniella, you already know it *is* all true. The fact that we did all of it for a good reason is no defense in the eyes of the law."

Grant was right. Within the next few hours, all hell broke loose, and Daniella had said "no comment" so often it was her automatic phrase no matter who said what to her. *Want some coffee? No comment.* It was enough to make her head spin, and Howard's death was far more personal to her than she could let on. That alone was a strain on her nerves.

The news storm when the A-Echelon story broke mid-March had been bad enough, but with Howard's help, they'd confined the bad news to that, and so far, they'd weathered the storm.

However, it had been nothing to what was hitting them now. The President implicated in murder, the invasion of an ally, Gestapo interrogation techniques...what could have been worse?

The news media was in a frenzy again. Words like impeachment, special prosecutors, jurisdiction of investigators, and more were in the mouths of all the news anchors and screamed from the headlines.

Political analysts were busy discussing the Constitution as it related to the potential arrest of a sitting president.

President Grant was embattled, his former supporters deserting in droves, his remaining friends painted with the same brush. Murderers! Torturers! Liars!

International allies and enemies alike didn't know what to think. Never had the United States been this unstable since the end of the Civil War.

The only people in the world who weren't watching the goings-on with horror were the Nabateans.

They were elated. At last! What should have happened weeks ago was now in full effect.

It was only a matter of time before all their targets were brought down in ignominy.

Jailed, or worse.

Chapter Forty-Eight

LET'S GET PROACTIVE

With Crane's "suicide" and the resulting media frenzy, Sean and Dylan were galvanized into action. They, of all the pro-Devereux players, were the ones unused to being passive and waiting for things to happen. The old joke went "There are three kinds of people in the world: those that make things happen, those that waited for things to happen, and those who wake up and ask, what happened?" Sean and Dylan were firmly in the first group.

About ten days before, they'd left Kelly White and Russell McCormick at their weekend getaway cottage after the interrogation. They'd made no progress in finding McCormick's handler. The aborted Congressional hearing had happened four days ago. It was frustrating them to sit around and wait for things to happen and then react to that.

When they heard that Crane's "suicide" was probably not suicide, it was the final straw, and they decided it was time to stop sitting on their thumbs waiting for the Nabateans to make the next move. In fact, it was time for a meeting of the brain trust—Bill, James, Irene, Carter,

Mackenzie, and they needed to be in the same room at the same time and hammer out a plan.

The safe house where Carter and Mackenzie had been staying for the past couple of days was a bit small for a summit meeting, so Sean offered his own luxury cabin in the hills west of Harrisonburg, near a little town called Rawley. It was a bit of a drive—two and a half hours—but they made good use of the time by all piling into a big SUV so they could talk on the way.

It was the first time since Carter and Mackenzie went into hiding they had seen James, Irene, and Bill. So, first, Bill apologized for his indiscretions towards Carter and Mackenzie in the early days of this drama. They spent another half an hour or so talking about personal matters before they got to the purpose of their get together.

Sean had already explained to each of them as he invited them he felt they'd been allowing the Nabateans to run the show while they all sat around biting their nails waiting for the next crisis. Doing so had placed them in a precarious position, where they had no control over anything. Everyone was prepared to brainstorm ideas about what the Nabateans' agenda was and what their small group could do to disrupt it.

By the time they arrived at the cabin, they had ideas for an agenda of items to explore. But first, Sean had to endure Dylan poking through every room in the four-bedroom, four-bath cabin, while loudly exclaiming, "You call this a *cabin*?" At one point, he spotted the guest cabin out back—a one-room bedroom suite with bath where Carter and Mackenzie would stay, and in a parody of an old movie, he declaimed in his best Crocodile Dundee accent, "This is not a cabin. *That's* a cabin!"

The others put their overnight luggage in their assigned

bedrooms and complimented Sean on his hideaway. For his antics, Dylan was relegated to sleep on the pull-out sofa in the living room. Their host put on a big pot of coffee and broke out the donuts and pastries he'd brought along, and they got down to business at the huge dining table.

First on their agenda was quantum computing, a subject Mackenzie had suggested on the ride. They'd known for some time the Nabateans used quantum computing. Mackenzie's question was, "Why don't we use it?"

Now, as they got down to business, Carter addressed it. "Every IT person knows quantum technology is the future of computing, but I for one am not sure what that means. Who in the US is working on it?"

Bill answered, "There are one or two companies based in D.C. who claim to have it. Both have government contracts, and you know what that means. They're hampered by the regulations they must adhere to, so their research isn't going anywhere fast. Everyone dreams about it, but few are doing anything with it."

Mackenzie asked her second pertinent question. "Why can the Nabateans do it when we can't? Remember, they don't have the benefit of the full library of the A- and E-Codices. We do. Why can't we search for it, translate it, and use it?"

Carter summarized the issue. "First, we don't even know if there *is* anything about quantum computing in the Codices. But assuming there is, this is why we haven't seen it yet—no one has asked for it. The way the translation works is our efforts are based on requests from authorized people and organizations. We've had a lot of requests for quantum physics information. DARPA, for example, has asked for antimatter, Zero Point Energy, and other quantum technologies. But nothing related to computing that I know of."

Sean leaned forward. "Assume something was there, maybe hidden in the other data concerning quantum technology. Who has been given access to translations over the past sixteen to eighteen months? Since the 'chocolate box' was installed in Russell McCormick's car?"

"Only DARPA that I know of. But to be sure, James has the list of who is getting what information. We can check that."

James spoke up. "Okay, I'll check that. Let's cut to the chase. What will it take to locate quantum computing technologies in the Codices, assuming it's there?"

"We just have to get the translators on it," Carter said. "The plates and the servers storing the scans of the plates were confiscated by the CIA during the mop-up operation and are in D.C.

"Therefore, we must take Mohammed to the mountain. The translation equipment is still on Freydís, I assume. As are the translators. We must load them all up and send them to D.C."

"Done," Bill said. "But there's some prep work to do as well. If we're actually going to build one, we need some help. I'll talk to my counterparts in several other agencies, including DARPA, about launching an IT project. It won't be fast."

Everyone started talking at once with ideas about the IT project and who should be included. Sean rapped his knuckles on the table for attention. "We can't wait for the usual government machine to get rolling. This is urgent. It should be handled like the Manhattan Project. Full steam ahead."

"It will still take some time. We have to assemble a team of the best IT minds we can find, maybe even from the private sector. Then we have to lock them in a deep, dark hole and feed them jelly beans and energy drinks until they produce a quantum computer."

Mackenzie wrinkled her nose at the thought of living on such a diet for more than an hour, but she understood the point. "Guys, maybe it's a long shot."

Bill said, "Oh, it's definitely a long shot, but it beats sitting around waiting for the Nabateans to take over the world. And even if we bring them down before this quantum computer magically appears, it will still be worth having.

"Carter, who is the key person you need working with you to get the translations done?"

"Liu, without a doubt."

Dylan shouted, "Yes! Now there's a proposal I can support wholeheartedly without hesitation."

Everyone started laughing as Dylan pumped his fist when Bill said he'd have her in D.C. the following day.

Bill excused himself to make some calls, saying he needed to get the ball rolling for the IT task force as well as giving Liu enough advance notice.

Mackenzie and Irene rolled their eyes at that. One day wasn't what they'd consider "enough advance".

Irene, who'd been quiet during most of the debate, suggested she could get some lunch together while Bill made his calls, and Mackenzie offered to help. They found the kitchen fully stocked. Sean wandered in behind them and explained he'd had his caretaker do some shopping, and everything should be quick and easy. Irene suggested, in that case, the men should be responsible for dinner, since she and Mackenzie were fixing lunch.

"Barbeque it is," said Sean with a grin.

Soon, they had a plate full of sandwiches, a bowl of salad, and a selection of soft drinks on the table.

The Nabatean Secret

While everyone ate, they engaged in a lively debate about what Carter and Mackenzie had found at the Smithsonian.

Carter explained he'd wondered about the Nabateans' grasp of technology and their sophisticated business practices ever since he'd learned of the existence of the modern group.

"Finding the libraries of the Giants, and knowing how much stock our ancestors put in the written word in our own civilization has made me wonder how the Nabateans got along without some kind of record. Mackenzie and I now believe we might've found a clue that could eventually lead us to the library of the Nabateans. I think it's worth going to look for it."

Bill shook his head. "Carter, you're needed here to help with the translation so we can build our own quantum computers. More to the point, you sound very uncertain if it's even there. Besides, how are we going to smuggle you out of the country?"

Mackenzie smiled. She'd made a couple of the same arguments to Carter already, and she knew he was ready for them. He didn't disappoint her.

"I know it's a long shot, Bill. Archaeology is all about lost knowledge, uncertainty, long shots—such as the Alboran Codex. This kind of exploration requires first thinking through and analyzing the history and what clues we can find. We found a good clue in the records at the Smithsonian. It was a symbol I remembered seeing somewhere before, a ring of dolphins in the shape of a pentagon. And it took a while, but I remembered where I'd seen it. The record in the Smithsonian that had the symbol was an image of it, carved faintly into a rock. Guess where?"

Mackenzie kept quiet, not wanting to spoil Carter's fun.

The others, baffled at his enthusiasm, shrugged, tilted their heads, and gave other non-verbal signals they had no guess.

"Petra!" Carter exclaimed in triumph. "It's carved into the very rock of the city where the Nabateans reached their pinnacle. Seeing it there in that image triggered a memory from a trip I took with my grandfather at the end of my sophomore year in college.

"I'd already decided my life study would be archaeology. As a reward for excellent grades that year, my Grandpa took me on holiday to the center of ancient civilization. We spent eight weeks traveling around Italy, and where I'd seen the symbol was in Matera." Carter paused for dramatic effect, but the blank looks on the faces of his audience disappointed him.

"Come on, *Matera*," he said again. With an exasperated sigh, he undertook their education. "It's one of the oldest cities in the world. The *Sassi*, the core of the prehistoric city, is thought to be more than nine thousand years old. Carved from the rock, like Petra. Now do you get it?"

James said, "Why don't you lay it out for us, Carter? We're not archaeologists, remember?"

"Okay, I'll spare you the lesson. Here's the bottom line. The fact that the symbols appear in both places could mean that some Nabateans from Petra went and lived in Matera at some stage.

"It could be that it was at the time when the Romans took over their country. It could be that those Nabateans took their library with them and hid it right under the noses of their new rulers. But it could have been the other way around—the people of Matera could have visited Petra and left their symbol there," Carter concluded.

Everyone except Mackenzie looked very skeptical. "Yeah, well, I don't know, Carter," Bill started. "It's as you said, 'lost knowledge, uncertainty, and long shots'. Why would they go and hide their library, that's if they had one to start with, in Matera? What makes you think that would be a good place? Also, I'm not convinced what advantage having the ancient Nabatean library will give us over the modern-day Nabateans."

Carter replied. "It's what we don't know about them that's dangerous, Bill. We might just learn a lot more about them than we know now, and as you know that's not much.

"As to why I think Matera could be the place—that dolphin pentagon for starters. Second, if you have a look at a map, you'll see it's almost a straight line by sea from Petra to Matera. Third, Matera is about five to six thousand years older than Petra. The Nabateans were known for their world-wide trading, and I'm willing to bet money on it there were Nabateans living in Matera at the time the Romans took over the Nabatean kingdom.

"I agree, it's a long shot. But if the dolphin pentagon is a clue, then shouldn't we follow up on it? The only way to know is to investigate."

Bill shook his head. "You may be right, but you still haven't convinced me how we can get you out of the country unnoticed."

"Who's got custody of our jet?" Mackenzie asked. She knew very well the CIA had snatched it from INSCOM after Kelly's admission she had no real grounds to hold it.

James and Irene started laughing when Bill slapped his forehead. "Okay," he said, "you can fly it out yourself, can't you? But what about bodyguards?"

"Excuse me?" Dylan exploded.

"Are you up for a trip to Jordan?" Carter asked him.

"Jordan? In your geography lesson a few minutes ago, I

thought I heard you saying Matera was in Italy?" Dylan said, confused.

"We need to go to Petra first. I'm all but certain the library isn't there, but we need to be thorough. First Petra, then Matera."

It was time for the men to bring on the barbeque.

After dinner, with the Nabatean library idea out of the way, it was Sean's and Dylan's turn to talk about what they thought they could do. They had McCormick, who should have been an asset but was proving useless.

"Why is that?" asked Bill.

"He doesn't know who his handler is, or even how to get a message to him to meet. We might as well have let Kelly use that knife on him just to make sure someone like him doesn't procreate," Dylan said.

Sean gave him an allaying look, but it was too late. Carter, James, and Bill had all winced at the implication, and James was looking at Sean for an explanation.

"We, ah, didn't think some of the details of our interrogation were important," Sean began hesitantly.

"I think you'd better fill us in," James said.

"Well, when Kelly discovered what a weasel McCormick had been, she was pretty hot under the collar," Sean explained.

"He admitted he'd abused a kid twenty-five years ago," Dylan stated flatly. "That's what the Nabateans have on him. When Kelly heard that, she went postal and offered to deprive him of his procreative parts. It was a surprisingly effective interrogation technique."

"Not so surprising," Carter mumbled. Involuntarily, he crossed his legs.

Bill clasped his hands over his ears. "I didn't hear that—plausible deniability."

"Yes, *sir*," Sean said. He shot Dylan another look, but based on his grin, Dylan was unrepentant.

"Can we get back to how we might use the facts we know about him?" Irene had been less than amused by the story. The men seemed to have forgotten the President was already in hot water for unconventional interrogation techniques. A Bobbitt situation was the last thing the President needed.

"Okay. Well, as Dylan mentioned, he's clueless. Doesn't know who his handler is or how to get hold of him. The only thing he's got going for him is the data collection box in his car. We might be able to use that."

"What do you have in mind?" James asked.

"Well… We might arrange an accident, smash up his car and the black box with it. Then they'd have to install another. We could put surveillance on it, and follow them when they come to pick up his new car," Sean mused. "We might also then get a chance to look at that box."

"Problem is, if *he* doesn't know who he's working for, or what he's even doing for them, the mechanics aren't likely to either. However, having the chance to pull that box apart might be worthwhile. But that in itself poses the risk they would know we've discovered the box," Dylan added.

Sean nodded. "He's right. Nor will it help to make McCormick disappear, as much as I'd like to turn the bastard over to Kelly. I'll tell you, it turns my stomach to leave him free, knowing what he's done. Not only to that child but also the people killed and maimed at Patch Barracks because of him."

"And only God knows how many others over the past twenty-five years while working for these evildoers," Irene added.

"Be that as it may, it sounds like he's a dead end for now. What if we attacked it from a disinformation approach?" Bill asked.

"What do you mean?" Mackenzie asked. She, of everyone in the room, was the most ignorant of spy-talk.

"Easy. We plant fake information in the translations they're stealing. Misleading stuff that will make them act on it. We'll watch for the action, and then we'll have them. Or at least some of them. Hopefully someone who'll have a better chance of leading us to the top."

"That sounds like a viable option," said Carter. "We'll need some time to come up with what we should plant. Let's table that for further discussion tomorrow and get a good night's sleep first.

The discussions continued the next morning, with James taking up the reins.

"Bill, you know this already, but I'll briefly explain for the benefit of the others. With Howard Crane's death, there's been pressure to step up the Congressional hearings. Of course, the revelations we were trying to avoid have both increased the pressure and have given the beloved Senator Michelle Davis more ammunition against us.

"What we need to do right now is brainstorm ways to delay the hearing as much as we can, to give us time to smoke out the traitor in the National Security Council. We're open to all ideas. Let's hear 'em."

"We've already considered some," Bill interjected. "Executive privilege, for one."

"What's that?" asked Mackenzie.

"Basically, it's when Congress says to the President, 'we demand an explanation for this thing you did,' and the President replies, 'well, you can't get one, because it has to do with national security.'"

"That sounds like just the right thing," Mackenzie replied. "Why do we need to discuss it any further?"

"Because he can't use it until he's already subpoenaed, for one thing," Bill answered. "We're hoping to avoid that altogether. It's one of the reasons we'd already decided to let James and Irene be the sacrificial lambs. If this goes forward, their ordeal will have been for nothing.

"For the same reason, we can't apply it to everything. We must give them something. It won't truly delay the hearings, just throw them off a bit. The objective is delay. Remember, we're trying to catch a traitor.

"Finally, and perhaps most important in the long run, it looks bad. People don't like it, and Grant doesn't want to use it more than necessary. It makes him look like he has something to hide, which of course he does. But the public would assume it was guilt, and it could very well hand the opposition the election."

Carter slapped the table. "You've got to be kidding! Forget the damn politics! This *is* critical to national security. Anyone in Grant's position should be prepared to look bad if that's the only way to keep the people safe. This is no place for election-year politics."

Mackenzie clapped her hands softly, while Sean and Dylan nodded forcefully. James and Irene were neutral on the subject or appeared to be. But then, they'd been privy to the planning session that had concluded executive privilege should be reserved for a last resort.

Bill replied mildly, "I understand your frustration, Carter. No one hates politics more than I do. I think only masochists like playing a political game. I know Sam Grant doesn't. But it's the price of democracy. Or at least the price as it's come to be. Politicians gonna politic, just like haters gonna hate."

"Sometimes I think a dictatorship would be more convenient," Carter said. Everyone understood it wasn't his literal opinion.

Bill thought to have the last word anyway. "It's like Churchill said. *'Indeed, it has been said that democracy is the worst form of government except all those other forms that have been tried from time to time.'*"

"You know what he also said? *'The best argument against democracy is a five-minute conversation with the average voter.'* Maybe he should have expanded that to the average Congressman," Carter added.

"Good one. Nevertheless, it's been decided above my pay grade. Executive privilege is the last resort. Let's move on."

"I say you all take the Fifth," Dylan offered.

"No good," Bill answered. "Same problem as executive privilege, plus a few more. Again, it won't delay the hearings. They'll just move on to the next person, and everyone who uses that tactic will end up in court eventually anyway. You know as well as I do that pleading the Fifth amounts to telling everyone you're guilty but you won't admit it. The President does that, and impeachment will follow like a rocket and the same for us. All that will do is guarantee Michelle Davis will dig harder and faster. Again, it doesn't serve our purpose."

"What's wrong with just telling the truth?" Carter asked, with a heavy dose of sarcasm. He was still disgruntled about the political aspect of the discussion.

The people around the table exploded. "Have you gone bonkers?" Dylan's voice broke through the others.

"Hear me out. We don't have to do it in public. What if we take the most influential members, or the ones with the highest security clearances—?"

"Everyone on the Intelligence Committee has a security clearance," Bill interrupted. "But it isn't top-secret clearance. They just make a pledge, and historically, they've honored it more in the breach than the spirit."

"Okay, but still. We need to insist on a closed-door meeting and show them some of the secret stuff to convince them."

"Go on. What would you show them?" Bill was still reluctant to consider giving any senator any secret information, but he had to admit that was force of habit. Maybe this was a special case.

"What about the ancient nukes? We bring in those two nuclear scientists who were on the ship when we retrieved the nukes from the Alboran Sea. That should get their attention.

"And maybe a video recording of some of our chats with the dolphins.

"After that, they should believe everything we tell them, including why they should stop this witch-hunt right now, in the name of national security."

Nods and smiles around the table convinced Bill that Carter was onto something. "Suppose we agree. What do you suggest as the next step?"

He wished he hadn't opened it for discussion when everyone agreed it was up to him to contact Michelle Davis, either directly or through one of the other committee members, to make the offer. He loathed the idea, and it wasn't just because of his natural wish to keep top-secret information out of her hands. She hated the CIA and him personally. The feeling was mutual. Several of her committee members felt the same about him and everything he stood for, which he'd always thought was an unfortunate situation given their oversight over his department.

Nevertheless, he agreed it was his duty and said he'd take care of it the following day.

Though they hadn't had much time to enjoy the beautiful spring weather at Sean's hideaway, it was time to get back to D.C. and put all their plans in motion.

Chapter Forty-Nine

ABOUT THESE QUANTUM COMPUTERS

April 23

True to his word, Bill contacted Scott Eadie first thing the next morning and wangled a short meeting with the President for later in the morning. Scott, in his usual irascible persona, asked several times if it was really important, because the President had meetings with party leadership scheduled for most of the day.

Bill, after the third such question, lost his patience. "Scott, if you ask me that again, I'm going to come over there right now and wring your scrawny neck. It is of the *utmost* importance, or I wouldn't ask. I've got better things to do than get on my knees and beg you for an audience. Now give me a time, and it better be before noon."

"Okay, okay! You don't have to get all pissy about it."

"Scott—"

"Fine! You can have fifteen minutes after the party chairman's slot. Be here at nine thirty sharp. That's when your fifteen minutes starts, and if you're late, you still end at nine forty-five." He ended the call before Bill could respond.

Bill looked at his watch. Two hours, and that was too long. Not to mention fifteen minutes was too short. "We'll see about that," he muttered.

His next call was to James, who told him to hold the line while he brought Irene into the call.

"I want you in the meeting with the President. Nine thirty sharp. Be there by nine fifteen."

His tone made it clear there were to be no questions or objections. James and Irene wisely agreed, and the call ended.

Bill spent the next hour and a half putting together a hasty PowerPoint presentation, rearranging slides, and timing it. There was no way he'd be able to present all the evidence and all the plans in under half an hour. But if he was kicked out after fifteen minutes he could at least leave the PowerPoint with all the information for the President to view.

Scott Eadie might get his knickers in a twist over the destruction of his schedule, but Bill was certain the President would back him up and allow him more time after seeing the first fifteen minutes.

Bill was the first to arrive, a couple of minutes before the deadline he'd given James and Irene. He was told to wait in the anteroom. In all his years of service to his country, from the time he was a raw recruit to the Agency, through countless perilous undercover operations, and over the past several weeks in the current crisis, he'd never been as unsettled as he was right now.

He felt the fate of the free world rested on his ability to convince the President the proposals he was about to make were not only imperative but urgent. Physically, he felt like what he imagined a guitar string would feel on a long, sustained, high note in a heavy metal song. He was surprised he couldn't see his arms vibrating, because they felt as if they were.

Just before he was about to jump out of his chair and pace, James and Irene arrived together. It was 9:16. He glared at them. "Where the hell have you been? You're one minute late."

Irene opened her mouth to protest, but James touched her arm, stopping her from saying anything. "Sorry, boss. We got hung up in security."

"Well, isn't that just dandy. They let traitors into the National Security Council meetings, and keep our top security officers out," Bill muttered.

James and Irene let the remark pass without response. They could tell Bill was wound tighter than a two-dollar watch.

At 9:29 a.m., the door to the Oval Office opened, and Scott appeared with one hand on the back of the party chairman, as he shook hands with the other. The guy probably didn't even realize he was being shoved out the door. He was only a few paces down the hall when Scott gestured to Bill. "Get in here, and make it brief."

It was all Bill could do not to snarl at Scott, but he managed a sickly smile. "Thanks, Scott."

James and Irene were on his heels as Scott closed the door. Before they even got to their chairs, he was opening his laptop and setting it in front of the President.

"President Grant, Scott didn't give me much time, so I'll dispense with formalities if you don't mind. James and Irene are here to help me answer any questions you have after you've seen this."

With that, he started his slideshow. He'd rehearsed it

once, timing the slides to open as his narrative got to them so he'd stay on track. Within the first few sentences, Grant stopped him.

"Slow down, Bill. Give me a chance to absorb this."

"With all due respect, Mr. President, I have half an hour's material to present in fifteen minutes. Scott said you were very busy with party business."

"Oh, he did, did he? Scott."

Scott approached confidently. He'd been listening to Bill but didn't have the benefit of the slides.

"Clear my schedule for however long Bill needs me."

"But sir, the party—"

"Can go to hell. There won't be a party if we don't take care of this business right now. So, go and clear my schedule."

Bill heaved a sigh of relief and felt his tension melt away. Now he could make the President understand everything. He left his laptop open but didn't start the slideshow again. Instead, he went through everything they'd learned, and not learned, from Kelly White and Russell McCormick. Everything Carter and Mackenzie had discovered or theorized regarding a potential Nabatean library and what they proposed to do about it. Carter's idea to lift the veil for some of the Intelligence Committee members to show them what was discovered and how serious it is. And the building of a quantum computer.

The President listened in silence until Bill stopped talking. "What can I do to help?" he asked then.

"You may be aware that I'm not Senator Davis's favorite person," Bill began.

The President burst out laughing. "I suppose you could say that," he agreed. "But you must also be aware she's out for my blood, too. You say you want the hearings postponed. How do you think I can help with that?"

Bill shrugged. "I thought you might know who *could* influence her."

"I'll give it some thought. I probably do. Maybe *your* boss. Sebastian Birch doesn't seem to have pissed her off as much as you have."

Bill nodded ruefully.

"What else?"

"Sir, to get all of the security agencies together for a project of the magnitude of the quantum computer proposal will take an order from you."

"No problem. I'll have to get Scott to look at funding for it, but go ahead and get started talking to your counterparts."

Bill was amazed at the President's grasp of it all. He'd expected to have to answer questions. James and Irene hadn't even opened their mouths, but the President was agreeing. Only one item remained.

"About the Devereuxs' proposal to go to Italy—"

"That's up to your buddies over there," the President interrupted, pointing to James and Irene. "If they agree and they have the funding, I have no objection."

Just then, Scott came back in. "I've cleared the next hour, Mr. President. Will that be enough time?"

The President and Bill exchanged glances. "In that case," Grant said, "tell me more about these quantum computers."

Chapter Fifty

THE IT PROJECT

April 25

Bill had made remarkable progress, in terms of government timeframes that was, by getting all his security agency counterparts to agree to meet only a couple of days after the President gave his blessing to the project. Even more remarkable was their agreement to bring the best minds in their IT departments with them. In a system where the best chance for advancement was cross-agency transfer, everyone was understandably leery of exposing their best employees to potential poachers.

He was mentally patting himself on the back when he opened the meeting, and he'd prepared opening remarks concerning the importance and urgency of the project.

"The project we're here to discuss and kick off is above top-secret. Think Manhattan Project urgency and importance. I want to say at the outset it's because of the work of A-Echelon that we have this opportunity. I know they've been under fire in the news media lately, but trust me on this, they have uncovered a threat that's worse than any this country has ever faced.

"Forget Pearl Harbor. Forget 9-ll, weapons of mass destruction, ISIS, and people tunneling under walls. What we face right now is nothing less than the complete destruction of not only our democracy, but any other democracy in the world."

He looked around at the curious faces, understanding he hadn't given them enough information to absorb the dire prediction. To correct that, he began with the truth about Patch Barracks, to low murmurs here and there. By the time he stated the mission—to build a quantum computer—the murmurs were a steady drone. And then all hell broke loose.

Bill was disgusted at the melee. It seemed the mild-mannered computer geeks had a different side to their personalities. Without waiting for permission to speak, or for others to finish what they were saying, several had stood up and begun shouting. Bill couldn't understand everything they were saying because they were shouting over each other, but he caught snatches of it.

"*...impossible... not proven... idiot...*"

The geek-speak was even more baffling. *Parallel universes? Millikelvins? Entanglement of quantum bits? Cubits. Are these guys even speaking English?*

The heads of the other agencies began shouting at him and at each other. He tried getting everyone's attention by rapping a gavel he found under the portable podium in front of him on the table. When that didn't work, out of desperation, he pounded his shoe, thinking he now knew why Soviet Premier Khrushchev had done such an uncouth thing decades before.

Still, no one paid him the slightest attention, except for his counterparts who were still shouting at *him*.

The IT people had gathered into several small knots, apparently along agency alliance lines. In one corner, two had resorted to fisticuffs and a ring had formed around them to encourage one or the other. The fighting pair were slapping at and pushing each other like kittens play-fighting. But the expressions on their faces said just because they didn't know how to fight didn't mean they weren't dead serious.

Bill attempted one more time to bring the room to order with no success. He wished he had gun so he could fire a shot in the air to get their attention or maybe even shoot a few of them. He stormed out of the room and had a couple of his operatives stand guard so none of the participants could leave.

Within minutes, he arrived breathless at the door of Scott Eadie's office. "I need to see him, *right now*," Bill said.

Scott had learned his lesson with the previous meeting and told Bill to follow him. He interrupted a photo-op session where Grant was signing a bill of some sort or other. One look at him had the President hurrying the signing ceremony along and all but shooing out the interested parties once it was done.

"What is it?" Grant asked when the three were alone.

Bill described the scene at his agency's conference room.

Grant turned pale, and Bill at first thought he was having a heart attack. He regretted bringing the matter straight to the top. Maybe he could have used an air horn or something to get things under control?

But it turned out Grant wasn't having a heart attack. Instead, it was an event so rare that his best friends had never even seen it. It was a fit of temper—compared to the one he'd seen a few days ago, when he told the President about the illegal surveillance of the National Security

Council members. That fit was like a light breeze—this was a tornado.

"Scott, get over there right now. Take a pistol with you to get their attention if you need to. Shoot one of the agency heads, if you'd like. When they're ready to listen, tell them every one of them is required to be at a rescheduled meeting at seven p.m."

"Tonight?"

"Yes, dammit, p.m. means tonight! No one is excused, unless he or she has died since this morning. In that case, I *might* accept an apology, but no guarantees."

Scott scuttled out of the office, leaving a shaken and slightly amused Bill in his wake.

"Thank you, Mr. President."

"You're welcome. Now get out of here and get to work. I'm going to set a lighted firecracker up their collective butt, and you'd better be ready to give them their assignments."

It was Bill's turn to scuttle. He had some prep work to do in the next few hours. Never again did he want to see the President that angry, and certainly not at him.

At seven p.m. precisely, Bill entered the meeting room again. In contrast to the way he'd last seen it, the participants were all in their seats, and no one was talking. They didn't need to. Bill could see from their expressions that if he wasn't about to introduce the President, he'd better have an escape route in mind. His counterparts alone looked ready to tear him limb from limb.

He made his introduction brief. "Ladies and gentlemen, the President of the United States." He watched with glee as mouths dropped open around the room, and every individual rose to their feet.

Samuel Houston Grant strode in from the side door looking like a thundercloud. He wasted no time on introductory remarks but got straight to the point. No thank you for coming or welcome.

"Sit down, and shut up.

"You have all been called here because you are the best minds we can pull together in the face of a crisis of world-shaking proportions. It's my understanding that you acted like drunken fans at a football game this morning. I'm here to tell you that nonsense will stop as of now.

"You *will* work together in the most efficient way possible, and you *will* accept the assignments that Bill Griffin gives you without question. There *will* be no more of this petty crap about who's better informed than whom. No more pissing contests. *Do I make myself clear?*"

The pale faces and tentative nods around the room didn't satisfy him.

"Let me tell you what *will* happen if you don't carry out my orders to the letter. I *will* fire your asses, every stinking one of you. Then I *will* have you charged with insubordination, endangering the lives of American citizens, and anything else the Attorney General can suggest, up to and including treason. I'll see you in jail, and if I have any say in it, I may just have you shot. *Now* am I clear?"

A chorus of "yes sirs" ensued, and one of the geeks started applauding, leading the entire audience to follow suit.

Grant continued, "In case anyone still believes I'm not serious, let me tell you what *will* happen if you don't produce results, and I mean *last week*. Bill tells me he informed you about the existence of the Nabateans and their superior technology. You all surely know about the explosion at Patch Barracks. That was the Nabateans. We have no way to predict when they might decide to do the same thing in the middle of our city or in Times Square. American lives depend on your quick solutions.

"They have infiltrated the highest layers of government. There may even be some of them among you, so if you see anyone, *anyone*, obstructing or sabotaging this project, you are to report it directly to me immediately. Your squabbles have already put us eight or more hours behind. That could mean the difference to the survival of your own families. I'm not kidding. And if you don't believe me, pay close attention to what I am about to show you." He nodded to Bill.

Bill had prepared several PowerPoint slides with the goriest photos of the Patch Barracks incident, which he now showed on the big screen without saying a word.

The audience had gone so quiet one could hear a pin drop.

"That, ladies and gentlemen, is what we're up against. All you have to do is imagine that happening in D.C. or any other city in America. That explosion there was just the prototype—our wakeup call."

Grant took a sip of water, looked out at his audience again, and gave them his last instructions.

"All right. I am now personally in charge of this project, and Bill is my voice. I want you working in shifts twenty-four seven, beginning right now. Don't expect to go home tonight. You have fifteen minutes from the time I dismiss you to call your spouses, significant others, parents, and children to tell them not to expect to see you for the foreseeable future.

"I'll have progress reports on my desk at eight a.m. and

five p.m. daily. I want a working quantum computer in six weeks and a prototype of a quantum, encrypted, *unbreakable* communications system in eight weeks. Get to it."

Grant turned to go when one brave soul called out, "Sir! Some of us haven't eaten."

Grant turned around. No one was pointing a finger. In fact, he hadn't eaten either, not since sometime the previous evening. These idiots didn't get it yet. With a heavy sigh, he returned to the podium.

"Order pizzas and soft drinks. Send the bill to the White House. But for the love of God, take this seriously. I don't know about you, but I have no wish for our nation's capital to be vaporized like Patch Barracks."

He gave a dismissive wave and walked slowly toward the exit. Bill took the podium but decided not to say anything. From what he could see, the geeks had already formed groups and were working diligently, discussing the problem and already making notes. He looked toward the President's retreating back. What was it about men who attained the highest office in the land?

President Grant was not a genius nor a general, but when it came to decisions of critical importance, he acted like both. *Reminds me of General George "Blood-and-Guts" Patton.* His admiration for his old friend had never been greater.

Chapter Fifty-One

A FAMILY VISIT

Mackenzie and Carter were desperate to see the children. When they'd left Freydís in mid-March, it was supposed to be an overnight trip as far as she knew. It was now near the end of April, and they'd lost count of the weeks.

"Is it four, five, or six weeks since I've seen my babies?" Mackenzie sighed.

"Liam would object to being called a baby," Carter replied.

"They'll always be my babies, even when they're grown and have children of their own. You're sidestepping my concern. I want to see the children, Carter. Can't we make that happen?"

Drawing her to him and putting his arms around her, Carter said, "I miss them, too, Mackie. I'll find a way."

The problem wasn't so much finding a place to meet in secret. It was getting word to Freydís. With electronic communications forbidden, the logistics weren't as simple as they might have been. The next time Dylan arrived to move them to a new safe house, Carter insisted he get word to

Freydís that Mackenzie's parents should take the kids to a safe location where he and Mackenzie could meet them for a visit of at least a couple of days.

"No problem," Dylan answered. "We have safe houses all up and down this coast. I'll send a message with the 'milk' plane." Then he couldn't resist a chance to tease Mackenzie, who never knew when he was being silly if he kept his face straight.

"The ranch may be under surveillance," he said. "Maybe we should disguise the kids. Best way to do that would be to make Beth into a little boy. You don't mind if we cut her hair, do you?"

Mackenzie sent a panicked glance to her husband, who was watching her with interest. She turned to Dylan. "Don't you dare! She loves her red hair. You can put a wig on her, or put one on Liam and make him into a girl instead—"

"Hey! *I* object to that," Carter interrupted.

Dylan held his hands up in surrender. "I was kidding!"

Mackenzie leveled a frown on him. "Now, tell me, when I can see my children?"

"I'll make it happen within the week," Dylan promised. As he left, he glanced back at Mackenzie, who had a wicked smile on her face. *Damn, she snookered me.* He grinned as he got into his car. Somehow, he'd get even.

The following Wednesday, the pilot of the "milk" plane hand-delivered a sealed envelope to Mackenzie's father.

"Mary, we're going to take a little trip," Steven called after reading the letter. His wife came into the room to hear what he was thinking.

"We're meeting Mackenzie and Carter in Maine," he

The Nabatean Secret

told her, speaking quietly so the children couldn't hear. "We won't have long with them, just a couple of days. But it will be good to see them."

Mary agreed. "It's been hard to keep answering the children's questions with 'soon,'" she sighed. "Does this mean they're out of danger?"

"Well, the meeting's clandestine, so probably no. But maybe it isn't quite as bad as it was before, or they wouldn't risk meeting us and the children at all."

"How are we going to do it?" she asked.

"We're to tell the children we're going to visit Bly and Ahote's children and grandkids. It would be best if they don't tell anyone where we're going."

"Liam wouldn't, of course, but Beth is a little chatterbox. I think that's best if she doesn't know until we're in the air."

Three days later, the Andersons and their grandchildren accompanied Ahote and Bly in their plane on a trip to Maine to visit Ahote and Bly's children and a string of grandkids.

They hadn't seen each other for quite a few months. Ahote and Bly had been getting messages via email and Skype, on a daily basis lately, hinting that it would be great for them to come over for a visit and how much their grandkids were missing them.

Two of their five grandkids were about Liam's and Beth's age and were asking about them. They had become good friends when they visited their grandparents on Freydís during school holidays.

At the airport, they were met by Ahote and Bly's children and grandkids—a crowd of four adults and five children. After the hugs and kisses, they all piled into three vehicles, Steven, Mary, Liam, and Beth were in the car with

Ahote and Bly's youngest daughter, Kay, and her husband, John, and their two kids, a boy and girl about the same ages as Liam and Beth.

When they got to John and Kay's house, a large three-story home with two living areas, the Andersons with their grandkids were taken to the top floor living area, which had two large bedrooms and enough space for all of them.

"Okay, Liam, Beth," Kay said while pointing to the bedroom door at the end of the hall, "that's your room. You can go and put your bags down there."

Liam and Beth thanked Kay and pulled their little wheeled suitcases to the room. Liam opened the door and froze.

Mackenzie lifted Liam off his feet, hugging him tightly. When Beth saw her mom, she squealed, "Mommy!"

Mackenzie passed Liam on to Carter and lifted Beth off her feet.

There was a momentary traffic jam at the door as Carter and Mackenzie greeted their children with hugs and kisses and more than a few tears on the part of Beth and Mackenzie.

When Carter let go of his son, Liam looked around and said, disgusted, "Beth, quit crying."

She stuck her tongue out to him and grabbed Mackenzie tighter around the neck.

Then it was Beth's turn to hug and kiss her dad.

They all cleared the doorway so the elder Andersons could get in, and another round of hugs were exchanged.

Kay led them to the lounge area on their floor, showed them all the amenities and the kitchen, and left them to be together.

As questions flew back and forth, those among the grownups only half-spoken so the kids couldn't understand them, Beth settled comfortably on her mother's lap and refused to move. Liam settled near his dad and looked wisely from his parents to his grandparents. It soon became clear to Carter his son understood more than he let on.

"Liam, you know not to talk about any of this when you get back home, right?"

Scornfully, the little boy answered, "Dad, I'm not an idiot. But Beth—"

"I know. We'll work something out with her. What have you been up to while we've been gone?"

"The wolves come to visit every day. Uncle Ahote says Keeva is going to have babies again. We're doing our school work, every day, we have lots to do. But we miss you and mom," he answered.

Carter struggled to swallow the sudden lump in his throat.

"When can you and Mom come back, Dad?" Liam asked.

"We'll be back on Freydís in another month... I think. That's one of the reasons Mom and I had to see you in person," Carter said. "You know when we went to get the dolphins to help us find that city under the sea?"

"Yeah."

"Well, we have another mission like that. In Italy, not under the sea. Remember Italy? We've been there a couple of times on vacation."

"I know, Dad. Italy is where Rome is, and the Coliseum, and the Pope, and all the statues."

"Yep, that's the place. Mom and I need to go there. Can you be brave and take care of Beth a little longer?"

"Yeah, but really Grandma and Grandpa take care of us. You knew that, right?" Liam grinned.

Carter winked. "I had an idea they were helping you. And we'll be back as soon as we can after that. Okay?"

"Okay, Dad. You can count on me."

Carter and Mackenzie were happy to forget all the worry and stress in Washington, D.C., for the two days with their kids and Mackenzie's parents. Mackenzie was in heaven and spent most of the time with Beth in her lap, reading to the children and listening to their prattle.

Carter got in plenty of snuggles with his daughter and realized with a pang his son was growing up too fast.

At bedtime on the first evening, Beth was a little teary, so Mackenzie sang her favorite lullaby until she slept. Liam seemed to also be asleep when she checked on him, so she tiptoed out of the room to join Carter and her parents.

"How are the children really doing?" Carter was asking his mother-in-law as Mackenzie entered the living room.

"Don't worry about them. They do miss you, but we keep them too busy to dwell on it. The translation staff and the EA people are spoiling them and their friends. And of course, having Jeha and the other animals helps. Keeva is especially watchful of Beth. It's amazing, the way she senses when Beth is sad and comes to comfort her."

"Am I about to be replaced as her mother?" Mackenzie asked, only half-joking.

"I'm sure Keeva will relinquish the role, especially if you come home around the time her pups are due. She'll have her hands full with them," Carter assured her.

"Hands, not paws?" Mackenzie laughed.

"You know what I mean."

Chapter Fifty-Two

HIS HOURGLASS WAS RUNNING OUT QUICKLY

Mathieu Nabati was sleeping soundly when his secure phone rang. He glanced at his bedside clock as he reached for it. Three a.m. It had to be his mother. Lately, she'd been growing anxious that the Devereuxs had yet to be arrested. He knew what was coming, despite his warnings.

"Yes, *Maman*, what is it?" he said in greeting.

"You know very well what it is," she snapped. "Why haven't the Devereuxs been arrested yet?"

Could this not have waited until morning? The ten-hour time difference between his hideaway in the Urals and his mother's in the Andes could easily have accommodated calls at a reasonable hour for them both, but his mother paid no attention. However, he didn't dare complain.

"*Maman*, we've discussed this. Someone is hiding them."

"It's time to call McCormick to account for his failure," she insisted.

"Agreed, he needs to be accountable. But it will mean exposing an operative to a face-to-face meeting for the first time in twenty-five years. Is this wise?"

"We have to do something. The data we're downloading from the Freydís translations has become useless. There's no more technical data, only history. I find it suspect that there's nothing but E-Codex material, and none from the A-Codex. One would think they'd be frantically working to determine the cause of the Patch Barracks bomb.

"Furthermore, the information from the National Security Council has also dried up. With the press and Congress calling for answers, surely something of top-secret importance is being discussed in the NSC meetings."

"You mentioned that Jason Sullivan has apparently had cold feet lately," Mathieu observed. "Perhaps he simply isn't passing it on."

"I made it clear what the consequences would be if he attempted to resign, either from the Council or from his Cabinet post. I don't think he's playing games with us. More likely, someone on the NSC suspects a leak, and now they are careful about what they discuss."

"*Maman*, that's ridiculous. They only exist to discuss secrets."

"Then you take my point. Have Sullivan and McCormick now come to the end of their usefulness?"

"Perhaps so."

Over a solitary lunch taken in his office, Jason Sullivan was considering the same question. As a non-statutory member of the NSC, he wasn't required to attend all meetings. Nevertheless, he'd been invited to all, or so he'd thought. Lately, he'd had hints that meetings had been called to which he wasn't invited. There was no easy way to verify his hunch, though. Not without exciting suspicion.

By the same token, he felt as if a target were on his back any time he attended the virtual meetings of the Council of the Covenant of Nabatea. As if he'd been the subject of discussion among the members, though no one pointed a finger.

Admittedly, it had been some weeks, since about mid-March, since anything of value to the Nabateans had come out of the NSC. There was nothing he could do about that, but the hints dropped in the Nabatean meetings weren't so subtle.

Nothing exciting for us today, Jason? We just need another good bomb out of the NSC now to tip the whole thing over.

He couldn't very well manufacture something like that, could he? Was it his fault that the information had dried up? There'd been times when he had something new for them almost every day, or at least updates on matters of interest.

Nor was he under any illusion that the sudden dearth of information he had to give would not be of concern to Graziella. It certainly would. And while she'd made it plain he could not resign from the Council, neither would she allow him to resign his Cabinet position.

The very outcome they'd been working toward—the downfall of President Grant—put him in a precarious position. In all likelihood, the President's troubles, even if they didn't bring him and his government down before the election, would give the opposition party the election come November. In that case, he'd definitely be replaced, and then his use to the Council would be at an end. Did the Council have a retirement scheme for members like him? Faithful members who, through no fault of their own, had been rendered useless?

They should, he reflected. It was dangerous work, in terms of his freedom. Risky, sacrificial—many such terms came to him regarding the work he did for his bloodline. But somehow, he knew there were no retirement schemes, or none that he had in mind. He recalled all too well how some members had "retired" since he'd become a member.

And while he'd never conspired against the Council, as Algosaibi had, whichever way he looked at it, it appeared he was on death row and just waiting to hear the date of his execution. Oh, he wouldn't *hear* it, of course. They say you never hear the bullet that kills you. The only difference between him and a death-row inmate was *he* had no right of appeal. Appealing to Graziella would only accelerate his execution date.

Appealing to the President would mean confessing and would get him arrested, which would also accelerate his execution date. He'd have to consider carefully whether he had any other options.

His gut told him he'd better come up with some in a hurry, because his hourglass was running out quickly.

Chapter Fifty-Three

A MIDDLE-FINGER SALUTE

May 1

After the rocky start with the quantum project, Bill was feeling a bit gun-shy when it came to approaching Michelle Davis concerning her intention of holding public hearings and the grave danger that would pose to national security. He'd kicked the negotiations upstairs—all the way to the top—only to have it kicked back. But then he and the President had agreed that perhaps a person of neutral interest to the powerful Senator Davis would be the best person to negotiate with her.

Michelle Davis's reputation preceded her. Before her long tenure as the senior senator from California, she'd cut her teeth in the business world, eventually rising to be among a rare few women to head up a Fortune 50 company. As was the case with her fellow female CEOs, she was forced to exhibit a more ruthless persona than her male counterparts and had developed a tough, no-holds-barred attitude because of it.

Once she was elected to the Senate, her quick intelligence and sharp tongue demolished many lesser men. Eight years prior to the A-Echelon scandal, she'd run against President Grant, and he'd only narrowly defeated her, thanks to her California constituency and their deep pockets.

During the pre-primary debates, Grant had found her weak spot. She could think quickly, it was true, but her ability to articulate her thinking while under pressure was not equal to his. At one of the debates, he'd unwisely mopped the floor with her. The resulting mud-slinging threatened to tear the party apart. Party leaders had stepped in, persuaded her to support Grant in the primary, and in return guaranteed her the chairmanship of any Senate subcommittee she desired, assuming she won re-election.

After handily doing so, Davis exacted her revenge by selecting one of the most powerful, the Senate Intelligence Committee. It was also her closely-guarded secret that she had a personal interest in, and hatred for, the CIA, having been dumped by a former Deputy Director for another woman.

Davis had never considered the possibility that her reputation for ball-busting was well-deserved. And that another woman might have been a more caring and supporting companion for the Deputy Director. Like the proverbial woman scorned, she blamed not only him but his entire agency. Bill Griffin had done nothing more to offend her than to be named the Director of the CIA. In her eyes, that made him her arch-enemy, and worthy to be her target.

As the proverb went, hell hath no fury…

No less distasteful to her was President Grant, who, though of the same political party, had humiliated her during that long-ago debate. She didn't forget, and she didn't forgive—not easily, not at all. It made no difference to her that her animosity might be responsible for the opposition party coming into power.

She was out to get Grant, anyone having to do with the CIA, and anyone else who stood in her way.

Therefore, when she met with Sebastian Birch, she did so with a predatory gleam in her eye. The Director of National Intelligence was a lofty title, but in reality, the position held little power. Prior to the establishment of the office with the passing of the Intelligence Reform and Terrorism Prevention Act of 2004, the head of the US intelligence community was the Director of Central Intelligence, who concurrently headed the Central Intelligence Agency as well.

When the 9/11 Commission exposed major intelligence failures, the bill was introduced to create the DNI position, but compromises were inevitably made to get the bill passed. Among them, several of the intelligence agencies were left in the hands of the Department of Defense, leaving the DNI too weak to adequately lead the performance of the US intelligence community in its entirety.

Senator Davis put Birch in an inferior position immediately, by having a chair brought in that would leave her seated much higher than his. She didn't offer coffee or extend any of the courtesies normally expected in such a meeting. Nevertheless, Birch forged ahead as he'd been instructed.

"Senator Davis, thank you for seeing me. I assume you are aware of my objections to your holding the A-Echelon hearings in public. May I elaborate on the need to do so?" he began.

"You're welcome to waste your time in any way you please," answered Davis tersely. "However, you are not welcome to waste mine. I've made my decision. The extensive coverage in the press has given the general public an extreme interest in seeing culpable parties pay for their indiscretions. Therefore, the hearings *will* be open."

"If I may, Senator. I'm not certain you've been made aware of the sensitive nature of the mission of A-Echelon. I'm certain if you heard what's at stake, you'd change your mind," Birch said.

Unfortunately, he was not firm in his convictions, and his shaky delivery gave it away.

"I'll give you credit for making an attempt, Mr. Birch. However, you try my patience. As the chairman of this committee, I am by law fully briefed on all covert activities. The fact that I knew nothing of A-Echelon prior to the media bringing it to the attention of the public is an insult, if not a criminal act. You surely cannot expect me to extend any favors under the circumstances."

"Not favors, Senator Davis. Consideration of the national security matters at stake. I'm authorized to tell you this is much bigger than has been reported, and public airing can and will cause immense and irreparable damage," Birch said. In fact, not even he knew the full extent of the issue, and he was feeling a bit insulted himself. Nevertheless, he was loyal to his President and willing to give it the best effort he could. However, his wording had an unfortunate effect.

"You are authorized! *Authorized?* Did you not hear what I just said? *I am already authorized!* You and the President go too far. You're a spineless jellyfish, and Grant is a lying bastard. I'll have him thrown out of office if it's the last thing I do.

And you! You can expect to be unemployed within the month. As soon as I've dug up every last criminal conspiracy you and Grant and that worm Bill Griffin have perpetrated on the American people." Davis was beside herself, standing and leaning forward over the desk, face red and spittle flying.

As soon as she'd jumped from her chair, Birch did the same, as much in self-defense as anger. However, the woman had made threats she'd have trouble backing up. He had one parting shot.

"You know, they told me you were a stone bitch, but they never said you were treasonous. If you don't agree to at least close the hearings when they approach matters of national security, you'll regret it."

"I know when to close a hearing and when not to. And I'll be the judge of what might constitute jeopardy to national security. *If* and when that comes up, though I seriously doubt it will, *then* I will close the hearings to all but the appropriate members of the committee. Now, get out of my office!"

She stalked toward him as he backpedaled to the door, keeping a wary eye on her. When he'd gone through it, she slammed the door with all her might.

Treason indeed. Grant made a serious mistake by sending that idiot. What he said was as good as an admission of guilt. She was convinced now they were trying to save their own skins by pulling her into their pathetic conspiracy.

She had another thought before she got two steps from the door. She opened it and yelled at the retreating back of the DNI. "I have this feeling your people know exactly where the Devereuxs are and are hiding them. I'd better not find out that's true!"

For his part, Birch was seething as well. With good reason, he was furious at Davis, though he waited until he was outside the building to flip her a middle-finger salute. But he'd also have a few choice words to Grant for putting him in this position.

Chapter Fifty-Four

LET'S GET GOING

May 1

Across town, Carter and Mackenzie were preparing to fly to Petra. It had been arranged with as much speed as possible, beginning the day after the summit meeting at Sean's cabin.

Bill had conveyed to the President Carter's request to investigate his theory on the existence of the Nabatean library. Grant had been difficult to convince the timing was right. With the country in an uproar over covert activities, sending the Devereuxs into a sovereign nation, even if it were an ally, was risky.

However, Grant also understood that Carter Devereux had an uncanny ability to unearth the most esoteric information, as well as a keen sense for when and how it could prove useful. At Bill's urging, he agreed to get behind the mission and help pull strings, those he still had control of, to smuggle them out of the country, on one condition. They'd be back to answer to the Senate Intelligence Committee when the hearing began.

Bill thought it prudent not to mention the condition to anyone until the time was right.

Work began on the Devereuxs' Dassault Falcon immediately. A team of properly vetted specialists who worked on Air Force One began equipping the Falcon with some of the secret features of Air Force One, including radar evasion equipment and high-tech communications equipment. There wasn't much to be done regarding extending the range of the plane or the speed. Even though the engineers were curious as to whose plane they were modifying, they knew not to ask questions.

The CIA, under Bill's direction, assembled everything they'd need. False passports, visas for Jordan, legends to match the passports, and a few simple accessories to disguise them without undue effort. Sean's friend Greta was helpful in that, saying the best disguise would be a little makeup, not much. She showed Carter and Mackenzie how to make themselves look ten years older with the application of a little contouring makeup and some eyeliner wrinkles at the corners of their eyes. Heavy plastic eyeglasses frames did the rest. Since the whole world was expecting the Devereuxs to be caught somewhere near Washington, D.C., it would be enough.

A couple days before the date they'd selected for the "great escape", the Falcon was taken for a shakedown cruise to make sure the radar evasion and other equipment was working. Convinced all worked well, the pilot who'd done the test in Carter's absence hangered the plane at a small private airstrip near Boston, and Bill put guards on it to make sure no one snooped.

Late in the evening on May first, Carter and Mackenzie, along with their security contingent, were taken to the plane. With the Devereuxs were Dylan and three Executive

Advantage operatives — one who was formerly Delta Force and two who'd been Secret Service in their former careers. All were highly trained, skilled, and experienced in VIP protection.

Dylan had a message from Bill. They'd need to be back in D.C. by May 12, to be briefed for the Intelligence Committee hearing.

"What the hell, Dylan!" Carter exclaimed. "No one said anything about this before!"

"Cool your jets, Carter. I'm just the messenger. I guess this was a condition of your going—from the President. It isn't written in stone, but Grant, Bill, James, and Irene are thinking of letting you turn up at the hearing unannounced. Maybe that will throw a wrench in Davis's plans."

"I don't like it, Dylan. Never mind the risk that Mackenzie and I will be thrown in jail on sight when we turn up at the hearing. To go and find something that's been hidden for two thousand years, and to be expected to do it in ten days—well, that's ambitious, to say the least."

"I get that," Dylan said. "That's one of the reasons we're bringing along someone else. This is Kyle Fields. He's a CIA pilot. If it's got wings, he can fly it."

"I pilot my plane," Carter snapped, still disgruntled at the last-minute news. He looked over the slim, average-height pilot and found him wanting.

"Carter, with this tight timeframe, there won't be much time for sleep," Dylan countered. "He's here to help. Don't bite his head off, and please stop biting mine off."

Carter grumbled a bit more. "If there weren't so much riding on the possible discovery, I'd call off the expedition. Finding ancient artifacts takes patience, meticulous planning, and above all, time. Ten days, excluding flight time, isn't enough time to even start."

"Come on, Carter, chill. You might as well use the ten days instead of just giving up. What have you been doing with your time since you saw the kids, anyway? Don't try to tell me you'd prefer to twiddle your thumbs for the next couple of weeks. You've been squealing about finding that library for some time, now that you have the chance, you whine about it."

Carter felt bad about arguing with Dylan. He was right; the time might as well be put to good use. He'd been shooting the messenger.

"Sorry, Dylan."

"No problem, buddy. I know you've been under a ton of stress. Let's get going."

Carter was well rested even for the late hour and insisted on taking the first leg of the flight, and Kyle didn't object. That raised him a notch in Carter's esteem. They took off from the airstrip near Boston at about eleven p.m. without filing a flight path. However, Bill, James, Irene, and Sean were aware of their route.

They flew directly to Queen Alia International Airport, Jordan's main and largest airport, located about eighteen miles south of the capital city of Amman. When they arrived on May 2, about six p.m. local time, Dr. Zachariah Sachs, a Jewish archaeologist who had obtained permission from the King of Jordan to work on the Petra site, was there to meet them.

The first part of the journey had been smoothed with the help of an old friend of James Rhodes. Ben Friedman, a Mossad operative James had dealt with before, had been very helpful to James during those dark days when

Mackenzie and Liam had been kidnapped, and Carter lay unaware of their fate in a Jerusalem hospital.

Dr. Sachs was unaware of the exact nature of their visit and of their real names. He only knew it was part of a top-secret mission that would eventually help his country, and he shouldn't ask many questions. He was to drive them to his camp, be as helpful as possible, and not get in their way.

He also had weapons for them. It made him nervous, but he followed Ben Friedman's directions and handed out 9-millimeter SIG Sauer P938s to each of them, along with three six-round magazines for each. The EA operatives made quick work of concealing the compact but lethal weapons then helped Carter and Mackenzie do the same.

From the airport to Petra, south via Desert Highway, Route 15 was a little under three hours, approximately one hundred forty-seven miles. On the way, Carter dozed occasionally while Mackenzie kept Sachs talking by asking about his work at Petra and what he'd learned.

Sachs, who couldn't be blamed for enjoying the attention of the beautiful redhead, chattered away and asked no questions. Exactly what they wanted.

They arrived in his camp at around ten p.m. By this time, the Devereux party was famished and exhausted, despite some being able to sleep a bit on the plane and Carter in the car. Such sleep is never as restful as that in a horizontal position, even if the latter is in a bedroll on the ground or a camp cot. After partaking of a light meal, they all turned in to get what sleep they could, for tomorrow would be a busy day.

Chapter Fifty-Five

THE DOLPHIN PENTAGON OF PETRA

May 3

The following morning, Carter discussed his objective with Sachs, while everyone enjoyed a breakfast in the pleasant spring morning. The last of the wildflowers perfumed the air of the camp. Mackenzie was transported by the green of the valley, the pink oleander blossoms, and her discovery of blooming cactus like the prickly pear of the southwestern US. Her mental picture of "desert" underwent a radical change that morning.

Sachs told her the city dates back to about 300 BC and is sometimes also called the "Rose City", because of the pink sandstone cliffs into which the tombs and temples were sculpted.

Carter had opened his laptop and was showing Sachs the dolphin pentagon, asking if it remained in the ancient city.

"Oh, yes, I know where it is. Would you like to see it?"

"Certainly, but don't take us directly there. In case we're observed, it should be part of a general tour of the city."

"No problem."

An hour later, the entire group stood in front of the magnificent edifices carved from the living stone. They were open-mouthed at the first sight of the most famous feature in Petra—the majestic temple with the elaborate Greek-style façade, the Al Khazneh, also known as the Treasury. They felt dwarfed by the structure, and Dylan remarked of the amphitheater that it was as big as or bigger than a football stadium back home.

To disguise their special interest in the dolphin pentagon when they got to it, they took hundreds of pictures of everything, from the mosaics of the fifth-century Byzantine church to the most modest dwelling that had been excavated.

When they got to the dolphin pentagon, which was carved into the side of the Siq where it opened opposite the Treasury, they not only took pictures, but covertly established exact GPS coordinates as well.

Mackenzie took the opportunity to gaze into the Siq as far as she could see. The narrow slot canyon held a mystique that sent a cold chill down her back. How many people had been swept away in flash floods roaring through it in rainy season? At some places, so narrow that only one person was able to pass through it, she couldn't fathom how they induced camels to travel its length. With a shiver, she turned back toward the sun to find the group had moved on to the next feature. She hurried to catch up.

Carter's head was inclined, the better to hear the much shorter Dr. Sachs. Mackenzie saw Carter jerk in apparent surprise and then bend to speak urgently to Sachs. She broke into a jog to catch up.

"Oh, there you are, Mackenzie. Dr. Sachs just told me something very interesting. He's seen the dolphin pentagon before." He took her hand and squeezed it. "I've just asked him where."

Fully expecting Sachs to say he saw it in Matera, Carter gave another surprised jolt when instead Sachs answered, "On Crete. I was working on a dig in Petras, just east of the modern Cretan town of Siteia. Beautiful area, situated on top of a small plateau that overlooks the sea north of Crete." Sachs raved on about the dig on Crete for several more moments, but Carter heard little of it.

His mind had seized on the similarity in the names of the places. Petra, in Jordan, Petras, on Crete. The Greek word, Πέτρα, Petra, meant "rock", and Πετράς, Petras, was its plural. Was it merely a coincidence, a naming of a place for its features? Or was there a deeper connection?

"What do you think the similarity in names means, Dr. Sachs? Given that the same symbol is found in both places?" Carter asked. The other members of the party had started listening closely when they heard Sachs say the name, but they let Carter do the talking.

Sachs shrugged. "Could just be that both places are rocky. But because of the symbol, maybe not." He snapped his fingers. "Maybe it's the ancient equivalent of a company logo! We know the Nabateans were great international traders. Perhaps they left their mark wherever they traveled."

"Maybe," Carter answered, drawing the word out. He decided not to mention he'd seen the symbol in Matera also. "Do you have any pictures of the Cretan symbol?"

"Probably. If you're ready to go back to camp, I could look on my laptop or the backup drive."

"Sure. I think we've seen what we needed to here."

They strolled to camp, as the sun felt warmer than the air temperature of around seventy-five degrees. When Sachs headed for his tent to get the laptop, Carter's crew gathered around him.

"What now?" Mackenzie asked, voicing the question on all their minds.

"Any of you ever been to Crete?" Carter quipped.

Sachs was back in minutes and showed Carter and the others the pictures from his time on Crete, including a few of the dolphin pentagon. He offered to transfer them to Carter's laptop, and Carter gladly accepted.

For the rest of the day, until it was time for the evening meal, Carter asked Sachs what he thought happened to the Nabateans, why they would have ceded their beautiful city to the Romans, and other questions about Petra.

Sachs thrived under Carter's interest. He was mindful of Friedman's instructions not to ask too many questions, but as it turned out, Carter and his beautiful wife were far too interested in what he thought to even explore what questions he'd ask if he were permitted.

Had Sachs known that the vaguely familiar-looking American was the famous Professor Carter Devereux, he'd have had questions in plenty. Fortunately, the minor disguise of the makeup held up, and he couldn't place the face.

Late in the afternoon, Carter told Sachs with feigned regret they'd decided to visit the Petras site, as it sounded very interesting and he'd never been there. Instead of staying near Petra for another day, they'd make their departure in the morning.

Sachs, though a bit disappointed, was gracious. "In that case, we must have the Middle Eastern feast which I planned for tomorrow night this evening." He excused himself to talk with the camp chef.

That evening, the group was treated to an array of delicious Middle Eastern fare. Carter and Mackenzie liked it very much, and several of the others who'd done tours in the Middle East during their military days were reminded of the flavors they'd enjoyed back in the day.

Carter remarked the only thing missing from the dinner was belly dancers, and while the bodyguards enthusiastically agreed, Mackenzie made her opinion known with a sharp elbow to his ribs.

Chapter Fifty-Six

WHO WERE YOUR VISITORS?

May 4

For the second morning in a row, the group rose early, this time to return to Queen Alia International Airport near the capital. Reluctantly, because no such arrangements had been made for Crete, they returned their weapons to Sachs, who concealed them inside the van.

Dylan and his men were on edge because they'd have no guns on Crete. The side trip left no time to arrange for them. They'd be doubly watchful there, and if trouble arose, they'd have to rely on hand-to-hand combat, unless they acquired knives. Dylan thought ruefully of the adage *never take a knife to a gunfight.*

He also pointed out to Carter they didn't have visas, either. Carter assured him that would be no problem, as US citizens were permitted to visit Greece for up to ninety days without one for tourist or business purposes.

"What about for spy purposes?" Dylan muttered out of

earshot of Sachs, who was bowing over Mackenzie's hand in farewell.

"For that, I'm afraid there are no visas issued anyway," Carter assured him unhelpfully.

They bade Sachs goodbye with thanks and saw him on his way before boarding the plane.

Sachs returned to camp to find it overrun with scowling Arab men. "How can I help you gentlemen?" he asked. He'd learned a mild demeanor went a long way toward more comfortable relations with the people of his host country.

"Who were your visitors? What did they want? What did you show them?"

Sachs was very glad he'd followed Ben Friedman's instructions to the letter by not being inquisitive with his visitors.

"Why, they were tourists, wanting an archaeologist's view of the city of Petra. I showed them everything, of course."

"What did they ask to see?"

"Everything. Of course, they didn't stay long. But I showed them all the important buildings, and the gentleman and I had very pleasant discourse regarding what happened to the original inhabitants. I believe he was a wealthy hobbyist."

"Why did they contact you? Did you know them before they came here?" the leader asked.

Sachs continued to give mild answers, as if this interrogation were nothing out of the ordinary. "No, no. They were referred to me by a friend in Jerusalem, Ben Friedman."

"He's a travel agent?"

"No, he's an international merchant, dealing in Israeli

technology products. He only told me they were friends of his." To prove he was speaking the truth, Sachs offered to show them the emails from Friedman, but he had to read the emails to them as they were written in Hebrew. The Arabs spat on the ground when they saw it but had Sachs read and translate it.

What he didn't tell them about was his face-to-face meeting with Friedman in Amman on a supply run. Nor did he tell them about the 9-millimeter weapons hidden in the panel of his van.

Still unsatisfied, the Arab leader then asked, "Where did they say they were going?"

"They said they were going to Crete for a few days to visit a few sites connected with Greek mythology and the Minoan civilization." Sachs began sweating in the sun and mopped his brow with a clean, white handkerchief. Was this questioning never going to end?

"And after that? Where will they go next?"

"Gentlemen, I'm not aware of their itinerary. I do believe I heard the lady say she wanted to spend some time in London on their way back to America. They're from LA."

The leader handed him a card written in Arabic. "Call me at this number if you hear from them again, or if they want to come back, or if you remember anything important."

"Of course," Sachs agreed.

When they left, he sagged in relief. His calm and poise must have convinced them he was telling the truth. *Baruch Hashem!*

That night, from Amman, the leader of the Arab men sent a report to his superior, whom he'd never met. It was a standard report about seven Americans who visited Petra and stayed for two nights. There didn't seem to be anything threatening about them or the reason for their visit.

To the report, he attached photos of the visitors taken with hidden cameras within the city of Petra. He didn't know what his superiors were on the lookout for, but the more than 460,000 visitors to Petra each year all had their pictures taken clandestinely.

It was his full-time job to keep a database of visitors and match names to faces by means of facial recognition software. In the ten years he'd been running the operation, there'd never been a mismatch between the face and a name, for those faces it recognized. But he knew the software was only successful in recognizing about forty percent of the faces.

Out in the desert, everyone wore dark glasses and wide brimmed hats. That made it very difficult to recognize faces at all, much less with certainty.

Chapter Fifty-Seven

THE DOLPHIN PENTAGON OF PETRAS

May 4

Carter, Mackenzie, and Dylan's team arrived at Heraklion International Airport, nicknamed "Nikos Kazantzakis", a little over an hour after taking off from Amman. The primary airport on the island of Crete, and second-busiest in the country after Athens International, was still eighty miles from their destination.

Carter's Greek was good enough to get them a van. He quipped he knew just enough of the language to stay out of trouble, order coffee and food, but nothing more.

They drove straight to Siteia and stopped for some lunch before continuing to the Petras site. Fortunately, they found someone who spoke Italian—in which Carter was fluent— among the diggers, and she was able to point them toward the area where they'd find the dolphin petroglyph.

Once they found it, they proceeded as they'd done in Petra, taking plenty of pictures of the dolphin pentagon and establishing an exact GPS coordinate, but mixing those activities in with other sightseeing activities to avoid exposing their true interest.

Although Carter wasn't an expert on Minoan civilization, he knew enough to keep up a running tour lecture for the benefit of anyone who might be listening and interested in what they were up to. As he spoke, he reflected that this site was much older than the Petra site and possibly even older than Matera.

The Minoan civilization was from the Aegean Bronze Age. It flourished on the island of Crete and other Aegean islands from approximately 3650 to 1400 BC, belonging to a period of Greek history before both the Mycenaean civilization and Ancient Greece. It was the first of its kind in Europe.

Late in the afternoon, they drove back to Heraklion and booked into the Aquila Atlantis.

"Isn't this a bit above our budget limit?" Dylan asked, looking around at the lobby of the five-star hotel.

"Bill doesn't have any problem if I kick in a little to get us some nice digs," Carter answered. "After making her camp out for two nights in Jordan, I'd like to put Mackenzie in something a bit more comfortable. Do you mind?"

"Not at all," said Dylan. "Do they have room service?"

Carter had already zoned out, thinking about the dolphin pentagons. The one at Petras was an exact replica of the one in Petra, or perhaps it was the other way around. His memory told him the one in Matera was also the same. He still planned to get to Matera to confirm it.

"Earth to Carter," Dylan said, interrupting Carter's thoughts. "Room service?"

"Oh, let's eat together. It will take Mackenzie at least an hour to get the dust off her and get ready. Let's meet in the restaurant at eight."

The Nabatean Secret

After a nice Mediterranean dinner in the hotel restaurant, Carter spent some time minutely examining the photos of the two petroglyphs and looking for clues. In the end, he admitted to Mackenzie that Sachs' idea of an ancient company logo could very well be a possibility.

"It's no crazier than anything else I've come up with," he remarked. "But I still wonder if it could have something to do with the library."

"I thought you said the library must have been moved from Petra to Matera," Mackenzie remarked.

"It's all conjecture, really. Not even strong enough to call a theory. They could just as easily have moved it from Petra to Petras, and then to Matera, or the other way around. We won't know until we explore all the areas. Maybe it doesn't even have anything to do with the library."

"That would be a bummer," Mackenzie mused. "Carter, why a pentagon of dolphins?"

"What do you mean?"

"Why five? Why not a hexagon, or octagon? For that matter, why not a dodecahedron? For the 12 sons of Ishmael?"

"That's a lot of dolphins to carve," he answered. But as he answered, he was also thinking. *She has a point. A dodecagon, with 12 sides. Or maybe it wasn't Ishmael's children, but Nebajoth's.*

"Mackie, I don't know how you do it. You always seem to ask just the right question to get me thinking. Listen—we know from the Book of Jasher that Nebajoth had three sons, Mayon, Mend, and Send. But no one ever mentions his daughters. Maybe he had a couple? Women didn't count for much in those days," he added, ducking as he said it.

His instincts were correct. Mackenzie hurled a pillow at him, but she laughed as she said, "They didn't have redheads among them, that's why."

"Don't think I haven't noticed you use that to mesmerize or intimidate men we want to put one over on," Carter joked. He ducked again as a second pillow flew his way. "But back to the pentagon. It could be that it represents all of Nebajoth's children, not just his sons. But I'm not sure how that will help us find the library."

After a minute, he spoke again. "I'll tell you what bugs me. Why dolphins? These people were desert dwellers—for millennia, before they suddenly took to the sea and became a power among merchants. Doesn't it seem strange that a desert nation would become a seafaring nation?

"Did the dolphins only become significant to them when they started sailing the seas, or were they important before that for some reason?"

"Could we ask Merrybeth about that?" Mackenzie asked.

"It would be nice if we could. But how would we explain to her what we're looking for? Even more problematic is the fact that we can't show our faces at the Alboran Sea dig. Remember, we're still in hiding."

"Well, it would certainly have been handy to get some help from our dolphin friends — Merrybeth and her pod." Mackenzie sighed.

"Maybe we'll think of a way," Carter said, kissing Mackenzie on the forehead. "Let's get some sleep. We have another early morning ahead of us."

"Hand me those pillows, love," Mackenzie wheedled.

"Oh, no. You threw them you pick them up—" Carter's words were cut off as *his* pillows came sailing through the air. "Okay, I'll pick them up!" he said, laughing.

Chapter Fifty-Eight

WELCOME TO THE BASILICATA

May 5

They were back on their original schedule as they breakfasted quickly and then flew from Heraklion to Bari, where the closest airport to Matera was located. Bill had arranged for them to be met by a CIA undercover agent, an Italian native by the name of Piero Rossi. His cover was a small tourist guide company with a few minibuses and drivers.

Carter had to smile when the flamboyant Italian introduced himself. "Welcome to the Basilicata."

Though accented, his English was perfect, and so were his continental manners, as he bowed and kissed Mackenzie's hand. That was happening a little too often for Carter's taste, but he thought he'd better tolerate it. Mackenzie was eating it up.

His smile, though, was for a different reason. Carter's Italian was much better than his Greek, and he therefore knew that the surname, Rossi, meant red. One of the most common surnames in Italy, it derived from the notion of a person with red hair or reddish skin. However, Piero had dark black hair, a neatly trimmed black beard with no hint of red, deep brown eyes, and olive skin. The red hair of his ancestors must have been a recessive trait.

Carter was wondering if Piero envied Mackenzie's red hair, which was more befitting of his surname.

Dylan, on the other hand, was openly staring at the loud Italian. Dressed up as he was in the most expensive tailor-made jeans, dress shirt, Gucci leather jacket, and Forzieri, handcrafted leather, cap-toe, dress shoes—looking as if he just stepped off the catwalk of a fashion show in Milan—he was hardly Dylan's idea of "undercover".

Next to him, they looked like hillbillies in their faded jeans, T-shirts, and baseball caps, even though the T-shirts showed off sculpted muscles. In fact, they'd have to change those to carry anything remotely resembling a weapon, but he appreciated the looks he was getting from *some* of the Italian girls. Liu would understand, he hoped.

Still, he wondered what Bill Griffin was thinking when he organized this bozo. They were supposed to draw as little attention as possible. But then slowly he became aware that everyone in the arrivals hall was dressed in similar fashion, and they were just as loud and boisterous.

Shit. We're the standouts. He couldn't see how he and his men were going to fit in, as they were used to blending into the woodwork, not being loud and flashy like their guide.

Piero gave every indication he was quite excited to see them. He took them to his ten-seater van, marked with his tour company's logo *Rossi's Italian Indulgence* on both side panels.

Rossi didn't have complete instructions yet. Bill had only told him to meet the group at the Bari airport, and he'd get further instructions from the group. He was to be at their disposal for the next six to seven days.

Once in the van, Dylan handed him Bill's written instructions.

Without opening the envelope, Rossi placed it in the inside pocket of his expensive leather jacket and said, "Coffee first." It was a statement, not a question.

Carter and Mackenzie made small talk with Piero as Dylan and his crew exchanged questioning looks.

Was this guy for real? A CIA undercover agent?

Before long, Piero spotted a small coffee shop and stopped, gesturing for everyone to get out. They followed Piero into the shop to order, and when Piero turned to Dylan with raised eyebrows, he said, "Cappuccino for my crew," thinking it was the most Italian coffee he knew of.

Piero snorted. These ignorant Americans didn't know it was rude to order anything other than espresso after ten a.m. He turned to the barista and said, "*Otto caffè, grazie.*" Eight coffees, thank you.

It would be his pleasure to teach the Americans. He noted with delight that Carter and Mackenzie already knew the proper etiquette, but he instructed Dylan and the rest. Taking the tiny cup holding the equivalent of two shot glasses of strong coffee, he remained standing at the counter as he gulped it down in two swallows. His audience followed suit.

When he finished his coffee, he ordered eight arancini, which the barista put in a paper bag and handed to him. It had taken less than five minutes in and out of the shop, and they were back on the road and on their way to Matera.

Dylan was wondering what was in the bag when Piero handed it to Mackenzie and asked her to hand it out to everyone. The little balls of deep-fried bread crumbs holding who-knew-what were new to Dylan and his crew.

Carter and Mackenzie had enjoyed them on their previous trip to Italy, so Carter bit into it, revealing a ball of rice stuffed with what Piero called *ragù*. Unlike the bottled spaghetti sauce known by the brand name in the US, this was meat and tomato sauce laced with mozzarella and peas.

The result was magical!

Dylan and his men wolfed theirs down and wished there were more. All of them decided there and then they were hooked on this little delicacy and would eat as much of it as often as they could while they were in Italy.

In practically no time, they arrived in Matera, only forty miles from the airport. As before, Mackenzie had upgraded their accommodation to a five-star hotel, the Palazzo Gattini. This time Dylan had no objections. If Bill was okay with it, he certainly was okay with it too.

The operatives were in double rooms on each side of Carter and Mackenzie's suite, while he, Kyle Fields, the pilot, and Piero were directly across the hall.

Carter had booked a suite so they'd have space for all of them to meet when required. This was the most delicate part of the operation.

Rossi finally read his instructions from Bill. He'd had enough of an idea of the importance when he heard the number of bodyguards accompanying Carter and Mackenzie that he'd come prepared with the weapons they'd need.

When he was done reading, he burned the paper in the fireplace of his room and got the gear ready.

An hour after they checked in, Rossi became all business as he handed each of the bodyguards a Glock G43 subcompact gun. They were ultra-concealable, accurate, and most important, comfortable for shooters regardless of hand size. He also handed each of them three six-round magazines as they'd had in Jordan.

After some discussion, they agreed to have a guided walking tour of part of the Sassi, the old city, after lunch.

Carter had a good idea where it was, but they'd only wander around until they "found" it, and that would be the following morning. Until then, they'd be American tourists, a little clueless.

Chapter Fifty-Nine

BE RID OF THEM FOR GOOD

May 5

On the day after questioning Zachariah Sachs, the leader of the group who'd done so received a disturbing report from one of his team. They'd fallen almost a day behind in matching faces with the names and passports of visitors to Petra but were nearly caught up. Even more disturbing, for the first time in the ten years he'd been running the program, there was a mismatch.

"What do you mean, a mismatch?" he roared, causing the man who'd brought the bad news to cringe.

"*Sayyidi*, it is just as I say. The facial recognition identifies this man as John Ellis. But his passport says he is Rodger Faye. I fear this man has a false passport." He bowed low, hoping to avoid another outburst from his superior.

The leader called in his entire staff and harangued them about falling behind, since the records at passport control showed Rodger Faye had left Jordan the day before. Then he dismissed them curtly to do a more thorough search for the days when Rodger Faye was in the area.

The team worked feverishly for half an hour, isolating the photos of Faye and those traveling with him. The leader began to get a bad feeling when he realized these were the people he'd questioned Zachariah Sachs about just yesterday. Even more so when the photos were enlarged, enhanced, and run through the program again. This time, they found two more mismatches. One was Chris Faure according to his passport but Kyle Fields according to the facial recognition system, a nobody, at least a nobody on their watch lists.

But the other was a big problem. Carter Devereux. The Arab leader turned as pale as the pigments in his olive-colored skin would allow. He'd be lucky to keep his head for this, much less his job. Hiding it would make things even worse. He must report immediately. With a trembling hand, he picked up his satphone to report to his immediate superior over a secure line.

In less than fifteen minutes, the order came back. Pick up Sachs and force him to reveal who these people really were and what they really wanted. Name, rank, and serial number if applicable—in short, every bit of information on every member of the party. Above all, what were they doing in Petra?

There'd been no order for the leader to step down, for which he was grateful. Perhaps it wasn't so serious after all. But he'd be worried until the matter was resolved.

Half an hour later, two canvas-covered troop carrier trucks blew into Sachs's camp at full speed. The twelve soldiers within jumped out and rounded up Sachs and his research team at gunpoint.

"What is this?" Sachs cried. "My permits are valid. You

have no right!" He stopped protesting as the man who'd questioned him the day before stepped forward.

"You lied to us. You will come with us peacefully, or you and your entire team will be arrested."

"But I didn't! I told you everything I know," Sachs protested, though his stomach was in turmoil at the lie of omission. No one had asked him about guns, and he hadn't mentioned them or his meeting with Friedman.

Now he regretted getting involved at all. His students were at risk. There was nothing to do but go with these dangerous-looking Arabs.

As an Israeli, he could be in very deep trouble.

Sachs was even more worried when they placed a black bag over his head while driving away from his camp. He'd seen the videos, hideous as they were. But those awful events had taken place in Afghanistan, Iraq, and Syria, not in Jordan though, which was considered one of the safer Middle Eastern countries.

He tried to relax and tell himself the bag was simply to keep him from knowing where they were going. But that alone was worrying enough.

When the trucks stopped, Sachs was dragged out of his seat and thrown to the ground. He felt the bag snatched from his head and blinked in the unremitting sunlight. When he could focus again, his heart sank. There were no buildings to be seen, no road even. They were somewhere in the desert, but he had no idea where or even in what direction he'd walk to find civilization if he survived the questioning.

The same man who'd questioned him before stepped forward and backhanded Sachs across the face. "That is just a small taste of what is to come if you don't answer truthfully."

Sachs reeled with the blow but didn't fall. He looked the man in the face and said, "I have told you everything I know. Please, I have no idea what to say."

The next blow came from the opposite direction. "We know your visitors were traveling under false passports. What are their true names?"

"I don't know! I swear it!"

"One of them was Carter Devereux. Am I to understand you, an archaeologist, did not know who he was?"

"I saw no one I recognized as the famous Doctor Devereux. If I had known—"

Whatever Sachs had intended to say was cut off by a vicious blow to his stomach. He doubled over and fell to the ground.

The questions came in rapid succession, and by the time Sachs's badly beaten, half-dead body was dumped on the Israeli side of the Allenby/King Hussein Bridge border crossing between Jordan and Israel, he'd given up nothing except that he'd armed the visitors at the direction of an acquaintance, the same Ben Freidman he'd mentioned as having referred them to him.

His last conscious thought was the hope his students were safe.

The news of Devereux's excursion to Petra and intention to go on to Petras made its way up the chain of command and finally reached Mathieu Nabati while Sachs was still being questioned.

Upon hearing it, Nabati threw a temper tantrum that rivalled the worst of his mother's. Only after a priceless Ming Dynasty vase lay shattered on his floor did he turn icy.

The Devereuxs were running around unchecked in the Middle East and Mediterranean, and not a word had Russell McCormick reported. The man had become useless and could now number his days in the single digits if Mathieu had any say in it. As soon as he'd issued orders to his contacts in the Middle East to track down the Devereux party, he'd urge his mother to give him permission to terminate McCormick, whose incompetence was an embarrassment to the Nabateans

Mathieu gave some thought to his own failures. Time and time again, Carter Devereux and those around him had escaped his clutches. Mathieu wasn't sure how much longer his mother would put up with the failures.

He didn't suppose she'd have him killed, but she was certainly capable of sidelining him and taking over his job herself. She'd done it for a very long time before he came of age, and she was very good at it.

It was days like this that he missed the uneventful lifestyle of a small banker in Zürich.

However, he must shake off this disappointment and deal with the Devereuxs. He paced as he analyzed the information he had. If Devereux and his wife were traveling in disguise and flying with fake passports and a team of five others, there must be a good reason for it.

That they'd visit Petra, the holiest of Nabatean sites, made his stomach roil. What were they doing there, if not attempting to learn Nabatean secrets? And then to go on to Petras. That meant they'd learned a fact not widely known, though not entirely a secret. In their heyday, Nabateans boasted a thriving community of merchants and traders in Petras.

It was imperative he catch up to the Devereuxs, wherever they were. It didn't take much imagination to determine that their jet would have been similarly disguised, and his contacts should be able to give him information about a new call sign and markings. That was the first step.

In fact, it took less than half an hour to have that information in hand and then to trace the movements of the jet. They'd arrived in Amman on May 2, left on May 4 for Petras, and then, what?

Matera? There were no Nabateans in Matera.
What's Devereux up to?

On second thought, Mathieu wasn't so quick to dismiss the possibility that Devereux was following a lead the Nabateans didn't know about. The man had an annoying habit of digging up things where they were not supposed to be. The evidence was strong that Devereux's trip had everything to do with investigating Nabatean history. He had to be stopped.

And that was Mathieu's brief. Carter Devereux, his wife, and more than a few of his associates were thorns in the sides of the Council of the Covenant of Nabatea, and as such, their lives were forfeit. It didn't matter what they were looking for.

Matera was as good a place as any to assassinate them.

This time, he wouldn't use spetsnaz troops. They had proven themselves incompetent on the Freydís mission and had no loyalty. As far as he was concerned, they were a bunch of loudmouth, unendurable, vodka-drinking, insolent, superstitious, overrated nincompoops.

This time, he'd use professional assassins, of which he had no shortage. And he'd send three without telling any of them there were two others with the same brief. As he communicated his orders, he provided the assassins with photos of the targets as they were disguised, the name of the hotel where they were staying, and the prices on their heads.

Carter Devereux, as the driving force behind the campaign against the Nabateans, was most valuable at two million dollars. His wife, almost an equal thorn, should not be so difficult to kill. Therefore, her price was one million. Out of sheer spite, Mathieu offered a quarter million for each member of the team around them. It would soothe his ruffled feathers to take out all of them, and the extra incentive to kill as many as possible would feed his assassins' greed.

In a city of only sixty thousand permanent population and a few thousand tourists at any given time, it should be easy to hide in plain sight and for the assassins to blend in as well. It didn't matter whether the targets died from apparent accidents or frank murder, so long as they *did* die.

He just wanted to be rid of them for good.

Chapter Sixty

I'LL GO TO YOUR RANCH WITH YOU

May 2 to 5

Bill Griffin was due at the Oval Office at nine a.m. on May 2. He'd had a good night's sleep for a change, having left Carter and his team in Dylan's capable hands. They'd left the night before, and the only thing on the to-do list for this morning was a report from Sebastian Birch to the President on his progress with Michelle Davis.

The President had invited Bill to sit in on that meeting as an interested party, though that invitation should have come through the DNI himself. The fact that Bill was much closer to the President than his boss proved the near-irrelevance of the position. Bill had nothing against his nominal boss. He just didn't think the man was effective in his mission. Still, it was better to send Birch than to go himself to that harpy's nest.

Birch's report proved him right. As Birch detailed the disastrous meeting with Senator Davis, quoting much of it verbatim, the President and Bill came to the same conclusion independently. As soon as Birch had left the Oval Office, Bill voiced it.

"Are you thinking what I'm thinking?" he asked

"Probably. How do you want to do it?" the President responded.

"Let's get Sean in here and get his buy-in, then give him the task."

It took an hour to locate Sean, who was having a bit of a sleep-in with his phone off after his late night. Nevertheless, he arrived at the White House in short order after his secretary personally rousted him at home. There, the President had Bill outline their plan.

"McCormick has been a wash. We need to get him out of the way so we can use the resources on more productive tasks. I assume you can handle that with no further direction?"

"Out of the way alive?" Sean responded.

"I won't condone an assassination on an American national," Grant answered.

"Gotcha. I'll take care of it."

Bill shot Sean a frown for his informal address, but the President didn't seem bothered.

"The second thing is, we're going to have to spike Davis's plans for her hearing somehow. President Grant and I think the best way to do that will be to bring the Devereuxs out of hiding and put them before the oversight committee. What's their status?"

"They're out of pocket right now, as you know, but they've already been notified they need to be back for the hearing. It won't be a problem. However, I wouldn't feel right about doing it unless they're granted immunity for their testimony."

"I have no objection to that," the President said. "We

already know they aren't guilty of anything, but I wouldn't put it past Michelle to try to pin something on them. Let's keep that under wraps, though. It will be my pleasure to watch her squirm when she learns of it at the last minute."

"Sounds like there's a story behind that remark," observed Sean, who was unaware of the bad blood between the President and the Senator.

"Old story. She did something stupid eight years ago when we were both running for this office," Grant said. "I've forgiven her, but she seems determined to nurture the grudge. And if she wants to go another round, then I'll oblige her." Grant's predatory grin was the last bit of explanation Sean would get.

"If that's all, I'll get right on the other matter," Sean said discreetly.

"That's all for now, and thanks for coming so quickly."

Sean reflected that he should have known Bill wouldn't want McCormick dead, even if the President hadn't made that perfectly clear. He'd been of no use to find the Security Council leak, and it was a waste of time and resources to keep tabs on him. But he might be of some use to testify against the traitor when he was found, as well as against the Nabateans. Therefore, he couldn't be arrested without letting on to their quarry that the CIA was onto them.

Two things needed to happen. They had to get a better look at that black box, and McCormick had to disappear; and although the two matters were linked, he had separate ideas to handle them.

Before he did anything else, Sean sent overnight mail to his brother, Jared. Jared lived on a ranch in central

Colorado, fifty miles or so west of Colorado Springs, where he raised alpaca. Jared had been cooperative a time or two before and would be glad of the extra hand. Along with the briefing letter, Sean included a check for McCormick's keep and a separate letter for McCormick.

Sean had to work quickly for the timing to be right. What he planned for McCormick had to be timed precisely to avoid endangering the man's life. He reported to Bill when he had all the elements in place.

"Do you need to inform Alec Burnett, so the FBI won't go nuts hunting for him?"

"Yes, that's a good idea. I'll tell him McCormick's going to disappear but will be all right. Anything else you want me to give him? Like the location where you'll be holding him?"

"Hell, no! I don't want the person who'll take care of him involved. Rest assured, he'll be fine. I give you my word on that."

"Good enough. Anything else you need that I can help with?" Bill asked.

"Better you don't know. Aside from our snatching him for his own safety, part of this is highly illegal. You want plausible deniability, yes?"

"You're right. I don't want to know."

"Then I'll get busy."

Sean had his cell phone out of his pocket before he even cleared the building. "Hey, buddy, long time no see. Want to meet me for lunch? My treat."

Over the best street tacos in Washington, D.C., he told a friend from his Special Forces days he needed a chop shop. His friend, a D.C. cop now, raised his eyebrows.

"Is there anything you want to tell me, Sean?"

Sean shook his head. "You know what I do now, right?"

His friend nodded.

"It has to do with a top-secret operation. Sorry I can't tell you more. Can you help me?"

"Yeah, I think I can." He went on to give Sean the name of a suspected chop shop, and contact information for the undercover cop who worked there. "You'll tell me someday?"

"If I can. Thanks, Joe."

His call to the undercover cop went pretty much the same. "We're looking for some non-standard equipment, a black box in the driver's side door panel. Give us that, and the rest of the car is all yours."

"More evidence for me, not a problem. Where will the car be, and how will we identify it?"

Sean gave him the address of Kelly's apartment building, a description of the car, and the license plate number. "Wait until at least two a.m., okay?"

"Sure. And how do we get the box to you?"

"I'll be in touch. And hey, make sure the battery is disconnected before you mess with that box. Then don't let it out of your sight. It's extremely important."

Sean's next call was to Kelly, who still wasn't keen on inviting McCormick to spend the night with her. "It's the last time, Kelly, I swear. And you don't need to do anything else for this operation. Just loan me your apartment key, and make sure McCormick is in bed before midnight. You can slip him a roofie if you don't want to make him sleepy the old-fashioned way." He grinned only when he'd finished the sentence, so she wouldn't hear it in his voice.

"Yuck. This is the last of him, you promise?" she asked.

"You have my word, Kelly."

At midnight, Sean and two of his men were at Kelly's door. They eased her door open and tiptoed to the bedroom, where they found both Kelly and McCormick asleep. Trusting that Kelly had done her part one way or another, they quietly hefted McCormick and carried him into the living room, where they administered another sedative and trussed him like a Thanksgiving turkey.

Sean noticed Kelly didn't wake either. *Must have been a good bottle of wine.* They held McCormick up between the two EA operatives, pretending he was a drunk companion until they got him in their vehicle. From there, they drove him to a warehouse near the same airport where the "milk" plane was hangered and loaded him into a crate with ventilation shafts that had been prepared for his transport.

They then had a truck pick up that crate and several others and deliver them to a freight transport service. McCormick's crate was labelled for delivery to Colorado Springs, Colorado. The pilot accepted the bill of lading without insisting on checking the cargo, as he'd been paid to do. The paperwork protected him.

Sean hurried back to Kelly's, where he'd arranged to meet the car thieves. He accompanied the undercover cop to the chop shop, where he took possession of the black box.

First thing in the morning, it was destined to be handed to the quantum IT project team. They'd be all over it like kids in a candy store.

McCormick's crate was met in Colorado Springs at noon by Jared Walker, who loaded it into his pickup and drove out of town before he opened it. When he pulled over on a dirt track off Highway 24, he could hear McCormick making a racket inside the crate.

Jared pried the lid off, and McCormick sprang up, ready for a fight.

But as soon as he noticed the mountain peaks around him and a familiar-looking but unknown guy in a cowboy hat with a pry bar in his hands, Russell stilled. It had been a while since he'd been directly involved in an operation, but he knew the evidence when he saw it.

"Who are you?"

"I have a letter here from my brother, whom I think you know. It explains everything." Jared handed the letter to Russell and then went to sit inside the cab of the pickup while McCormick came to terms with his situation.

McCormick read the letter with growing disbelief.

Russell, we apologize for the inconvenience, but we've placed you with my brother for safekeeping for the time being. You are best advised to stay put and do as you're asked. Enjoy the peace in the Colorado Rockies, and stay out of sight of your former masters if you value your life.

The letter was signed "Sean W."

McCormick jerked open the passenger door on the pickup and said, "What the fuck?"

Jared shrugged. "You know as much as I do. My brother asked me to pick you up and feed and shelter you until further notice, and said you'd be glad to give me a hand on my ranch in return for the favor."

"Fat chance of that. Take me to the nearest airport," McCormick demanded.

"No can do, friend," Jared answered. "Firstly, my brother told me your life would be in danger if you were seen by anyone else. He went to a lot of trouble to get you here, and he must have a good reason. I just got his mail this morning. If you want to risk it, you'll have to walk back to Colorado Springs, because I don't have time to take you back.

"Secondly, picking you up has cost me three hours, and my alpacas are hungry. The least you can do is come help me feed them. Then we'll talk about what's next."

Russell had no intention of helping with any alpacas, but neither did he know how far it was back to Colorado Springs as the truck had been moving when he finally woke up.

That bitch, Kelly White, must have roofied me.

And it was cold, much too cold for the garb he was wearing. He didn't even know where the jeans and plaid shirt had come from, but he wished whoever had dressed him in them had sent along a heavier coat than the denim jacket he had on.

"Fine, I'll go to your ranch with you," he huffed in defeat.

Chapter Sixty-One

LATELY HE COULDN'T DO ANYTHING RIGHT

May 6

Mathieu sighed in satisfaction after reading the latest message from the last of his three assassins. She had arrived in Matera. With the plan to deal with the Devereuxs in place, he turned his attention to McCormick. It was time to get his mother on board with his plans.

"*Maman*, I trust you received my analysis of Russell McCormick's performance lately," he said by secure satellite uplink.

"I did, and I have read it. I concur," she answered.

"Then I have your permission to proceed?"

"Absolutely." They needn't bother with a vote in the Council; security matters were part of their duties.

While talking to his mother, Mathieu's eye caught the statuette which he always kept on his desk. It was an exact replica, mini version of Maman, the huge sculpture of a spider by Louise Bourgeois on display at the National Gallery of Canada in Ottawa. It was supposed to allude to the strength of Bourgeois' mother, but always reminded Mathieu of how predatory his own could be.

Mathieu kept his expression solemn until he'd closed the video link and then broke into a big smile. Perhaps his most favorite part of his job was the elaborate planning that went into an operation of this type.

He had a rather elegant solution to the McCormick problem—one that would also implicate Kelly White while taking McCormick out of the picture entirely.

He needed no permission to render Kelly irrelevant in any manner he chose, as she was only an unwitting pawn. However, he was displeased with her ineffectiveness. Ruining her would add spice to the task.

Mathieu contacted his undercover operative within INSCOM and gave him two names, along with instructions to carry out his plan. If they were successful, McCormick would be found dead in his apartment, and Kelly White would be arrested for his murder.

Within two hours, his INSCOM contact was back with a disturbing message. Russell McCormick was missing! He'd disappeared from White's bed without a trace in the early morning hours of the previous day.

"How could that happen without her knowledge?" Mathieu asked, dubious.

"Apparently the two shared a bottle of wine, and she is a heavy sleeper when drinking. She reported him missing around noon, after he failed to show up for a planned meeting at ten and then also missed a lunch date.

"Evidently, she woke to find him gone and assumed he'd gone to work early. When he missed their meeting, she called his office and learned he hadn't been there. By the time he missed the lunch date, she felt something was wrong and raised the alarm."

"Keep your eyes on the situation and notify me immediately when he turns up. I don't like coincidences."

"I will."

Mathieu considered his options. He couldn't hide this for long. *Maman* would have to know.

He sighed.

It seemed lately he couldn't do anything right, ever since that damned Carter Devereux had stolen the Giants' library from the City of Lights.

Maybe Devereux's death would stop the downward spiral.

He should be hearing the good news any time now.

Chapter Sixty-Two

IT'S A TRIANGLE

May 6 early morning

In the crisp early morning, Carter, Mackenzie, and the rest of their team, led by their "tour guide", Piero, strolled out to explore Matera. Acting like the other tourists in town, they were headed for the Sassi.

Carter's trip to Matera in his youth was prompted by the history of the region. He'd been between college semesters, about to embark on the advanced undergraduate classes that would eventually lead to his work as a leading archaeologist. Thanks to his grandfather's interest in archaeology and his wealth, Carter was often treated to such excursions, priceless in memory. It was during that trip he'd seen the dolphin pentagon they were seeking now, and he thought he knew just where it was.

Nevertheless, to maintain their cover as tourists, they strolled through the winding paths of the Sassi, taking pictures, pointing and exclaiming at the sites, and making their way to the carving by an indirect route.

The Nabatean Secret

The morning was a beautiful example of the mild spring weather in Southern Italy. Sunny, but not too hot, it was perfect for their purposes. Judging by the crowds, it was perfect for the other several thousand tourists in the area as well. They often had to stop and wait for the way to clear before moving on. However, they worked to appear as if they were unhurried, though Carter was itching to confirm his memory.

When they finally came to the spot, they took pictures, and one of the team inconspicuously took the GPS coordinates as Carter and Mackenzie posed with the carving between them. Afterward, they continued to wind their way through the ancient city.

Just as it had been in Jordan and on Crete, the outing was enjoyable for its own sake. Carter was perhaps the most interested, but the history of this ancient town was fascinating. Considered the third-oldest continually inhabited settlement in the world, after Aleppo in Syria and Jericho in Israel, the Sassi was a jumble of cave dwellings carved into the side of a deep ravine. It had been occupied for more than nine thousand years.

People still lived in some of them, though the Italian government had forcibly evicted some fifteen thousand citizens in the 1950s because of the squalor and terrible living conditions. Now many of the cave dwellings had been cleaned up, restored, and returned to service. The churches among them had been deconsecrated and now served as living museums.

The cave areas, or "sassi" meaning "stone" in Italian, consisted of thousands of man-made caves cut into the hard stone. Ascending the slopes of the valley, it was evident that one cave's ceiling was often the next cave's floor.

Stone-brick fasciae presented a veneer of civilization,

but as they were meandering through the narrow ways coursing through the caves, they unavoidably had to walk over the roofs of some homes.

Walking through this part of Matera was like stepping back into Biblical times. No wonder movies like *The Gospel According to St Matthew*, Mel Gibson's *The Passion of the Christ*, and the new *Ben-Hur* were filmed there.

They'd explored only a small portion of the area when it was time for the mid-day meal. Afterward, Piero insisted they remain in the hotel as most of the places of business would be closed, and they would stand out if they were on the streets before four in the afternoon.

They used the time to brainstorm again what the carvings meant, whether they had anything to do with a Nabatean library, and if so, how to find it. Carter plotted the GPS coordinates on a map he'd brought along.

Carter remarked to the others, "I don't know why, but a physical map is just so much more satisfying than a map on a computer screen. And it makes it easy to draw lines between the three sites."

He did so and then examined his handiwork. Dylan came to look over his shoulder.

"It's a triangle," he said.

"Yeah, I expected that," Carter quipped. "Since we had three points and all. But I don't see a clue in it."

Despite his joke, Carter was frustrated. He had a gut feeling there must be more to the carvings than the idea of the company logo, or even a family crest of the patriarch, Nebajoth, or a specific trader. The surroundings where each of them appeared didn't particularly resemble each other. There was no common element other than the carvings themselves.

Even Mackenzie's trick of stream-of-consciousness ques-

The Nabatean Secret

tioning didn't give him an idea for further exploration this time. The others tried to emulate her with questions of their own. But nothing came to his mind.

Eventually, he said, "We need more information. Either another one or more of these carvings, or… and this is just a shot in the dark… simply more contemporaneous carvings of dolphins."

Dylan grinned. "You mean, like breadcrumbs? Individual carvings of dolphins pointing the way?"

"Something like that. Pointing the way to what, I can't say. Hopefully, it would be the Nabatean's library."

Everyone in the room turned to look at Piero.

"What about that?" Carter asked. "Know of any such carvings?"

Piero shrugged. "I don't remember seeing any, but it might be worth asking locals and other tour guides."

"Only if you can do it without raising interest in why we're looking for dolphins," Carter answered. "I still want to keep a low profile. And it's possible we missed something at the other sites and will have to go back sometime. Do it if you can."

Chapter Sixty-Three

THEY KNEW ABOUT HIM

After four p.m., rested but restless, they set out again as soon as Piero gave the okay. Now they were looking for something, anything, that caught their eyes. No one knew what it would look like, but they'd know it when they saw it.

This time, as they strolled through the Sassi again, they noted the way the shadows fell at different angles now, and stopped from time to time so Piero could talk to other guides.

At one such stop, Piero, who'd been playing the part of their tour guide with an actor's flair, was speaking to the middle-aged woman guiding the group just behind them and noticed something from the corner of his eye. A trained and highly-effective CIA agent, he caught a glimpse of someone he'd noticed before. The man seemed to be following them, though it was difficult to say he did so intentionally, as the group he was with was moving in generally the same direction, and many other people were behind them, also waiting for a temporary blockage to clear.

Something about this man bothered him, though. He'd

stood out when Piero first noticed him. He was convinced he'd seen the man in another context.

He felt the cold shiver between his shoulder blades as recognition kicked in. He'd seen the man's face many times before, all in photos accompanying "wanted" notifications. In countless photos, old, bad, and newer, he'd seen the face of the known assassin from Germany. The guy was wanted by every security agency in Europe.

Piero knew him as Karl Stossel, but no one knew his true name. Rumor had it that he went by several, maybe one for every security agency that had him on their payroll for black ops, while simultaneously pretending to want him brought in. He was credited with dozens of kills, but again, no one knew how many were real and how many were simply thought to be his because of his fearsome reputation. Like Carl the Jackal, he was legendary, and only he knew where reality ended and the legend began.

Politely but quickly, Piero finished his conversation with the other guide and approached Dylan. Under the guise of pointing out an interesting site, he whispered that they should return to the hotel at once.

Dylan began moving the group along more quickly, and Carter caught his urgency. Before long, they were all back in the Devereux suite, and Piero was a changed man. There was no more foppish behavior, and even though he was still dressed like a runway model, he was deadly serious as he described who he'd seen.

"I don't like it," Piero stated flatly. Like most people in his profession, he hated coincidences. Especially those that brought highly-sought targets and one of the world's most deadly and elusive assassins to the same small town in Italy at the same time.

"I don't either," Dylan said after hearing Piero out. He

could now appreciate why Piero worked for the CIA and why Bill had sent him to help them. Despite appearances, Piero knew what he was doing.

Matera wasn't a known holiday destination for assassins. *Do assassins take holidays?* Dylan didn't know, but he wasn't about to second-guess their new friend when it came to the German. In fact, he'd never second-guess him again. Sure, Piero's style was different from the no-nonsense Dylan was used to, but he'd proven himself worthy of respect. Dylan hoped Piero would help back him up when he made his next suggestion.

Dylan drew a deep breath. This was going to take some persuasion. He opened his mouth to say they should all get on the plane and get out of there. It was that or take the assassin out so they could stay and complete their mission. He liked the Devereuxs' odds better with the first idea.

Before he could get any of it said, Carter interrupted. "Don't say it. I know what you're going to suggest, Dylan, and I don't want to hear it. We came here to do a job, and I need to finish it. I'm not running away. But I do want you to get Mackenzie out of here and to safety. Then get back here, and we'll go after this killer."

Dylan didn't have a chance to respond to that, either, before Mackenzie unleashed her famous temper.

"Carter Devereux, don't you dare try to send me away if you're staying. I'm not a piece of luggage or furniture you can just shove out of your way. This is as much my fight as yours, and I'm not going anywhere." She stood with her hands on her hips, her hair almost glowing with the heat of her argument, and a look on her face that would have felled an average man.

"Mackie, no. What about the kids? They need you," Carter began.

The rest of the party looked on in awe as they saw for the first time ever just how forceful Mackenzie could be.

Piero was lost in admiration. *What a magnificent woman!*

"They are *our* children. They need you as well. This is not the first time I've told you we must stay and fight these monsters. *We*, not you. My vote is to stay here and finish our mission. We've been running from these people far too long. But if I must go, you're going with me. Final answer." Mackenzie visibly fought back the tears that sometimes came when she was overcome with anger.

Dylan hesitated to get in the middle of it. But *his* mission orders were to protect the Devereuxs and make sure they made it back to the US alive.

"Carter, Mackenzie, in this case, I think discretion is the better part of valor. It's admirable that you want to deal with that killer and whoever sent him yourselves, but this isn't the time or place for heroics. You're needed elsewhere, and may I remind you, it isn't just your kids who need you. Your country needs you, too." He stopped abruptly when he saw both Devereuxs were glaring at him.

Piero tried to calm the storm. "I'm here to support whatever decision you make. But if I get the slightest opportunity to take the assassin out, that's what I'm going to do. It isn't just you I'm sworn to protect. This man is a menace. Europe and the world will be safer with him gone."

The argument went on for a few minutes longer, but Dylan finally realized he was getting nowhere. Carter was adamant he'd stay and finish what he came to do. Mackenzie was immovable in her stance that if Carter stayed, she was staying too. And with Piero eager to take the rare chance to eliminate a prolific and notorious killer, Dylan was frankly outnumbered. Even his own men, according his interpretation of their body language, were leaning toward helping Piero.

In the end, they agreed to make a stand. And they did have the advantage in having spotted the assassin. Therefore, their next task was to form a plan to deal with him so they could then get on with what they'd come to do.

He'd been following them most of the day, they assumed. Piero had seen him twice, and the second time the assassin had been staring directly at their group. Cocky bastard. *He must think he's invincible.*

Dylan pointed out that Stossel would probably recognize any of them and even knew where they were staying.

Dylan hated the plan Carter put forward, although it made some sense. Carter and Mackenzie were the targets. Had to be. None of the rest of them were high-profile. Therefore, Carter suggested he be the bait. Mackenzie was having none of it and insisted she be with him. The two of them would lead the guy into a trap in a relatively secluded area, and the rest would summarily deal with him before he could harm them.

It was the last part that gave Dylan heartburn. It would require split-second timing. This kind of assignment usually relied on the killer making the kill quickly, almost always from a safe distance, and then getting away without being seen or caught.

The only advantage they had was the assumption that Stossel didn't know they knew about him.

Chapter Sixty-Four

EXCURSION TO SAN PIETRO CAVEOSO

Piero knew the area well and suggested the church of San Pietro Caveoso, the only church in the Sassi district not carved into the rock. With the help of online maps and many photos, he showed them where he thought they could pull off a plan that wouldn't expose Carter and Mackenzie to unnecessary danger while luring Stossel into a trap.

Piero put his flamboyant personality on like a uniform, transforming before the eyes of the team into the man they'd thought he was when they first met him.

Dylan shook his head. The guy was a chameleon, and what a useful trick that would be! Piero winked at him on his way out the door.

At the concierge desk, Piero made quite a scene as he flirted with the woman behind the desk and booked tickets for his party to tour the church the next morning. By the time he was done, the young lady was flushed with embarrassment at the attention of everyone in the lobby. Not a soul within yards was unaware Piero would be taking his clients to the church the next day and at what time.

May 7

A few hours before the others left, Dylan and Conrad, his ex-Delta Force operative, went to the site and took up well-concealed positions. The rest of the Devereux party was due while it was still early, as they wanted a few other tourists around for better cover but didn't want a big crowd in harm's way.

A few hours later, the rest of the party arrived. Dylan observed with relief that Carter and Mackenzie were on alert. Their casual stances didn't fool him. He knew what to look for because he'd overseen their training. They could take care of themselves, though they weren't as highly trained as the rest of his crew. Nevertheless, he hoped it wouldn't be necessary.

Piero and the other two operatives were also alert. Even the CIA pilot had been drawn into this operation, because the more watchful eyes, the better. They were all tense, but trained not to show it. Dylan felt it himself—that itching between the shoulder blades, the instinct that was the difference between a sniper's bullet finding its mark and living to make it home.

Thus far, all of them had made it home, every time. And that was exactly how Dylan wanted to keep it.

The larger group had been in the church only a few minutes when Dylan signaled Conrad and cast his eyes in the direction of a new group that had just come in. Kurt Stossel was with them, hanging back a bit and drifting ever more slowly behind them, pretending to be engrossed in some feature on the walls.

When Stossel came to a door and started to push it open

with a slight squeak, Dylan seized his chance to close the gap between them and shoved him all the way into the room.

He had his Glock G43 pushed hard into the back of the killer's head. "Don't move, asshole."

"Wie bitte?"

Dylan recognized the German phrase, "What did you say?" but he wasn't in a generous mood. The tension had left him with an excess of adrenaline.

"Listen, you son of a bitch. I know you speak English. One more German word and I pull the trigger. Hands on your head!"

Stossel remained silent, stood still, and slowly raised his hands to his head.

Conrad, providing cover for Dylan, had been following what was said on his earphones and entered the room just as the German placed his hands on his head. Dylan stood slightly to the side so that Conrad could zip-tie him – he kept the gun against the back of Stossel's head.

When Conrad grabbed Stossel's right hand to pull it down behind his back, the German moved and spun around, breaking Conrad's grip. His left hand went for the inside pocket of his jacket but never reached it.

Dylan was ready for him, expecting anything, Stossel hadn't gotten his reputation because he was a patsy. The butt of the Glock 43 in Dylan's right hand hit him between the eyes. His eyes turned up, and he dropped to the floor like a bag of potatoes off the back of a truck.

Dylan and Conrad quickly zip-tied his hands and feet and relieved him of his weapons.

Holy cow! This guy came loaded – literally — ready to kill people, many of them. Under his right arm, in a holster, a Walther PPQ .22. The gun was small, made almost no noise compared to bigger caliber guns, but was lethal at short distances – the ideal assassin close-quarter killing weapon.

In the small of his back, they found a Bersa .380 CC, and in an ankle holster, he had a Gerber Ghoststrike Fixed Blade Knife, with a rubber handle for superior grip and black ceramic coating for minimal reflection.

"Shit! Don't you think we should check to see if he perhaps has a few sticks of dynamite shoved up his ass as well?" Conrad quipped.

"Be my guest," Dylan grinned.

They also checked him for mics and earphones to see if he was in communications with anyone. But no, it looked like he operated alone. He had a cell phone, which they took. They removed the battery so that no one could track its GPS signal. They would study the contents of the phone later.

They stuffed all Stossel's belongings into the small backpack Dylan carried.

Dylan let the rest of the team know via his throat mic they'd neutralized Stossel.

Piero's van was close by, and they wanted to get Stossel into it without anyone noticing or with as little fuss as possible and then out of town.

Piero would get a coded message through to Bill and ask him how he wanted to handle this little distraction. It would probably involve getting Stossel out of Italy and to an undisclosed place where the CIA could have a chat with him.

Everyone sighed in relief, but it was going to be short-lived.

Dylan and Conrad made sure Stossel was still unconscious before they cut the zip ties and propped him up between them. They left the church carrying him like they would a drunk, prepared to explain to anyone who might ask that their friend had fainted, fallen, and hit his head—thus explaining the swelling between his eyes where Dylan had cold-cocked him with his pistol—and they were taking him to a hospital.

However, as they stepped outside, Stossel exploded into action. He kicked Conrad with his right foot and then tried to headbutt Dylan, all the time attempting to wrestle himself out of their grip. He very nearly succeeded before he suddenly went limp again.

Dylan felt a spray of something wet and glanced sideways as he took the sudden dead weight again. In that split second, he saw a gaping hole in the side of Stossel's head.

"Sniper! Take cover!"

He knew the bullet had been meant for either Conrad or himself and must have missed him by less than an inch. The only thing that had saved them was Stossel's timely struggling. He let go of Stossel and hit the deck as Conrad did the same. They rolled in opposite directions, Dylan hearing the thumping sound of another bullet striking the sandstone wall behind them where they'd been standing milliseconds ago. He hadn't heard the report of the gun, though.

"Bastard's got a silencer!" he shouted.

Piero and the rest hadn't reached the scene yet. They were about three yards away from the corner, which would have brought them into the sights of the sniper. He was leading the group when he heard Dylan's shout, stopped, and repeated Dylan's warning.

"Sniper! Take cover!"

He didn't even look back at them. He knew the bodyguards would take care of their charges. He left them there and dashed over the open space to take cover among the few vehicles near the retaining wall. His eyes met with Dylan's. The big man pointed to the rocky outcrop above them to their right, where he was sure the shots came from.

When the two former Secret Service agents heard the shouting, they unceremoniously threw Carter and Mackenzie to the ground and fell on top of them— protecting them with their bodies. But they were not near the danger.

It took the crowd of about fifty people a bit longer to realize what was happening. When they did, chaos erupted in many different languages – *terroristi*! (Italian) *les terrorists*! (French) *terroristen*! (German) terrorists! Everyone was screaming and shouting and running for cover.

This pandemonium gave the Secret Service agents the chance to get off Carter and Mackenzie and pull them to their feet and through a nearby door into the chapel.

Inside, they found a melee, as several panicked tourists had also taken refuge when the screaming and shouting began, and even more poured in from outside. By then, Carter and Mackenzie had their weapons drawn but kept concealed inside their jackets, looking around for more threats, while the former Secret Service agents and Kyle herded them together, backs to them and looking outward, ready to shoot anyone or anything that made a wrong move. Like Carter and Mackenzie, they had their weapons drawn from the shoulder holsters but kept them concealed inside their jackets. They didn't want to scare the tourists by brandishing their guns.

Outside, Dylan, Conrad, and Piero had found better cover and were trying to ascertain the sniper's location.

Piero ventured a peek around the edge of his cover and felt a sting as a bullet grazed his right cheek.

Che cavolo! That was too close for comfort!

Dylan got the idea the sniper must have been getting nervous or was inexperienced. He'd taken that shot too soon. But Piero hadn't given him much lead time, so maybe he was farther away? The angle for any shot from the top of the nearby crag above them was problematic, too. He and Conrad were about five paces apart from each other.

When the sniper fired again at Piero, they heard the soft *whump* of the silenced gun, and both turned their eyes and guns to the spot it came from. They'd never know who spotted him first in the tree above the wall, or if they even did spot him before they fired, instinctively, twice each.

The double-tap shots were so perfectly timed it sounded like only two shots, *one-two*, only a lot louder.

The sniper's lifeless body, a bullet through the right eye and one through the heart, tumbled out of the tree, over the wall, and crashed onto the top of a car parked below.

Inside the church, the people who'd taken refuge heard the shots, the first that weren't silenced, and screamed even louder. Some cowered behind pillars, and others crawled under the benches.

Only Dylan, Conrad, and Piero remained outside.

Carter and Mackenzie had allowed themselves to be herded by their bodyguards into the farthest corner from the door where they'd rushed in earlier. They stood with their backs to the wall, centered between the bodyguards as all faced outward in a semi-circle, ready to fire, desecration of a place of worship or not.

After a few moments, when no more shots were heard outside, people began making cell phone calls. Carter assumed the calls were going to the police or some emergency number like the 9-1-1 number at home.

He gave a brief thought to whether their guns would get them in trouble or not. He thought the gun laws in Italy were like those in the States, but having what were clearly concealed weapons and no license could prove a problem.

Chapter Sixty-Five

THE CLEANUP

Outside, Dylan, Conrad, and Piero were scanning the surroundings, especially above them. Were there more snipers? Nobody wanted to find out by stepping out of cover. But they could hear police sirens in the distance, and they needed to clean up the problems at hand.

Piero hoped the sound of the police sirens would have chased off any other assassins. He shouted to Dylan to help him, and then took a chance and broke cover to run to the car where the dead sniper still decorated the roof. The two men muscled the body off the car.

A quick look showed them two bullet holes. "Well, either you each pumped one into him, or one of you missed twice," he said with a grin.

Conrad had joined them. He and Dylan grinned back. Each knew at least one of his shots had hit the killer—no doubt about it. Either one could have shot the eye out of a rat at fifty paces on a full gallop. Then Conrad noticed the blood streaming down the right side of Piero's face from under the handkerchief Piero had pressed against it.

"Oh, man, you're hit!" he exclaimed, causing Dylan to snap his head up for a look as well.

"Just a scratch," Piero replied. "Look, we've got to move quickly. We've got to hide the weapons. Everyone's. If the *sbirri* see you have them, there'll be a lot of explaining to do. Italian prisons are the pits. You don't want to spend any time there."

"Conrad, you find Carter and Mackenzie and the rest, collect their weapons and your own in your backpack and bring them to the van."

Conrad gave a thumbs-up and hurried away.

Piero turned to Dylan. "Give me your weapon and holster. Let's go." They hid the weapons and cell phone and Stossell's stuff inside a hidden panel of the van. A few moments later, everyone else turned up.

"Quick! Give me the weapons!" They could hear the sirens nearly upon them. Conrad swung the heavy backpack over, and it, too, went into the hidden panel, just before the *polizia* in the first car swerved around the corner.

Mackenzie, who'd spotted the blood-soaked handkerchief Piero held to his face, went into nurse mode, fussing over him and demanding Carter hand over his own handkerchief so she could tend to Piero's wound.

As he handed it to her, Dylan muttered, "It's not serious, but keep that up." Mackenzie winked to show she understood.

A few other people had ventured out of the church by then, but everyone froze as three police cars came to a stop a few feet from the crowd with lights still flashing and a deafening wail from the sirens. Police officers poured out of the cars with weapons drawn, scanning the crowd. Many of the already-frightened tourists threw their hands in the air and kept them there.

The Devereux group stood out—eight people clearly together, one wounded. And the bodyguards looked like exactly what they were. Their stoic faces, the way they were dressed. Even their body language, tense and wary as their eyes continually scanned the terrain above them and the edges of the buildings, gave them away.

Most of the police kept the rest of the crowd gathered but herded them back away from the Devereux group, while two approached Carter and Mackenzie. Standing in the circle of protectors, they were clearly the principle members of the group. In Italian, the senior officer asked, "What happened?"

Everyone in the group, even Carter, who was fluent in Italian but didn't care to expose it yet, looked at Piero. Most of the group didn't know what the officer had asked. Carter was content to listen and follow Piero's lead.

Piero explained that the group were his clients, and he'd brought them to the church on a tour.

"These two," he said, pointing to Dylan and Conrad, "fell behind and saw that man faint and collapse." He pointed to Stossell's body. "They went to help him, and I followed to see what was going on.

"When they came out, someone—I think that man—shot him." Piero indicated the body of the sniper, now laid out on the ground next to the car he'd fallen onto.

"Why is that man dead?" the officer asked.

"When we heard the shot, and saw this man dead, we all took cover. It was a terrorist attack."

Piero was speaking loudly. When the closer edge of the crowd heard him say terrorist, they started buzzing with the word in half a dozen languages.

Even the crowd-control officers started listening more carefully.

"I looked around that car, where I was hiding, and he shot at me and hit me in the face." Piero took Carter's handkerchief away from his face and everyone got a look at the wound for the first time.

Even Mackenzie hadn't seen it clearly when she'd swapped Carter's linen for Piero's. She gasped. The wound was definitely more than a scratch.

Piero continued. "I shot back in self-defense in the direction from where the shot had come. Two shots. He fell out of the tree and landed on the roof of that car and then rolled off onto the ground.

"These people," he continued, gesturing to the crowd and to Carter, Mackenzie, and the rest of the group, "took refuge in the church, and they came out a few minutes ago. None of them could have seen what happened out here."

"Stay here," the officer ordered. He went to his car to call the ambulance that all was clear, and it could approach.

The ambulance and paramedics had been hanging back by about a mile at the direction of the police, who didn't want them in harm's way if the shooter was still active. Given the all-clear, they moved in fast.

Two paramedics first confirmed that both bodies on the ground were dead, while another attended to Piero's wound. "That's going to scar," he told Piero, who shrugged.

Meanwhile, the police were now making sure no one else in the crowd was injured. A few were badly shaken, but there were remarkably, considering the panic earlier, no injuries. Everyone was told they weren't allowed to leave until they'd given their statements, and that required that translators or bilingual officers be brought in.

Mackenzie had a twinge of guilt that so many people were inconvenienced, but at least they hadn't been harmed. And the world, minus two killers, was a safer place.

After hours of questioning, the police were frustrated. The tourists' stories ranged from seeing masked gunmen who shouted *Allahu akbar* before opening fire with automatic weapons to "I saw nothing. May I go now?"

The most convincing story was the one from their wounded countryman, Piero Rossi. His version at least matched the evidence at the scene.

One or two of the police eyed the distance between the car Rossi had taken refuge behind to the tree from which the gunman had allegedly fallen and speculated that Piero was either a very good marksman or a very lucky one. The wound on Piero's face led them to conclude it was the latter.

That the shooting was in self-defense was not in question. What *was* in question was why was Rossi armed, was he licensed to carry a concealed weapon, and was his firearm licensed to him?

The investigating officer voiced those questions in a tone that didn't leave room for argument.

"To protect my clients, of course. You can see from this incident that it is necessary to carry a gun. Think of all the terrorist attacks in Europe. Not to mention common criminals who think nothing of mugging wealthy tourists.

"As to my authority to carry, check my registrations. All are in order."

Within an hour, it was confirmed. Rossi was who and what he said he was, and the licenses checked out. After taking his contact details and those of his clients, the officers allowed them all to go.

"Don't leave Matera, though, until we say. There may be more questions."

Carter and Mackenzie exchanged worried glances when Piero translated that order. They were due back in the States in only a few days. Meanwhile, they still had a job to do. They'd cross the bridge when they came to it, if the matter of leaving hadn't been cleared up by the time they were due to leave.

Piero was allowed to go with his group, but with the admonition from the paramedics that he should go to an emergency department to have his face stitched and dressed properly.

Chapter Sixty-Six

I, TOO, LOVE DOLPHINS

Dylan drove the van to the hospital at Piero's direction. On the way, Carter regaled the others with Piero's enhanced version of the sequence of events.

Dylan and Conrad ribbed Piero about taking credit for their kill, but it was good-natured. He was rising in their esteem. His quick wit had saved them from a tight spot.

At the hospital, an old and experienced nurse tended Piero's wound, cleaning and stitching it up, all while he flirted with her outrageously. He did experience a fit of temper when she insisted on shaving his beard off, though, and again when she handed him a mirror.

Piero was going to sport an ugly scar on his face for the rest of his life. Lucky or not, the graze on his cheek pissed him off when he viewed the nurse's handiwork. He'd liked his face the way it was, and so did the ladies—he liked to believe. Hmm. Maybe he could tell the story in such a way that the ladies would think him a hero? He had a good version already.

He pretended to be offended when the others subjected

him to a barrage of jokes. But he was truly pleased. In the way of men everywhere, they showed their acceptance by joking inappropriately about him and the incident. It meant he was one of them now, and a better group to be part of he couldn't name. It improved his mood, and he began joking back.

"That was a face only a mother could love in the first place," Conrad said. "Now you'll have to wear a bag over your head when you see her."

"I'll wear the bag when I visit *your* mother again," Piero returned.

The others roared and slapped him on the back. Conrad had to shake his head and grin. He'd heard worse in the Army.

The nurse, Paloma Festa, didn't speak English. She questioned Piero. "Why are your friends laughing and pointing at your wound?" she asked. When he translated, and explained, she laughed so hard she had to wipe tears from her eyes.

Before discharging Piero from her care, Paloma asked if the group were enjoying Matera. "Except, of course, being shot at by some lunatic." She went on at length about how upset she was by the violence in the town of her birth and where her ancestors had been living since time immemorial. "I have never seen such violence as this. Never a terrorist attack!"

Carter, who'd dropped his pretense of not understanding Italian, had been participating in the conversation. When he heard she was a local, he began to steer the conversation to sights they'd seen, and especially the dolphin pentagon.

"My wife loves dolphins," he explained. "They are truly special to her. Have you seen this carving?"

"Yes, many times. It is near my home. Where I grew up, I mean."

"It seemed almost out of place. Do you know what it means? Where did it come from?" he asked.

She shrugged. "It is just there. It's been there since long before I was born. I don't know if it means anything. No one has ever told me if it does."

"Have you ever seen other dolphin carvings like it anywhere in the Basilicata?"

"No others like it, with the five dolphins in a ring," she answered. "But I have seen a few images of single dolphins etched into the rocks around Matera. I, too, love dolphins."

Carter translated for Mackenzie, and within minutes she and the nurse were talking like old friends about their mutual love of the sea mammals. Carter and Piero had a hard time keeping up with the translation as the two women chattered.

In the end, Paloma had to attend to other patients, but she said this was her last shift before her three days off. She offered to take them on a tour of the area where she grew up and show them the dolphin petroglyphs.

Mackenzie offered to pay her, but Paloma wouldn't hear of it.

"As a Professional Nurse, I make a very good salary. Even after taxes, the average salary for my profession is the US equivalent of over $1,500 per month, and in Matera, my salary is above average."

It was indeed a handsome salary for the area, Mackenzie knew. Still, she persisted. "I think we should give you €750 for giving up a day of your off time."

When Paloma continued to protest, Carter stepped in. "Listen, Paloma, Romeo here," pointing to Piero, "charges us €750 a day—he is going to be a client on this tour so he will not be paid—or do you prefer we give it to this women-chaser?"

That settled it. Piero, aka Romeo, had showed her his true colors as he flirted. She laughed at him as she accepted the deal.

Piero played along, giving an exaggerated pout when he heard the lie that he wouldn't be paid. But his wink showed he would be a good sport about his new nickname. Even though the older woman wasn't the vision he'd want in his bed in the morning, he never failed to flirt with any woman he met, young or old.

It paid to keep his skills sharp, and it never hurt to have an old woman on your side.

Chapter Sixty-Seven

THEY WOULDN'T HIDE

Back in the hotel room, Mackenzie declared herself too rattled to be seen in a public restaurant. Dylan said it was just as well, as innocent bystanders would be in jeopardy if there were other assassins out there.

Mackenzie exclaimed, "Others! You think there are more?"

"We were taken by surprise that Karl Stossel had an accomplice. That didn't fit his usual MO based on what Piero told us about him. We can't afford to take the chance, anyway." Dylan said.

Carter agreed. "But I think we'll be okay on our tour with Paloma. It promises to be not only private, with no chance of someone having overheard our plans, but also it sounds as if it's not on the regular tourist routes."

Conrad had been tasked with ordering room service, but he came back with a bemused expression just then. "The manager heard about what happened today. He's sending up a complimentary dinner for us. He wouldn't let me order. Said it would be the dinner of a lifetime."

Piero replied, "You are in for a treat, then. The food of Southern Italy resembles not at all the food you Americans think of as Italian. It is a blend—your television chefs would call it a fusion—of all the other cultures that have influenced this region. Greek, Arabic... just wait, you will see!"

"My mouth is watering already," Carter said. "I suggest we relax until it arrives and collect our nerves. We can discuss our next moves over dinner."

The feast was just that, with a celery-based soup to begin, a main dish of succulent *pollo al mattone*, which Piero translated as "chicken cooked under a brick", and *ciamotta*, or mixed-vegetable stew. Since there were so many of them, the manager had also supplied a casserole of mussels and rice with vegetables. Finally, a dessert plate of fresh fruits and aged cheeses.

They were so busy eating and exclaiming over the flavorful dishes, they barely got any discussion in before they pushed away their plates and claimed they were stuffed.

However, the discussion was too important to put off until morning.

It was fortunate they'd found a local guide who could shorten their search for what Dylan had suggested might be like breadcrumbs leading them to some great discovery.

However, the fact that they were told they couldn't leave Matera until the police said they could was of concern. What would they do if it wasn't settled before they needed to show up for the hearings in Washington?

In the end, they decided it was above their pay grade. If it looked like they'd be detained longer, perhaps diplomatic channels would be an option.

They still hoped to find the Nabatean library before they returned. Stossel and his companion's appearance on the scene had cost them more than a day already.

If they found the library, getting it out of Italy was another can of worms, but that, too, depended on whether they actually found it before they had to return.

The question of more assassins, though Mackenzie shuddered every time it was brought up, remained an issue. But short of locking themselves in their hotel rooms for the rest of their time in Matera, or go home earlier, there was nothing to be done except to take care. That's why the bodyguards were with them. The incident that morning only confirmed what they'd known all along—it was a risky mission.

Getting the library, if it existed, was crucial in their battle against the Nabateans. Until they prevailed, there would never be a time when they could stop looking over their shoulders. Therefore, it was settled.

They'd be vigilant, but they wouldn't hide.

Chapter Sixty-Eight

THE LATTER COULD GET HER KILLED

Mathieu Nabati had reached the end of his rope.

When he learned what had happened in Matera, he burst into tears of frustration and rage. Had there been anyone to witness it, his contorted face, teeth bared, and shouted growls of hatred would have made them believe he'd gone insane.

The remaining assassin was just as enraged but for a different reason. The woman, as lethal as the late Karl Stossel but much younger, had never been so insulted when she realized there were others with the same target.

Half Brazilian, half Asian, a smoking-hot beauty in her mid-thirties, she'd never been burdened with the emotion of a normal woman. In fact, she was a stone-cold sociopath, and she'd never failed in her contracts before.

She'd worked for this client before but had never met him, or them. She knew nothing, other than she'd always been paid well and had no way to contact the client if anything went wrong.

As far as she knew, she'd always been given an exclusive contract. Never before had there been interference such as the morning's disaster.

She'd been reconnoitering the area and studying her targets as part of a group of tourists at the church. She wasn't planning on making the kills that day, when the events unfolded like a train wreck.

First Stossel, whom she recognized, went down with a bullet in the head.

The men with him reacted with admirable speed and professionalism—special forces, no doubt. And then more shots were fired, and the result was a sniper tumbling from a tree like rotten fruit.

It didn't escape her that when the trouble started, her primary targets, the Devereuxs, were immediately shielded by their bodyguards, professionals no doubt.

Her preparations always made her one hundred percent effective. She wouldn't have botched the mission. And now she knew what she was up against. Normally that would have given her an advantage.

But now she was pissed off.

Her client must not have trusted her to accomplish it on her own, and that was unacceptable.

His distrust had made her job almost impossibly difficult. The quarry was now alerted.

And if it wasn't a trust issue, it was stupidity. Didn't her client know the adage "too many cooks spoil the broth"?

Whether distrust or stupidity, she didn't like either option. She now had to decide—stay and try to salvage the operation, or strategically withdraw?

It didn't take long for the answer to come to her. She wouldn't work for a client who didn't trust her, and even more revolting was working for a stupid client. The latter could get her killed.

She started packing her bags.

Chapter Sixty-Nine

ON THE DOLPHIN TRAIL

May 8

The day promised to be a long one, especially if the dolphin trail, as Carter began calling it, led to anything interesting that required further exploration. After a very early breakfast—complete with cappuccino—the whole crew set out in Piero's van to pick up Paloma.

With Piero driving, the front passenger seat was reserved for Paloma as their tour guide for the day. Piero showed her how to use the built-in sound system and microphone to send her voice throughout the luxury vehicle. She turned in the seat and spoke into the microphone so everyone could hear her answers to Carter's and Mackenzie's questions.

At his suggestion, she started with a review of the history of the area. The team had been immersed in it for several days, and Carter for even longer. But hearing it from the perspective of a native whose ancestors spanned many generations of locals gave them a different and very interesting angle.

None of them had thought of the town as a fortress before.

Thinking about it as it must have looked from the Gravina River valley below, it would indeed look like a fortress, with the *grotto*, or caves, occupying row after row of a towering limestone cliff. Even in ancient times, they had been farther hollowed out, the entrances fortified with brick or mud walls. They'd walked among them in the Stassi, some now abandoned, some modernized and utilized as residences for a young, hip, new citizenry or for stores, museums, and the like.

Carter was almost salivating with the desire to excavate some treasures of his own discovery as Paloma described the remains of a one hundred fifty-thousand-year-old hominid, or tools and bones from ten thousand years ago.

Matera had already been a significant settlement in the Bronze Age and had been continuously occupied ever since. She described one dig from early in the previous century that had uncovered layers from early Christians, Saracens, the Byzantine Empire, Greeks, Romans, and even ceramics from three thousand years before. Layers of civilizations on top of each other like a lasagna.

Carter sat forward, so fascinated by Paloma's narrative he forgot to translate for the others who were listening. "Did your family ever live in the Sassi, Paloma?"

She glanced at Piero beside her and took a deep breath. "We don't like to talk of those times," she said. "But I will tell you.

"When I was a little girl, maybe ten years old, my family was evicted from our *grotta*. It was in 1959. The conditions then…, they were not as you see them now. Everyone was poor, and the caves had little in the way of modern conveniences.

"The government cleaned out the Sassi and moved everyone out."

Mackenzie leaned forward and rested her hand on Paloma's arm. "I'm sorry remembering makes you sad."

After Carter translated, Paloma said, "Not sad. Ashamed. Conditions were so primitive! We lived like savages. Our animals, even a pig! They all lived in the cave with us."

Carter tried to comfort her. "Some Americans keep pet pigs. I wouldn't be ashamed if I were you."

"Many of us are," she admitted.

Piero broke in with a flood of Italian Carter couldn't even follow, and Paloma answered. Piero took the next turn, and then several more as Paloma paid close attention to their surroundings.

While her attention was otherwise occupied, Carter contented himself with watching the old city as they passed by ancient buildings still in use. He wondered if either of his and Mackie's children would find an interest in archaeology one day. Liam was almost old enough to be taken on his first dig.

Another flurry of Italian questions and responses from the front seat culminated in the van coming to a stop at the edge of a belvedere, where Paloma said they'd have to go down a flight of stairs carved into the limestone to see the dolphin. Carter translated and then opened the van door and gallantly helped his wife out. The others piled out as well, following Paloma down the uneven steps. Piero stayed close to her, his arm outstretched to catch her should she stumble. But she skipped down the steps like a young girl and beamed as she pointed out the dolphin.

Mackenzie played her part like a pro, exclaiming over the "sweet" petroglyph, asking the others to take her picture, and distracting Paloma while Kyle took a GPS reading. After fifteen minutes or so, she had Carter ask Paloma how many more she knew of.

"Quattro."

Even the non-Italian speakers understood. Four more.

Carter caught Mackenzie's eye and raised an eyebrow. She responded with a broad smile. They didn't have to say anything to know they were both thinking the same thing. Five dolphins on each of the petroglyphs they'd seen in Petra, Petras, and now in the Sassi.

This was the first of five single dolphins. Could there be a connection? Carter had learned from Sean and Dylan to distrust coincidences. But this could very well be a happy one.

Paloma watched the group, and how they interacted around the petroglyph, with interest. The redhaired lady, her new friend, was most excited. She and her husband took many pictures and spoke in whispers. Wherever they walked, three of the others walked close by and usually scattered around them, but close.

Others had come right on her heels, before the married couple, looking from side to side and forward as if they expected a threat. One had an instrument of some kind that he held up briefly to the petroglyph while Mackenzie was talking to her, and two more never approached the 'glyph but looked back frequently along the way they'd come.

Paloma asked Piero, "Who are all these people? Why are they acting this way? Are some of your clients uninterested in the site?"

"The lady and her husband, Carter, are very rich. They always travel with bodyguards. Understandably, the incident yesterday shook them up—they're just extra-vigilant."

"They're nice people. I like them." She smiled.

When they were finished examining the first carving, she led them to the next, and then the third, with a stop on the way for espresso and arancini.

Piero told the amused Paloma that his guests had fallen in love with the delicacy on the first day of their visit and now demanded it every few hours. "It is fortunate that your tour includes much descending and climbing, or my clients may return to America much fatter than before."

Paloma giggled and took the arm he offered as she led the way to the next dolphin.

After the third dolphin, on their way to the fourth, she suggested they explore a rupestrian church near an interesting modern artifact.

The church, she explained, was a delight of Byzantine frescoes painted directly on the rock walls of the underground chapel. It was worth seeing, and the fourth dolphin was nearby. As she led the way, the group was astonished to see an enormous railroad bridge that connected to nothing at all towering above it.

Paloma explained the bridge was part of a failed attempt to link Matera to the main national railway lines.

"More amazing," she said, "was that this church was completely forgotten during the Second World War and when the government removed the population from the Sassi in the 1950s and 1960s, except for rumors.

"As you can see, it is not very noticeable from the road. Monks lived here twelve hundred years ago and did not want to be disturbed. It has only more recently been rediscovered and restored. I think you will enjoy the artwork."

Indeed, they did. Images of the Holy Family and St. Peter were warm and inviting. St. Peter had a beard and mustache, like a Levantine patriarch.

Mary was depicted less as a saint and more as a mother, her baby in her arms.

A naked and curvy Eve held out a fruit to an equally naked Adam, but it wasn't the usual apple. Instead, it was a wonderfully suggestive fig.

Paloma told them this fresco was the reason for the site's name—The Crypt of Original Sin.

A riot of flowers connected one painting to the next in style.

Mackenzie looked around for signs prohibiting the taking of pictures but didn't find any, and she took plenty of photos before Paloma led them outside and down a steep path to a small cave in the cliff.

It was in deplorable condition. The ancient engravings had been defaced by modern graffiti. Despite the vandalism, somehow the dolphin was still intact.

The group went through their usual photos and GPS readings ritual here, but there was not much else to see. After climbing back to the level of the Crypt of Original Sin, everyone agreed it was time for lunch and persuaded Paloma to let them eat before she showed them the fifth and last dolphin.

After dining on more Southern Italian delicacies, they finished the tour with the fifth dolphin.

It had been a tiring but stimulating day when they dropped Paloma off at her home around four p.m. Before leaving Paloma, Mackenzie extended an invitation for her and her husband to join them for dinner at their hotel later that night.

At first, Paloma protested that it was too expensive and she couldn't accept such a lavish gift on top of what they'd paid her. Though she and her husband had been inside the hotel, they had never been able to afford the luxury of having a meal there.

"Then you must *certainly* dine with us. Our treat, of course. You have been more than kind to show us your marvelous dolphins and that church of Original Sin. Please say you'll come!"

Mackenzie could be very persuasive. Eventually Paloma accepted the invitation with a blush.

"My husband will think we won the lottery!" she added. "Thank you."

Chapter Seventy

THE DOLPHIN PENTAGON OF MATERA

Though the rest of the town was just coming back to life, after the siesta, Carter, Mackenzie, and their team were ready for hot showers after wandering through the dusty and warm streets and hillsides all day.

They had about four hours to kill before dinner, so after freshening up, they all met again in the Devereux suite to determine if they'd learned anything.

It didn't take long to determine there was indeed a connection between the single dolphins they'd seen that day and the pentagons. All Carter had to do was plot the locations on a map of the city. The array looked very familiar, and connecting the dots with lines confirmed it. The single dolphins made a pentagon, too. But what was the significance?

"Does that mean we have five places to dig?" Dylan asked.

Carter was looking from photo to photo, not only the singles, but also the three dolphin pentagons they'd seen in three different parts of the world. Something was trying to catch his attention, but he couldn't quite get it. And then he did.

On a sheet of paper, he drew two pentagons. In the first, he sketched the original three dolphin pentagons, with the dolphins swimming nose to tail in a clockwise direction. In the second, he put arrows in, representing the direction of the dolphins as they were depicted in the petroglyphs they'd seen earlier in the day. Starting at the bottom, he drew a clockwise arrow for dolphin number one, and continued until he reached dolphin number four. That arrow had to go counter-clockwise.

"Swimming upstream," he muttered. He put in the fifth dolphin, and then began to grin. "It's the only one that doesn't follow the pattern," he said, looking at the drawing instead of the people in the room.

It caught Mackenzie's attention, and then Dylan's, who was talking to Piero about something. They all drifted over to the table where Carter was working.

"What are the chances that is a coincidence? Meaning nothing?" Carter asked, pointing to the widdershins arrow, representing the dolphin petroglyph in the cave at The Crypt of Original Sin.

"No chance in hell," Dylan breathed.

Mackenzie nodded. "I'd have said very little, but I like Dylan's answer better."

"We've got to go back there. Preferably late at night. What we might have to do wouldn't be smart during the day," Carter said with satisfaction.

"Have to be really careful," Dylan added. "If we were seen today…"

"That would mean we're still being followed," Piero finished.

They spent the rest of the early evening planning the

expedition and gathering supplies before they met with Paloma Festa and her husband in the hotel restaurant.

The rest of the team took shifts, half eating at tables scattered near Carter and Mackenzie, and the other half keeping discreet watch from elsewhere in the hotel—making turns so that everyone could enjoy the elaborate four-course meal.

Carter and Mackenzie managed to contain their excitement while they entertained the Festas. Or rather, the Festas entertained them with more stories about Matera, the Basilicata region, and the changes they'd seen in the last forty or fifty years.

Mackenzie promised to stay in touch with Paloma by email before the Festas left with many thanks and smiles.

They were gone by ten thirty.

Chapter Seventy-One

THE CRYPT OF ORIGINAL SIN

After that, it was a matter of an hour or so before Dylan deemed the night quiet enough for their expedition. They made their way to the Crypt of Original Sin, and then took great care on the path down to the cave where the fourth dolphin was found.

Inside that cave, most of the party hung back, providing light when asked, but otherwise staying out of Carter's way as he studied the dolphin, peered closely at the other carvings, and finally dropped to his knees to examine the floor.

When he found it, he marveled at how easily he might have missed it if not for the handheld, ground-penetrating radar Kyle retrieved from the plane late that afternoon, and his extra-powerful tactical flashlight.

The GPR unit was originally designed for locating voids under concrete, along with metal objects and cables. It was capable of detecting targets up to twenty inches in depth and displaying them on a built-in digital screen.

In a wall and near the floor, he found a hairline crack. Following it produced an outline on the display about two feet square. The GPR showed the stone to be less than twenty inches thick with a void behind it. It could have been a tunnel, but the GPR wasn't powerful enough to say how far back it went. The only thing it proved was there was a stone inside the area outlined by the crack with an empty space behind it.

However, the seam was too narrow for a tool or even a thin knife blade to penetrate the crack.

"There must be some way to get it out," Dylan said, frustrated.

"Look for a lever," Carter answered, already running his fingers over the surface of the rock wall around the crack."

"You mean like Indiana Jones? That kind of a trigger? What if it brings the walls down on us?" Dylan responded nervously.

"You watch too many movies," Carter mumbled. "But yes, something like that. You'll know it when you see it."

Mackenzie was examining a section of the wall that had an unusually dense batch of graffiti on it. "Carter, look over here. This part of the rock doesn't look right."

Carter joined her and moved the beam of his flashlight to the section she indicated. "Roman concrete," he said. "It's like Paloma was telling us today. The modern has overlaid the ancient everywhere in the city."

"If you could call Roman cement modern," Mackenzie contributed. On their recent vacation, Carter had explained to her how the material allowed the two thousand-year-old buildings of the country to stand into the present day.

"What's Roman cement?" Dylan asked.

"Special recipe," Carter said absently. He was examining the extent of the addition to the wall. "Made with volcanic sand. Bonds with the limestone in a way that prevents cracks from spreading." He looked up. "I think this is here to hide something even older."

"Kyle, do we have anything that will penetrate that?" he asked. "Nothing drastic. I want to see what's behind it. A small hole will do."

"I've got a drill and a cement bit," Kyle said. "I thought the bit might work on rock, too."

"Let's try it." Carter thought the stronger mixture might foil the cement drill, but it turned out Kyle had brought one with a diamond tip, and it made short work of the two inches of Roman cement that plugged the hole.

Dylan supplied the device to look inside, a tiny camera on a USB cable he'd had modified to use a mini-USB connection with his cell phone. Mackenzie and Carter watched the view from the phone's camera lens as Dylan threaded the cable through the small hole.

When the camera approached the end of the tube, and just before it would have flopped over, Carter spotted a lever behind the concrete plug. "Stop!" he shouted. Dylan froze.

"The trigger's in there, I'm sure of it," Carter said.

They worked feverishly to figure out how to pull the lever without completely destroying the covering and finally managed with an ingenious lasso on the end of a wire they cannibalized from the USB cable.

"That was $10 on eBay," grumbled Dylan. "Plus the modifications."

"I'll buy you a new one," Carter said, laughing. "Hell, I'll buy you a dozen. Give it a pull."

Amazingly, when the lever was pulled, it did remind everyone of an Indiana Jones movie. With a groan, the stone plugging the tunnel receded into the rock wall and disappeared.

"I'll be damned," said Dylan.

"Stay here. I'm going in to see what's back there." Carter was speaking to the entire group, and some of them were grateful to be left behind. All but Kyle were trained to ignore claustrophobic feelings, but that didn't mean they liked crawling through small tunnels, especially one that had been engineered at the dawn of history.

Mackenzie refused to be left behind, though. "I'm going, too."

"Honey—" he started.

Dylan interrupted. "Me, too. Let Mackenzie come. If it doesn't cave in on you or me, it surely won't on her, either."

"Good point," Carter said. He didn't have claustrophobia under most circumstances. An archaeologist couldn't afford to, but he'd never had the problem in the first place. And Dylan was twice Mackenzie's size. "All right. Me first, then Dylan, then Mackenzie. You can come if you want to. Chances are if it leads to a dead end, we'll all have to back out. The tunnel isn't big enough to turn around in."

Carter got on hands and knees, then slithered on his belly, "swimming" through the passage with relative ease. The rock below was padded with a good amount of sand, which allowed him to pull himself through with hands pressing sideways and backward on the rock walls and pushing with his toes. He could hear the others behind him but couldn't turn far enough to see them.

He'd crawled perhaps five times his body length when the end of the passage opened into a chamber, and he could stand.

He scrambled out of the tunnel and stood, sending the beam of his flashlight above and around him to discover a cave about the same size as the one they'd come from. Dylan and Mackenzie crawled out, too, and stood waiting for Carter to decide what to do.

His flashlight crossed what looked like an empty space, or perhaps a deep shadow.

"Carter, what's that?" Mackenzie said, pointing.

On closer inspection, Carter discovered a passage, which wound around behind a rock and kept going. For another hour, the trio followed openings from one underground room to another, sometimes crawling or squeezing through tight spots.

When they came to the dead-end, it was a shock.

Before them stood another stone door. This one was large enough to admit the three of them walking abreast, but it was firmly closed. Encouraged by the success of the last search for a trigger, they fanned out and found this one in short order. It hadn't been disguised, but it was massive. But it operated with surprising ease. Dylan pulled it with little effort, and the massive stone in front of them slowly slid sideways.

Mackenzie was the first to see what was behind it and gasped in shock.

The others turned from their task to see a colossal room, the ceiling more than twice as high as the cave in which they stood. Inside were rows of shelving, in their flashlights it seemed like hundreds of them, stretching from floor to ceiling. And on every shelf were stacked dozens of what looked like copper cylinders. Carter couldn't even venture a guess at how many there were.

For several minutes, they were speechless with awe, each remembering a different event that had made them feel the same.

Mackenzie remembered sitting with Carter in that cave in Cusco many years ago. She and Carter hadn't even been engaged then, but it may have been when she began to love him. Looking at that thirty thousand-year-old city inside a mountain in Peru, the Golden Garden of the Incas, with Carter and his grandfather, Will, had been like peering into Heaven. This came close, though there was no gold.

Dylan remembered his first sight of the city of the Giants underwater in the Alboran Sea.

Carter was remembering his grandpa Will, the man who had instilled in him the love of archaeology from an early age. He looked up, imagining the stars that would have been visible if they hadn't been dozens or hundreds of feet below ground. He'd lost track of the direction half a dozen turns ago. For all he knew, they were directly under the center of Matera. "I hope you can see this, Grandpa," he said softly.

Mackenzie heard him. She moved to his side, put her arms around his waist, and looked up at him. "He does, Carter. He's looking at it with you, right now."

They moved farther inside the room and came to an open spot that could have been the center. There they found a table carved from the cave rock, and on it were a few of the cylinders, one open. Gingerly, Carter slipped a coil of thin copper out of the cylinder and spread it out. He saw writing etched in the surface. At least it wasn't nano dots…

He recognized the writing as cuneiform, an ancient form of Semitic and very similar to the Giants' language. He could even read most of it, with his knowledge of Arabic, Semitic, and the Giants' language. His hope was to confirm this was the long-lost Nabatean library, but he was looking for something to confirm it.

After a few minutes, he found what he was looking for.

Silently, he read the passage, piecing together from what he could read the parts he wasn't sure of.

The Nabatean Secret

I, Rabbel Il Soter, King of the Nabatean people, commission the construction of a library to hold our ancient secrets. This knowledge must be preserved, and it must be hidden from the Romans who will force us to become part of their Empire very soon.

"And they did," Carter said aloud.

"What?" Mackenzie and Dylan asked in unison.

Carter realized then that Mackenzie and Dylan were staring at him. He read the passage to them and went on to explain.

"In 106 AD, shortly after Rabbel Il Soter died, the Roman emperor, Trajan, annexed the Nabatean kingdom without a battle. History has always wondered why the Nabateans didn't resist. This record shows that the last king of Nabatea predicted that to happen and commissioned this library to hold their knowledge in secret. His prediction came true. The Romans did force the Nabateans to become part of their empire, but the Nabateans expected it and ceded without losing their people to war. Pretty smart. They remained free, unlike some of the Romans' conquests, and eventually most were assimilated into Roman culture."

Dylan and Mackenzie exchanged glances. Carter seemed almost too calm if...

Mackenzie put her hand on Carter's shoulder. "Then, is this...?" She hardly dared finish her question.

Carter looked up at her, unshed tears glimmering in the unsteady light. "Yes, Mackie. This is the library of the Nabateans!" Speaking it aloud broke his shock, and he leaped to his feet, hugging Mackenzie and dancing her around with joy. "We've done it! We've found the secrets of the Nabateans! We can beat them once and for all now!"

Mackenzie was no less excited, and she did shed tears of joy as Carter whirled around with her. Dylan felt like dancing a jig, too. But soon Carter sobered. "Let's see if this is all of it."

Dylan moved to the door and began circling the outer walls for another exit, while Carter and Mackenzie, hand in hand, moved in the opposite direction. Dylan found it first—a passageway that led into another large, domed cave with more shelves and tightly-stacked cylinders. "Here!" he yelled. "I've found another one!"

They'd been gone from the outer cave for over an hour now, so rather than examining any more of the artifacts, they concentrated on making sure they'd come to the end of the cave system. There'd be time enough to explore farther after this discovery was secured.

When they reached a room with only one way in or out, they counted. Five rooms, packed to the very edges with cylinders. Five dolphins, five halls. Now it made sense.

The only exception to the layout of the rooms was the second one. There, instead of the "library table", they found the remains of about twenty people, laid out neatly on their backs, skeletal arms folded over their chests. Without touching the remains to be sure, it was impossible to determine how they'd met their deaths. No obvious signs of violence were visible. Poison, perhaps?

"Killed to guard the secret?" Mackenzie asked, shivering.

"That would be my guess," Carter replied.

The shape and layout of the rooms was strange. Accustomed to square rooms, the explorers didn't at first understand. It was plain that the rooms had been purposely carved from the limestone; therefore, they would have expected more or less square rooms. However, Mackenzie was the first to visualize the shapes as they were intended—as parts of a whole.

"It's a dolphin!" she exclaimed, delighted.

"What?" Carter asked, looking around for another etched dolphin.

"The layout! It's in the shape of a dolphin. We came in through the blow-hole. How clever!"

"Mackenzie, that was a clever observation! Just like a real archaeologist," Dylan wisecracked.

"Dylan, never fear when Mackenzie is near," she snickered.

Carter was working on something else, and he smiled absentmindedly. "That 'blow-hole' is probably not how they got in here," he whispered. "The ancients often had a way of hiding or blocking the main entrance of places they wanted to hide, and then they'd leave a hidden escape way like we have seen here.

"Someone killed those twenty-odd souls to keep this secret. They placed their bodies like that and then got out the way we came in. And then, after that, it's anyone's guess what happened.

"But one thing is sure—the location of this place was lost."

They took pictures as they double-checked they hadn't missed anything. But because of the five rooms and five dolphins' juxtaposition, they were almost certain they couldn't have missed another room.

On the way back, they stopped at the stone table again, retrieved the scrolls from their cylinders on the table, and took pictures of them after blowing away the dust on them. They checked the pictures to make sure they were clear enough to read the text in the photos.

Carter was arguing silently with himself as he was tempted to take at least the first scroll he'd read earlier with him. From the dust and stale air in the caves, it was evident even the Nabateans hadn't visited it in many centuries, if ever, since it was commissioned. It could assist in convincing skeptics or maybe the Nabateans about their find.

In the end, experience took precedence over emotion. Even if there was no record of its existence, and no one but they would know about it, and despite the fact that it might serve a higher purpose, the backlash, justified or not, of doing that at the City of Lights for that very reason, was a painful deterrent.

They'd have to go through diplomatic channels to get their hands on the contents of the library, which would take time. And time was precisely what they didn't have, but there was no way around that. Reluctantly, they turned their backs on the first chamber, pushing the lever to reclose it as they started back toward the cave through which they'd entered.

As Mackenzie emerged on hands and knees from the small entrance tunnel, a cheer went up among the anxious security detail waiting for them.

"We didn't know how long we should wait before organizing a search party," Conrad said. "We were just about to draw straws to see who should go in after you."

Carter popped out next, followed closely by Dylan, who heard the last sentence. "Glad you didn't. I wouldn't have wanted to push your limp body out of that passage after you passed out from fright," he joked.

"I'm surprised Mackenzie didn't have to drag you behind her," Conrad retorted.

"Okay, okay. Time for that later," Carter said, laughing. "Let's get this place back the way we found it and get back to the hotel." He fussed with the lever again, finally getting it into the right position to move the entrance block back in place.

Shining his flashlight at his handiwork, he could clearly see the unnaturally square outline. He grabbed a fistful of dirt from the floor of the cave and blew it into the cracks, concealing it once more.

The drill-holes in the Roman concrete, however, required a bit more ingenuity. Kyle produced a tube of superglue from Carter's bag of tricks and patched the holes with a paste of it mixed with dirt from the floor. He didn't have a solution for the graffiti, though.

They all stared at the gaps in the reddish paint, scratching their heads. Then Mackenzie stepped forward with a lipstick. She quickly filled in the gaps and then closed the tube and put it back in her pocket. She was grinning when she turned to ask, "How is that?" only to find everyone staring at her.

Carter said, "You carry lipstick on a midnight mission?"

"Hey, you never know when you'll need to touch up your lipstick," she said, winking at him.

"Oh, okay. If you say so." Carter smiled.

"Certainly came in handy this time," Piero added.

They stepped back and looked at their handiwork. Only if someone knew exactly where and what to look for would anyone be able to detect they'd been there.

"What's next, boss?" Dylan asked.

"We can talk about that on the way back to the hotel," Carter answered.

"I say we carry everything out and hide it somewhere else," Piero suggested.

Dylan nodded.

"No, that gets us in as much trouble as taking it out of the country without permission. Besides, you're talking about a massive amount of material." Carter opened his phone and set his photos to play on slideshow before handing it to Piero to watch. "We'd never get it out in two days anyway, even if all eight of us could work on it around the clock.

"But I agree, we need to secure it immediately. We have no idea if someone has noticed our interest in the dolphins and could work it out for themselves. I'm afraid it's up to our President and your government.

"We need to get a message to Bill right away. It has to be done in hours, not days."

With his words, everyone was tense again. Mackenzie was drooping with weariness.

"Come on, let's get back to the hotel. We have to figure out how to get a message out securely and post haste."

Carter and Dylan hashed it out in the car. They were reluctant to even trust the satphones, and their cells were out of the question. In the end, Dylan said he'd just have to talk to Sean in riddles until he got it, and then he could move the message up the line. Carter couldn't see a better plan, so it was settled.

At the hotel, Dylan worked out the time difference. It was evening in D.C., but not so late a phone call from Italy would panic Sean. He took out the satphone and made the connection.

"Man, it's good to hear from you," Sean said as he answered. "I saw the news. You guys okay?"

"Same here," Dylan said. "Yeah, we're fine. Got the package."

Sean thought for only a second. Was Dylan saying they'd been successful in finding the library? *Unbelievable.* "Bringing it home with you?"

"No can do. Need you to meet us here. Bring the secretary."

That one stumped Sean. The secretary? "Uh…"

"Sorry, I mean the CEO's secretary. Top guy."

Sean tumbled. *Top guy. The President? They need the Secretary of State?* He said, "Oh, *Connie!*" Constance Pierce was the Secretary of State, and although he had never met her, he was sure she'd no doubt have something very unpleasant to say if she'd heard him refer to her as Connie.

"You got it. Oh, by the way, you wouldn't want your wife to know, even though it's a business trip."

He means come incognito. And the business must be diplomatic. "Gotcha. When do you need us there?"

"Take your time, as long as you hurry up and make it before yesterday."

Sean just smiled at that old saying from their military days.

Chapter Seventy-Two

SHORT BRIEFINGS

May 8, evening in D.C.

Sean couldn't believe it. They had the library! Carter had done it again!

He looked at his watch. Just past nine p.m., which meant Dylan had called him at three a.m. Matera-time. That put even more urgency into the request they get there as soon as humanly possible.

By nine fifteen p.m., Sean had contacted Bill, and by ten, they'd briefed the President—maybe the shortest brief in history. "They've got the Nabatean library! They need the secretary of state and me over there now. Actually, the exact word was 'yesterday'."

The President knew urgency when he saw it. Protocol would have been to have Scott Eadie summon Pierce, but that would have taken more time. He had a Secret Service member text her. "White House. Now."

Fifteen minutes later, a hastily-dressed but wide-awake Constance Pierce hurried in. "You hollered?" She smiled.

Constance was a slim blonde woman whose Texas speech patterns were more suited to her cattle ranch than her exalted position in the US government. Sixty-eight years old and a veteran of the CIA and the Senate herself, she exuded competence and good cheer in equal measure. Her weathered face had seen more than its share of the hot Texas sun, but her smile was infectious. "Bill, good to see you. Mr. President, where am I going?"

"Italy. Sean will fill you in on the way."

If Constance was bewildered, she didn't show it. She looked Sean up and down and liked what she saw. "Do I have time to pack?"

"No, ma'am," he replied.

"Then let's go," she said, smiling. "My, you're a handsome one."

She kept Sean off-balance with her combination of earthy humor and sharp intelligence. A CIA car whisked them to Dulles, where they boarded a CIA-owned Gulfstream G550. The plane was overkill for their purposes, with the ability to sleep eight on long-haul trips of up to 6,750 nautical miles. Matera was only 4,090 nautical miles away, but neither of them would get any sleep, because the briefing Sean was about to give the Secretary would not only take all of the almost eight hours of their trip, but it would no doubt leave her unable to sleep anyway.

They were airborne by eleven thirty p.m.

Sean couldn't start the briefing until they'd made themselves comfortable in the Gulfstream, received their drink order from the steward, and were alone.

He began, "What do you know about human history?" he asked.

Pierce blinked owlishly. "That might take a while to tell

you," she said. "But I'll bet you're about to tell me I have it all wrong. Why don't you go ahead?"

As succinctly as possible, Sean recounted the events from the time A-Echelon had recruited Carter Devereux until the present.

Pierce felt as if she'd been pulled backward through a time warp and catapulted hundreds of years into the future at the same time. Surely most people would have taken weeks or months to assimilate what Sean had told her. She had less than eight hours.

Everything she'd been taught to believe, believed her entire life, and relied upon had been yanked out from under her feet like the proverbial rug. But she knew her Bible. Giants on the earth? Okay, that was a start.

Ultra-modern technology in the hands of people who lived before people were supposed to even be people yet? That was a bit harder to swallow.

She'd seen Carter Devereux's name in the news.

"We talkin' about that traitor?" she demanded.

Sean realized he hadn't given her much detail about the reprehensible Nabateans yet. So, he told her all about them and what they were capable of and had actually done since the CIA became aware of their existence, when Perrin Durand handed them Algosaibi's laptop and flash drive.

Pierce was staring at him in utter shock when he finished. "Goddamnit! Are you saying none of our world-renowned security agencies knew about this outfit since... what's it two years or so ago? How is that even possible? .... Two thousand years in hiding..."

"Yes, ma'am, that's what I am saying. And therefore, I can tell you Carter Devereux isn't a traitor. The Nabateans are spreading lies to discredit him and get him out of their hair. I'll step you through all the evidence we have of how they did it."

Pierce just nodded for him to continue.

Sean gave her the details and was often interrupted by single-word and lengthier expletives from the Secretary. "And now, Devereux and our team have found their ancient library. My guess is they want to take it out of Italy. That's where you come in."

"Holy shit!" she exclaimed. "Pardon my French, but do you know how hard it is to get sovereign nations to give up their ancient artifacts? They're like my former constituents back home. *'You can pry it out of my cold, dead hands.'*"

"Yes, ma'am," Sean said, uncomfortable again. He'd had no previous dealings with Constance Pierce, and he couldn't get a read on what she might say next. "That's only my educated guess, ma'am. The Devereuxs are due back in the US to testify before the Senate Intelligence Committee within the next few days. We'll know soon enough what they'd like you to negotiate."

"Son, if you call me 'ma'am' one more time, I'm gonna show you how much life this old gal still has in her."

"Yes, m... uh... okay, Conn... ah... Constance."

She beamed at him. "That's better. Now, let's go over this again. I'll need to know it backwards and forwards when I talk to the Italians."

In Matera, Dylan had given his team instructions to pack their backpacks and by turns go wandering around the ravine and walkways surrounding the Crypt of Original Sin. The idea was to observe and record anyone who went in there and how long they stayed, whether they carried anything in or out, and whatever other observations seemed prudent. Each man would be relieved every twelve hours until the Italian government made alternate arrangements.

At least, he hoped the government would step in to protect the precious contents of the cave.

Upon landing, Sean and Constance got a taxi to Matera and went straight to their hotel, the Palazzo Gattini. They dropped their bags in their rooms and waited in Sean's room. Before long, there was a knock at the door. Dylan's smiling face was behind it.

He took them to Carter and Mackenzie's suite, which he explained they'd been sweeping for bugs since their arrival, every time they returned from a trip or let someone in to clean. They also had counter surveillance measures deployed against the possibility of anyone attempting to listen in on their conversations. Sean approved, and Constance was impressed.

Dylan introduced Constance to the Devereuxs and the security team, along with their pilot and Piero. Her eyes were drawn to the dressing on Piero's face. "What happened, sugar?"

Piero's eyes brightened; he liked her immediately—that scar didn't put the ladies off. Dylan was the one who spoke. He brought the Secretary and Sean up to speed on everything that had happened since they'd left on May 1, including the assassination attempt and the previous night's discovery of the library.

Sean was outraged at Dylan for not getting the Devereuxs out when he recognized the German assassin. Before he could dress Dylan down for it, Carter and

Mackenzie jumped in, explaining they'd given him no choice.

"As you can see," Carter concluded, "it worked out well. A dangerous assassin, or possibly two, are off the streets, and unless you want us to undiscover the Nabatean library, I suggest we move past the incident in the Sassi."

Constance hooted at the suggestion they'd be willing to "undiscover" the library. Everything she'd learned about Carter in the past ten hours or so led her to believe he'd find another way if she didn't cooperate with him. "Okay, so what exactly would you like me to do about this?"

Sean stared at her in amazement. Where had her Texas accent gone? She winked at him. *Damn, I wish she'd quit doing that!*

"At the moment, ma'am, all we want is for the Italian government to take responsibility for securing the hiding place of the library and agree to let us take a closer look as soon as we're free to do so.

"And speaking of free, we're under detention here because of the gunfight in the Sassi. But we're due in D.C. So, if they'd agree to let us return home on the stipulation we'll return for questioning if we're needed, that would be helpful, too."

Sean held his breath, waiting for Constance to do something crazy to follow through on her threat. Apparently, Carter got a pass for calling her ma'am.

"All right. I'll need you to act as my top hand," she said, gesturing at Sean. "Get hold of my office and have 'em get me a meeting with Enrico Fellini. In secret, if possible. That's the Italian Prime Minister, if you didn't know," she added. "Then talk to my Chief Deputy and have him handle getting the local police to lift the travel ban on these folks. I don't care what he tells 'em. Tell 'em we're extraditing them if he has to. Just get these folks back to D.C. so they can clear up the crap that's going on there."

Now the rest of them were staring at her while Sean grinned. *There it is. She can switch from smooth D.C. politician back to her Texas ranch owner persona at will. Nice trick!*

"Well, hop to it!" she snapped, causing Sean to stop musing and literally jump.

Chapter Seventy-Three

CIAO TESORO

May 9

Within two hours, the meeting with Fellini was set up, the Secretary of State had obtained appropriate clothing with Mackenzie's help, and Sean was at the wheel of a rental car Piero had found in the nearest town. Carter was with them as they tore up the highway to Rome. He could only hope the Prime Minister would step in if the Materan police caused trouble because he'd left town without permission.

For the next almost five hours, Sean experienced Italian driving first hand, especially the closer they got to Rome. He quickly concluded the tales he'd heard were all true— as the Italians lived up to their reputation as the worst drivers in the world, bar none.

Fellini had agreed to a secret meeting, provided it take place that evening. The fact that it would be after ten p.m. by the time they could reach Rome, despite the speed at which Italians drove, helped. No one would question his movements at that time of night. He'd directed them to come straight to his residence and his security detail to let them in.

Constance strode into Fellini's elegant entry with both hands outstretched. "Enrico, *ciao tesoro*."

Fellini pulled her forward and kissed her on each cheek. "My dear friend! What in the world brings you here at this hour, and in secret!"

"It's a long story, Enrico. May we sit?"

"Of course, of course!" He clapped his hands, and a manservant appeared. "Bring refreshment for my guests." He then led them to a cozy study and bade them to make themselves comfortable.

"Enrico, I'm afraid this is a very long story. You may not sleep tonight. But my friend, Carter Devereux, is the best person to tell it."

Fellini showed his surprise. "The famous Carter Devereux! What are you doing in my country, if I may ask?"

"As Secretary Pierce has said, it's a long story. However, if you know my name, you may already know some of it. You're aware I'm an archaeologist?"

"Of course. Your reputation precedes you. You don't intend to steal precious artifacts from us, I assume?"

Carter concealed his surprise that the Prime Minister knew that much. But then recalled the bad publicity he and A-Echelon had received the past two months and realized it would not have been contained to America only. That made his job tonight a bit easier.

"No, sir, I don't. And the fact that I've done it before has extenuating circumstances. Let me tell you about them." He spent the next half an hour giving a very abbreviated account of the history of the E- and A-Codices, including the actions of the nefarious group that was trying to discredit him and take the information for their use only.

Throughout the narrative, Fellini looked at each of the Americans in the room and made a few judgements based on their body language. He was the third-youngest man to ever become Prime Minister of Italy, and he'd met the Secretary of State on several occasions and admired her greatly. It was her influence that led him to appoint women to replace several heads of state-owned companies whom he'd forced to resign for corruption. More than ten years her junior, he adored her outrageous flirting and encouraged it whenever they met.

He was inclined to trust anything Constance told him, but he was a little disturbed that she'd turned up incognito and unannounced. Now he was glad he'd reserved judgment.

He was still not certain of the role of the second man, Sean Walker, but Professor Carter Devereux had impressed him with his sincerity. Honesty shone from the man's eyes.

Carter's recitation soon put the PM's concerns to rest. He would have done the same thing as Constance under the circumstances. Her requests were reasonable, and given the circumstances, necessary.

Enrico gave a shudder as he considered what might have happened if Carter or his wife—or God forbid, both of them—had been killed in the assassination attempt. Or if the dreadful Nabateans had found their library first.

It was up to him to prevent the disaster that would befall the world if he didn't act immediately. Therefore, he risked the not inconsiderable wrath of his President to wake him at midnight. He made the call in the presence of his guests, without whom he would have known nothing of the threat.

In Italian, he explained the situation and secured the

President's agreement to send the Italian Carabinieri, the national gendarmerie, responsible for policing both military and civilian populations, independent of the other services, to protect the site of the Crypt of Original Sin.

Almost as a side thought, Fellini sent word to the police in Matera that they were to let the Americans leave any time they wished to go. He promised they'd be available for questioning in Matera if needed. Piero, being Italian, they could have at will.

All this Carter explained to the others when Fellini briefly excused himself. Fellini returned, took Pierce in his arms for the formal kiss again, and whispered to her in Italian, "If only you were Italian, my sweet, or I were American!"

Pierce gave him a smile worthy of the Mona Lisa and patted his arm. "Thank you for seeing us, *caro mia*."

Back in Matera, they held a celebratory breakfast while waiting for the Italian troops to take over guarding the hidden library. They'd leave as soon as the troops arrived on site, except for Piero, who would hang around to make sure nothing untoward happened. If anything seemed off, he'd call in help from other CIA operatives in Italy.

On the tenth of May, the Devereux party departed Italy bound for Washington, D.C., arriving two days before their deadline. The mood on the plane was jubilant, though they were all tired, and it would be a very long day as they regained the five-hour difference in time.

Carter pushed away the sobering thought that this was only one battle in the war with the Nabateans.

The victory was exhilarating, and major. But the next battle would be epic.

The Devereux party hadn't even landed in Maryland yet when the Italian press got wind of the military presence in Matera. Only a little snooping brought them the understanding that the Carabinieri were guarding a previously unimportant cave near the Crypt of Original Sin, but they either didn't know or wouldn't say exactly what they guarded.

Understandably, the region surrounding Matera was an archaeological paradise. It was widely touted as having been continuously occupied for nine years or more. Some even whispered it could have been one hundred fifty thousand years. Certainly, new discoveries would be made now and then, or one might even say often.

And of course, it was also understandable that new discoveries would be kept quiet until confirmed. But never in the memory of the oldest residents had those discoveries been guarded by the military. That this one, if in fact it was an archaeological discovery, *was* being guarded by the military caused an apprehensive stir among the populace.

Over the next week, the media, ever on the lookout for a sensational story, stirred the pot. Aggressive journalists would corner the soldiers and demand answers. The soldiers, having none, would push back, sometimes physically, until the rumor started that it was something dangerous in that cave.

When a military spokesman tried to calm the waters by hinting that not all WWII secrets were known yet, and it was a matter of national security, the ploy backfired. They reported a possible weapons and ammo cache left over from the war. The more daring newspapers speculated it was a secret Nazi weapon that conspiracy theorists had been hunting since the war ended in 1945.

The people who knew for a certainty what was actually hidden in that cave numbered less than a dozen. But among those who "knew" because they felt it in their gut were Mathieu and Graziella Nabati. They didn't need direct, firsthand knowledge to put it together. Their hated enemy, Carter Devereux, had been in Matera until just hours before the news broke and had left with his wife and five others despite Mathieu's assurances they were being detained in Matera.

Graziella had seldom been in such bad temper. The worst part of it was she had no way to satisfy her need to punish someone. Her own son was the miscreant. It was such a disaster it necessitated a face-to-face meeting. She summoned him to her lair high in the Andes and paced around Mathieu, as he cowered and endeavored to keep her in front.

"Mathieu, what am I going to do with you? You have failed again. Carter Devereux's alive, and he's made an important discovery. I don't have to tell you what a catastrophe it will be if that discovery is what we believe it is! And two of our best assassins are dead, one at the hands of the other!

"You actually sent three assassins, none of whom knew of the others, to kill the same people? How could you have made such an imbecilic mistake? Have you lost your mind?"

Mathieu could offer no defense. The true reason he'd made the mistake couldn't be admitted to his mother. He'd been driven insane by Devereux's narrow escapes. The man was like a cat with nine lives. A buzzing began in his brain as his mother continued her rant.

"From now on, I'm in charge of these operations. You are now my assistant again, and you'd better pay attention and learn. I'm not going to be around forever to hold your hand, protect you, and clean up after you. And I won't let you destroy what we've built."

The veiled threat in the last sentence was the final blow. Had he lost his mother's love and protection? Would she have him killed, as she'd had so many before? For the moment, though, she seemed to have turned her attention to a different frustration.

"Why can we not gain direct access to information about what's in that cave? The one thing we have in our favor here is that we have thousands of contacts. And not one of them can tell us what's going on."

Mathieu was all too aware this could be laid at his feet as well. Indeed, they did have thousands of contacts in the hallways of power throughout the world, including some high in the Italian government. But the President and the Prime Minister were not among them. And they were playing this discovery very close to their vests. Try as they might, through their contacts in the Italian government, they could not get answers, but they highly doubted it was anything to do with WWII.

He risked direct eye contact with his mother. She'd gone from blaming him to blaming their contacts, perhaps he was safe for now.

The burning question was how the hell Carter Devereux could have solved the puzzle that had stumped the Council for centuries? How did he find the library of legend?

His heart seized again when he met her stormy eyes, just as she hissed, "Incompetent fools!" through clenched teeth. If she numbered him among them, he faced the most precarious situation of his life.

Chapter Seventy-Four

PREPARING FOR THE HEARING

May 10

On the flight from Italy, Sean brought Carter, Mackenzie, and Dylan up to speed with what had happened in D.C. in their absence.

They had a good chuckle over Russell McCormick's disappearance. Sean had them rolling with his description of McCormick's adventures so far on his brother's alpaca ranch, which he got in reports from Jared.

"He should be grateful they aren't llamas," Carter quipped, remembering a few encounters with cranky llamas when he was in Peru.

"Aren't they both just miniature camels?" Dylan asked. "I'd hate to be on a camel ranch. Nasty beasts."

"Actually, llamas are friendlier than alpacas, but Jared isn't interested in them as pets. The alpacas have soft fleece. He harvests it and sells it to a co-op in Colorado Springs that hand-spins it into yarn."

"Is there money in that?" Conrad asked. "I grew up on a farm. Might be a good retirement plan."

"Alpaca yarn can go for up to twenty dollars a skein, depending on the type of yarn," Mackenzie offered.

Sean cleared his throat. "Can we get back to the subject? So, McCormick has disappeared for all intents and purposes, and the President's people have been trying to stall the hearing with that and anything else they can think of. But Senator Davis insists on moving forward. The hearing is going ahead as scheduled, for May fifteenth, five days from now."

"We might as well start preparing for it as soon as we land. We can't avoid testifying, can we?" Carter asked.

"I'm afraid not. We'll get to that in a minute. First, I want to tell you about the hint we got from McCormick on who assigned Kelly to the Patch Barracks investigation.

"Terrence Ham is her immediate supervisor. He says he got a call from General Fleming on the night of the explosion. The General told him what happened and to get a team of investigators together immediately. Then a few minutes later, he called back and said he wanted Kelly assigned as lead investigator.

"Ham told us Kelly would have been assigned to the team anyway. She was one of the best they had, and she'd gained attention from the higher ups. They were giving her every opportunity to shine in high-profile cases, preparatory to promotion. So that was a dead-end.

"Then we talked to Fleming. He said he made the first call, but not the second. He gave us permission to look at his phone records, and it checked out—he made only one call to Ham that night. However, he had no doubt Kelly was the right person for the job, so he didn't wonder about it."

"Another case of faked voice," Dylan observed.

"Looks like it."

They fell silent, each thinking his own thoughts about how they'd manage to track down the person responsible for those faked calls or the technology that made it possible. Eventually, most of them went to sleep to try to prevent jet lag.

Carter and Mackenzie were overjoyed to see Liu on the tarmac waiting for them when they landed. But it was nothing like Dylan's joy. Not standing on protocol, he rushed down the air stairs ahead of them and caught Liu in his arms.

Mackenzie laughed as she saw him lift Liu in a perfect imitation of all the romance movies she'd ever seen. He was turning around and around with her, kissing her in complete disregard for the catcalls of his teammates of "Get a room."

When he finally put her down, Dylan turned to the others and winked. "Some of us have a gorgeous lady waiting for us and some don't. Get over it."

The fun over, they piled into a couple of SUVs and accompanied Carter and Mackenzie to a safe house they'd never seen before. Mackenzie sighed. Back into hiding, but at least the end was in sight. They had five days to prepare for the hearing, but that was going to have to wait until she'd showered and had a rest. Transatlantic flights were no joke, even in their luxurious jet. Mankind wasn't meant for thirty-hour days.

They began their preparations with Carter asking a second time if he and Mackenzie could avoid the hearings. They missed their children, Mackenzie's family, and their home.

They just wanted it to end so they could rest for a while before digging into the Nabatean library.

"I'm afraid not. Davis is bound and determined to bring the CIA to its knees and the President with it. It's part of our strategy to spring a surprise on her in your turning up at the hearing." Sean said.

"What do you expect her to do?" Mackenzie asked. They'd been in hiding to avoid arrest. What would happen now, if they strolled into the Senate hearing chamber unannounced?

"She'll probably order your immediate arrest, but don't worry. The President has the Executive Privilege Order signed and ready. All we have to do is hand it to the Senator, and they can't touch you."

"Okay. What do we need to do to get ready?"

For the next few days, everyone involved studied like they were cramming for the bar exam. Bill, James, Irene, the Director of National Intelligence, Sebastian Birch, in their respective offices. Carter, Mackenzie, Sean, and Dylan at their safe house. They all had copies of every bit of information about A-Echelon that was in the public arena—every opinion, speculation, theory both reasoned and from conspiracy nuts—they could dig up.

Computer analysis sliced, diced, and tracked down common origins to help them prepare truthful answers that didn't give away national security information.

The latter condition turned out not to be an easy task. In fact, it was going to be impossible to answer truthfully to every question they anticipated. About eighty percent of the truthful answers would tread on national security. For those questions, they'd have to refuse to answer, but doing so without proper grounds would land them in jail for contempt of Congress. The only proper grounds were the

Fifth Amendment, which they knew would only delay things.

At least, they hoped it would delay things long enough to get another run against the Nabateans. Maybe investigations would reveal the true conspirators. In truth, that could take years, but the discovery of the Nabatean library could help, if only they had time to get their hands on it and find some hints.

As far as Carter and Mackenzie were concerned, they'd done nothing wrong. Not even in making the illegal copy of the Sirralnnudam and removing the library of the Giants from the City of Lights. In hindsight, those actions had been wrong at the time, but extenuating circumstances made both actions excusable as well as lifesaving in more than one sense.

The slight damage Carter's actions had done to relations with Egypt had been cured by the President more than a year ago with the promise to return the plates immediately. They'd done so. In addition, the President had made a small donation to the Egyptology Department of the Cairo University. But Carter and Mackenzie didn't know about the donation and therefore couldn't testify about it.

The same went for the copying of the Sirralnnudam. The Armenian government had pardoned Mackenzie and thanked her for the copy she sent them. If not for her doing that, it would have been lost entirely. The original had gone missing shortly after she'd handled it for the last time, so they had only the copy she'd sent them, and its illegality was no longer of concern.

Those things they could testify about, justify, and not have a care about. The A-Codex was a different matter, even though its retrieval had been completely legal. The worry was about the damage to the US and to the world if the information they'd already gleaned from it became public knowledge.

Carter and his translation team hadn't gone through even ten percent of the information contained in it. That was damaging enough in the wrong hands. What might be lurking in the other ninety percent could be even more so. Just look at the trouble the ten percent had caused—close to four hundred people dead and another six hundred injured, half of Patch Barracks vaporized.

Fortunately, the committee members didn't know that the Patch Barracks incident was connected to A-Echelon's work. In fact, they didn't know about the A-Codex, thanks to the media not having discovered it. They knew nothing about the ancient nukes, the dolphins, or the attacks on Freydís. And with any luck, they never would. Certainly, none of the players had any intention of opening those lines of inquiry. Unless they were asked. At which point, they'd have to fall back on the sanctuary of the Fifth Amendment, even though they had no personal incrimination to worry about, just worldwide panic.

The trouble was, quite a few other people did know about it, Kelly White and Russell McCormick among them. Far too many for comfort. And what if the committee or any of its members had been fed information in the same manner it was fed to the late Howard Crane and Kelly?

They were happy McCormick was out of the way and Kelly wouldn't cause trouble. It was the unknown that bugged them. In fact, if the Nabateans could set up one McCormick, what's to say they hadn't set up two, four, or many more? With their unlimited resources, they could easily have done so.

Another thing that worried them was that witnesses called before Senate committee hearings were typically sent a list of questions in advance, along with a list of documents to bring to the hearings. However, that wasn't the case this time. As far as they knew, the inquiry was all about the illegal existence of A-Echelon and the flagrant waste of taxpayer money on frivolous investigations. But the lack of advance questions meant they could be thrown a curveball at any moment while testifying.

Michelle Davis had them right where she wanted them —off balance, with a wide-open field of investigation and squirming public. No private hearings for the good Senator. She wanted the galleries packed with both the public and the Fourth Estate. She had some serious grandstanding to do.

In the meantime, Senator Davis had been doing her own preparations. Unaware that the missing Devereuxs would crash her party, she didn't factor them into her plans. Although she would have loved to.

Her intention was to start with those she considered the little fish, James and Irene. Her beef wasn't with them, though she did honestly believe their operation was a reprehensible waste of taxpayer money, not to mention the questionable legality of it. Her beef was with none other than the CIA itself, and Bill Griffin specifically. Lately, she'd also been insulted by the National Intelligence Director as well, so it would be a bonus if she could take him down, too.

She counted on the fishing expedition. Hopefully, by the time she got to Bill and Sebastian, the lower ranks would have given away so much condemning information to cover their own asses they would have completely compromised their bosses. And then there was the ultimate prize. If she could damage Samuel Houston Grant enough, her own party would have to turn to her to rehabilitate its image before the election.

What a pity I couldn't start with Professor Carter and Doctor Mackenzie Devereux. Rich, spoiled elitists who would probably do anything to keep their faces clean, their reputations untarnished, and the extent of their obscene wealth hidden from an envious public. The media wouldn't hesitate to shred them over that alone.

Davis knew a little about Carter Devereux from reputation. He was the hotshot professor who'd made all those earthshattering discoveries a few years ago and was big in the news at the time. Some people thought very highly of him and praised him as one of the leading archaeologists of our time. Others made him out as the biggest hoaxer and pseudoscientist of *all* times. Because there were a number of leading scientists among the latter, she was inclined to rather believe that version.

She just wished she could have them in front of her committee. This was her turf—not a classroom at a university or a dig out in the sticks. She would put them through a few classes of her own.

She flipped nonchalantly through the Devereuxs' file, and her attention was arrested by a picture of Mackenzie Devereux. *Hmm, our Professor's lovely wife. Wonder how she caught him—what the prospects of money and status won't do to a girl's principles?* She occupied herself with a few minutes' fantasy of skewering Dr. Devereux with pointed interrogation, calling her integrity into question.

"Ah well, it's not to be," she whispered as she shoved the file out of the way to the side of her desk.

Chapter Seventy-Five

QIT PROJECT UPDATE

May 12

Bill took time out from his preparations to give everyone an update about the Quantum IT project, dubbed QIT and pronounced like "quit". Liu gave an update on how the translations for it were coming.

The QIT team had been at it for only fifteen days, but working at breakneck speed, twenty-four seven in shifts. A few, the top one percent of the brilliant scientists and engineers who were involved in the project, pushed themselves around the clock, sometimes resting only a couple hours before getting up to attack the problems again.

Early on, Bill had given the team leadership permission to reach out to the private sector in return for promising them access to the new technology as long as it wouldn't jeopardize national security. IBM, D-Wave, Samsung, Intel, and a few universities sent anyone they had who could contribute meaningfully to the project.

With so many involved, it became difficult to properly

vet new participants or even to know where they came from. Security was on the minds of very few of the operations team. They relied on the admins to take care of all that.

The project team had developed an effective routine to keep everyone up to date on the progress of the project. Each morning at eight a.m., everyone gathered for a brainstorming session, where new ideas were welcome, no matter how outlandish or weird they may be. Everyone discussed them, and then it was decided by consensus which of them they'd try.

At these sessions, the outcomes of previous ideas would be reported, along with an overview of the progress vis-à-vis the timeline the President had given them. That hadn't changed and would not.

One morning, shortly after the project started, a couple of new consultants turned up at the brainstorming meeting, and after that they appeared every day. No one knew where they'd come from and knew even if they asked they wouldn't get an answer, but they stood out in the crowd of sloppily dressed geeks. They wore suits and ties, appeared to have gotten plenty of sleep, and always had fresh, exciting, out-of-the-box ideas.

It got to be a game, betting among themselves which of the crazy ideas would work and which wouldn't. But the game soon became boring when someone pointed out that all the ideas did work. Every single weird idea paid off. And that was the strangest thing of all.

Soon everyone who attended the brainstorming sessions trusted the outsiders, and they were eager to test the new suggestions presented by these mysterious visitors.

They would've been stumped if they were to learn the ideas and suggestions from these well-dressed consultants came from a seventy thousand-year-old library.

So, when they brought a black box in one morning and suggested it might help with the communications part of the project deliverables, the scientists tasked with the invention of an unbreakable, encrypted communications device seized it with enthusiasm and studied it carefully. Their trust in the outsiders proved well-founded.

It didn't take them long to figure it out, reverse engineer it, and hand it over to the CIA. The CIA technicians added a few modifications, including miniaturizing it, and were delighted with the end result. It was now the size of a packet of cigarettes and would give their field agents an enormous advantage in covert data collection efforts.

The spooks would be able to carry one of those devices on their person, hidden from sight, walk past any modern-day computing device, and copy all data off it in just a few seconds, the owner of the computing device none the wiser.

They called it a Blackjack.

Bill's estimate was that the project was on target or perhaps a little ahead of schedule.

Chapter Seventy-Six

SAVED BY THE BELL

May 15

The media, including newspaper journalists, bloggers, TV journalists, and their cameramen, were out in full force on the morning of the opening session of the Intelligence Committee hearing. Sebastian, Bill, James, and Irene squeezed their way through the packed hallways and into the hearing chamber, ignoring shouted questions from the media.

They took their seats in the front row directly backing the witness tables nearly half an hour early. None of the committee members had arrived yet, but their administrative assistants, aides, and a bevy of interns bustled around the committee's elevated desks. The noise level was lower inside the chamber than out in the hall, but only by a little.

Spotting the witnesses, Senator Davis's senior aide went to inform her.

"I'll be right there," Davis replied. She'd use the extra time to get a feel for the audience.

As she entered the chamber, Davis nodded to her committee members, who were drifting in as well. She took her seat and looked around. The ushers had opened the doors a few minutes before, and now the public gallery was packed, the outer walls lined with TV crew and cameras. Everything was just as she wanted it.

It was almost time to begin when Davis noticed a bit of commotion at one of the entrance doors. An aide hurried to her side and whispered, "The Devereuxs are here."

"What did you say?" she asked.

Her aide repeated his statement, and a triumphant grin broke out on Davis's face. "Let's not keep our honored guests waiting then. Do we have a quorum?"

The aide looked up, quickly counted the one or two empty chairs and nodded. Davis rapped her gavel and called the hearing to order.

Carter and Mackenzie hurried to gain their seats before the noise died down. "Are we late?" he asked James.

"No. I suspect she started a few minutes early. She must be excited to have all of us here."

Davis was making a show of ignoring the Devereuxs as she wasted the next fifteen minutes on administrative detail and red tape. Finally, unable to wait for the next phase to begin and hoping she'd put the entire witness list on the defensive, she looked at Carter and Mackenzie and spoke into her microphone.

"Mr. and Mrs. Devereux. We are honored that you could join us." She watched closely to see if they blinked at her deliberate omission of their academic titles but could see nothing but cool, neutral expressions.

"In fact, in order to secure your future attendance at these hearings, I'm going to issue an immediate warrant of arrest for the two of you."

Sebastian was on his feet before she'd finished the sentence, and he held his arm out in a protective barrier as the sergeant-at-arms stepped forward to carry out the arrest.

"Not so quick! I have an Executive Privilege Order signed by the President here."

Davis's temper flared, and she raised her eyebrows. If she had stopped to think, she'd have realized she'd been outflanked. She'd have assumed the Devereuxs had made an immunity deal with the President in return for their testimony. But to have these two slip out of her grasp and receive a figurative slap in the face at the same time was enough to make her see red and think only of revenge.

"I take it then," she snarled, "that the President is making himself responsible to assure the attendance of these two... alleged traitors... at future hearings."

Sebastian bristled at the unwarranted description but decided to pick his battles. "I will pass the message on to him, Senator."

Davis believed she'd scored a point. To her, that Executive Privilege Order was as good as an admission of guilt, and she didn't even stop to consider any other possibilities.

Next, she looked to score another point by calling what she thought to be the weakest link to the witness table first. "Mackenzie Devereux, take the witness stand."

No one else expected that. Indeed, Davis hadn't had the opportunity to prepare for it, but her motto for the moment was *carpe diem*. She rapped her gavel once to quiet the buzz that had started among the gallery, the other witnesses, and even her own committee.

At the witness table, everyone was concerned except Carter. The others, concerned about Davis pushing

Mackenzie too far, had to stop whispering about it, but they were still worried. Mackenzie could be the loveliest, soft-spoken, self-effacing person anyone could imagine. But they'd all had occasion to witness what happened when someone pushed her too far. She personified the reputation of redheads, especially if that someone was targeting her loved ones.

Carter, on the other hand, grinned, crossed his arms, and settled himself more comfortably in his chair—to watch the show. The Senator probably thought she had a pushover in Mackenzie. He couldn't wait to see how the senator was going to get her ass handed to her.

Mackenzie took the oath and sat down, waiting calmly for the first question.

Sen. Davis began. "Mrs. Devereux, I take it you are aware of the gravity of the matter brought before this committee."

Mackenzie replied, "Yes, Miss Davis, I am."

Davis, let it go that Mackenzie didn't address her correctly, never thinking she was the one who started it.

"Mrs. Devereux, the media for the last seven or so weeks has raged with serious allegations about A-Echelon and its activities. What is your response to that."

Mackenzie responded, "It's true, Miss Davis."

Davis again ignored the incorrect address. She was too keen to jump on that admission of guilt.

"Are you saying the allegations are true, Mrs. Devereux?"

Mackenzie answered, "No, Miss Davis, I'm saying it's true that the media, for the last seven or so weeks, has been raging with serious allegations about A-Echelon and its activities."

Davis almost exploded. Her face turned red, the

committee members started chuckling and shook their heads, and the public gallery erupted in raucous laughter.

Mackenzie sat there expressionless. Carter and the rest had a very hard time not smiling. When she had collected herself, Davis banged on the desk with her gavel and glared at the public gallery until they quieted.

"Mrs. Devereux, I noticed you don't know the correct form of address for the members of this committee— "

She got no further before the senator next to her touched her arm and whispered something in her ear.

Mackenzie rejoined, "My apologies. I know how to address the members, but I thought we were going to keep this informal and do away with formal titles."

Mackenzie smiled. Another round of laughter followed among those who knew her title, but a glare from Davis was sufficient to quiet them this time.

No one wanted to be removed. This promised to be the best show in town.

Davis shrugged and continued without apologizing. However, from then on, she addressed Mackenzie as Doctor Devereux, and Mackenzie responded in kind by addressing her as Senator or Madam.

After a few rounds of pointed questions with no better results, Davis was struggling to control her emotions and ready to take a break. The damn witness brilliantly side-stepped every question without being insolent. What was worse, she was swaying the audience in her favor. By now, she regretted making the mistake of calling Mackenzie first, too enraged to make rational decisions, instead of stopping the questioning and call another one of the witnesses, she pushed ahead.

Hoping another senator might do better, Davis ceded

the floor to another committee member. But it soon became apparent he would have no better luck.

Half an hour later, Mackenzie was getting annoyed at the same question being asked in different ways. Carter shifted to a more alert position as the committee member asked it for the sixth time, and Mackenzie lifted her shoulder to signal she understood not to lose her cool.

Instead, she answered in a sweet tone, "Senator, I have answered that question exactly five times already. I really can't help it that you don't like the answer."

Someone in the audience stage-whispered, "Bazinga!" and Davis lost it.

"Do you think some of us are idiots?" she shouted at Mackenzie.

Mackenzie gave a ghost of a smile. It was really not fair to take advantage of a woman not in her right mind, but the opening was too good. "No, some of you are not idiots." The very faint emphasis on "some" was the last straw.

The gallery detonated. Even the media, well-trained not to become part of the story, couldn't contain themselves.

Davis banged her gavel so hard the head broke off and flew back to hit her. She was all but foaming at the mouth and used the distraction to point to her nearest neighbor, the vice-chairman of the committee. "Adjourn for lunch," she gasped before scrambling for the door.

"Medic," she wheezed as she collapsed. *A heart attack. That will teach that redheaded bitch to have some respect.*

A few minutes later, an EMT completed her humiliation by telling her, loudly, "You had a panic attack."

One journalist took out his cell phone, forbidden in the chamber but smuggled in with the camera equipment, and tweeted: *"Davis vs. Devereux: Round 1: Davis saved by the bell."*

Chapter Seventy-Seven

LUNCH TIME

If Davis had thought she'd get a break to collect herself after her "medical emergency", she was sadly mistaken. During lunch time, her office became the frontline in a war zone when her party leaders, apprised of the debacle by her committee members of the same party, stormed into her office, uninvited and accompanied by the committee members. Her head began to pound, and she could barely keep up with who was speaking as they gave her an ass-chewing the likes of which she'd last had as a rebellious teenager from her mother.

"After lunch, you go back in there and treat Doctor Devereux with respect."

"Stop being vindictive—you're no match for her, and you should've realized that within the first few minutes."

"You change your attitude, or she is going to ruin you and your career – you'll never recover from it."

And the final blow, from the party chairman, "If you don't back off on her, we'll destroy you, and you might as well hand in your resignation. You're ruining every chance

—and it's already slim—for our party to elect the next president."

With angry men and women shouting at her from every side, Davis was reduced to tears. Taken aback, they softened their tone and tried to persuade rather than threaten, but it was too late. They'd already backed her into a corner, and she didn't take that lightly. Those were tears of anger, not of unhappiness or fright.

"*I'm* the chairwoman of this committee, and I'll conduct the hearing as I please. Don't for one moment think you'll get away with bullying me," she screamed.

The party chairman patted the air as he tried to mollify her. "Michelle, you're right, and I'm sorry. We shouldn't have ganged up on you. But surely you can see your approach has only made Doctor Devereux a heroine among the gallery that *you* wanted there. All we're saying is please think about changing your approach."

Davis crossed her arms and lifted her chin. "I'll *think* about it."

That was the best they were going to get. Sighing heavily, they filed out of her office. They could only hope she'd moderate her obvious bias when she resumed questioning the witness.

The Devereux camp, in contrast, were having a celebration over their lunch. Everyone was elated with Mackenzie's performance. Carter had expected nothing less, so he was sitting back and smiling as Sebastian, Bill, James, and Irene congratulated her. Occasionally one of them would quote one of her zingers, and the whole group would break out into the laughter they'd had to suppress during the session.

She'd done what no one besides Carter knew she could—diverted the attention from A-Echelon and focused it squarely on the rude, brash, and vindictive Senator Michelle Davis from California. Those who'd attended had begun to hate Davis, and once the footage from the major networks was aired, everyone else would, too.

In fact, those reporters were outside the building, screaming to the lenses of the video cameras about the debacle so far. Most of them blaming the vicious Senator Davis for the chaotic state of affairs and the unnecessary battering of this beautiful, soft-spoken, obviously innocent woman.

Sebastian and the rest cautioned Mackenzie that Davis would be right now receiving attitude adjustment training from her party members.

"When the hearing gets back underway after lunch, things will become really serious, Mackenzie," Sebastian concluded.

"I'm sure they will," Mackenzie answered. Smiling at her husband, she said, "I'm ready for whatever happens. Trust me."

Carter smiled back. After the morning's performance, he wasn't the only one who did.

Chapter Seventy-Eight

WHAT DO YOU DO FOR A-ECHELON?

Davis gaveled the hearing to order. She looked refreshed compared to her panic as she'd left the chamber an hour and a half earlier. She'd managed to get over her tears with the help of a Valium and chain-smoking three cigarettes. She even had on fresh makeup—war paint, as her ex-husband always called it.

Her attitude had undergone a remarkable change as far as anyone could tell. She even smiled as she reminded Mackenzie she was still under oath.

Mackenzie thought the smile looked remarkably like those she'd seen on the faces of the deadly African Black Mamba snakes. As she confirmed she understood she was still under oath, Makenzie knew the cat and mouse game was over as far as Davis was concerned. The fake smile hiding its sinister intent meant that though the good senator may have put on kid gloves, her bite was still extremely toxic.

Mackenzie took a deep breath and prepared to do mental battle as Davis nodded at another committee member to ask a question. She turned her attention to the senator questioning her—a member of the opposing party.

"Doctor Devereux, were you involved in, or aware of, investigations into alien visitation?"

Mackenzie suppressed a twitch of her lips, only a little surprised at the ridiculous implication. "No, Senator. I am unaware of any such investigations."

"Is that because the military and intelligence community have concluded their investigations? Perhaps before you were a part of A-Echelon?"

"Not to my knowledge, Senator," Mackenzie answered.

"What about Hitler's children?"

"I am unaware that Hitler had any," she answered. "In any case, there is no such investigation that I'm aware of."

"Elvis?"

"If you are referring to Elvis Presley, I believe he died in 1977."

Another member of the opposite party tried to come to the rescue of his colleague and ask a more intelligent question. "What about Nazi secret bases in Antarctica or the Arctic? What about their secret weapons programs, such as the Glocke?"

"Science fiction, Senator, as far as I know."

"You seem to be qualifying your answers, Doctor Devereux. Let me ask you directly. Are you, or have you ever been, involved in investigating any of the subjects my colleague or I have mentioned?"

"No. Never." Mackenzie's firm answer was given in a sweet tone of voice with a smile.

Davis indicated a member of her own party next.

"Doctor Devereux, if you are not involved in any of these investigations, what *do* you do for A-Echelon?"

That was the first question, since the whole circus started that morning, which was worthy of a sincere answer.

"My research has to do with ancient medicine. I track down ancient texts, and with the help of translators, investigate what we might learn from them. If we can apply it to modern medicine, I also perform experiments to test its worth."

"So, what have you learned?" The senator smiled, charmed with Mackenzie's dignified and decidedly non-whacky answer.

Mackenzie smiled back. "I have been and still am very surprised at what the ancients knew and stunned by how much knowledge has been lost or suppressed over the ages. Much of it is being *re*discovered, not discovered as we sometimes claim." She held up a folder. "I have here just a few examples, of which I've made copies for the committee, if you are interested."

Davis nodded to one of the clerks to collect the folder and hand out the copies.

"We'll look at that with great interest, Doctor Devereux," Davis said. "But give us just a few examples off the top of your head."

Another of those Mamba-smiles warned Mackenzie to pick a few of the most believable examples.

"Well, let me think. The Chinese in 300 B.C. already had government medical aid. Doctors received their compensation from the government and medical aid was free to all."

"Like Medicaid?" Davis sneered.

"As I understand it, no. Theirs were free to all. No one received better medical aid than anyone else. Another example is a pharmacological encyclopedia from India that's more than four thousand years old. We're still going through it. There are over five hundred herbal medications listed, along with instructions for their use. Modern scientists have experimented with some in double-blind tests, and many are better than modern pharmaceuticals."

"None of this sounds new, Doctor Devereux. People have been claiming herbal remedies are better than drugs for decades."

"That's true, Senator. But now we have the means to prove it. There's more. Surgical instruments and techniques that rival today's, for example. Obsidian blades have been found to be a thousand times sharper than modern day platinum surgical blades. So sharp they don't bruise cells. Dental cement that's still holding up after fifteen hundred years. This research is not frivolous, as the news media has been reporting." Mackenzie stopped. She'd said enough, and her primary research into respirocytes was top-secret. She couldn't speak about it in an open hearing. Fortunately, no one asked.

When she fell silent, Mackenzie became aware of a stir in the gallery. A quick sidelong glance to each side showed her people were whispering to each other excitedly.

Her heart ached. These weeks in hiding could have been put to better use extending her knowledge of the technology that could prove to be the answer to many health issues.

Davis, too, noticed the interest in the gallery as well as among her committee members.

This couldn't be allowed to go on. Things weren't going her way, because of Mackenzie Devereux's almost supernatural ability to sway her audience. Her credibility, whether it came from her calm demeanor, her obvious intelligence, or the indisputable fact that she was telling the truth was hurting Davis's own, simply because she'd called it into question.

The senator who'd opened that door was about to ask another question. His expression said he was now highly interested in what Devereux had to say. Davis cut him off and took over the questioning again herself.

Davis went on the attack again. "It's been reported you played fast and loose with the rules of an Armenian museum in which you were a guest. Did you or did you not illegally copy an ancient document known as the Sirralnnudam?"

Mackenzie swallowed. *Here it comes.* "Yes, I copied it, and I admit it was illegal at the time. However, in hindsight, it was the right thing to do. Even the Armenians agreed and condoned it. They thanked me, because shortly after I handled it last, it disappeared from the library. All they now have is the copy I made."

"You are quite certain you do not yourself have the original in your possession?"

"Quite." Mackenzie bit off the rest of her retort. She'd already been investigated and cleared of that accusation. Davis knew it.

That was a low blow.

"And would you decide again that your opinion counts more than the rules, Doctor Devereux?"

"I can't say if I would do it again. That would depend on the circumstances. I would always do what I feel is right, as an American citizen and a person who has only the good of the public in mind. But I admit that back then – given the circumstances then—I was wrong. There was no emergency that required I copy the document. I merely wanted to be able to study it at leisure. It was fortunate only because someone took the document and then lost it afterward."

Davis took her admission of guilt as a victory. She tried to capitalize on it by asking Mackenzie about the rumors of Carter having stolen from an ancient library in Egypt. She didn't mention the City of Lights, or the Giants.

"I was not there," Mackenzie answered. "I have knowledge of it, but not firsthand knowledge. Perhaps you should ask my husband directly."

Davis pounced on her answer. "Am I to understand from your reply you're refusing to answer the question?"

"Not at all, Senator. I am willing to answer, but wouldn't it be better if my husband gave you the correct facts? Wouldn't it be better to hear it from him firsthand? Or do you prefer my secondhand version? It wouldn't be as comprehensive as his."

Davis walked right into the briar patch with her next question. "Why do you keep saying second-hand version? Where were you when it happened?"

Mackenzie paused a beat, instinctively waiting for the hush in the room that would make her next statement all the more dramatic. Then she spoke quietly.

"My son, daughter, and I were being held captive in a research facility in Saudi Arabia. A place just outside of Mecca."

A collective susurration as the gallery drew in a shocked gasp, and then the audience went deathly silent again. The media had reported Mackenzie was colluding with Saudi dissidents at the time. The one or two reporters in the room who remembered the original story felt a skipped heartbeat. Their source had said that, and they'd never verified.

Davis felt as if she'd stepped on a merry-go-round and had her feet swept from under her. Nevertheless, she forged ahead, determined to discredit Mackenzie at all costs.

"So, the reports in the media are wrong? *All* of them?

Are you trying to make us believe that not one journalist investigated and is now able to prove your claim?" Davis made an incredulous face.

"Yes, the reports are wrong. I did not work for or with the Saudis at any time, ever in my life. I can't think of any reason why I ever would. Not voluntarily."

Leaning heavily on a sarcastic tone, Davis tried to shake the story. "How did you come to be... *captured*? Why and how did that happen? Why hasn't it been reported along with the rest of the scandal? We've heard nothing about it in the press."

Mackenzie again answered evenly. "I can't say why the press hasn't mentioned it now. But they certainly knew and talked about it at the time."

Davis recalled nothing of the story. Befuddled, she asked Mackenzie to explain.

Sensing she'd gained a lot of sympathy and support, not only from the audience but from some of the committee as well, Mackenzie seized the opportunity to tell the whole story.

"We, my family and I, were in Jerusalem on holiday. We'd just gone into a restaurant, and Carter excused himself to go to the restroom. The next thing I knew, my son and I were grabbed by masked men and bundled into a van. The men held ether-soaked cloths over our faces, and the last thing I heard before I lost consciousness was a huge explosion and people crying and screaming.

"We woke up in the place where we were to be held prisoner for nearly a year. I didn't know it then but shortly learned I was pregnant. My daughter was born in captivity. I learned later everyone had believed us dead the entire time.

"Then we were rescued and reunited with my husband,

along with another American woman who was also being held prisoner. Not much was printed about it at the time. I think another big news story took precedence, probably.

"It's strange, though, that in all the hoopla that's been going on in the media about us in the past few weeks, no one has ever bothered to mention what happened back then, when the information has been available all this time."

This was the longest answer Mackenzie had given, and as she continued, Davis felt her gains slipping away from her again. These facts were easily enough checked. She knew Devereux wouldn't be stupid enough to lie about such a thing while under oath. It must all be true. She could see and feel the audience felt the same way. They were almost all now siding with Mackenzie.

Desperately, she seized on the one thing Mackenzie hadn't elaborated on. "Tell us about the operation you alluded to when you said you and your son were rescued. Who rescued you, who authorized the operation, when, and how did it happen?"

Mackenzie paused, this time to think through the consequences of the answer. If she gave it in full, she would reveal top-secret information, and she wasn't going to let that happen. She neatly sidestepped.

"It was actually my son, my infant daughter, and me. You'll recall I learned while I was in captivity that I was pregnant. I gave birth to my daughter while in captivity. And the other American. She was rescued at the same time, too." Mackenzie withheld Liu's name. She didn't need to be dragged into this as well.

Murmurs of sympathy rose from the gallery until Davis picked up her gavel and looked in the direction of the noise with purpose. They quieted without making her resort to verbally warning them.

Mackenzie had the upper hand now, and she decided to capitalize on it. "I can't tell you about the details of the planning and execution of the rescue operation. Obviously, I wasn't involved in them.

"What I can say is I thank God we *were* rescued. Can you imagine what it feels like not to see the sun for close to a full year? To not know where you are, not even what country you're in? To be subjected to wearing a black niqab day in and day out?

"I was required to work under constant threat that my children would be taken away, perhaps harmed, if I didn't cooperate. I didn't know if anyone knew we were alive or even cared. I thought my husband was dead, killed in that explosion.

"Can you imagine wondering if you'd ever see the sun again? Wondering what would happen to your child if you were to die? And to top it all, to be pregnant with another baby, knowing you'd bring another child into that miserable existence? Can you understand that I *wanted* to die, but couldn't bear to leave my son unprotected, or to destroy my unborn baby along with myself?"

Mackenzie had almost succumbed to her own hypnotic story, remembering the horror. Her eyes were damp, along with many in the gallery. A few were unabashedly sobbing. Even on the committee, she could see faces full of shock and shame.

Davis, however, seemed unaffected. Oblivious to what was happening to the mood of the room, she pushed harder.

"I can see that you must have endured a terrible ordeal. However, you haven't answered the question. Would you please do so now?"

Mackenzie first looked down at the table in front of her

for a second or two and then slowly looked up. She said, "I was trying to avoid answering the rest of it. You know as well as I do, Senator Davis, that I can't answer the rest of your question in public… because—"

Davis tensed like a big cat getting ready to jump onto its prey. She interrupted. "Are you refusing to answer? I promise you there will be serious consequences if you do."

Mackenzie looked Davis straight in the eyes and said, "In that case I have to inform you that my legal counsel has advised me—"

Davis interrupted again. Smugly, she said, "Oh, I see. So now you are going to hide behind the Fifth Amendment. Is that how it's going to be from now on?"

Mackenzie shook her head. "It doesn't have to be like that. If you and your committee members will promise to stop this witch-hunt right now, I will answer every question. I'll make you a deal—"

Davis dropped her jaw in an exaggerated parody of surprise. "You're in no position to make deals, Doctor Devereux! This is not a flea market where you bargain for the best prices!"

She was about to continue her tirade when she saw the admonishing look from one of the committee members who'd read her the riot act during lunch break. The senator next to her, another one of those who was in her office during lunch, leaned over and whispered something in her ear.

She shook her head violently in obvious disagreement. He leaned over again, and her demeanor changed. Now she looked like she'd taken a big bite out of an unripe lemon.

"This goes against my grain, but I'll give you some latitude. What's your proposal?"

Mackenzie thanked her and said, "Clear this place out—

and I mean everyone except you, the committee members, and the witnesses behind me. Clear out your staff and the public, and I'll tell you everything you want to know. Because what I have to say is top-secret, and believe me, I am very, very serious. National security is at risk. I will not discuss it in an open hearing."

Davis tried to save face—and the remnants of her authority. "This is an open hearing. It will remain open. End of story. You can't dictate terms and conditions to this committee! We are here to protect the American people and act in their best interest. They *will* hear it."

"Well then you leave me no choice. I have been advised by my legal counsel—"

Davis waved her hand impatiently and interrupted. "Yes, yes, yes, I know we won't get any answers from you. What about the rest of the witnesses?"

She looked at Sebastian, Bill, James, Irene, and Carter. They stood as one, and Sebastian answered for them.

"We will do the same as Doctor Devereux. We'll take the Fifth."

Davis was furious. She stared at them, seeing not the faces of enemies but a future that included her ouster in the next election. She mumbled, "How am I supposed to conduct a hearing if they can take the Fifth just to avoid my questions? It's a damn circus." Without meaning to, she pounded her fist on the podium, but the uproar in the room meant that few saw it and even fewer heard it.

Mackenzie saw her chance, correctly guessing the source of Davis's frustration with a little help from lip-reading. She said, "Madam Chairwoman, it's easy, as far as I am concerned, and I am speaking now only for myself. The rest of the witnesses must speak for themselves.

"I ask you again to clear out this room as I have

suggested, and I will tell you everything you want to know. You have my word – I will not invoke the Fifth. After that, you and your committee will own the information, and if you decide to place this country's security on the line by making what I tell you public, you're to blame, not I.

"So, what's it going to be? The truth or the Fifth?"

Davis knew she had lost. It was a reasonable request, and the important thing was to get the incriminating information. She looked at the other witnesses questioningly. They all nodded their agreement with Mackenzie. She looked at the committee members. They all nodded as well.

She was alone—the gallery had deserted her during Mackenzie's touching story. Only the media representatives looked unwilling, but they were only thinking of their stories, not the big picture.

"So, just for the record then," Davis said reluctantly, "we clear out this room, only the committee members and you remain, and you answer all questions truthful and honestly? No one takes the Fifth?"

Mackenzie turned to look at the rest of the witnesses as Davis spoke, and all were nodding. "Yes, that's it," she said, turning back to face Davis.

Davis rapped her gavel. "We'll take a half-hour break while the room is cleared." She stood, gathering the shreds of her dignity, and strode out of the room. Once out of sight of the gallery, she almost broke into a run as she scurried to her office.

She needed a cigarette, maybe two, and another Valium. If she'd had her wish, she'd have had a double shot of the strongest alcoholic drink she could get her hands on. Even moonshine would have done in a pinch.

Chapter Seventy-Nine

IT WOULD ONLY GET WORSE

Graziella and Mathieu had been watching the newsfeed from their respective lairs. The latest development had them almost foaming at the mouth. Nothing was going as planned, and they were devastated to see their scheme slipping away from them—again.

Every time the cameras showed Carter's face, one or both erupted like a volcano, spewing smoke, fire, and molten rock.

That redheaded bitch had wrapped the public, and now the committee members, around her pinky. The final straw was how she finally convinced the committee to have the meeting behind closed doors.

They did have a few senators and representatives in their pockets, but none on the Senate Intelligence Committee. They knew once those doors closed they would soon become the topic of conversation.

By the time Davis called for the break to clear the room, Graziella and Mathieu had a very long list of people whom they blamed and whom they were going to have killed. And the list was growing.

If the hearing going off the rails hadn't been enough by itself, they'd had even more bad news just hours before the hearing started. They'd had communication with a sleeper plant, who broke her long silence with a report that the President of the United States had ordered and was personally overseeing a secret project code-named QIT. She had been fortuitously assigned to the administrative team for the project.

Having gathered sufficient information to believe it would be of interest to the Council, she contacted her handler to ask what they'd like her to do. She'd never seen her handler and didn't even know if it was a man or a woman. Meetings took place in a confessional booth in the National Shrine of the Immaculate Conception, where she could neither see nor hear the full voice of the handler, who spoke in whispers only. She highly doubted the person was a priest, though. Even though she took care to confess a few "sins" each time, she never received a penance.

That such a project could have escaped the Council's notice except for the accident that their plant was assigned to it was a shock. But the project itself shouldn't alarm them. It had taken their own savants years to develop their system. This wasn't something a bunch of government IT people, notoriously hampered by budget restrictions that left them with obsolete equipment, would be able to do in a decade, much less the six- to eight-week timeline their informant mentioned.

Their confidence faltered a bit when they were told that private sector technology companies and a few universities were lending their expertise. But they lost it completely when their informant told them about the visits from the mysterious, well-dressed consultants.

It seemed after every such visit, the project leaped ahead.

The handler had questioned the informant in detail, knowing the Council would want to know everything. She didn't know much because she wasn't part of the coding team. But she did know what progress had been made, and there'd been a rumor going around about a black box they'd brought in. Apparently, understanding how it worked would help them with the secured communications part of their project.

When Graziella and Mathieu heard that, they nearly lost their minds. The only conclusion they could come to was that the outsiders' information was coming from the A-Codex, which was just about the worst thing they could think of. Absolutely the worst was the news that the project team had one of the Council's own devices, the black box, to reverse engineer.

It could only have come from McCormick's car. The fact that he and his car had disappeared without a trace was ominous. They were beginning to feel incompetent, and that didn't bode well for the fate of anyone who'd crossed them or would do so in the near future.

Their days of exclusive access to quantum computing were rapidly coming to an end. And with the knowledge gained from digging into the black box communications device, their access to private communications with quantum security could very well be in jeopardy as well.

This day was proving to be the worst in their lives, and they had a gut-wrenching feeling it would only get worse when the hearing reconvened.

Chapter Eighty

ENOUGH IS ENOUGH!

Sebastian had pulled a few strings to commandeer a private meeting room on-site for them. When Davis announced a half-hour break, they gathered there to wait and have some refreshment. No sooner had they entered than Carter scooped Mackenzie off her feet into his arms and kissed her in front of the others until she begged for mercy. She had single-handedly turned the threat around and had given them the upper hand.

Sebastian was more than a little embarrassed that Mackenzie had succeeded where he'd failed in getting Davis to hear them out behind closed doors. But he was enough of a team player to congratulate her with the rest of them. Irene, Bill, and James hugged her.

When they'd settled down, Sebastian also had a question. "So, what now? We go back in there and spill our guts?"

Bill shook his head. He was disappointed with Sebastian's lack of understanding, but he managed to hide it. Though the man was his boss, he was more of a political appointee than a person who truly understood security issues.

"No. We feed them bits and pieces. I'll see if Davis will agree to let me give them a short address about A-Echelon and what they've been doing. I'll make it interesting and give them enough to ask questions about. We'll stay away from anything too sensitive to even tell *them* about."

Once in her office with the door locked and her assistant told she wasn't to be disturbed, Davis got through two cigarettes before popping that much-needed Valium. She wisely decided to forego any alcohol.

While smoking, she mentally berated herself for not listening to Sebastian in the first place. If she had, she wouldn't have lost face in having to finally close the hearing. Her reputation had taken a heavy blow, and voters had memories like elephants. They'd never allow her to forget she'd been bested by a soft-spoken scientist.

She started thinking about retiring from politics. Life was just too short to deal with this kind of crap on top of everything else.

Both sides, the committee and the witnesses, reconvened in the hearing chamber with a sense that things would go better from then on. With the meeting now behind closed doors, the witnesses could be more forthcoming, and the questioning could be less adversarial.

As soon as Davis had called the hearing to order, Bill stood.

"Madame Chairwoman, may I address the committee?"

"Go ahead, Director Griffin," she answered. Glad she'd not have to face Dr. Devereux again, at least not for as long as Griffin was talking.

"I'd like to propose that I take the stand now and give the committee some background information. It will help give everyone on the committee an understanding of what A-Echelon does. I believe it will help us get your questions answered much quicker," Bill said.

"You're saying you'd like to begin with an information session rather than questioning?"

"No, Madame Chairwoman, the committee would, of course, be welcome to ask questions as they arise, as well as afterward," Bill conceded.

Davis, though it was too little, too late, and her constituents wouldn't see it, was eager to make herself look better. She polled the committee members before answering. They were just as anxious to put the entire matter behind them so they could also assure *their* constituents they'd been thorough but fair. She turned back to Bill with a smile that belied her personal animosity toward him.

"You have the floor, Director Griffin."

Bill began, "A-Echelon investigates unexplained archeological phenomena, conspiracy theories, and ooparts. There are so many wild ideas and strange beliefs out there it makes my head swim. I'm talking ancient astronauts, aliens, star gates, time travel, Atlantis, the lost continent of Mu, or UFOs."

He got no further before someone interrupted him to ask what ooparts meant.

"Out of place artifacts," he explained. "Like what we think of as modern inventions encased in solid rock, or objects in paintings that resemble items we think of as not having been invented until long after it was painted."

Though some of the senators still had puzzled looks, he forged on.

"I know it sounds crazy, and to the uninformed, it may sound like a waste of money. But our government can't afford to ignore those. We *have* to investigate and decide if it's fact or fiction. Most turn out to be exactly that—fiction and fantasy, but a few have proven absolutely true and the technology has implications for national security.

"We simply can't afford for advanced or incomprehensible technology to fall into the hands of people who may use it for purposes contrary to our security. Whether those people are other governments or organizations with wicked intents.

"Rather than give you examples and sidetrack the intent of this hearing, I'd prefer to tell you about the biggest threat to the United States, and indeed the world, we've uncovered in A-Echelon's existence."

After all that, Bill could see he had the rapt attention of everyone on the committee, even Michelle Davis.

She leaned forward, apparently eager to hear what came next. "Please continue."

For the next hour, Bill summarized everything he knew about the Nabateans. He shared with them just a few of the horror stories that had come to light through A-Echelon's activities. How the Nabateans killed Algosaibi's children, the information Durand gave them, including how the Nabateans assassinated him while he was in US custody. He went on to describe what they were capable of, including how the head of the Council, Graziella Nabati, and her son, Mathieu, disappeared after those killings.

He told them about the attack on Freydís and the

circumstances that led to the capture of nine of the attackers, who gave up information about who had ordered it. Then he talked about the Director of the Federal Security Service (FSB) of Russia, Peter Nikolaev, who was behind that.

One of the committee members raised his hand at the mention of Russia. "Are you telling us that Russia is in league with these Nabateans?"

Bill answered, "No, Senator. I was just about to get to that. We have every reason to believe that Nikolaev was one of the twelve members of the Council of the Covenant of Nabatea. However, before we could act on our information, Nikolaev was killed in a skiing accident, or so it was reported. Based on our knowledge of their MO, we believe he was murdered to preserve the Council's security."

Davis was puzzled. "Getting back to the attack on Professor Carter's ranch. I assume a man of his wealth—and given the secret nature of his association with A-Echelon—he would have had the latest in security measures installed. How did these Russians get as far as they did?"

Bill explained, "That's a very good example of why A-Echelon exists. The assailants had a device advanced enough to defeat the latest and best security measures, including those of the CIA. Fortunately, it was captured during the attack, and it's now been reverse engineered. It is no longer an advantage to them or a threat to national security."

Bill deliberately left out the role of Executive Advantage in defeating the raid. No one had mentioned them in the press or during the questioning, so it was his hope that's how it would stay.

Satisfied with Davis's nod that she understood, he went on. "I'd like to conclude by helping you understand that between the media making this ruckus and you taking all of their rambling seriously, you've been playing into the hands of the Nabateans. We have discovered a senior member of one of the security agencies working for the enemy. He called himself Shadow, and he was the source of everything you've heard.

"This man traitorously gave all this top-secret information to a journalist who recently died under suspicious circumstances after starting this media circus. Though the lead detective's ruling was suicide, we suspect he was murdered.

"We now have reason to believe that someone even higher in government—someone who has access to highly sensitive information—is leaking it to the Nabateans. Can you now understand why we have been reluctant to further expose A-Echelon operations to the public?"

The silence that followed his question was fraught with tension. The majority of the committee believed him outright with no further proof required. If Davis had polled them, the hearing would have ended immediately.

However, Davis still had an issue with Bill, and even though she was beginning to see the error of her ways, she was determined to salvage some of her authority before she let it go.

"I assume you have proof of what you've told us," she said. "Can you show it? Or are you still going to hide behind the national security smokescreen?"

Bill shook his head. He'd thought his words alone would sway the committee, and in fact, he was sure he'd swayed most of them. But Davis still seemed to be after blood.

He nodded. "If I may, I have some information on my laptop that will interest you."

Davis gave him a moment to set up his laptop and

connect it to the projection device so they could all see it on the big screen. When he had it done, he opened a folder labeled "Patch Barracks."

He flipped through picture after picture of the gruesome scene, and when the silence in the room told him he had everyone's undivided attention, he said, "You thought this was a meteorite? Let me tell you what it really was. This, Senators, is the aftermath of an antimatter bomb."

The committee erupted in tumult. Two common questions emerged. "What's an antimatter bomb?" and, "I thought that was nothing but science fiction?"

Davis rapped her gavel for almost a minute, calling for order. Bill waited it out patiently suppressing a grin. He knew what was coming next would be even more explosive, no pun intended.

"An antimatter bomb is simply the collision of matter and antimatter. Antimatter was once indeed the subject of science fiction, but any physicist today will tell you it is quite real. In fact, it's being produced in minute quantities by various scientific facilities across the globe. The biggest producer so far has been CERN, known as the Large Hadron Collider, in Switzerland.

"And the result of the collision of just a small quantity of antimatter particles with matter will produce devastation that looks exactly like this. No crater, no fire from the explosion itself. It simply vaporizes anything within the blast radius as it did here. This, Senators, was a warning shot. Oh, and before I forget, the experts think this antimatter bomb, at Patch Barracks, could have been the size of a woman's lipstick or smaller."

The senators were gob smacked. But Davis wasn't convinced. "Why should we take your word for this? Who can verify it?"

The Nabatean Secret

Bill sighed. "We have scientists, at DARPA, who can verify it was not a conventional explosion. Beyond that is process of elimination. I can bring them here if need be, but let's move on to something else if you aren't convinced."

He then proceeded to tell them about the dolphins.

Now Davis had an expression of complete disbelief. "Are you presuming to disrespect this committee with an outrageous claim like that? I'll have you charged with contempt of Congress!"

Murmurs of support came from the committee.

Bill said, "Okay, give me a minute." He didn't have the images he needed on his laptop. A short consultation with Carter bore fruit as Carter confirmed he had some video and audio. They switched laptops, and Carter showed them what he had.

When Carter's presentation ended, Davis stated, "Any Hollywood producer could have created those. That isn't proof."

Exasperated, Bill replied, "Okay, then, why don't we call the Chief of Naval Operations in? He knows all about it. What do you say? Or better yet, why don't we go out into the mouth of the Chesapeake Bay, and we can all have a chat with Joanna and her pod? Hell, I'd bet she'll be glad to hear from us. We haven't had a chat since that video was taken. That was Joanna talking to us."

Davis shook her head. "Move on, Mr. Griffin."

Bill was beginning to wonder if it would take the Nabateans attacking the building to convince this stubborn woman of anything. He'd hoped not to have to play the next card but had no choice.

"You know about the discovery of an ancient library in the Egyptian desert, the City of Lights as we call it. That city existed more than sixty thousand years ago. Upon studying the library, Professor Devereux and his team discovered that the race of Giants who inhabited that city had the secret of nuclear energy, as well as the nuclear bomb. Because it was imperative we find any still in existence before anyone else got hold of them, Professor Devereux launched a global search and was able to find them with the help of the dolphins you don't believe talked to us."

Bill wasn't about to give up the information about the location in the Alboran Sea, nor about the technology to neutralize them. If *that* got out, well, he didn't want to think about it.

Once again, Bill's revelation was met with skepticism. One of Davis's supporters flatly called him a liar. "*We* were the first humans to build a nuclear bomb."

Saying nothing, Bill once again hooked up his own laptop and showed the pictures of nukes being hoisted out of the sea. In the shocked silence, he spoke. "I'll be happy to let the scientists at LANL come and testify concerning what they found. In fact, I'd be more than happy to take every one of you to Los Alamos and let you see and touch the five-hundred some-odd sixty thousand-year-old nuclear bombs in person!"

Davis looked uncertain. "You can back up all of this with physical proof?"

Bill wanted to snarl, but he drew upon all his patience. It was late, everyone was cranky from hunger, and besides, Davis would simply push back if she were challenged.

"Yes, Senator Davis. We can back it all up with physical proof. I know you have a poor opinion of me for some reason. But even you can't believe I'd be stupid enough to spin a fantastic tale like this without physical proof.

"I'd be happy to show you every speck of it."

It was enough, at last, to convince the rest of the committee. What he'd just said swept away all doubt.

One by one, they came to the same conclusion.

They'd been duped. They'd been persuaded by the half-truths and falsehoods in the press and nothing more than Davis's passion to destroy Bill Griffin, her old enemy the President, and anyone associated with either of them.

And the committee members were shamed by their gullibility.

With Davis paralyzed by the conflict between her ego and the irrefutable evidence, her vice-chairman stepped in.

"What can we do?" he asked. "I think I speak for the majority when I say we see we've done damage to the security community of our country. How can we help repair that damage?"

Bill's shoulders lifted with the removal of the burden, and he had a ready answer. "First, get off our backs and let us do our jobs.

"Second, now that the damage has been done, you can help mitigate it by delaying your rulings while we continue to hunt down the high-level spy."

The vice-chairman nudged Senator Davis and whispered they should have a private consultation. She nodded and dismissed the witnesses for a fifteen-minute break so the committee could air their opinions in private.

Davis was a dejected woman. Everything she'd believed in her whole life was now suspect, and she'd made a complete fool of herself with this hearing.

When a member of the opposition party suggested they do as Bill had asked and create delaying tactics as a smokescreen, Davis found she had no support to argue against it. She said that as chairwoman she'd have to abstain, thereby avoiding a reversal of her previous position, and with no nays, the vote carried to do exactly that.

When the fifteen minutes had passed, the witnesses filed back in and were given the good news. It was the best outcome they could have hoped for. And it was all thanks to Mackenzie schooling the committee.

Carter had never been more proud of her.

Despite the late hour, the public and the media were still waiting outside. They understood something big was going on inside and were not at all happy to have been kicked out. They were going nowhere without some resolution.

The media especially were up in arms. They had a feeling the Gold Rush of news was over, and they'd missed it.

When darkness fell, the crowd became restless. Mackenzie had become their darling, and they imagined she was being grilled inside.

A few began to chant, and eventually most of them picked it up. *"Leave Mackenzie alone. Enough is enough! Free Doctor Devereux!"*

Chapter Eighty-One

LET'S TAKE IT TO THEM

May 15, late night

The crowd had dispersed except for a few die-hard journalists with midnight deadlines by the time Davis gaveled the hearing dismissed for the evening. The journalists made a half-hearted effort to stop someone, anyone, for a report on the outcome.

All they got was a curt "No comment!" from Michelle Davis.

Carter and Mackenzie were whisked away to a new safe house, where Sean and Dylan waited for them with hot pizza. Carter stuffed most of a slice into his mouth, with a muffled, "Thanks! Starving!"

"How'd it go?" Sean asked. He'd already heard some of it from James, but he wanted to hear firsthand how Mackenzie had gotten the best of Davis. Carter had immense pleasure in relating the drama to Sean and Dylan. When the story was done, the Devereuxs taking turns between wolfing down their pizza, Sean and Dylan applauded.

"Okay, we've got the Intelligence Committee off your backs now, but we're no closer to finding the traitor in the NSC," Dylan noted.

"I've been thinking about that the whole day while Mackenzie was schooling the senators." Carter grinned. "Let's take it to them. Divert attention away from us to the Nabateans."

"Interesting thought. How do you propose to do that?" Sean asked.

"Scare them into making a mistake," Carter answered. He had the beginnings of a grin playing around the corners of his mouth.

Sean put his hand to his chin. "And? How do you propose to do *that*?"

"Let's break the story that we have their library! There's no time to translate it, but that doesn't matter. Just the fact that we have it and we can prove it could bring them out of hiding, or at least cause them to make stupid mistakes."

"Could be dangerous," Dylan muttered.

Mackenzie got excited by the proposal. "Next, we break the story about them—the Council—and show them for what they are. Show the public the contents of Algosaibi's laptop. That will certainly take the attention off us and at the same time make them furious enough to make the mistakes Carter's talking about."

Mackenzie and Carter missed their kids, Freydís, and their friends. It was time to kick ass, take names, and go home.

Carter tag-teamed Mackenzie's suggestion. "We'll tell the public about McCormick, just using the name Shadow, and how he was the one stirring up the ruckus in the media all this time, interfering in our political system and all. We don't have to reveal any of the top-secret stuff, just expose him as a traitor."

Sean thought for a moment. "Dylan's right. It could be dangerous. Rattling their cages might bring them out in the open, but they're powerful, sneaky, and vindictive. They won't just roll over. Chances are if they do come out to fight, it will be with a bang. Then they'll disappear as they always have."

"By bang, do you mean you think they'll explode another antimatter bomb?" Mackenzie asked.

"Could be. They had one, and I can't believe they'd use their only one on Patch Barracks. I mean, it was quite a symbolic statement, but they could just as easily have crippled our government by planting it in the Congressional Building. They have an end game. I reckon your plan could throw a wrench into it."

Everyone was too wound up by the victory in the hearing to go to sleep yet, so they started brainstorming how to pull off Carter and Mackenzie's plan.

Foremost in Carter's mind was to get his hands on some of the copper leaves from the Nabatean library and translate them. That would lend credibility to their claim that they had it. They'd need Italy to cooperate and go along with the story afterward. Sean said he thought he had a line on how to accomplish that. The grin he gave them was infectious, and Carter started laughing.

"It wouldn't have anything to do with a certain lady from Texas, would it?"

"Good lord, don't ever let Sam hear you say that!" Sean said. But he had a twinkle in his eye.

"Remember, too," Mackenzie said, "that Durand's laptop hinted they had the means to paralyze the stock markets. We should warn them, in case the Nabateans go for retaliation first."

"Good idea," Sean responded.

"And everyone who's been exposed by this media circus needs extra personal security," Dylan added.

"What else could they do?" Mackenzie mused.

"The biggest thing I'm worried about," Sean said, suddenly much more serious than he'd been a minute before, "is *if* they have more antimatter bombs, which they surely must, *where* they're likely to set them off."

"I think you hit the nail on the head earlier," Carter said. "We need to double down on protection for Capitol Square."

Carter and Mackenzie got up later than usual the next morning because of their late night. As she prepared breakfast, Mackenzie had a thought.

"Can we go home now, Carter? I miss the kids more than ever. And we're no longer on the Most Wanted list."

Carter took her in his arms. "Mackie, I wish I could say yes. Maybe you could, but I need to stay here to help. And remember, we're both targets for the Nabateans. I'm sure it would be easier for EA to guard us if we were together. That's why we're still in a safe house now instead of a downtown hotel."

She sighed. "You're right, of course. I just miss them so much."

"I'll see if there's anything they can do about that. Don't worry, Mackie. It's going to be over soon, now that we're taking the fight to them."

Carter left the room until Mackenzie called that breakfast was ready. When he came back, he had a grin a mile wide, but he wouldn't tell Mackenzie what it was all about.

Within the hour, Dylan and Sean arrived and asked if the Devereuxs were ready to go.

"Go where?" Mackenzie asked. "We've only been here overnight. We have to move *again*?"

"One last time," Sean said. He winked at Carter, mystifying Mackenzie even more.

"Okay, you guys, what are you conspiring about?" she asked.

Carter put on a look of innocence. "I don't know what you're talking about," he said.

Mackenzie knew there'd be no use asking further. She'd find out soon enough. The second surprise came when Sean and Dylan took them to a nearby private air field, instead of to another safe house. When she saw the helicopter, she got her hopes up for a trip home, but the flight didn't last long.

They settled on a helipad in a clearing in what appeared to be a woodland park.

"Dylan, you'll see to their luggage while I take them up to the Lodge?" Sean asked. Dylan gave a thumbs-up, and the other three took a waiting golf cart to a rustic but elegant lodge. They passed under a hanging sign that said "Camp David".

Mackenzie gasped. "Are you kidding me?"

"Nope!" Sean laughed out loud, and Carter was grinning from ear-to-ear. It had been hard to keep the secret from her, and he was glad he hadn't had to keep it for long.

"I called Bill and gave him your request. He went straight to the President with the suggestion there could be no better place to keep us secure than this. James and Irene with their families will be joining us soon, but that's not the best part."

"What is?" Mackenzie challenged, still overwhelmed that they'd been taken to the Presidential retreat.

"The kids and your parents will be here later today. Your brother's going to hold down the fort at Freydís, but he'll be able to make a short visit before we get the ball rolling on our plans for the Nabateans. The rest will stay for the duration."

Mackenzie was speechless, but the tears glimmering unshed in her eyes and the big smile on her face said it all.

Before the rest of the family got there, the four of them set up their "war room" in the conference room where so many historic meetings had taken place before.

Chapter Eighty-Two

BREAKING NEWS

May 22

With the help of Press Secretary Daniella Stewart, they laid out the plan for releasing the bombshells they hoped would flush the Nabatean council members out of hiding. After securing the cooperation of the Italians, Constance Pierce helicoptered in with a few of the copper leaves from the Nabatean library, the very ones Carter had photographed on the table inside the cave.

They had called Bill in to advise what to do about the stock market issue. The markets all had their own circuit-breakers in place to shut down in a financial free-fall, but the Securities and Exchange Commission had instituted a rule that allowed them to open more easily after a circuit-breaker shut-down.

Changing that would expose the plan to the SEC, and with proof the Nabateans had plants in some of the highest levels of government, even among Presidential appointees, they were reluctant to involve the head of the SEC.

Bill solved the problem by communicating in person with the heads of the Dow, Nasdaq, and the S&P 500. He made it very clear heads would roll if anyone else got wind of his warning.

"What about world markets?" Mackenzie asked. "Shouldn't we warn them? At least those of our allies?"

"Logic tells us the Nabateans would go after the US first, just because we're the biggest thorns in their sides. We expect the other markets to follow our lead if we must shut down. It's the best we can do.

"There's no time for Bill to go globe-trotting, and we don't trust any other communications methodology until we have the quantum system ready." Sean's explanation mollified Mackenzie, but they all agreed she had a valid concern.

There was just nothing more they could do about it.

Within a week, all was in readiness, prompting the President to congratulate Bill. He'd never heard of such efficiency. Bill replied they couldn't have done it without Grant's generous offer of the use of Camp David.

"Brace for impact," Bill said. "Daniella advised us to release selected portions of news at a time, but in rapid succession—every four to six hours. We'll saturate the news on every medium and keep it coming until the A-Echelon flap disappears from view." He looked at his watch. "I believe the first release is scheduled for early tomorrow morning. Should be fun to watch."

"Brilliant!" the President replied. "Care to watch with me?"

Bill smiled. "I wouldn't miss it for the world."

At five forty-five a.m. the next morning, Bill was back at the White House. His chief deputy knew where to reach him if the very first release triggered a blowup anywhere in the world. The White House staff was instructed to put through any call from the CIA.

Bill and the President settled on the sofa in the Oval Office to watch the big screen.

Everyone else, including James and Irene, Sean and Dylan, and the two Devereuxs, were at Camp David.

Mackenzie and Irene passed out cups of coffee before taking their own seats.

There was a festive atmosphere. They'd set something in motion. It remained to be seen how quickly things developed.

The first portion of news had to do with the discovery of the Nabatean Library but was prefaced with some background about the Nabateans and Petra. To ensure the safety of the library and avoid trouble for the Italians, they had deliberately avoided mention of where the library had been found, which left the impression that it was somewhere near or in Petra.

A few minutes later, following the plan, they flooded the internet with articles made to look as if they'd been hastily researched. Those articles delved into the history of the Nabateans, how they'd all but disappeared as a distinct culture, and then stating that they were still around. But the hint was that some of them were not nice people.

Bill's prediction was spot on. It *was* fun to watch the ripples spread from the initial news release. It was even more fun to follow the progress of the internet articles as conspiracy theorists seized on them and spun even more shocking theories, tying the Nabateans to alien abductions and, more accurately than they'd have thought, to ooparts.

Carter observed, "They're really going to have a field day when we release the translations."

The initial uproar was just about to die down when it was time to release the next bombshell.

They'd chosen the contents of Algosaibi's laptop, spilling all the secrets of the Council of the Covenant of Nabatea, to release next. Along with those contents, they mentioned how Algosaibi's children had died and tied his beheading to the council. A few of the newspapers balked at the potential for libel suits but gave in when their sources pointed out that no one had given the names of the council members. There was no one who could bring a suit without exposing themselves to public questioning.

By close of business on the East Coast, there was public outcry for justice for the Algosaibi children. They'd been murdered! No one questioned what kind of people *they* had been. What mattered was two young people had lost their lives because this shadowy council thought they were a law unto themselves.

Almost ninety percent of the adult residents of the Eastern portion of the US were glued to their TVs for the five o'clock news.

They weren't disappointed.

This part of the plan called for the release of information about an unnamed, high-ranking FBI agent who'd been working for the Nabateans. Accusations against him were he'd fed misleading information to the press, infiltrated a top-secret INSCOM investigation, and stolen top-secret information and passed it on to the Nabateans.

It was reported he'd been taken into custody and would be brought to trial for treason.

At the end of the day, the subject of A-Echelon had all

but disappeared from traditional media and would have required a very specific search to be found on the internet.

By then, the nation had seen all the news from coast to coast, and the foreign press had picked it up as well.

Everyone in the know about the plan from the President down was satisfied it would dominate the news for days.

Carter and Mackenzie, Sean and Dylan, James and Irene, and the newest member of the inner circle, Daniella, knew all it would take to push this news out of the forefront would be a world disaster.

They expected that to happen as soon as the Nabateans formed a plan for a response.

In his Washington townhome, Jason Sullivan turned off his TV after learning the devastating news that McCormick had been taken into custody. Even though his name hadn't been mentioned, Sullivan knew it had to be him. Why else would he have disappeared?

Sullivan knew McCormick wouldn't be able to identify him by name. But the mere fact that he existed and had been giving McCormick sensitive information would set a hunt in motion. And from the other side, he wasn't at all certain the council would believe him. Even if they did, they didn't take chances with their anonymity.

He could feel his time ticking away rapidly.

What, if anything, could he do to save his own skin?

Chapter Eighty-Three

A PLAN OF ESCAPE

May 23

Members of the Council of the Covenant of Nabatea across the globe were wakened by emergency summons to a virtual meeting immediately after the news release that the Americans had their library.

How could it be true? Of course, it had to be Carter Devereux. No one else could have found what they themselves had been seeking over many centuries. It shook them like a magnitude eight earthquake.

There weren't enough swear words in the languages of the world to express what they thought of Devereux. He was Satan incarnate, the most diabolical adversary they'd faced since the beginning of time.

Whichever it was, he had to be destroyed, utterly and completely. Along with his wife, children, and any speck of DNA that belonged to him or his family.

This was the last straw.

As if the first news release on its own wasn't enough,

bad news kept hitting them in aftershocks. First the internet articles, then the copycats. It simply couldn't get worse! They were exposed. They'd never be able to operate in secret again—and even worse, Devereux would soon have every secret of their ancient forebears, some of which were keeping them technologically ahead of their time to this day.

What else might be in that lost library?

What knowledge might defeat them as soon as Devereux translated it?

Questions pelted Graziella without mercy until the second wave of news hit. With it went every last vestige of privacy. What they'd done to Algosaibi's children was being shouted from every rooftop, and speculation about their methods and who they were sent them into a full-scale panic.

Further news about Durand's revelations, his murder, and the suspicion that Nikolaev's accident had been no accident pounded them.

The crisis meeting went on for hours, and each time, just when they thought they had a handle on what they should do, a new wave of disaster sucked them under again.

The news about one of their primary sources of information from the FBI being taken into custody was the last straw. The last time they'd faced such a crisis was in 106 AD, when the Romans had taken over their empire.

Graziella pulled herself together to preside over their last resort. Always in the past, when faced with a crisis that threatened their existence, the council had done what they did best. What they'd done in 106 AD. They'd retreated and disappeared, to emerge again when it was safe.

This time, however, their tentacles spread farther than ever before. It wouldn't be easy, and they couldn't just disband the council and walk away. There were preparations to make—a modern library to hide, evidence to destroy, and some tough decisions on operations cleanup to make.

The takeover of their empire by the Romans way back then was peaceful, but this takeover was going to be different—it was going to be vicious.

Everyone not on the council who could potentially inform on them must go. They began to realize with dismay that this part of the cleanup, more than anything else, could expose them. There were just too many to make disappear or "die unexpectedly."

Worse, their modern library contained some seriously damaging information. Not just their history since 106 AD, but their savant program, full specifications on their advanced technology, their medical secrets, and the algorithms that allowed them to control the stock markets to their advantage. Full records of the people they'd terminated over the millennia. Information concerning their contacts and plants in high places throughout the world, including those who were council members themselves.

Some of it had to be destroyed completely. The majority had to be concealed and this time left where the members of the next Council could retrieve it when next they emerged from obscurity to take up the mission of restoring the progeny of Nabatea to world dominance.

And then there was the matter of retribution. To a man and woman, the council members believed in the superiority of their bloodline. Hitler's views on a Master Race didn't begin to rival their own. When Mathieu mentioned that if he had to go, he'd prefer to go with a bang, he got unanimous agreement from the rest.

One last operation, or maybe two, in addition to the

destruction of that demon, Carter Devereux. Then their legend would grow among the inferior beings who lived on the planet with them. Next time they came into their own, people would respect and fear them, making their mission of world domination that much easier.

As their enemies had done, they'd do as well, not with news, but with disasters. They'd collapse the stock market first. When things got back to normal, they'd deliver another one-two punch. First, a bomb to vaporize the seat of government in Washington, D.C. It would have been nice to kill two birds with one stone, so to speak, by destroying a more populous city, but D.C. had several advantages.

First, America, and specifically Washington, had a special significance for them. It was there that their downfall had been plotted and executed.

Second, destroying the government would cripple the country for some time to come, leaving them free to operate and track down everyone they had to terminate.

And finally, it would leave the country reeling and set up the knockout blow.

That would be the pièce de résistance, the final statement of their power. An antimatter bomb large enough to leave a mudflat where New York City once stood.

Again, it would have been preferable to take out a bigger city, such as Tokyo with its thirty-eight million inhabitants. New York City, by contrast, had only eight million or so. Nevertheless, their main gripe was with America, and New York City represented the United States and all its most reprehensible qualities to the Nabateans.

After the first day, the bad news slowed down, and though the story was still the top news in the world, the council felt they could settle down, take a figurative deep breath, and do what needed to be done.

Among their priorities was a distributed record of where each was located, what information or system they controlled, and where and how they would secure it before disappearing. They didn't want a repeat of 106 AD, when the collective knowledge of their forefathers had disappeared from their own grasp.

They knew what it would mean if that happened again. The knowledge of some of the secrets had lived on in the council members of old, but they'd had to start afresh with a fraction of their secrets going forward. Next time, even if they lost some, which would be doubtful, the majority would be readily available.

They'd be able to gain the advantage again quickly. Next time, it wouldn't take two millennia to again be ready to rule the world.

Next time might even come within their own lifetimes.

During the crisis meetings and throughout the planning, Jason Sullivan was a participant. He took pains to keep up appearances but wasn't fooled by the lack of a hint of his own demise. He had a special circumstance. His direct contact, McCormick, was in custody, they didn't know where, and the Council couldn't be certain he didn't know about Sullivan.

He wasn't stupid. His name was on someone's hit list as part of the cleanup operation.

Therefore, he'd been working on a plan of escape for himself. When it came to personal survival, bloodline be damned.

Chapter Eighty-Four

AN EERIE QUIET

Suddenly, the pressure was off the Devereux contingent. They'd set their plan in motion and the ball was in the enemy's court.

For now, there were no more libraries to discover, though Carter had an idea about that. Secure at Camp David, there was no more hiding, worrying about being caught. The children and Mackenzie's folks were with them. They all missed Freydís, their friends, and the wolves, but Camp David was delightful and the best they could do under the circumstances.

Michelle Davis and her one-time band of vicious, self-serving senators were singing a different tune after their briefing about A-Echelon at the last hearing.

Most were now ardent supporters. All played their part in keeping the media at bay by being vague, evasive, and ambiguous—any good politician's specialty.

Those very senators who, up till a few days ago, were ranting about *"getting to the bottom of this"* to *"protect and inform the American people"* to *"stop this lunacy"* and *"hold officials accountable for the way they spend taxpayers' money"* were now answering with *"National security is at stake here,"* or, *"It's being investigated thoroughly,"* or, *"No comment yet,"* and *"We'll root out this evil."*

Not mentioning, of course, what evil they intended to root out.

There wasn't even any more news to release about the Nabateans. They'd spent all that currency and were happy with the result, if a little apprehensive about the fact that they hadn't yet had any pushback from the council. Most likely, the Nabateans had enough to deal with themselves that Carter and Mackenzie had become secondary projects.

Nevertheless, the adults at Camp David and those who came daily to support them felt the other shoe had to drop soon. The quiet had come too suddenly.

Were they in the eye of the hurricane? What havoc would be wrought when the eye had passed?

It had to have been a low blow to the Nabateans to learn that outsiders were in possession of their library. Because of the assassins in Matera, no one believed the smokescreen about its location would last long, yet the Italians hadn't reported any assaults on the defenses of the cave.

Maybe the Nabateans, every member of the council, would run and hide, but a bunch of psychopaths like that would surely not go out without a statement.

The uncertainty was getting on everyone's nerves. Not being able to adequately prepare for an unknown eventuality was the worst. It made for unbearable tension among the group and even a few near-misses when arguments flared among the men.

All that alpha-male testosterone was like a tinder-box hidden in a pile of dynamite.

Even Carter and Mackenzie had an argument—something which almost never happened. Afterwards, they couldn't really recall how the argument came about. It probably started when Carter mentioned it would be nice to get breakfast in bed one day, and Mackenzie responded with, "If you want breakfast in bed, go and sleep in the kitchen."

Somehow, that struck Carter as funny. He started laughing, and in a moment, she joined in.

Chapter Eighty-Five

SHAKING ONE MORE TREE

May 28

Part of the tension among the group came from the knowledge that Bill's illegal surveillance of the NSC members had turned up not a shred of evidence. He was in danger of being in big trouble for nothing.

Out of desperation and a last-ditch effort to shake every tree they could find, Sean and Dylan told everyone they'd be out of touch for a couple of days and flew to Sean's brother's ranch.

It took them just over three hours to get to Colorado Springs with the CIA jet and another forty minutes or so to get to the farm by rented helicopter, which Dylan piloted. They landed on Jared's farm shortly after eight a.m. Zulu, having followed the sun to arrive when the *clock* said they'd left less than an hour before. It promised to be a long day.

They had a quick word with Jared, who was surprised to see them, and then they took McCormick away from the house, far enough that no sound would reach where they'd asked Jared to stay, preferably with his sound system on loud.

Jared told them there was a small shed there, suitable for what he suspected they needed.

McCormick's heart sped up when he saw the visitors. When he glimpsed their faces, he knew it was not the time to mess around. He searched his memory frantically. Telling these guys, he didn't know was going to get him punished, even if it was the truth. And by punished, he expected jail, probably with broken bones and possibly with bullet wounds.

Both of them were carrying.

The only thing he could be grateful for, as he thought at the last minute before they reached the shed, was they hadn't brought Kelly White with them. He suspected they were in a mood to treat him the same way she would, but he hoped that, as men, they'd be reluctant to resort to that crazy woman's tactics.

When Sean started talking, McCormick realized he'd been wrong. Kelly's option might very well have been better.

"I guess you know why we're here, McCormick. Do I need to tell you we're both in a hell of a bad mood?"

McCormick shook his head.

"Then you're aware that if you don't cooperate this time, we don't particularly care if we kill you, right?"

Thinking broken bones, bullets, jail, and even missing his family jewels were probably the best he could hope for, McCormick started talking fast.

"Guys, please, I get it. I truly wish I could help. But I told you all I know last time. I swear it!"

"Let's just test that theory, shall we? Let's go through it again, from the beginning."

Sean and Dylan both had really good memories, and in any case, they'd listened again to the recordings on the flight out. They asked him the same questions and compared the answers. To their frustration, they couldn't find any incongruities except in maybe the word choices and order of sentences.

His story matched, and there was no escaping it.

It didn't make sense, though. An asset in his position had to have more than he was telling them. Threat of bodily harm hadn't produced anything but another unpleasant pants-pissing episode.

Disgusted, Dylan knocked McCormick down, but he still claimed he didn't know.

Sean held Dylan back when he would have followed that punch with a kick to the ribs. "Wait. I believe him. I think he's not deliberately hiding anything. We need to try something different."

"Hanging for a minute?" Dylan asked hopefully.

"Maybe later," Sean answered, distracted by his own thoughts. McCormick was telling the truth as he knew it, Sean was convinced. He wasn't hiding anything, but there had to be something he just wasn't thinking about. They were asking the wrong questions.

He said, "Now listen carefully, asshole. You've had time out here in peace and quiet in this lovely place, among your new friends, the alpacas, to think for more than twenty-five days.

"There *is* something you're not telling us. So, let me be succinct – Dylan is going to kill you right here and right now, and I won't lift a finger to stop him. The world will be a better place without you.

"Just so you know what your future looks like, you're looking at the electric chair or the needle if you go to trial. I can't save you from that, but I can help you out of a long wait to die by letting Dylan shoot you right now. He'll probably get a medal for doing it, especially if he and I are the only ones remaining to tell the story of how it *actually* happened.

"On the other hand, we might also be able to help you out by telling the prosecutors how cooperative you were and how much remorse you showed for your wrongdoing.

"Hell, we *might* even tell them you were blackmailed into doing someone else's dirty work. We can't give guarantees, but with that sort of testimony and calling in a few favors, who knows?

"You might just escape the death penalty."

Dylan grinned ferally and took his pistol out of his shoulder holster.

McCormick shook his head in desperation. "What do you want me to say or do? I've already told you everything, and I mean *everything* I know. I've been honest, I swear!" Sweat beaded on his forehead and trickled down his cheeks.

"You must have some inkling who your handler is." Sean overrode McCormick's attempt to answer and continued, "Yes, I know you 'saw him twenty-five years ago, once, for a short while in a poorly illuminated place'. You've said that. But I'm sure you must have wondered who that person was. You must have seen people that maybe looked like him or reminded you of him. Tell us about them."

McCormick sat quiet for a long while. They let him, because they could see he was thinking hard—he was thinking for his life.

He had no doubt Sean or Dylan would execute him—he could see it in their eyes, and they could see that knowledge in his.

Finally, he said, "Yes, I've been thinking and wondering

about that cursed man every day for twenty-five years. And I still don't know... rather I can't be sure... or... I just don't know—"

"McCormick!" Dylan yelled. "Any more, silly rambling like that and I put a bullet between your eyes."

McCormick looked up and slowly shook his head and said, "It's not possible... it can't be... I... it's been driving me to the edge of insanity... For almost eighteen years I never saw or heard anyone that reminded me of that man, but for the last seven years or so—"

"*Who?* I'm not asking again," Dylan yelled. He cocked the gun.

"Jason Sullivan... but it can't be... him... it just can't be... yet..." McCormick had been reduced to babbling, and they noted with disgust he'd pissed himself again.

Sean and Dylan looked at each other. The only Jason Sullivan they knew was the Secretary of the Treasury of the United States, and... he was one of the President's NSC members.

"Jason Sullivan, as in the Secretary of the Treasury of the United States?" They asked in unison, as if they'd been practicing it.

McCormick nodded slowly. "Yes. Every time the last few years I saw his face on TV and heard his voice and way of speaking, it reminded me of the man I saw twenty-five years ago, and who has been holding this sword over my head for all that time.

"But... it can't be... him. It's... not... it's not possible."

"Why not?" Sean demanded.

"I don't know. I just can't imagine a man in his position would do it. Also, he is known as a very good manager. The people in his department are crazy about him. He's just not the type of person that could do something like this," McCormick babbled.

"Well, he hasn't been the Secretary of the Treasury for all of the past twenty-five years. He's been in that position only about seven and a half years," Dylan pointed out. "McCormick, we're going to check up on that. And you might just have saved your own life. Honest to God, I was ready to kill you today. You have no fuckin' idea how close you were to your death a few minutes ago."

Sean nodded decisively. "Dylan, we need to check this out." To McCormick, he said, "We're going to leave now, but you stay put on this farm until I come and fetch you.

"Jared says you've been good so far and have been a big help. Just carry on doing that. Don't even think about running away. We *will* find you, even if we have to go to the ends of the earth. We'll find you and *kill* you. Understood?"

McCormick nodded.

"Okay, get your ass out of here, and go feed the alpacas. They must be missing you."

After he left, Sean and Dylan stared at each other again. *Jason Sullivan?* He was known as one of the friendliest and most efficient high-ranking officials in President Grant's administration. His staff and people in his department loved him. He was known as a fair and good-natured executive—in short, he would have probably been the last man they would have suspected.

"A friendly, good-natured, soft-spoken, people-pleasing, and beloved psychopath?" Dylan mused.

"Not unheard of. Remember Ted Bundy," Sean answered.

"You have a point. Listen, we need to get back to D.C. immediately. There's no time to lose."

Chapter Eighty-Six

SORRY, YOU GOT BUMPED

May 29

Jason Sullivan had been thinking about his future for a while, but he got more serious about it when McCormick disappeared. And the last two days, with all the breaking news about the Nabateans and the crisis meetings he attended, he had read between the lines and recognized the signs the council found him too dangerous to let live.

An analytical man, he'd considered several options and narrowed them down to one. But it was going to require very careful planning.

There was only one man he felt could get him out of his predicament, and that man was Carter Devereux.

In Nabatean circles, Devereux had become legendary. He, and he suspected some others, had come to believe Devereux was a demi-god. In all their long history, the Nabateans had never been faced with so formidable an enemy. Not only did he beat them to every critical discovery, but he had somehow escaped every plan they'd made to destroy him.

Sullivan had one big problem in his scheme, though—how to contact Devereux without raising suspicion of his motives? More importantly, how to do so without the council learning of it?

But he was out of time—he had to act immediately. Between the news of late, the panic among the council members, and Graziella's constant temper tantrums, his hourglass had only a few grains of sand remaining.

There was no time to ponder his next move any longer.

Sean and Dylan left the ranch mid-morning and were back in D.C. by afternoon. They didn't even stop to eat, going straight to Bill with their information.

Bill leapt to his feet at the news. "Impossible! He's lying. You guys probably used torture techniques, and that's the trouble with them. McCormick would have said anything to save his skin and stop the pain."

Dylan crossed his arms, and his face assumed a stubborn expression. Sean tried to explain. "We did threaten him, but I swear we didn't touch him, just one little love-tap. All we did was threaten to shoot him." He grinned, but Bill was in no mood for levity.

"Damn it, Sean, that's just what I mean. Think about it! Sullivan has an untarnished reputation. He's a gentleman in both senses of the word and highly regarded from both sides of the political fence.

"One of the few in this administration that gets things done without ruffling feathers. The President likes him for that, and relies on him.

"How am I going to go to the President and tell him a traitor under duress has named him as the mole in the NSC?" As he ranted, hardly drawing breath, Bill paced his office and ran his hand through his grey hair.

Sean signaled Dylan to let him do the talking. "Bill, it's the only—" He got no further.

"No! Just stop. There's no way I'm taking this to the President. Shit, man, Sullivan is without a doubt the only Cabinet member who's likely to continue in his position irrespective of which party wins the election. Even boneheads like you must know about his good reputation."

Sean and Dylan didn't even risk a glance at each other. They just stared at Bill. What he was saying was all true, including the accusation of enhanced interrogation, though they hadn't taken that as far as Bill assumed.

On the other hand, it was the only lead they had. There was literally nowhere else to look.

Bill wasn't done, though. Apparently, they'd opened the floodgates of his stress.

"What's more," he said, "I've put my head on the chopping block by ordering the illegal surveillance of the NSC members.

"I did that based on a notion from *you* guys. And I admit, I agreed with it at the time, but you know as well as I do we couldn't even find one of them having an argument with his wife.

"I study those wiretaps every goddamn day, and I'm telling you, Sullivan is squeaky clean. And you're asking me to stick my neck out even further?"

Sean lifted his hands in frustration, but Dylan beat him to the answer. "Yes, that might be so. But remember the Nabatean's superior technology. Just think about how they managed, almost successfully, to frame the Devereuxs.

"Think about how they were able to escape detection of our NSA—hell man, all our security agencies. *And* those of every country in the world for close on two thousand years.

"Just remember their almost-free access to our security agencies' databanks. They have the ways and means to avoid any electronic surveillance techniques we can throw at them."

Bill stopped to consider Dylan's point. Then he answered, "Okay, that might be so, but it still doesn't explain the discrepancy in personality traits. Psychopaths usually display disinhibited behavior, low anxiety, and feckless disregard—Sullivan displays none of that."

Sean agreed. "You're right. But we're just calling these guys psychopaths. It doesn't mean they necessarily fit the profile. And as I reminded Dylan earlier, we've seen some who don't conform to the usual traits we as laypeople think they have, at least on the surface.

"Let's call in one of the shrinks and hear what he or she has to say. We're convinced McCormick wasn't lying."

Dylan nodded vigorously. "Bill, we did put a lot of pressure on him. Like Sean said, we threatened to shoot him, and I'll admit he was convinced we would. But I swear, we didn't use extreme measures on him. Yes, I hit him once, but not very hard, and only once.

"We didn't even tie him up during the questioning. Sure, he could have been making it all up just to make us stop, but we're convinced it's not the case."

Sean took up the refrain. "Bill, we were there. We spoke to him. Just trust us on this one."

"Yeah, well, your definition of 'speaking' to someone and mine might differ, I suspect," Bill growled.

Dylan snorted. "Bill, you're harping on that, and we've both already said exactly what we did and did not do. Why not do as Sean suggested? What can it hurt? Just call a shrink in and ask!"

Bill threw his arms in the air. "All right! Shit, you guys *are* a pain in the ass. But I'll do it, just to shut you up."

He buzzed his secretary. "Get hold of Dr. Banks and have her come in here on the double."

While they waited, Bill tried to relax. "How was Colorado?"

"Shit, Bill, we were only there a couple of hours. And we were a little too busy to notice the weather," Sean retorted.

Dr. Banks arrived breathless. "You wanted to see me, Director?" She was a lanky, almost anorexic-looking woman; she had big black glasses and dark hair cut in a straight bob. She probably wouldn't break any mirrors, Dylan thought, but neither would she turn any heads.

Without telling her what it was all about, they fired hypothetical questions at her for the next half hour. Her answers revealed that psychopaths could be master people-pleasers and manipulators. The skillful ones could get literally anything they wanted from people, which would be incredibly useful to them in furthering their self-serving nature.

"So, you're saying not all psychopaths are killers," Sean clarified.

"Yes, not all psychopaths are killers," she answered. "Many of them, because of their people-pleasing and manipulative traits, are very successful business leaders, CEOs of big corporations, and even head government departments. Even some of the *killers* can appear normal and charming. Ted Bundy, for example."

Sean shot a triumphant glance at Bill.

After dismissing the shrink with thanks, Bill immediately called for an appointment with the President.

As usual, it was a battle of wills with Scott Eadie to get in.

"All your appointments are urgent, Bill. You don't have to tell me. Eight tonight, take it or leave it."

Within an hour after Bill's call, Scott took a call from Jason Sullivan.

"I need to see him on a personal and private matter, Scott," Sullivan said.

"I can slot you in for next week sometime," Scott answered.

"It's urgent." For the next ten minutes, Sullivan used every manipulative trick in his arsenal to persuade Scott to give him just a few minutes immediately. Scott soon felt so good about himself and Sullivan that he said he'd clear the President's schedule for fifteen minutes. At eight p.m.

With that done, he called Bill. "Sorry, you got bumped. Best I can do is seven a.m. tomorrow."

Bill exploded. "What the fuck! Who got my slot? This is serious stuff man! I'm telling you, this could be more serious than anything else I ever brought to the President. You know I'm good friends with Sam Grant. I want my appointment tonight, and if I don't get it, I'm going over your head."

Eadie wavered. He liked Sullivan and didn't want to disappoint him. His business was urgent, too, he'd said. Yet, he feared Grant's wrath if he blocked Bill from bringing a critical matter to his attention. He pushed back, and Bill pushed harder, finally demanding to know who was the person who got priority over him.

After a long argument, Eadie said, "Jason Sullivan."

Bill felt an ice cube slip down his spine. "No! You can't! Wait right there in your office, Eadie. I'm on my way."

"What? What are you talking about?" Eadie replied.

Bill said, "Don't go anywhere, not even to the bathroom. When I walk in there, you'd better be in your office. Don't make me search for you." He slammed the receiver down in its cradle and called for backup.

Bill sped from Langley to the White House in a mini motorcade with sirens blaring and lights flashing. The nine miles, which in normal traffic should've taken sixteen minutes, was done in ten. On the way, he called Sean and Dylan and told them to get their asses to the White House, *pronto*.

Eadie was behind his desk when Bill, Sean, and Dylan marched in, followed by his flustered secretary. "I'm sorry, sir. I tried to stop them."

Eadie stood. "What the hell is this, Bill?"

Bill silently motioned the secretary to leave, shut the door, and sat down. Backed up by Sean and Dylan, he told Eadie what they suspected was going on, psychoanalysis and all.

By the time they finished, Scott Eadie was as pale as bleached-white linen. "Oh, my God! What do you want me to do right now?"

He was shaking like an October aspen leaf, wondering if he'd unwittingly exposed the President to an assassination attempt. *Thank God, they set me straight!*

Bill answered crisply, "Clear the President's schedule. We go in immediately, tell him what's going on. Then, depending if he agrees, you call Sullivan and tell him a slot just opened, and he can come in immediately."

Scott dialed the President's next appointment with shaking hands but managed to keep his voice steady as he apologized. "I'm sorry, the President has had a priority one matter come up. I'll have to get back to you to reschedule." He suspected he'd be doing the same for the rest of the appointments that night and probably the next day, if not more.

Fifteen minutes later, they were briefing the President, who was as incredulous as Bill had been earlier. He was more than a little upset with them. "This guy is my best Cabinet member by a long shot. He's beyond reproach."

"Yes, Mr. President," Bill agreed. "I said the same thing. But I've been persuaded we must at least check it out. Here's what we've learned…"

Bill had Sean and Dylan report on their early-morning interrogation of McCormick. They went through the same objections with Grant as they'd endured from Bill, with the same answers that their methods hadn't been as extreme as they could have been.

The President conceded McCormick could have been telling the truth. "But I'd hate to lose a friend and a key Cabinet member over an accusation the accuser isn't even certain of," he concluded.

"That isn't all, Mr. President." Bill took over again, summarizing what they'd learned from the psychologist. "As you can surmise, Sullivan is exactly what we're potentially looking for."

Eadie backed him up. "Mr. President, in fact, I've just fallen for those very tactics. Sullivan persuaded me to bump Bill and this meeting from its original slot and put him in it instead. Who knows what could have happened if Bill hadn't come straight here?"

It took more batting the subject back and forth before the President conceded. "All right. But you'll all be looking for other jobs if this doesn't pan out."

While Eadie left to place the call to Sullivan, Bill, Sean, and Dylan gave the head of the Secret Service a briefing to make doubly sure Sullivan would not carry any weapons of any nature when he entered the Oval Office later. If they had to subject him to a cavity search as part of a "new security directive" to do random searches like that, then they were to do so.

Chapter Eighty-Seven

THE LAST KING OF THE NABATEANS

May 29, 7:00 p.m.

All was in readiness when Sullivan was led into the Oval Office. A nervous Eadie and still-shocked President Grant were there to greet him. The President was a consummate actor. He'd spent most of the past decade in the position of portraying calm no matter what his inner thoughts. He could hide his shock and dismay.

As he greeted Sullivan, he asked him to take a seat. If Sullivan noticed Grant was keeping his distance, he didn't say anything about it.

The President studied Sullivan's face for any signs of anxiety but saw none. He remembered what Bill had told him—that low anxiety when normal people would panic was a trait of psychopaths.

Bill, Sean, and Dylan were in Eadie's office nearby watching the meeting on the closed-circuit TV screen.

The President started on a light note. "Jason, to what do

I owe the honor? Please don't tell me you're here to discuss some crisis in the Treasury, or worse, your resignation?"

Sullivan smiled. "No, Mr. President. None of that. I have a strange request, and I believe you might be able to help me with it. I've been wondering if you could assist me to get a face-to-face meeting with Professor Carter Devereux. I can't get any messages through to him." Sullivan smiled. "I don't know where or how to contact him. I know since they have extracted that library of the Giants from the Alboran Sea, every request to get access to it has to go past you first."

He was telling a half-truth. It had to go to Bill first, and then James and Irene would examine the request as well as the requester and give Bill the yay or nay. Only then would the President sign off on it.

"Urgent matter, my ass," a fully-alarmed Scott Eadie whispered quietly to himself. *At least we have the assurance from security he's not armed.*

The President, on high alert himself, didn't correct Sullivan, keeping up the subterfuge. "Oh, that shouldn't be too much of a problem, Jason. But may I ask, what is your interest in the A-Codex that could relate to the Treasury?"

Sullivan answered smoothly, "Well, it took me a very long time, and I'm sure most people who learn about this remarkable discovery, to come to terms with it. The idea of civilizations that existed so long ago and were much more advanced than ours, that is. I was wondering if there could be something we could learn from those wise ancients about economic and financial systems? I think it's at least worth having a look. You can never be too sure that you know it all."

Now alert to the possibility, Grant had to admit Sullivan was definitely a master spinner—no doubt about that. But what was the real reason he wanted to meet with Carter Devereux?

When the group in Scott's office heard Sullivan asking to see Carter, Sean said, "Let's get Carter over here right now."

Bill agreed. "You see to that, and I'll let Scott know they should keep the meeting going so we can get Carter here." He wrote a note for Scott on a piece of paper then went to the President's personal assistant and asked her to take the note in to Scott immediately.

Scott read the note. *Devereux is on his way. Stall the meeting as long as you possibly can. Show this to the President.*

He nodded and said, "Apologies for the interruption, Mr. President, Jason. Just a quick note for you, sir." He handed the note to Grant, who read it quickly and nodded.

"Jason, you're in luck. Professor Devereux is actually on his way here right now, and my schedule is clear for the rest of the night. Isn't it, Scott?"

Scott thanked his lucky stars he'd foreseen this possibility. "Yes, Mr. President."

Grant smiled, turned to Sullivan, and said, "Why don't we use the time and you bring me up to speed with how things are going in your department? When Devereux arrives, we can get you two acquainted and set up the terms of your joint research project as we did with all the others."

It was not entirely how Sullivan wanted it to happen. He preferred to meet with Carter in private, not in front of the President. But he'd take what he could get. It meant he'd have to reveal the sorry mess to the President and Scott Eadie as well.

But, beggars can't be choosers.

It wasn't ideal, but better than not being able to talk to his only hope. Carter Devereux had become mystical to Sullivan. He'd been placing so much hope in Carter he'd lost contact with reality and thought of him as an immortal, not a normal, fallible, human being of flesh and blood like others.

"That's great news, Mr. President. I appreciate it very much."

At Camp David, Carter heard the helicopter approach as Sean gave him the message. "Get your ass on the chopper, which will land at your doorstep in about two minutes. I'll see you soon and explain then."

As the pilot took off the second he'd cleared the door, Carter asked, "Where are we going?"

The pilot answered, "All I know is I'm supposed to get you to the White House without delay."

Must be some serious stuff. Carter didn't waste time trying to figure it out. He'd know soon enough.

Sean met him outside on the south lawn, where the President's helicopter, Marine One, always landed and took off. "Jason Sullivan wants a word with you."

"The Treasury Secretary? Why?"

"Well, he's told the President it's because he wants to learn if there's anything in the A-Codex about advanced financial systems or some such bullshit. But here's what's really going on..."

Sean began the briefing as they jogged to Scott Eadie's office, where Dylan was waiting to help bring Carter up to speed about events leading to this meeting.

Carter expressed the same shock as Bill and the President when he heard they suspected Sullivan of being the leak from the NSC. But he was intelligent and quick-witted enough to keep his mouth shut and listen, process it quickly, and do his best to prepare himself for whatever was coming.

The President's secretary showed him into the Oval Office, but before she could announce him, the most bizarre scene any of them had ever seen began to unfold.

Sullivan started up from his seat on a sofa facing the door where Carter had just entered. Before reaching his full height, he dropped to his knees. He bowed his head and kept it like that, staring at the floor, not daring to look directly at Carter.

Sullivan started speaking in a loud voice. "My master and my King. I'm your eternal and humble servant, Jason Sullivan."

Carter's mouth dropped open as Sean and Dylan rushed the door, guns drawn and pointed at Sullivan, yelling, "Hands on your head! Do it now!" Secret Service agents streamed in, pointing their guns at Sean and Dylan, yelling, "Drop your weapons!"

No one knew how it happened, but the President was flat on his stomach behind his desk, Scott Eadie on top of him. He struggled to rise as Sean and Dylan lowered their guns, looking sheepish at their mistake.

Later, when the surveillance tapes were reviewed, it would be seen that Scott had dived onto the President like a Secret Service agent to protect him from the bomb blast he'd believed would come.

Sean and Dylan apologized to the Secret Service agents

for pulling guns in the Oval Office, explaining they, too, had expected a bomb or something of that nature.

Everyone would joke with Scott from then on he'd have no need to look for a different job after the new President took office—the Secret Service would hire him in a heartbeat.

In the moment, however, Sullivan was on his knees still, hands on his head, with six guns pointed at him. He seemed to be unaware of what was going on around him. When the yelling and hysterical explanations had stopped and things were quiet again, he began speaking again.

"Your majesty, I bring you a message of extreme importance. Please bear with your humble servant as he gives your majesty this crucial information."

Carter, who was stunned speechless and motionless while all this unfolded somehow managed to get his equanimity back. Based on his quick briefing about Sullivan's possible mental state, it struck him what could be going on.

He motioned to everyone to be quiet and started speaking—like a king.

"Approach, Sullivan. What is this important message you have for your king?" Carter knew he was never going to live down the jokes that would follow from those who saw and heard him—assuming he and they got through this alive.

Sullivan began to get off his knees. The Secret Service agents tensed, and Sean moved to keep him down, but Carter motioned Sean to stand down. Sullivan got to within six feet of Carter and dropped to his knees again, keeping his hands on his bowed head. He started speaking again.

Everyone in the room was agape, staring at this medieval scene as it unfolded, but their amazement was soon replaced by shock and awe as they listened to the words coming out of Sullivan's mouth.

Pouring it all out in a stream of consciousness, Sullivan raved about the Nabateans, his role in the Council of the Covenant of Nabatea, and their latest plans.

Everyone in the room had plenty of questions, and they tried in vain to get Sullivan to answer them directly. He ignored them as if they weren't there.

Grant was the first one to figure out how to get his questions answered—ask Carter. But Sullivan would only answer if anyone talking to Carter addressed him as "your majesty."

His thoughts of earlier about the jokes that would come in the days and years to follow became stronger every time the President addressed him as "your majesty." The smile on Grant's face every time he did so told Carter everything he could expect—if they survived this. Carter was just happy that all Sullivan's attention was on him. There was no telling what the man would do if anyone broke his fantasy by showing they didn't take it seriously.

Bill, Sean, Dylan, the President, and Eadie, who knew what these Nabateans were capable of, wondered nervously if Sullivan could somehow have been rigged up into a living bomb the White House security measures couldn't detect.

Could he be about to push a button at any moment?

Carter seemed to be the only one who didn't worry, or maybe he was so immersed in his role he didn't think about it.

Sullivan remained on his knees on the carpet for more than two hours.

Slowly, it settled on the others that the man was heavily burdened and deeply troubled, as the words kept pouring from of his mouth.

King Devereux now and then ordered one of his other "servants" to give the messenger a sip of water. Each time, he praised Sullivan for his diligence and good work before asking him to continue.

No one dared to ask Sullivan why he thought Carter was his king—keeping it up and playing along with Sullivan kept him talking and divulging information. It was as if they had opened the floodgates of an overflowing Hoover Dam.

As Sullivan corroborated every assumption A-Echelon and the CIA had made, and added much, much more, the stunning revelations about the full reach and power of the Nabateans alarmed everyone in the room. It was clear they were not safe, and they'd need every ally they could pull in to avert a world disaster.

Sean had a quick whispered conversation with Bill and got his agreement to bring James and Irene in immediately.

It was only days later, when Sullivan was secured in an isolated cell and heavily guarded, that they learned Sullivan thought Carter was Rabbel II Soter reincarnated —the last king of the Nabateans.

Chapter Eighty-Eight

LETTERS OVER GRANT'S SIGNATURE

May 29

They learned from Sullivan the Nabateans were planning to set off two big antimatter bombs—one in D.C. and one in New York. But he didn't know precisely when or the exact location where the bombs would be placed.

He also knew about plans to crash US stock markets, but again, didn't know exactly how or when.

All he could say was it would happen within the next forty-eight hours. The bomb explosions were going to be the signal that the Council of the Covenant of Nabatea had ceased to exist. They'd been preparing to vanish, destroying everything they couldn't take with them.

As Sullivan started revealing the names and exact locations of the twelve council members, the President's mind went into overdrive. He had to plan the diplomatic delegations he'd have to send to the various countries where the perpetrators lived.

He was of the opinion the apprehension of the Nabatean

councilors in India, the UK, Japan, Peru, and Saudi Arabia wouldn't pose much of a problem—the US had good relations with those countries, and their governments were expected to be complaisant with his requests. That would take care of five of the council members, six including Jason Sullivan, and of course their prime target, Graziella Nabati, in Peru.

However, Grant found himself with a few intractable issues when it came to the remaining six councilors. They, unfortunately, were living in countries whose governments weren't exactly known for their friendliness and cooperation with the US.

Four of the twelve Nabatean councilors lived in Russia and China, two in each country. The second highest value target of the whole operation, Mathieu Nabati, who resided in the west Ural Mountains of Russia, was one of them.

Although the US had diplomatic missions in both countries, Grant thought they would still be hard nuts to crack. It was highly debatable, if they got an audience with those heads of state in the first place, whether they would get any cooperation from them. Grant could only hope they would listen to his delegates and understand the danger facing themselves and the world.

Getting their hands on the final two Nabatean council members was going to be near impossible.

Councilor Alireza Karimi-Shah, a very wealthy engineer, businessman, and humanitarian was an Iranian, living in Tehran.

The US's last diplomatic mission in Iran had closed during the Iranian Revolution in 1979. The only way to get in touch with the Iranian government was through the embassy of a close ally such as the UK or another. That was how the US, from time to time, communicated with the

Iranian government. The problem was, in this case, there was not enough time to make all the arrangements. And even if they could, there was very little to no chance the Iranians would collaborate—US-Iran relations had been at an all-time low for more than a decade already.

The twelfth and final councilor, Hassan Al-Suleiman, the leader of the True Sons of the Prophet, referred to by many as the Sultan of Syria, was going to be even more difficult to get their hands on than the Iranian.

The United States closed their consular services in Damascus, Syria, in February 2012, and since March 1, 2013, only a US Interests Section operated through the Czech Republic's embassy in Damascus.

Syria, in the throes of a civil war since 2011, was probably the most chaotic and treacherous place on earth. Hassan's base of operations was close to the Syria-Iraq border, the hotbed of ISIS activities.

When Sullivan got to the end of the list, Grant asked Carter to pause Sullivan for a few minutes and called Bill, Sean, Dylan, Irene, James, and Scott into Scott's office and told them what had been going through his mind.

They all agreed that no one of the councilors could be allowed to escape—they had to be either apprehended or eliminated. It was immediately clear that Alireza Karimi-Shah in Tehran and Hassan Al-Suleiman in Syria were on the termination list. And that meant Grant, in the heat of the moment, had to make another decision with far-reaching consequences—authorizing the assassination of citizens of another country.

Everyone was looking at him.

"Do we have any other options?" he asked.

Bill and the others were shaking their heads.

"Then it is as Harry Truman said, *'The buck stops here'*. Bill, how do you want to take care of it?"

Bill nodded and pointed to Sean and Dylan. "That's why Executive Advantage exist."

Sean looked at Dylan and asked, "Phantoms?"

"Yep," Dylan replied without hesitation.

Grant and Scott looked at Sean and Dylan questioningly.

Sean explained, "The Desert Phantoms, sir. They are the Omani Special Forces. There is nobody on earth that knows the desert better than they do. They are the hardest men I've ever encountered. They train British and American Special Forces teams in desert warfare and survival, and we have often embedded some of them when we were on special operations in those parts of the world. We have a few of them working for EA. They know the Middle East and will take care of this."

Grant nodded. "Okay, make it happen."

At ten p.m., Scott was tasked to call in the National Security Council members to help brainstorm the massive operation.

Sean called their commander of Middle East Operations, Omar Said, a former Desert Phantom, to the White House and then joined the rest in the Oval Office to continue Sullivan's questioning.

When the NSC members arrived, the group moved to the John F. Kennedy Conference Room, unofficially known as the Situation Room. A five-thousand-plus square foot conference room and intelligence management center located in the basement of the West Wing of the White

House, it was not only large enough to accommodate the crowd, it was also very secure.

Carter, Irene, and James, protected by two Secret Service agents, continued Sullivan's debriefing in a secured room.

Bill immediately informed the NSC members that electronic communications were out until the operation was over, and that ban included personal calls. The Nabateans would intercept any such transmissions and the element of surprise would be lost. That also meant in-person diplomatic missions to India, the UK, Japan, Peru, Saudi Arabia, Russia, and China.

Bill and the President agreed not to tell anyone about the Iran and Syria missions, so as far as the NSC was concerned, there were only nine council members to deal with.

Someone mentioned several of the countries, notably China, Saudi Arabia, and probably Russia, would no doubt want to take immediate action, which would jeopardize the element of surprise for others. It was imperative every member of the Council of the Covenant of Nabatea be apprehended at once, leaving no one to give the order for the bombs to be set off or to escape.

If any one of them escaped the net, the threat to the world would remain. Not just the threat of bombs, but the greater threat of Nabatean world dominance. One remaining seed to replant the evil conspiracy was all it would take.

Coordinated missions then, tightly timed, so every country involved received word at precisely the same time.

Each of the groups who'd be tasked with taking the message would be virtually flying by the seat of their pants to reach their assigned target at precisely the same time, taking pains to arrive at the US embassies in time to secure the help of the ambassadors in gaining the ears of the respective heads of state. Then it would be up to the US delegations to convey vigorously that it was imperative all missions to capture the Nabateans also be synchronized.

Grant had Constance Pierce, the Secretary of State, put her wordsmiths to work. Each foreign dignitary required a different approach if the plan were to have the best chance of success. Letters over Grant's signature would appeal to each, and in some cases, an offer of an incentive for cooperation.

Chapter Eighty-Nine
OPERATION ROCK CONCERT

May 30

At twelve thirty a.m., they had worked through all the options, and the State Department employees were summoned and locked in under the watchful eyes of Secret Service agents. There'd be no more assumptions that high-level government employees were above suspicion. Only when the missions were complete would these employees get their cell phones and mobile devices back and be allowed to go home.

Sean and Dylan had been awake for close to twenty-four hours, but their military training made it possible for them to focus with a clear head for at least thirty-six. They refused Grant's offer to let them take a rest. Dylan muttered something about resting when he was dead.

It was a sobering reminder that if this didn't work, it was likely they'd all be dead within days, vaporized by the antimatter Sword of Damocles hanging over their heads.

The two of them had briefed Omar Said and arranged

for him and one other former Desert Phantom to be flown to Oman on a private jet.

Carter, too, was looking at some long hours and sleepless nights as he'd been forced to continue the job of interrogating Sullivan, who still wouldn't talk to anyone but him.

At least Sullivan's willingness to divulge information without being tortured or threatened worked for them, and it didn't waste time.

At one thirty a.m., the contingent in the Situation Room took a short break as coffee and snacks were brought in. As they snatched bites of the food and sipped coffee, they began the task of putting the timeline in order.

Everything hinged on the flight times to the countries involved and would be choreographed like a ballet. Once in motion, one misstep would create the risk of bringing down the rest of the dancers in a disastrous chain reaction.

When they were notified the group in the Situation Room had a coffee break, Carter gave Sullivan a bit of a breather and went to get coffee and some food for his group.

He arrived in the Situation Room just in time to hear one of the advisors talking about choreographing the operation like a ballet followed by someone asking what the code name for the mission would be.

Carter whimsically suggested "Operation Rock Concert"—for the meanings of the names Petra, Petras, and Sassi, each meaning "rock'" or "stone'" in its respective language.

President Grant approved. Quipping, "If that's the

name your Royal Highness desires, that's what thy humble servants will name it."

Carter just shook his head—*the jokes have started, sanctioned by the highest authority in the country.* He grabbed the coffees and pastries and scooted out of the room before more bantering could follow.

To create the timeline, they calculated the longest flight time—from D.C. to New Delhi—fifteen and a half hours. The delegations would leave at predetermined intervals so as to reach their destination countries at the same time. They allowed fourteen hours for meeting with the various heads of state and preparation to launch the strike response.

Zero hour for Operation Rock Concert was set for exactly thirty hours from the starting gun, which would sound as soon as the delegation to India were airborne at four a.m. in D.C. On their heels would be the delegations to Japan and China, both of which would leave an hour later for their fourteen-hour flights.

Saudi Arabia's mission would leave two hours later for their twelve-hour flight, Russia's an hour and a half after that for a ten-and-a-half-hour flight, Peru's three hours later, and the mission to London for the UK would leave only half an hour behind Peru's delegation.

The mission to Russia was the second most critical of the seven. Grant would have liked to lead it himself, but his place was in D.C. if the Nabateans managed to set off the bombs before Operation Rock Concert got them.

Grant and Russia's President hadn't been on the best of terms for most of his tenure in the White House. And since the capture of the nine Spetsnaz operatives in the raid on

Freydís and their transfer from Canada to the US, the already shaky relationship had only deteriorated.

Russia claimed the transfer was a violation of international law and half a dozen treaties, and her President had been pouting like a toddler ever since. Therefore, Grant sent his Vice President, who would be accompanied by Dylan and six of his Executive Advantage operatives.

The target was none other than Mathieu Nabati, whom Sullivan had named as the second in command of the Nabateans behind his mother, Graziella. Sullivan confirmed that Mathieu Nabati had been responsible for the Freydís debacle, as well as the murder of Peter Nikolaev, the former head of the FSB.

If Russia would agree to help capture Mathieu Nabati, Grant was prepared to exchange the Spetsnaz troops for him and would throw in a few pieces of vital information for the Russian President to make a deal even more alluring.

Therefore, it was decided if the Russian President agreed to the exchange and Mathieu Nabati was handed over, Grant would also release the information that the former head of the FSB, Peter Nikolaev, was a member of the Nabatean council responsible for the attack on Freydís. That Nikolaev's ski accident was no accident but an action taken by the Nabatean council to protect their secrecy.

In addition, the Russian President would be alerted to the fact that he had a viper in his bosom—his closest confidant, Igor Ustinov, was Nikolaev's replacement on The Council of the Covenant of Nabatea.

Consequently, Ustinov was the only Nabatean council member who was not targeted for capture during Operation Rock Concert. Cautious diplomatic maneuvering was required, partly because of the kneejerk reaction expected from the Russian President if he were to receive this devastating information about his bosom friend, often speculated to be Russia's second-most powerful person.

Those revelations would be alluded to in vague terms and only if the circumstances during discussions called for it.

The letter the Vice-President carried contained only the outline of the Nabatean conspiracy and the proposed terms of cooperation. The rest, it explained, would be given to him verbally by the delegation. The Vice-President himself knew not much more, but Grant assured him Dylan would fill him in during the flight.

The most critical of the missions, the one to Peru, would be almost the last to leave. Constance Pierce would lead it accompanied by Sean and six more Executive Advantage operatives.

Sean had to endure an almost serious scolding from Sam after confessing the Secretary of State's flirtation with him on the trip to Matera. He just grinned when he thought about the repercussions it would have this time if he told Sam he and the coquettish Secretary *had* to go on an urgent trip—again. He shrugged. *I'd rather take my chances with Sam and Connie than with an antimatter bomb.*

Mercifully, he'd get some rest on the flight, since he only had to fill Pierce in on what had happened since their last excursion, mostly the last twelve hours or so since Sullivan's arrival at the White House.

Before they left, Carter took a few minutes away from Sullivan and gave them the history of his involvement in Peruvian archaeology. It had begun about ten years ago, when a former student of his, Jacob Wilson, working on a dig at Cusco, had smoked out an illegal artifact dealing ring, and with Carter's help, returned most of the stolen artifacts to the Peruvian government. After this, Carter was placed in charge of the dig, and Jacob was appointed as the onsite manager. He and Jacob had gone on to discover the fabled Golden Gardens in an underground city in the mountains near Cusco.

It was their honest and cordial dealings with the former Minister of Culture, now the Prime Minister, that resulted in Carter's former university still overseeing the dig and Jacob still in charge of it.

Carter still had an affable long-distance friendship with Prime Minister Alvarez and would have gone himself if it hadn't been for the necessity of keeping Sullivan's illusion intact. He asked Constance to convey to Alvarez his warmest greetings and an apology that he couldn't be there himself.

There was little Grant could offer the Saudis to induce them to wait for Zero Hour, except to remind the King that he owed the US one. If Grant hadn't revealed to him former council member Algosaibi's plan to overthrow his rule, it might have been accomplished and the King's own head on a pike along a desert road.

There was only one council member left in his kingdom, unfortunately a member of his own family, a prince who was third in line for succession.

Grant had no doubt the King would cooperate. Third in line was too close for comfort. But whether His Majesty would wait for the signal was another matter. They could only hope he would understand the gravity of the situation and oblige.

Also at issue was the interrogation techniques the Mabahith would likely employ before the traitor was executed by public beheading. Their enhanced interrogation techniques, which included waterboarding, de-nailing, flagellation, beatings, sleep deprivation, starvation, and the old favorite, electrocution, made what the US called "enhanced" look like child's play.

Nevertheless, if the King would agree to allow it, Bill would have two of his agents sit in on the interrogations. They'd probably have nightmares for the rest of their lives, but it was crucial to get all the information firsthand and act upon it.

Chapter Ninety

ONE MORE QUESTION

It was already three a.m. Carter, with the help of Irene and James, had been questioning Sullivan for close to five hours, not counting the almost three hours when he was spilling his guts in the Oval Office before he was taken to the secure room.

The effects of the stress and anxiety of the past weeks were taking their toll on Sullivan. With every passing hour, his speech became more slurred. At times, it was inaudible and incoherent.

Notwithstanding the urgency, they agreed the man needed a rest.

The White House physician was called in to examine Sullivan. He concurred, "You're running the risk of driving him over the edge if you continue. The anxiety and stress is causing his body to produce too much adrenaline. It's causing his rapid heartbeat, high blood pressure, anxiety, sweating, and palpitations. He might have a stroke or heart attack at any moment.

"You have to lay off and give him a break. I can give

him a Xanax injection. It's an anti-anxiety medication and will calm him down, but it also has a sedation effect. In other words, it could put him to sleep."

The three of them agreed and asked the doctor if they could ask Sullivan just two more critical questions before he administered the drug. The doctor agreed reluctantly and said he would wait outside the room. They had fifteen minutes.

The twenty-minute rest during the physician's examination, diagnosis, and advice had a positive impact on Sullivan's condition. He sounded marginally better than before.

Carter still had to do all the talking as Sullivan seemed oblivious to James's and Irene's presence.

"Sullivan, when is your next council meeting?"

"Five o'clock this morning, Your Majesty."

Carter's eye caught the time on the wall clock—it was 4:10 a.m. He looked at James who nodded and left the room in a hurry to inform Bill and the President.

Carter would not get to the second question. If Sullivan didn't attend the mandatory council meeting, the Nabateans could get nervous about his absence and possibly move up the timeline of their operations.

They had to improvise a plan to keep up appearances so the Nabateans wouldn't conclude he'd defected.

After a short consultation with the doctor, Carter concluded it would be dangerous to let Sullivan attend the meeting, even if it would mean they could get better intel. In his delusional state of mind, and as exhausted as he was, he might set off alarm bells among the already panicky Nabateans, even reveal he had changed sides.

Within minutes, James was back with Bill in tow. They had a quick discussion with the physician and a plan of action was formed.

Chapter Ninety-One

COLLECTIVELY SUSPICIOUS

As predicted, the members of the council were immediately on edge when Sullivan was a no-show at their meeting. Graziella roused her contact in D.C. at 5:10 a.m. from his sleep and ordered him to find out where Sullivan was and not make her wait more than ten minutes for his call.

He called back in seven and reported that Sullivan had been at the White House, pulling an all-nighter on a critical piece of financial legislation when he suffered a brain aneurism at about four thirty a.m., was rushed to Walter Reed Army Medical Center, and admitted to the ICU.

When Graziella and the rest of the councilors heard the news, they were immediately and collectively suspicious.

Sullivan's situation looked unnervingly similar to that of a previous councilor, George Robertson, the former Vice President. He'd supposedly had a stroke while in the White House and was rushed off to a private hospital where not even his wife and children could see him. There he'd committed a very suspect suicide, but the world was told he died from a second stroke.

Closer investigation of Sullivan's situation was ordered immediately.

The councilors were only satisfied this time it was real when they got the report, shortly after seven a.m. D.C. time that Sullivan was really in hospital, really in the ICU, and only his family and closest colleagues could visit him, and then only if in possession of the ICU code.

Graziella's messenger was one of those colleagues who were allowed to visit. Though they couldn't be in the room with him, they could see him through the window.

Sullivan was reported to be in a bad way. Graziella's contact was there when the doctors told his wife and children that the prognosis was bleak. He'd probably not make it past the forty-eight-hour mark, and if he did, he'd most likely never regain consciousness.

The doctor didn't actually use the word vegetable, but that was the situation in laymen's terms. Another episode would kill him instantaneously, and the next forty-eight hours was the most critical time for that to happen.

Only after hearing all that did Graziella relax and put on a wretched face while suppressing a smile. There'd be no need to plan his death now. He'd saved her the trouble.

It tickled Carter to be admitted to practice as a "brain specialist" at Walter Reed Army Medical Center.

The White House physician assisted in setting up the subterfuge with the administration of a light sedative, which put Sullivan out for about an hour. During this time, his family could see him hooked up to medical equipment—an array of frightening monitors, tubes, cannulas, and wires. No one—except "the brain specialist", his assistant, and a couple of nurses who were in the know—was allowed into the ICU.

Chapter Ninety-Two

EN ROUTE

Each of the teams of CIA and EA operatives embedded in the diplomatic missions would carry at least one of the Blackjacks and perimeter scanning devices. Those were the devices which they got from the Spetsnaz troops who raided Freydís and reverse engineered. Sticking to naming conventions the CIA techies aptly named it the PeriD'ice.

They'd take these devices with them in case they were allowed to go with that country's forces to apprehend the Nabateans. They would use them to defeat any electronic perimeter protection measures they expected the Nabateans would have. And of course, if allowed inside the Nabateans residences, the Blackjacks would scan all electronic devices and download information. This would negate the need to rely solely on the word of the various countries' heads of state to share information.

Of course, these devices had to be kept hidden from the eyes of the other countries' security forces at all times.

The flight to New Delhi took off at four a.m. from D.C. with the Under-Secretary of State for Indian Relations aboard and Irene along to brief her on the background of the Nabateans. There'd barely been time for the two of them to gather a change of clothes before they were off.

They expected that the Under-Secretaries for India, the UK, and Japan, leading their respective missions, would have the easiest of all the undertakings.

India and the US had cordial relations, as did the US and Japan, whose mission was to take off shortly after their own, and of course the US and the UK were allies. All three delegations would have with them a pair of CIA agents for each target to accompany the taskforces who would do the arrests and to observe the questioning of the Nabateans afterward.

The UK was also expected to be a walk in the park. In fact, if they'd been allowed electronic communication, a simple call from Bill to his counterpart in MI6 would have seen the London-based Nabatean council member in custody almost before they'd ended the conversation.

Although the Japanese delegation was expected to achieve the same outcome as the UK and India groups, the CIA agents assigned weren't expected to have an easy time of it in their observations during the interrogations.

Japan's interrogation techniques weren't nearly as barbaric as the Saudis. But in a modern country with such a high standard of education and advancement, it was shocking to learn their pre-trial techniques were undoubtedly the reason for their ninety-nine percent conviction rate.

While the number did include guilty pleas without undue force, most were obtained by confessions made to the police under duress.

It was an eyeopener for many to learn that techniques which would result in an acquittal in the US were standard procedure in a highly-cultured country like Japan.

The mission to China was one calling for acumen. Chinese memory was long, and it hadn't been that long ago when the US Navy's showdown with them in the Alboran Sea had embarrassed them. That incident would no doubt have left a lingering bad taste in their mouths.

The assessment was they wouldn't be keen to work with the US on anything, especially not anything involving security agencies. Bill was dead set against sending any of his agents to China.

Constance Pierce's predecessor, the former Secretary of State, was tapped as a special ambassador to convey the news to China. He was the last to have had neutral if not mildly cordial relations with China, and though now retired, he had informed Grant upon his departure from office he stood ready to help his country in any way they needed him. Grant respected him greatly and trusted him to get the job done.

The former secretary would try to convince President Zhang his country was literally sitting on a time bomb. He'd explain who the Nabateans were, what their mission was and had always been, what the rest of the countries who had an infestation of them intended to do, and that there were two of them in his country. After that, it would be up to the Chinese.

If nothing else, the Chinese were expected to deal with the problem swiftly, decisively, and in complete secrecy.

Even if they jumped the Zero Hour gun, the two Nabateans in China would simply disappear, very quickly, with no clues left as to what had happened.

Chapter Ninety-Three

THE FRENCH CONNECTION

The whole stratagem to pull the wool over the Nabateans eyes about Sullivan took about three hours and had the advantage of giving him some much-needed rest. By the time, Walter Reed Army Medical Center's latest "brain specialist" with his "understudy", Dr. James Rhodes, could talk to Sullivan again—in his hospital bed in a private room with the blinds drawn—he looked and sounded a lot better. He was eager to please his king.

Carter made a big fuss about his loyal servant who, despite his serious wounds, was so loyal and brave to put his king's well-being above his own. Sullivan was smiling proudly.

Carter explained there was just one more important topic to cover before he would let his faithful servant get his merited rest.

Where were the laboratories and IT centers of the Nabateans located and how to get to them?

Sullivan's face brightened up, he smiled, and started talking.

The main medical and all technical labs, as well as the IT control center, with the servers holding every bit of information about the Nabateans since 106 AD were in underground chambers below Graziella's mansion in Paris.

He'd been there a few times. Carved out of the limestone substrate, it was not in any way connected to the known Parisian catacombs, as far as he knew, and could only be, as far as he knew, accessed through a secret passage in her library. At least that's how he and Graziella accessed it the few times when he was there.

Sullivan also explained that from what he understood about their technology, the triggering of the two antimatter bombs was controlled by the quantum computers located in those underground facilities.

"What is the plan with those facilities?" Carter asked.

"They are to be destroyed as soon as the bombs in D.C. and New York have detonated, your majesty."

"How?" Carter dreaded the answer Sullivan was about to give.

"Your majesty, the whole place has been rigged with thermobaric explosives. It will incinerate everything and everyone inside."

"Everyone?" Carter asked incredulously. "Are you saying they plan to kill the people that work for them?"

"Yes, your majesty, all of them, there are more than one hundred people working there."

"Oh, my God!" James whispered measuredly. "Thermobaric explosives yield six to seven times more explosive power than TNT of the same weight—every living being in its path will be evaporated."

Images of the neatly-stacked pile of decayed bodies in the Nabatean library in the caves of Matera flashed before Carter's eyes. "This is how they are going to try and guard their secrets. They must have already copied everything they want."

James nodded, the blood having drained from his face. "And we still don't know when it's going to happen."

Five minutes later, shortly after seven thirty a.m., Sullivan was in a medically induced coma. Carter and James were speeding to the White House in a military helicopter to inform the President and Bill.

Securing those laboratories and IT center in Paris had become their number one priority.

A hurried conference with the President and Bill took place before they brought the grim news to the rest of the NSC members.

Their assessment of the French was that they were unpredictable at the best of times. Nominally allies, they had a prickly way of showing it, and it was by no means a given that they would be easily swayed to cooperate, at least not in any way that would see the US removing the contents of that underground complex.

Carter and Bill couldn't help but smile when James was heard mumbling something which sounded like, "Damn Frogs only exist as a country because we liberated their sorry asses in WWII. I would've expected a bit of gratitude from them."

Grant heard it and smiled, but his mind was working on the concern about another illegal operation. And even more concerning was the carefully coordinated schedule would be thrown into disarray if they had to first convince the President of the French Republic there was a clear and present danger.

Even if the French cooperated and stormed the facilities, they didn't have the technical knowhow to operate quantum computers. If the US were to supply the skills for that in a joint operation, admittedly theirs were limited to the people working on the QIT project. It was debatable how much of it the French would be prepared to share with the US after the operation on their soil.

There were no arguments about it—the contents of the laboratories and IT center were more important than the apprehension of the council members. Not only did they have to stop the clock on the trigger of the antimatter bombs, they had to save and apprehend the hundred-odd scientists who were about to be killed, and they had to get their hands on all the information in those facilities—it contained every fragment of information, technology, history, and much more about the Nabateans from 106 AD up till now.

The Paris mission, everyone agreed, had become the top priority.

Bill explained to the President that the CIA had an "asset" within the *Direction générale de la sécurité intérieure (The General Directorate for Internal Security),* a French intelligence agency responsible for counter-espionage as well as counter-terrorism, countering cybercrime and surveillance of potentially threatening groups.

He didn't elaborate about the "asset", and no one asked. Even if they had, Bill would not have divulged that information. Having someone over there who could help them pull it off was a relief. The only catch was Bill was the only one who had contact with this asset.

It didn't take much for Bill and the other security advisors to convince the President the Paris mission required Bill's personal oversight.

Three of the top experts on the QIT team received taps on the shoulders and were escorted to the White House in a hurry.

By eleven a.m., Bill found himself on an eight-hour commercial flight heading across the Atlantic for the capital of France, where he would enlist the help of his asset and assist her in planning and executing the mission. He had not a moment's hesitation or doubt that Simone would be willing to do what was asked of her, but he needed time to convince her of the urgency of his request—there were only twenty-two hours left to Zero Hour. He made a quick calculation—by the time he had landed in Paris, cleared customs, and contacted Simone, he would have twelve hours left.

His team of nine, on the plane with him, included the top three QIT quantum computing experts, three FBI bomb disposal experts, and three EA special forces operators.

An hour before Bill and his team departed, he had dispatched one of his Deputy Directors to London with a brief for the head of the Secret Intelligence Service, commonly known as MI6. As in the case of Simone in Paris, he also had no doubt that MI6 would be keen to join the party and send the necessary manpower over the channel to assist in his operation.

When the plane took off from D.C. and reached cruising altitude, Bill reclined his seat and closed his eyes. He sighed long and deep, exhausted. Since Sean and Dylan walked into his office and told him about Jason Sullivan, he had gone through the most taxing eighteen hours of his life, and he had a gut feeling the next twenty-four was going to be worse.

But even as fatigued as he was, his mind was just too busy and too excited to allow him to fall asleep right away.

A little smile broke across his face as he allowed his brain to meander away from the perils of his coming mission to something more pleasant.

He and Simone Bouvier had a history. It had been over a decade since he'd last seen her, but the pull they'd had toward each other in their youth still made itself felt.

Forty years ago, during the Cold War era, their affair had held all the passion of youth combined with danger. Simone at twenty-five was an exquisite woman, exotic and sensuous. Bill, also in his mid-twenties, was a newly-minted CIA agent. He was good-looking in an American collegiate way, but his looks concealed a mind as sharp as a stiletto.

Both appealed to Simone.

Thrown together in a joint US-French covert operation, they fell hard for each other. After six months, Bill was reassigned and begged Simone to marry him and leave France. She, in turn, challenged him to leave the CIA and stay with her in Paris. With the fervency of youth, they argued as passionately as they had loved, and in the end neither would give up country or job for the other.

When Bill left, Simone promised him that whatever she could do for him or his agency, she would, short of betraying her country. He'd made the same promise. And from time to time, they had lived up to that promise when they had helped each other to overcome bureaucratic hurdles in each other's government that would have hampered the successful outcome of missions.

They went their separate ways, and eventually each married other people.

They'd had correspondence intermittently throughout their years apart, and Simone always ended with what he'd thought was a teasing reference to her youthful declaration that someday she'd track him down and *make* him marry her.

Now, he was on his way to ask for Simone's help in a covert mission in Paris. He knew she would help him, but given their history, he also reflected that he'd been alone for a long time. He missed his wife, nine years' dead, but the grief had faded and become an old friend.

Simone divorced her unfaithful husband seven years back. She had been alone as well—that's what her letters said. And in those same letters, she had been threatening, again, that she was just waiting for retirement before she would get over to America and *make* him marry her.

At the age of sixty-five, he'd thought he was passionate only about his job, except now, at the prospect of seeing Simone again, he had to admit, his body was telling him something different.

Chapter Ninety-Four

DIPLOMATIC MANEUVERING

Meetings with the heads of state of the UK, India, and Japan went as expected. As soon as they received agreement and were introduced to the heads of the security agencies who would execute the captures, they began joint operations planning.

Meeting with the King also went as planned. Surprisingly, and to their relief, the King agreed to wait for Zero Hour. He was also delighted to agree to have CIA agents present from the beginning to the end.

They met with the Mabahith to jointly plan the arrest and be ready at Zero Hour.

Former Secretary of State Abraham Goudy was granted a meeting with China's President Zhang, who conveniently was also the head of the National People's Congress and the People's Liberation Army.

The US ambassador to China wanted to accompany

Goudy but was told in no uncertain terms that President Zhang would see Goudy alone—no one else of his entourage was welcome.

The ambassador and Goudy understood. This unusual request and purported urgency that was communicated with the request to meet with the President would have raised red flags for them—the Chinese didn't like surprises.

Goudy had a few objectives; first, convince the President about the danger posed by the Nabateans and the need to take action. Second, convince him it was imperative to synchronize Chinese actions with those of the other countries involved in Operation Rock Concert and wait for Zero Hour.

However, Goudy was mindful the thorniest part of this meeting was going to be the disclosure of the identity of one of the two Nabatean councilors in China, Zhang's long-time friend and ally in the party, Vice-Chairman Lin Zhou Li.

Goudy was fully aware disinformation about key people in an adversary's government and security agencies was a favorite strategy of spy agencies across the globe. He was equally aware Zhang would know it, too.

Goudy's naming Zhang's friend as a Nabatean plant would be as difficult as convincing Zhang of the Nabateans' threat in the first place.

Therefore, he began by listing everything he'd been told about the Nabateans, emphasizing their acts that would be most dishonorable in Chinese tradition. He accentuated the threat the organization posed to every country on the planet.

Zhang finally indicated he believed Goudy and agreed these people should be apprehended, examined vigorously, and then kept in custody or executed as the circumstances warranted. He also agreed to issue orders that his taskforce had to wait for Zero Hour.

Goudy was relieved. *So far so good. Just one more bridge to cross.*

Zhang stayed quiet but stared at Goudy in anticipation.

He knew the President was waiting for the name; he hesitated. What he was about to say could undo everything he had gained so far. He couldn't help but think about ancient times when messengers were often killed for bringing appalling news.

But there was no way around it. Finally, he looked Zhang in the eyes and said, "One of them is Vice-Chairman Lin Zhou Li, Mr. President."

And indeed, Zhang exploded in wrath. From the impassive and outwardly gracious host he'd been, he turned into the tyrant Goudy knew him to be.

It quickly became much worse than Goudy had expected when Zhang summoned his security detail and ordered them to take Goudy into custody!

To Goudy, in an ice-cold voice he hissed, no longer speaking English, "I will consider what you have told me and let you know what I have decided. Meanwhile, you will remain as a 'guest' of the People's Republic of China."

Goudy understood enough Chinese to appreciate his position—a feeling of despair descended on him. When he'd agreed to come out of retirement, he hadn't thought he may spend the rest of his days in a Chinese prison, or worse.

Constance Pierce arrived in Lima with Sean and six of his Executive Advantage operatives.

As the representative of the US government, Connie was afforded a befitting greeting, the Prime Minister welcoming her to his country. His hospitality grew even warmer when she conveyed Carter's greetings.

Between her charm, her fluent Spanish, and dropping Carter's name often, the Prime Minister was won over in short order.

The message Connie conveyed about the Nabateans caused him a great deal of distress, but frequent mention of Carter's role in discovering them convinced the Prime Minister without much persuasion needed.

Not only did he agree to the raid on Graziella's Machu Picchu compound, he suggested Sean lead it, and ordered the head of his military to provide a squad of six Fuerza Delta—the best he had.

In Moscow, at times, the negotiations were threatening to take the same course as Goudy's in Beijing.

It took all the Vice President's tact and flair to finally get the Russian President to eventually agree to the operation to capture Mathieu Nabati.

In a major coup, he also persuaded the Russian President to allow Dylan and his men to go along as observers.

Even so, the Russian was not prepared to talk about the prisoner swap now. As far as he was concerned, it was a separate matter. "Besides," he said, "those Spetsnaz troops were on an unsanctioned mission, and even if they were not, then they were idiots to get themselves captured by the Americans and Canadians. I don't need idiots in my military. You can keep them."

Therefore, the Vice President made no mention of the

information he had been holding back about the late, former head of the FSB, Peter Nikolaev, or the President's confidant, Igor Ustinov. Those would be topics for another day—after Nabati was captured.

This outcome was not entirely what the Vice President hoped for, as he would have liked to take Mathieu Nabati back to the US with him.

Nevertheless, what he got in the end was a very good second prize. In fact, it was one of the possible scenarios which they'd foreseen and prepared for. Dylan would get a chance to put the Blackjack gadget to good use.

"So, given the circumstances, being able to go with the Russians on the operation is a major win," he said to Dylan when he met with him after the meeting with the Russian president.

Dylan agreed.

Bill and his nine men were scattered in seats throughout the commercial flight to Paris. On arrival at Charles de Gaulle Airport, they gave no indication any of them knew the others as they deplaned and made their way to separate lodgings, all within a few miles' radius from Simone's apartment, where they'd wait for Bill's instructions.

As he cleared customs, Bill was more than a little concerned. A visit by the Director of the American CIA to France was a rare event and usually would not happen without prior official arrangements. On the other hand, there was no travel ban on Americans wanting to visit France for business or holiday purposes. That the French border control systems and facial recognition would have identified him the moment he walked through customs he didn't doubt for one second. Therefore, he'd deliberately not try to disguise himself; that would have undoubtedly raised the alarm bells immediately.

As he left the arrivals terminal, he subtly studied his surroundings to see if there was anyone following but found none. However, he fully expected by now the message would have gone up the chain and his unannounced arrival in France would have raised some eyebrows. He shrugged. There was not much he could do about it other than to act as a tourist. Though he fully expected a French official to make contact with him at some stage during his stay in their City of Lights.

Bill hailed a taxi and gave the driver the address of Simone's apartment. It was 2:20 a.m. in Paris when he called her from a phonebooth opposite her apartment.

"Simone," he breathed when she answered with a sleepy voice. "It's Bill."

"*Mon Dieu*, Bill! What is going on? It's… it's two in the morning."

"I know Simone, I'm very sorry. Are you well?"

"Oui. What is wrong, Bill?"

"Simone, I'm here, in Paris, and I need to meet with you urgently."

"You are *here*! Why did you not let me know you were coming?"

"That's what I need to explain to you."

"Where shall I meet you?"

"I'm outside your apartment on the street."

"Go to the foyer, type in my apartment number, and I will let you in. You still remember the number?"

"Yes, Simone, how could I ever forget it?" Bill felt his heart re-start. He was grateful she didn't tell him to get lost and was prepared to see him despite the ungodly hour.

Walking across the street, he got a text message from the head of MI6—*6@XA03 in 4.*

Bill sighed in relief. Six MI6 operatives would be ready at the safe house, codenamed XA03 in four hours. He replied, *THX!*

When Simone opened the door for Bill and he saw her, as elegant and breathtaking as ever, even in her nightgown and with no makeup, his heart started racing.

She threw her arms around his neck, kissed him, and then pulled him inside. It took more than a few minutes for Bill's heartbeat to return to normal.

She was still in his arms when she looked up at him and said, "What's wrong? You looked tired, and you are tensed."

Bill looked down and said, "We need to sit down. It's going to take time to explain it all to you."

She nodded and said, "Let's go to the kitchen. I'll make us coffee and something to eat." She took his hand and steered him to the kitchen.

Most people who'd learned of the Nabateans required days of explanations and proof. He had eleven and half hours left before Zero Hour.

Four hours later, after many cups of coffee and croissants, he had given her as much information as she could assimilate. When he told her of the criminal acts the Nabateans had performed and the Machiavellian tactics they had employed over the centuries, especially lately, her eyes had narrowed.

Bill was relieved at how quickly she came to grips with it all and agreed to help him save the people, stop the bombs, and recover the priceless information hidden beneath Graziella Nabati's Paris mansion.

By dawn, when they got to the end of the information

session and discussed the first high-level plan, an uneasy silence erupted.

She was staring at him. "And then," Simone concluded sadly, "I suppose I will not see you again?"

It was time for a personal moment.

"No, Simone, that's part of the reason I'm here. I wanted to tell you, I never stopped loving you. Even when I married Beth, and I did love my wife, she was a wonderful woman... ah... it's difficult to explain... but now... now that she is gone, I love only you."

Simone's eyes shone with unshed tears. "This is true?"

"It's true," he said as he stood, held out his hand for her, and collected her in his arms. At last, Bill felt he could draw a full breath.

For what felt to them as only a fleeting moment, the kiss they shared transported both to their lost youth.

There was not enough time for more; they had a lot to do before Zero Hour.

Simone, always the chirpy one, had an idea. "Let's leave a marker here so we know from where to continue when this is all over?"

"*Chéri d'amour*, I wouldn't have it any other way," Bill whispered in her ear.

It was seven and a half hours before Zero Hour.

Chapter Ninety-Five

THANKS TO HIS NEW AMERICAN FRIENDS

Precisely twenty-five hours after the first plane took off carrying the delegation to India, Dylan and his men accompanied Russian Spetsnaz troops as they were in the air on their way to Mathieu Nabati's location to reconnoiter and plan the takedown. They had four hours to Zero Hour.

Dylan and his men suspected the Russians spoke better English than they let on, but antagonizing the Russians was not part of their assignment. One of Dylan's men understood enough to quietly translate some of the muttering.

"They're talking about their comrades who were killed in Canada and the ones still in US custody."

"Do they know if they play nice with us they're getting the ones we have back?" Dylan asked.

"Not sure. But it's obvious the spin on the story was a lot different here. They think those guys were on holiday and were attacked by US and Canadian special forces. Heavily out-numbered, blah, blah, blah. They think those guys were big heroes and wonder if we have any knowledge of it."

"Better not tell them what we do know," Dylan said, his mouth tight and a grim expression around his eyes.

Dylan accepted the fact that it was a Russian operation and that he and his men were given observer status—as a favor. But when the arrogant SOB started pestering him about the purported attack on the Spetsnaz troops in Canada and making a few snotty remarks, he had a hard time not setting the guy straight there and then—with a right cross. That would have been a serious mistake and would have been the misstep that brought down the entire mission, so he bit his tongue, denied knowledge of the raid, and managed to avoid escalating the conflict.

Once on site and after some reconnaissance, half an hour before the attack, Dylan was shaking his head in disbelief. He supposed he should have been grateful the Russian shared his plan of attack with them, but he couldn't agree with it. He and his crew were to stay back, like a camera crew in a warzone, which was frustrating enough.

The worst part was the plan was foolish and dangerous. For this, he couldn't keep quiet. The PeriD'ice told him there were lots of invisible, electronic surveillance obstacles between them and the house. He couldn't let the Russian know how he knew, but he could try to persuade him to change his stupid plan.

"You're going to get your men killed. It won't work." He wanted to point out the weaknesses in the plan, but the Russian overrode him.

"You Americans are pansies. You will stay behind and watch how real men do it." He walked off with a swagger, making Dylan really wish he could take the guy on and wipe the floor with him. His orders were clear—follow and observe. Do not engage without permission from the leader. And it was obvious the leader didn't pay attention during the briefing, not heeding the warnings about the technical capability of the enemy—making the rookie mistake of underestimating his opponent.

Dylan had a bad feeling, and it was soon apparent to be well-justified.

The idiot led his men in a full-frontal assault on the house, which, as Dylan would have told him if he wanted to listen, was going to be suicidal.

The Russian troops set off surveillance alarms in the house while still more than one hundred yards away from it.

Nabati's guards were waiting for them.

They were mowed down by landmines and small arms fire from the house as they rushed the front door. Their weapons had no effect on the bulletproof glass of the windows. More than half of them were killed or seriously wounded within seconds of the launch of the attack, the leader himself becoming a casualty when he took one bullet through the left shoulder and another through his right thigh.

From their concealed position, Dylan and his men could see this was going south fast, and the worst part was the occupants of the house would have time to communicate with their counterparts around the world. Dylan knew he had no option but to act immediately—his problem was he and his men were not armed—another stupid decision by the leader.

He split his men into three groups of two each. He ordered two of the groups to stay put while he and the remaining group of two rushed to aid the fallen Russians, move them to a safe spot, and get their weapons.

Fortunately, the gunfire from the house had become sporadic and wild because the guards couldn't see them. He and the others dragged the Russians to safety and then commandeered their guns.

Dylan and his men, with the nonwounded Russians, moved the wounded to a safe location. The Russians were all truly shaken up. Dylan told the unharmed Russians to take care of their comrades while he and his men took care of business. He would call them in later if needed.

Thankfully, the Russians had destroyed the satellite dishes on the roof of the house when the firefight started.

He and his two men returned to their original position, handed out the Russians' weapons, grenades, and body armor, and sent two of the groups to flank the house from the left and right.

Taking care to observe and avoid more landmines, tripwires, and other electronic perimeter security systems detected by the PeriD'ice devices as they approached, Dylan's men, with their three-pronged approach, quickly worked their way toward the house.

This was like old times in the Sandpit. They knew how to fight house to house and how to clean out buildings with fanatic enemies inside. It was nerve-wracking, painstaking, and slow work, especially now that the occupants of the house knew they were there.

Dylan cursed the foolishness of the Russian leader, whose arrogance had put every man in more danger than they should have faced. Before long, gunfire from inside the house told him that some of his men had penetrated and were busy clearing from room to room.

With the occupants otherwise engaged, he and the men with him stormed the front door. One of them shot the lock to smithereens, kicked it open, stood to the side, and the second threw a hand grenade in to clear the area inside.

Dylan took in the layout of the house and made a guess

about where Nabati would be. Most likely his bedroom, or if Dylan's luck was bad, he'd be in a panic room. If the latter, all Dylan could hope was his men had by now managed to cut all other communications from the house as he'd ordered. In situations like these, there was no time to wonder and check. He assumed his men would have done it and proceeded.

The house was a maze. After a couple of wrong turns, Dylan finally found what he thought must be the master bedroom. It had grand double doors worthy of a ballroom. It was located in the southeast corner of the mansion from where the view of the mountains would be most spectacular in the mornings.

He tried the knob. Stranger things had happened than someone forgetting to lock a critical barrier, but no such luck this time. He tried to kick in the door, but it held. The bullet that came through it immediately afterward missed him and confirmed someone was inside. He guessed it was Nabati.

Dylan had no time to finesse it. Shooting the lock risked hitting and killing Nabati, but there was no choice. He set the Russian weapon to automatic and demolished the lock mechanism.

His second kick opened the doors. He dove into the room and rolled away, shots flying over him in the space where his upper body would have been if he'd rushed in.

At first glance, the room was empty. His eyes darted across the room, looking for where the occupant was hiding. Then a bullet from underneath the bed took him in the left calf muscle, through and through. Without a second's hesitation, he rolled to the left, spotted Nabati, and shot him in the shoulder. He would have preferred to kill the bastard, but his orders were to take Nabati alive if at all possible.

"Tell them to stand down, asshole," he yelled as he dragged a moaning Nabati out from under the bed.

"No," Nabati gasped. Dylan took out his rage in the kick to Nabati's jaw, feeling it breaking under his boot. Nabati's body went limp. He would only regain consciousness when the transport choppers arrived. Nabati was going to have his meals in liquid form, through a straw, for the next two to three months.

In the battle for the rest of the house, Nabati's men refused to surrender. One of Dylan's men was seriously wounded, and two others received minor wounds. Most of the guards were killed when they refused to surrender. They probably knew all too well what was in store for them from the Russian secret service if they were to be captured alive.

Dylan and his men zip-tied Mathieu Nabati and his few remaining men.

They attended then to the Russian leader and his wounded. The few Spetsnaz who'd been called in after Dylan and his men had entered the house and participated in the takedown were showing great respect and appreciation to the Americans, especially to Dylan, whose lead they were now happy to follow.

During the hour they had to wait for the evacuation choppers to arrive, Dylan and his four able-bodied men went through the house gathering Nabati's electronic equipment, documents, and anything that looked as if it could be useful to learn about the Nabateans.

Dylan instructed them to gather all electronic equipment and plug them into the power in the lounge. He took the Blackjack out of his backpack, booted it up, and placed it on the table to scan and collect data from all the devices. His men didn't ask about the device; they were intelligent enough to figure it out for themselves.

It would be hours later before Dylan, his men, and the Russians were finally all back in Moscow. By the time Dylan, who refused to be evacuated with the wounded, and his men arrived in Moscow, a celebration was underway.

The Spetsnaz troops, including their leader, had experienced a profound change of heart. Many had already consumed their first bottles of vodka and were starting on the second.

After the third Spetsnaz had bear-hugged him and thanked him for saving their asses with tears in their eyes, he was in a pretty good mood himself. The Spetsnaz leader was confined to a hospital bed, but he'd sent an apology and his profound thanks to his new American friends.

The Vice-President intervened before Dylan and his men could get into the party mood. Time to go home, and time for Dylan to be glad they weren't searched on departure.

They would have liked to take the Nabatean scoundrel, Mathieu Nabati, with them, but it was not to be. At least they had a copy of all the information on his vast array of electronic devices.

Chapter Ninety-Six

EIGHT MORE COUNCILORS

Barely two hours before the strikes in the rest of the countries were to take place, the President of China made his decision. Better safe than sorry, former Secretary of State, Abraham Goudy, had urged, and China's President had pondered a bit of history before deciding to risk his friendship with one of the Vice-Chairmen of the National People's Congress by allowing the Ministry of State Security to pick him up and question him.

Polite but cold, the President thanked Goudy for his information and assured him China would take care of the problem. Just as politely, he suggested Goudy waste no time in returning home.

Goudy was not entirely happy with the outcome, but there was nothing more he could do. At least he got President Zhang to agree not to jump the gun and agree to wait until the other operations started. And at least he'd be able to go home.

There was no discussion of allowing US representatives to sit in on the questioning, despite Goudy's urgent pleas.

Nor was any information shared. No details of the arrest were made available.

Careful observance of Chinese government rolls later showed the vice-chairman's seat vacant, but no death notice appeared. From those facts, Bill Griffin concluded the man had been kept alive for questioning, determined to be untrustworthy, but not killed. One could never be sure, but the Nabatean appeared to be out of circulation in any case.

It would only be weeks later that information from US covert operators in China revealed someone who'd been of previous interest in Shanghai was killed in a shootout with the MSS police. The name matched that of the second Nabatean in China, and the date corresponded with the day of the coordinated roundup of the Nabateans.

Missions to close allies went almost as expected. With full cooperation of the respective governments, US personnel were involved in the apprehension of every Nabatean council member.

Rather than resist, two of them, the one in London and his counterpart in Tokyo, committed suicide.

MI6 rushed in at the sound of a handgun but found the Nabatean with a small hole in his right temple and the left side of his head gone—most of it still dripping off the wall on his left.

The Tokyo scene was just as messy. The Nabatean woman was pushing a sword through her stomach in classic hara-kiri style when Japanese security personnel entered the house.

They rushed her to a hospital, but she'd lost too much

blood and damaged too many internal organs. Doctors were unable to save her.

In Japanese tradition, she had performed what was considered an act of restoring honor by one who had failed and shamed friends and family.

In India, the Nabatean councilor calmly surrendered. When told his co-councilors were dead or detained, he became very keen to secure a deal—he'd inform against them for any sort of comfort in prison, where the Indian special police assured him he'd spend the rest of his life.

An initial search of the Saudi's residence had the Mabahith taskforce think he has escaped. But then a locked and impregnable room led the Mabahith men to believe he was inside. They waited him out, and when he emerged, arrested him promptly.

Well aware of what was in store, he began talking before he was out of his house. They didn't even have to use enhanced interrogation techniques on him, though the two CIA agents thought they eventually would, just to make sure they got all the information he had and that what he told them was the truth.

Within an hour after the launch of the final phase of Operation Rock Concert, President Grant was handed a note from one of the senior CIA members. He was part of the group in the Situation Room monitoring the unfolding of the global operation.

The message from Omar Said consisted of only three words—*Done. Coming home.*

It would only be three days later when Omar and his companion were back in D.C. that Sean got the details about the missions to Iran and Syria to take out Alireza Karimi-Shah in Tehran and Hassan Al-Suleiman.

Hassan Al-Suleiman was taken out by a sniper with a high-powered rifle from about eight-hundred yards.

Alireza Karimi-Shah in Tehran was taken out with a car-bomb, which was remotely detonated at ten minutes past Zero Hour.

Chapter Ninety-Seven

HE DIDN'T CARE

Sean couldn't decide whether to be annoyed or amused at Connie's insistence she could help with Graziella's capture. The Secretary of State was all for putting on a Peruvian Army uniform, arming herself, and if there were horses, saddling one to ride out with them. He had to believe she was kidding; nevertheless, he explained to her in all seriousness that President Grant would have his ass in a sling if he allowed Connie to be anywhere near a dangerous operation.

"This isn't a horse ride out on your ranch to catch a few cattle-rustler wannabes," he finished.

"Honey, you are so sweet. I know that."

"You scared me there for a minute, Connie."

She turned a look on him that was devoid of her usual teasing glint. "Sugar, I know you have a girlfriend waitin' for you. If I were twenty-five years younger, she wouldn't have a chance, but as it is, you're like a son to me.

"You take care, for both our sakes, you hear?" She kissed his cheek. "Now get goin'."

Sean's jaw dropped. He'd had no idea Madame Secretary knew anything of his personal life. Wondering what being "like a son" to her would mean for him in the future, he grinned, gave a snappy salute, and left to join the rest of the raiding party.

He was to lead his six Executive Advantage operatives and six Peruvian Fuerza Delta troops. The Fuerza Delta was based on America's Delta Force model and was one of two Special Forces units in the Peruvian Marines. The six had been chosen partly because they could speak English well enough to follow Sean's instructions.

Sean and both teams boarded two Mil Mi 17 choppers in Lima and headed to Machu Picchu, approximately three hundred miles distant. They had just under two hours to finalize the plan of attack they'd formed in Lima before leaving.

With the help of satellite photos, they knew the layout of Graziella's compound. What they didn't know was how many guards she had, their weaponry, and how they were deployed within the mansion or the grounds.

Sean was a careful leader. He preferred to scout first and give his men the best chance of survival. Therefore, he assigned his troops to each major area of the compound in twos, instructing them to observe and report back but not to move in until his order.

They had an advantage in the PeriD'ice anti-surveillance devices, which proved effective in defeating Graziella's electronic security measures and allowed Sean and his troops to surprise Graziella and her guards.

As he'd suspected, she was heavily protected. One of the Peruvians literally stumbled over a guard as they approached, and in the ensuing scuffle, the guard got off a shot. The Peruvian killed the guard with his knife, but the damage was done—the alarm raised. Before Sean's men had a good read on the situation, guards were streaming out of the house to meet the threat.

Sean's two-man squads immediately sought cover and strafed them with automatic fire. They mowed down eighty-percent of the storming guards within seconds, the rest went to ground.

When the shooting started, Sean gave orders to two of his men to use their grenade launchers to take out the satellite and other communications antennae on the roof of the mansion so Graziella couldn't get messages out to the rest of the world. A few well-aimed shots took care of that, and then the raiding party inched toward the house, making sure they left no live enemy behind them.

Sean assumed Graziella would have kept some of her guards with her. He led four of his men into the house while the others assisted the Peruvians in the mop-up outside. They cleared the rooms methodically, working their way from the front entry right and left, with Sean cautiously moving between them, taking cover behind furniture as he went.

It took nearly half an hour to clear the way before they found a room guarded by two men.

On approach, one of Sean's men stumbled over a rug, alerting them. Sean and his companion opened fire, but one of the guards was able to shoot and kill the fallen operative before he could recover. Both guards succumbed to double-tap gunshots immediately afterward.

Sean was in a savage mood over the loss of his friend and teammate when he kicked Graziella's door down, dodging back around the wall immediately. He called out.

"Graziella Nabati! Surrender now, and no one else needs to get hurt."

The response was a burst of fire from an automatic weapon that shredded the door frame where Sean's head was a split second before. Sean's right forearm was grazed by one of the rounds, but it didn't slow him down.

His remaining teammate was unhurt and answered the gunfire with a burst of his own.

Sean shouted at him over the noise to cease fire. They needed Graziella alive.

When no further gunfire from inside the room ensued, they assumed either the person who'd shot before had been killed, seriously wounded, or had given up.

Nevertheless, Sean and his man peeked quickly around the damaged doorframe and pulled back immediately. They repeated that several times, each time allowing their eyes to make quick snapshots of the layout of the room, as well as where someone could be hiding, waiting to kill them when they came in.

After a minute of the standoff, Sean knew someone would have to make a move. He dropped to the ground in a belly-crawl position, held up three fingers and lowered one at a time. When the third finger folded down, he and his man slithered into the room, leopard-crawling as fast as they could.

From his vantage point on the floor, Sean saw Graziella huddled in a corner next to the bed. She was sobbing uncontrollably.

An automatic rifle lay on the floor nearby.

Sean surged to his feet, ran the few yards toward Graziella and kicked the weapon out of her reach. His man cleared the rest of the room, finding no one.

Sean took Graziella by the arm and urged her to stand. He could hear no more gunfire from outside, and the lack of a response from inside the house told him it was secured by his men.

He frog-marched Graziella outside and told her to call out to her guards to stand down, which she did.

Two Nabatean guards rose from their concealed positions and were covered by Peruvian troops immediately. When the clean-up was complete and Sean had a tally, he'd lost one Executive Advantage operative and one Peruvian. Three were wounded, two Peruvians and himself. Although he didn't regard his as a real wound.

Sean had the wounded tended to first, then had the medic sedate Graziella, who'd gone into a screaming fit when she'd seen the devastation and the lifeless bodies of her guards.

It was a merciful relief to everyone when her high-pitched bawling ended as the sedative rendered her comatose.

The two remaining guards were handcuffed and pushed unceremoniously into the chopper, followed by an unconscious Graziella and the two wounded Peruvians.

Sean sent the able-bodied men he had left to ransack the mansion for anything useful or informative, and they returned with various records, computers, and electronic devices they didn't recognize. They loaded it all into the chopper.

Sean boarded last, looking over his shoulder at Graziella's mansion. The front door stood wide open. He looked at the body bag containing his fallen comrade and was tempted to set fire to the house, wipe it off the face of the earth.

Instead he just clenched his jaw, got into the chopper, and signalled for the pilot to take off. Once in the air, he asked the medic to bandage his wound.

Perhaps indigenous people would find the house, or more likely looters and other criminals. Maybe even a drug lord would take it over. He didn't care.

In Lima, Constance Pierce had been working her charms on the Prime Minister. After telling him about the Nabateans' goals and methods, how they'd stayed below the radar anywhere they had operations, and everything else they were capable of, she had the poor man spooked.

She relieved his anxiety by volunteering the US to deal with the diabolical leader, Graziella Nabati.

"In that way, Peru would not become a target of the Nabateans, should they ever raise their ugly heads again," she said.

The Prime Minister wasn't entirely naïve. Before allowing the valuable Nabati woman out of the country, he extracted a promise that the US would share all information with Peru and negotiated a beneficial trade deal as well.

Chapter Ninety-Eight

THE RISKS

Bill and Simone were painfully aware of the risks for both of them. Simone's involvement, if discovered, was not going to go down well with the French authorities. She could very well be facing subversion charges—emotional as the French could get, they'd probably revive the use of the guillotine just for the occasion. Bill would probably be arrested and thrown in jail for espionage, at the very minimum, and the political fallout between the US and France would be catastrophic. Other allies might even side with the French.

Notwithstanding their predicament, both were equally aware that an hourglass was running out, and no one had any idea how much sand was left in it. The Operation Rock Concert's Zero Hour was nine hours away, but no one knew what the Nabateans' Zero Hour was.

The thermobaric explosives in the chambers below Graziella's house, threatening the lives of the people working there, plus the threat of an antimatter bomb that could take out Capitol Hill and much of the surrounding area, not to mention one that would wipe out New York City, trumped every other consideration.

There was definitely no time left to go through diplomatic channels.

If this operation went pear-shaped and their involvement became known, that would be their only justification for their actions—they could only hope and pray the authorities would also see it that way.

Bill had explained to her that only the US, with its firsthand knowledge of the Nabateans, had the skills and technical knowhow to prevent the imminent disaster.

As a senior agent for the *Direction générale de la sécurité*, Simone's duties included counter-espionage, counter-terrorism, countering cybercrime, and surveillance of potentially threatening groups. This operation would have fitted one hundred percent into her job description was it not for the fact that she was not going to inform her agency.

Their first major issue was the information about the subterranean complex below Graziella's house was scanty at best. In fact, the only information they had, provided by Sullivan, was that it consisted of at least four levels, and there were more than hundred people working there.

Simone had access to detailed maps of the Paris Catacombs—her agency, working closely with the police, had been keeping an eye on them for years because of the ideal hiding place it provided for criminals and terrorists.

While she and Bill were talking, she logged into her work account from her laptop via an encrypted virtual private network and downloaded the maps. With the maps in front of them, she disconnected the link, and they quickly figured out that Graziella's house was apparently surrounded by catacombs. Although they had no idea where the edges of the compound below her house were, it was clear that in some areas there would be common walls.

"Sullivan told us the only way to access the chambers is from Graziella's house, but I'm wondering if that's correct. Not that I think Sullivan would have lied about it; maybe he wasn't told about it," Bill said. "The thing that has been bugging me since I heard about it is how those hundred employees get in and out of that place? They can't all be going through the house every day. That would've raised red flags with the neighbors and police ages ago."

"Hmm, that's true, but only if the people who work there are living on the outside—they could be living inside," Simone responded.

"Like moles...," Bill mused. "That's what I call a crappy working environment. I just can't imagine how people could live like that for extended periods of time. There *must* be other entrances."

"It would be very helpful if we can find another way to enter the facility than through Graziella's house. Especially if we could do so from the cover of the catacombs," she said.

"Well, if we can figure out the layout of the facility and determine where the shared walls are, we might be able to use a few carefully shaped C4 charges to provide us with a new entry if required—if the walls are not too thick."

Simone went quiet for a while as she worked on a plan to get into Graziella's house discreetly. She used her special access rights to the City Council, Postal Services, and Police networks to find out if the house was occupied by anyone in the absence of Graziella Nabati. Within a few minutes, she had the information. The house was still registered in Graziella's name but currently occupied by one person, Jean Aubert, a seventy-six-year-old bachelor. "Probably the butler," she said. "If we just had more time to investigate..." her voice trailed off.

Simone also found the plans for Graziella's three-story house on the City Council servers and downloaded them. None of them were surprised that the plans did not show any underground rooms.

Bill's mind had been busy as well. "Maybe it would be best to take a team and a few Walabot devices and see how much we could learn about the chambers and map whatever we can."

"Walabot?" Simone inquired.

Bill laughed. "Don't ask me about the technology. I wouldn't have a clue, but I do know it's a 3D-imaging sensor, which you connect to a smartphone, and then you can look right through walls. It will show everything inside the walls like pipes, wiring, cavities, and it will show structural foundations, and even people in the room."

"I always thought a window is the only way to look through a wall!" Simone giggled. "Anyway, that sounds a lot better than blowing the walls away. I take it we'll be able to buy those at a mobile phone shop?"

"In America, you can. I am sure you'll have it here as well."

Simone also had a solution for Bill's concerns about the French authorities asking questions about the Director of the CIA's impromptu visit. She was going to phone her superior to let him know she had a surprise visitor and would like to take a few days off from work. She would leave enough hints during the conversation to make him curious enough to ask the obvious question, which would enable her to reveal who it was.

She assured Bill the news would travel fast from there

and would probably have the desired results—they'd leave him in peace.

Shortly after nine a.m., with a little less than five hours to Zero Hour, Simone phoned her office and spoke to her manager. She explained in the sweetest tone she'd gotten the surprise of her life, a very pleasant one, in the early morning hours and would like to take two days off. This was enough to peak the curiosity of her manager who asked what the surprise was. With that, Simone had him in her pocket and elaborated. She dropped Bill's name, managing to sound a bit self-conscious about the purpose of his visit—to spend a few days with her, before he was due to travel to an undisclosed location elsewhere in Europe.

The French, always excited by anything that sounded like romance. Her manager, no exception, was more than happy to let her take a few days off and told her to enjoy it.

"You're a star, Simone. It feels just like the old days." Bill chuckled when she put the phone down and stole a quick kiss before he contacted one of his team members with a cryptic text message to meet for coffee in fifteen minutes about two blocks away from Simone's apartment.

Chapter Ninety-Nine

ENTER LIKE CIVILIZED PEOPLE

It was nine thirty a.m. when Bill and Simone met with Peter Cusack, the senior EA operator on the team, and gave him instructions. He had to get the message to the rest of the team and the MI6 agents.

Simone showed Peter a map of the relevant parts of the catacombs and the different entry points, which the team had to use to get to the rendezvous point. She handed him a copy of the maps on a flash drive, which he and other team members would transfer to their tablets.

Bill also told Peter to make sure they got a few Walabot devices and installed them on some of their smartphones.

Shortly after eleven a.m., they were all gathered in a cavernous room in the catacombs adjacent to the Nabatean underground facilities.

The MI6 team, as per request from Bill, brought weapons, explosives, and other tools of the trade with them and handed it out to the rest. No one asked how they managed to get their hands on it or smuggle it into France.

There were three hours left to Zero Hour when Bill and

Simone gathered everyone around them and in whispered voices shared the plans with them. The first and preferable option, Plan A, was to try and find one or more entryways into the Nabatean facilities from somewhere in the catacombs. If they couldn't find one in time, they had to resort to Plan B, which was to go in through the front door, and Plan C was the highly undesirable idea to blow holes through the walls.

The revelation that the facilities they wanted to enter were rigged with thermobaric explosives made most of the team gasp. One of the MI6 agents, an explosives specialist, summed up the general feeling, accentuating every word as he spoke. "No bloody way I'm fokkin around with that stoff. Apologies, ma'am."

Bill grinned. "Yes lad, that's why I prefer Plan A—find a door and enter like civilized people."

The little interlude broke the tension for a short while and had them all smiling.

Simone's maps showed there were at least five walls in the adjacent passages and rooms that could be shared walls.

A few of them kept a lookout for unwelcome visitors while the rest got busy with their Walabots, fine-combing the walls and mapping out what they could "see" on the other side.

However, it was slow and frustrating work. The Walabots were nowhere as powerful as they hoped they would be, and they were heavy on the phone batteries. Many of the images produced were unreadable.

The team was getting more and more frustrated and nervous as time passed. They had portable chargers with them to recharge the phone batteries but decided not to use that unless absolutely necessary. They needed their phones when the attack started. All their phones were configured with push-to-talk software, which would enable them to use the phones as walkie-talkies.

After an hour, they managed to cover about thirty percent of the walls but already used up half or more of the phone batteries.

Bill, Simone, and the computer experts were collating the images coming from the Walabots and started to get a vague idea of what it looked like on the other side of the walls. But it was nowhere near enough information to launch an attack without risking the lives of everyone involved.

Bill made the call. "One more hour, guys. If we haven't found a door or weak spot, we'll have to go through the front door, or take the chance and use the explosives to get in."

"One hour is also the maximum the phone batteries will last," Peter commented.

About forty minutes later, one of the scanning teams returned and reported the battery on their phone has been depleted. Over the next ten minutes, two more teams returned with the same news.

Bill told them to recharge their phones from their mobile chargers while they wait for the last team to arrive.

Just then, Peter, who was part of the remaining team, rushed into the room, sounding quite excited. "Looks like we've got it! Come and have a look."

He explained they found a spot in the wall the images showed to be about the size of an arched double door. But it looked like it was sealed with concrete or similar material; the scanner showed it was enforced with steel.

They were all gathered at the spot, staring at the area pointed out by Peter in the beams of their flashlights. It was impossible to see the difference between the area Peter showed them and the surrounding limestone walls with the naked eye. But when they looked at the images on the phone, it was clear the natural-looking façade was hiding something else.

"Must have been an opening or door here in the past," Bill said. "They sealed it, probably with concrete as you said, and skillfully hidden it behind this fascia."

"Peter, can you move the scanner to the area on the left side of the door, please?" Simone asked.

He did so, and slowly images started appearing on mobile phone's screen. There was clearly a cavity in the wall to the left—large enough to accommodate the "door"' they looked at.

This got them all excited, but then the phone went dead —out of battery. They quickly plugged the phone into one of the mobile chargers and started it up.

Further scanning revealed there were what looked like rails at the top and bottom of the "door" and in the top and bottom of the cavity. No doubt there was a sliding door behind the façade. Their problem was they couldn't find any way of opening it from their side.

They scanned the surrounding areas, looking for a concealed opening mechanism but could find any. A little less than one hour before Zero Hour, Bill called a halt and had them gather around him, explaining the final plan.

He and Simone plus one of the EA operators, one IT expert, and one of the MI6 agents would go outside. He and Simone would go to the front door of Graziella's house and try to take down the butler and see if they could get the layout of the underground facility from him. The three men accompanying them were to stay out of sight and be their backup in case things did not work out as they hoped.

The remaining twelve would stay down there and wait

until that door was opened from the other side or they were called to come up to the house.

"Any comments?" Bill asked when he came to end. He looked around the group to see if anyone had reservations.

Peter replied, "I can't say I like the idea of you and Ms. Bouvier going up there, Sir. I'd prefer to be the one doing that." Joe, the team leader of the MI6 contingent, agreed.

"Any other ideas?" Bill asked. When no one else responded, he looked at Peter and Joe and said, "I appreciate your concern, but Simone and I *have* to go. She speaks the language. She's the one carrying the official badges and authority to get us into the house. And don't tell me you'll go with her. I'm the one who's drawn her into this; I'm the one going with her. But I have no objection if you two come along with Shane as our backup instead."

The fact that they would have to pull this off in broad daylight was worrying, but there was nothing they could do about it. It was absolutely critical they launched their attack in sync with every other operation across the globe.

They would have liked to have more information, more options, and more time—they had none.

Chapter One Hundred

WE'RE TRAINED TO HANDLE THIS

At one forty-five p.m. in Paris, fifteen minutes before Zero Hour, Bill checked his satellite phone—no messages from D.C. That meant the attacks would proceed as planned. He nodded to Simone. "Let's go."

Fortunately, Graziella's mansion was located about thirty yards away from the street, and the space in between was covered by lush lawns, trees, shrubs, and garden features. This gave their three companions ample places to stay out of sight when Bill and Simone approached the front door.

It was one forty-seven p.m. when Simone pushed the button on the extravagant oak double door of Graziella's mansion. They heard the bell chime inside, and twenty seconds later the door opened. They immediately recognized Jean Aubert, the seventy-six-year-old bachelor. He was a tiny man with thick glasses and snow-white hair.

He looked and sounded cranky when he said brusquely, "What do you want?"

Simone displayed the most beautiful and disarming

smile when she greeted the old man and apologized for the intrusion.

She showed him her badge and explained she was investigating a case and required his help. She took a slight step closer to him in a non-intimidating way while she was talking. It had the desired effect. His mannerism changed when she spoke again, and he invited them in, a smile on his face.

Aubert held the door while he waved them in. Simone stepped out of Bill's way as they entered, Aubert's back was turned to them as he locked the door. Bill took one step, placed his right arm around Aubert's neck and clasped his left hand over his mouth.

"Listen carefully. Do as I say, and you'll not be hurt," he whispered in perfect French. Bill felt sorry for the old man as he felt him starting to tremble. "Is there anyone else with you in the house?"

Aubert shook his head. Bill nodded to Simone, who unlocked the door and spoke into her mobile phone now acting as a walkie-talkie. "Come in."

Peter, hiding among the plants close by the front door, took a quick look around to make sure no one was watching and strolled to the front door.

Joe and the IT expert, Shane, heard the message from Simone. They were hiding on either side of the house, waiting to get Peter's message to enter once he had secured the house and opened the side doors for them.

Bill was apologetic when he zip-tied and gagged Aubert. He promised him he would be released when they were done and that no harm would come to him. Bill had him sit down on a chair in the living room while Peter and Simone quickly scanned the ground floor and called Joe and Shane in.

Bill was grateful they met with little resistance from Aubert, who was quiet but wide-eyed and shaking.

Bill started questioning him while the rest of them secured the remainder of the mansion. Simone's map of the layout was very helpful. They had three goals; make sure there was no one else in the house, find and deactivate the communications system, and find the entry to the underground chambers.

At first Aubert refused to answer, just shaking his head to every question Bill asked. Bill quickly got more than a little irritated and told him what would happen if he didn't quit his stupid behavior immediately. He took a few minutes and explained to Aubert they knew about the secret subterranean complex and the Nabateans.

It didn't encourage Aubert to talk, but when Bill told him he was literally sitting on a bomb, a thermobaric one to be sure, which was going to blow his ass to kingdom come at any moment, Aubert's eyes shot wide again, and he started sweating profusely.

Some pieces of the puzzle must have fallen into place for him. Although his voice was muffled by the cloth over his mouth, Bill was able to understand Aubert was asking what could be done to prevent the disaster.

In short order, he showed them what they asked for. First was the secret entry to the chambers below—bookcase that concealed an elevator. They would come back to that soon. Next, he led them to Graziella's communications control room, the entry cleverly hidden behind the full-length mirror in Graziella's luxurious bathroom.

Shane let out a soft whistle. "Shit! This is the most sophisticated setup I've ever seen. I'm... wait... the power." He looked around and found the power plugs but didn't switch it off immediately. "There'll be a UPS... uninterrupted power supply, somewhere here. I'm sure." He looked at Aubert. "Where're the backup batteries?"

Bill translated, and Aubert nodded his head to a wall closet.

Shane opened the door and stared at the shelves filled with rows and rows of what could be batteries, but he had never seen that kind. He shook his head. It didn't matter what type it was. All he had to do was disconnect them from the equipment. He quickly retrieved a set of pliers and went to work. Within twenty seconds, it was done. He went to the power board on the wall and flipped the main switch. The next moment, the lights on all the equipment were out. He unplugged everything and looked at Bill.

"Done?" Bill inquired.

"Yes, boss. That would take care of anything in here. What we don't know is if this was linked to what they have underground. If so, we're okay, and this could have stopped the countdown for the antimatter bombs," Shane replied.

"We better make sure about that," Bill replied.

They sprinted down the stairs to the ground floor, dragging Aubert with them.

Aubert volunteered that there were only two armed guards down in the underground chambers. They were stationed outside the elevator on the second level. They'd be ready to fire when the elevator doors opened, he warned.

Bill wanted to go down, but Peter and Joe stopped him. "No way I'll let you go down there first, old-timer," Peter quipped. "We're trained to handle this." Peter had no doubt he would hear more about it after this was over. But he was definitely not going to let the Director of the CIA do his job for him.

Peter and Joe went down atop the elevator car with the access panel open. When the guards saw an empty elevator, they entered to investigate. Peter and Joe dropped on top of them and overpowered them before they could make a sound. Joe stayed behind to zip-tie and gag the unconscious guards while Peter went back up to get Bill.

Simone and Shane would stay with Aubert for now.

While Joe and Peter went down to take care of the guards, Bill had Aubert draw a rough layout of the underground chambers and mark the spot where they would find the sliding door they had found while in the catacombs.

When Peter arrived, Bill grabbed the paper, asked Simone and Shane to keep on questioning Aubert and get him to draw a new detailed layout while he, Joe, and Peter went and opened that door for the rest of the team waiting in the catacombs.

Sullivan's intel about the place had been woefully incomplete, as it soon became evident the floors covered an area much bigger than just the perimeters of Graziella's mansion. By Bill's approximation, the area must have covered below the properties on both sides and the back of hers.

"Which means those houses could be occupied by collaborators and could be providing more ways to enter this place."

It turned out Aubert wasn't lying, and his map was good enough to guide them down a hallway on the first level below ground, past the sleeping quarters, and down a limestone spiral staircase to the fourth level. The staircase ended right in front of the sliding door.

Joe found the button that would open the door and pushed it. But nothing happened for a few seconds. They were looking at each other—*what now?* The door started moving slowly after what felt like an eternity, and in chorus, they let out a breath.

Chapter One Hundred One

ZERO HOUR

It was 1:58 p.m. when the twelve men, waiting in the catacombs, stepped through the door. Peter's instructions were short as he ordered the men to split into four groups, one group for each floor to secure it and find those bombs. He also quickly explained Bill's thought that there might be other entrances from houses adjacent to Graziella's, told them to be on the lookout, and to secure it if found.

As they went up the stairs, the designated groups peeled off on their assigned floor to explore and secure it. They crept silently, assault rifles aimed, peering through the sights of their weapons, ready to fire. Fortunately, the floors were well lit.

It had been quite some time since Bill had been in the field. Truth be told, it had been more than thirty years. His heart hammered as he worked his way up the stairs with the men.

Just when they reached the basement's second level, a short burst of gunfire sounded from the level below them— basement level three, Joe's group. Bill's heart rate doubled.

Peter, who was leading, said over his shoulder, "Keep on going. Joe will take care of it."

Joe was leading three of his MI6 men when they rounded a corner and ran right into one of the workers. Joe acted in a flash and cold-cocked the worker with the butt of his assault rifle. But then two more men came running around the corner. Joe's men shouted at them to freeze, but they just kept coming—the operatives had no choice but to shoot them down.

"Shit, I hope those shots weren't heard on the outside," Bill said.

"Impossible," Peter replied. "These walls are too thick to let out any sound. But everyone inside would have heard it."

Bill and Peter found it strange that despite the fact that the whole place must have been on alert after those shots that there was no eruption of gunfights.

Then the leader of the level four group reported, "Level four secured. No resistance. Ten rounded up and secured. But man, they are weird!"

"What do you mean?" Peter asked.

"They were all sitting at computers when we came in. They didn't even look up at us. When we pulled them off their chairs and tied them up, they were moaning a bit but didn't resist. Now they're just staring at us. None of them has said a word. And you're not going to believe this, but they all look the same."

"What do you mean they look the same?" Bill interjected.

"They look like clones."

With a sickening shock, Bill remembered Carter's report —these monsters had programs to *make* their own savants.

"Oh, my God!" he sighed. "Listen, those people are autistic. Make sure no one hurts them."

"Will do," the team leader replied.

Peter and Bill, with the last team, reached the first level. The sleeping quarters, kitchen, and dining area were on this level. They found twenty people asleep in their beds and discovered the same experience as the team on level four. The people all looked the same—tiny, fragile, bleak-skinned humans with dark hair and big, dark eyes, wordlessly staring at them. It was like a horror movie.

"What do I do with these poor people when the operation is over?" Bill muttered. Before he could think any further, the reports started streaming in.

"Basement level three secured," Joe reported. "This is the medical lab. Twelve here, two dead, nine more clones, and one normal. Says he is a brain specialist."

Joe was sickened as he stared at the liquid-filled jars on the shelves—fetuses *in vitro*. The doctor had explained these were savants in various stages of development. The doctors would, at the right times, insert different chemical substances to create the conditions for determining the exact type of genius the Nabateans required.

"But be warned," Joe said, "you'll need a strong stomach for this one."

"Basement level two secured," the team leader reported. "This is the IT hub. There're two 'normals' and eight clones. Send the IT experts in. The 'normals' are cooperating."

"Okay, sending them in now," Peter replied.

Bill had been adding the numbers—fifty-two. He turned to Peter. "We were told to expect more than a hundred people. We've only got fifty-two."

Peter nodded. "Yes, I've been wondering about that. As

far as we know, there's no place in this facility where they can hide. They could have escaped or could've been evacuated as part of the Nabateans plans to disappear."

Bill paused for a moment. "Animals! They've evacuated the best and left these poor souls to be killed."

Peter raised his phone to his mouth, "Okay, everyone, listen carefully. Leave two operators with the IT gurus on level three. The rest of you all up to level one. We need to work level by level and find those bombs, *now*."

Bill went up to the ground floor and told Shane to join the IT team on level three. He questioned Aubert to find out if he had any idea where the bombs could have been hidden. But Aubert had no idea. He had very little empathy when he tied Aubert's arms and feet to the chair and wrapped a few pieces of duct tape around his mouth.

"Bastard! You knew exactly what was going on down there. I have a good mind to shoot you right now."

Simone put her hand on Bill's arm to calm him down.

Bill took Simone's hand, led her into an adjacent room, and told her what they had found so far. Simone had tears in her eyes when he told her about the people. "I'll have to go back down now, Simone, but in the meantime, you'll have to think what we're going to do with those unfortunate people down there.... If we get out of this alive."

"Don't talk like that, Bill. We're going to make it out of here—all of us. You and I have some unfinished business to take care of." She smiled and rose to the tip of her toes and kissed him. "Now go and find the bombs and deactivate them."

When Bill arrived in the IT hub on level three, he found room after room of what the computer geeks identified as highly advanced computer servers, used as databanks.

The two "normals" they captured in the IT hub became

extremely helpful when they were told their bosses had abandoned them to die in an explosion.

Unfortunately, they had no idea where the thermobaric bombs could have been placed. Neither did they know about the antimatter bombs, nor if they were controlled from the IT hub. However, they told Bill and Shane that more than half of the workers were moved to a new facility over the past two days.

"I believe you *now* understand why they did that?" Bill said.

The two men nodded in shocked silence.

Shane asked them about their external communications link, and the leader explained they had fiber-optic cables running to one of the houses on the outside, where it was connected to small but very powerful satellite dishes.

"Shit!" Shane exclaimed. "We've to assume that if we cut those, it will trigger the bombs."

"Okay," Bill started with as much calm as he could muster, "if you want to save your asses and the rest of the people here, we need to find the server that's controlling the antimatter bombs. It's linked to the thermobaric bombs—all of it will go off at the same time. That much we know."

The two men asked that the rest of their team be untied and promised none of them would cause any trouble—they would do exactly what they were told. Shane looked at Bill.

He hesitated. "Okay, but tell them one wrong move and… no, just tell them about the bombs and that they'll be dead if they don't find that controller."

Bill's phone crackled. It was Peter's voice. "We got one in the kitchen. The experts are looking at it, but you better come and have a look."

Bill ran up the stairs and was out of breath when he arrived in the kitchen. Peter and one of the bomb disposal experts stood in front of a cavity in the wall, which was previously blocked by a stove. He saw the bomb—it filled the entire cavity and was rigged with wires and a device, which looked like a smartphone.

He looked inquisitively at Peter and the explosives expert.

"No touching that thing, sir," the expert said. "That device there" —he pointed to the smartphone— "is wirelessly connected to some other device. Breaking the link will set the bomb off."

Bill took a step back, and before he could say anything, Joe came through on his phone. "Found another in the sleeping quarters."

Bill, Peter, and the expert rushed to the sleeping quarters. Within a minute, they reached the same conclusion as with the first bomb—hands off.

"Damn! We're down to one option—find the controller. Okay, Peter, let's stop the search for the bombs, and evacuate the people and as much of the medical lab and IT equipment into the catacombs as we can."

"Yes, sir," Peter replied and started issuing the orders.

Bill turned and went down the stairs back to the IT hub. "I'm too damned old for this," he muttered.

Chapter One Hundred Two

IN TEN MINUTES

Shane's voice came over his phone before he reached the third level. "They've found it!"

"The bomb controls?" he retorted.

"Yeah. And you're not going to believe this—"

"Spit it out, man! We don't have all day."

"Sir, it's... It's going to detonate them in ten minutes."

By now, Bill was inside the IT hub. "Can they stop it?" he asked in an almost inaudible voice.

"Sir, there are safeguards. They're working as fast as they can to break the password or pin code or whatever. I'm not sure what they're up against, but it doesn't look good."

Bill's blood ran cold. That wasn't enough time to warn the President to evacuate Capitol Hill. And the antimatter bombs wouldn't be stopped even by the hardened shelter below the White House. His friends... Grant, James... They'd be annihilated. His head dropped. Simone!

He ran to the room where they found the control server and skidded to a halt behind a knot of computer scientists in front of a server and looked at the numbers on the screen. It displayed 9:30, and just then it ticked down to 9:29.

He shouted, "Stop that fucker!"

It seemed to break the collective trance, even for the savants.

Bill didn't look back. He sprinted out of the room, skipping the stairs two at a time up to the first basement floor to the elevator. On the way, he got his phone out, pushed the button, and shouted, "Simone! Get in the elevator and come down immediately. We have to get you to safety."

Simone jumped up and entered the elevator, leaving Aubert behind, whose eyes were wide—he knew what was going to happen to him.

Bill literally dragged Simone out of the elevator while the doors were still opening and dragged her with him to the stairs leading down to the fourth floor and the sliding door. Out of breath and with a heartrate that must have been exceeding two hundred, he explained what was going on.

When they reached the IT hub level, Simone stopped and shouted, "Bill, if you're not going with me, I'm not going out. I stay with you."

Bill stopped and was about to shout at her that there was no time for arguing but saw the determination on her face. For a moment, he considered throwing her over his shoulder and carrying her down then realized he had almost no strength left to walk, let alone lifting and carrying her. He gave up and instead said, "Come this way."

Hand in hand, he and Simone entered the server room. Bill's eyes sought the screen first—2:28.

One of the savants was in the seat in front of the server, his fingers a blur over the keyboard. It looked like a science fiction movie set. Everyone else was quiet. It was if they have stopped breathing.

Moments passed.

The counter showed 2:10.

The savant's hands came to an abrupt halt. He didn't say anything—he just rested his hands on the desk on either side of the keyboard and stared at the screen.

Everyone's eyes move from the person's hands to the screen.

The clock showed 2:08 and below it a message:

> *Confirm Shutdown of Countdown Sequence.*
> *Press "Y" to stop or "N" to continue.*

Shane took a step forward, leaned over the person's shoulder, and pressed the Y-key.

> *Countdown Sequence Ended.*

It was exactly two forty-five p.m. in Paris.

"I am *really* too old for this shit," Bill growled.

Everyone except the savants started laughing and high-fiving each other. Simone put her arm around Bill's waist and hugged him.

"Okay, Shane," Bill started after a deep breath, "shutdown everything. Unplug and dismantle everything on this floor. I'm going to meet with the others and figure out a way to evacuate everyone and everything from these chambers of horror."

With the assurance that the Nabateans' global communications system had been deactivated, Bill felt it was safe to let the President know. He and Simone went up to the ground floor where he switched his encrypted satellite phone on and called President Grant.

Chapter One Hundred Three

I'M PROUD OF HER

The French situation was a prickly problem from the outset and only became worse in the aftermath. The French President was informed of the details of Operation Rock Concert through a briefing by the US ambassador to France, and of the fact that one of his citizens was the leader of this nefarious group. However, he was oblivious to the operation that took place on French soil.

After stopping the countdown to the bomb explosions, Aubert was brought down to show them the hidden entrances to the adjacent houses. Peter and Joe took some of their men and searched the three residences and were not surprised when they found no one inside.

That made their next decision much easier. They rented two furniture removal trucks and packed all the equipment. By six p.m., they had emptied the place and dispatched the trucks, driven by their own men, two from each of Peter's and Joe's teams, to 21st Theater Sustainment Command, Kaiserslautern, Germany.

Kaiserslautern was two hundred seventy miles from

Paris— about four and half hours' drive. With the European Union's open borders, they didn't expect any problems with crossing into Germany and reaching the US Military base at Kaiserslautern from where the equipment would be flown out to the US.

Their next big issue was what to do with the captives. They couldn't smuggle them out of the country, and they couldn't just abandon them. But even more of a problem was, what happened to those people who were evacuated in the days leading up to Operation Rock Concert? Who took them? Where were they taken? And adding to their already throbbing headache was learning from the "normals" that some of the equipment was evacuated with the people two days ago.

The problem was they couldn't start a manhunt for them in Europe, or anywhere for that matter, without divulging the background information about the Paris operation.

This situation presented the potential mother of all lose ends and the father of all diplomatic catastrophes.

Eventually, after much deliberation with the NSC members, it was decided that there was no way around it— President Grant and the Secretary of State, Constance Pierce, had to pay an urgent visit to the French President.

The personal call from President Grant came through five hours into their flight from back from Lima to D.C.

When the call ended, Constance let out a few very unladylike expletives, looked at Sean, and said, "You guys really know how to stir up shit properly, don't you?"

At Sean's inquisitive look, Connie explained. All Sean could say was, "I'm sorry, ma'am, ah… Constance. I'll be more than happy to go with you if I can be of any use."

She just smiled. "Thanks, Sean, I appreciate that, but

what we need now are people who can talk their way out of trouble, not shoot their way out. But trust me, if I need anyone shot, I'll be on the phone to you immediately."

Grant was waiting for her on the tarmac when they landed, and they were immediately escorted to the waiting Airforce One.

Neither of them were looking forward to the meeting with the French President and his advisors.

When Airforce One reached cruising altitude, President Grant got hold of Bill and told him he had seven hours to get himself and his men and Simone out of France and into the UK before Airforce One landed in Paris. Once in the UK, MI6 would take care of them and escort them to RAF Lakenheath, from where they would be airlifted back to the US.

"Bill, don't worry about Ms. Bouvier. I know you well enough to know there's more than just a professional relationship between the two of you. You can let her know we'll not throw her under the bus. Constance and I'll be discussing her situation with President Robichaux. And if we can't get the necessary guarantees from them, we'll take care of her—US citizenship and a job if that's what she wants."

"Thank you, Sam." Bill sighed in relief. "I'm grateful for that. I'll pass the message on to her."

When the call ended, Bill walked over to Simone, sat down next to her, and told her about the call with Grant, his instructions for them to move out, and his offer to protect her.

She stared out into middle space for a long while before she spoke. "I knew what I let myself into when I agreed to help you. Now that it's over, even with the wisdom of hindsight, there's nothing I would've done different.

"I love my country, and it is that which kept me from marrying you forty years ago and going to America with you. I still love my country, and what I did here was as much as anything I ever did to protect my country. If my President can't see that and acknowledge I was acting in the interest of France, then so be it.

"Of course, I would prefer to not be labeled a traitor by my own people, but if I'm to be persecuted by them for doing the right thing, then I'd prefer not to stay in France. "

Bill took her hand and looked her in the eyes. "Simone, let's not put the cart before the horse. President Grant is an old and loyal friend of mine, and he gave me his word. I'm confident he's not going to drop the ball.

"We've got very little time to wrap things up here, but before we do, let me just say this. I want to spend the rest of my life with you. Whether that's in France or America, I don't care, as long as I can be with you from now on."

Simone wiped the tears from her eyes and said, "And that's exactly how I feel."

Bill got up from the couch and called the team together to plan their withdrawal.

By the time, Airforce One touched down in Paris, Grant had the assurance that the stash of equipment removed by Bill and his team were already en route to D.C. That was one less thing to worry about. He and Constance agreed it was best not to volunteer any information about the removal of the equipment unless the French brought it up.

President Robichaux of France was visibly cranky when they sat down for the meeting. The US ambassador had given him very little information about the Nabateans, but it was enough to infuriate him that he was not informed months earlier. After his meeting with Robichaux, the ambassador called and informed President Grant what to expect.

Robichaux welcomed them curtly and got right down to business. "I take it this has to do with the Nabateans, which your ambassador told me about earlier?"

Grant nodded, but before he could say anything, Robichaux continued.

"As a NATO member and ally and supporter of the US for many years, I have to place on record my disappointment about being kept in the dark about this until now."

Grant held his hand up and started with an apology and then asked Robichaux to allow him to explain and give him the full picture.

At times, they spoke to each other in raised tones, and at times they managed to allow a grin and even a smile to decorate their otherwise grim-looking faces.

Grant and Constance operated like cogs in a Swiss watch.

Within the first half hour of the meeting Grant had told him about the unauthorized and totally illegal raid on Graziella's mansion and the underground facility but managed to explain about the urgency and timing. It took some nifty footwork from both Grant and Constance to placate Robichaux after that revelation.

But in the end, they got him over the line as he accepted part of the blame for his security agencies' ineptness for never knowing this was happening right under their noses for so many years. It was embarrassing, and he had the courage to admit it.

He immediately issued orders to the Chief of Police to

take everyone at Graziella's house into custody and report back to him.

It took another almost four hours before they convinced President Robichaux everything was still good between the USA and France and that this operation was in the best interest of both countries. Grant had to throw in a few guarantees that all information, technologies, and advancements gained from the Nabateans would be shared with France and other close allies.

Robichaux didn't mention anything about the equipment removed from French soil. He must have believed them when they told him the equipment had been moved with the people who were evacuated before the US team arrived.

In the end, Robichaux was gracious enough to thank Grant for saving France and the world from the Nabatean tyranny through their timely actions.

After this, Robichaux was looking around the room asking if there were any other questions or comments when Grant cleared his throat and said he had one more small matter.

Robichaux grinned. "Why do I feel it's not going to be such a small matter?"

Grant chuckled. "After what I put you through the past four hours, I don't blame you, Pierre." He continued and explained Simone Bouvier's role in the operation.

When Robichaux heard what Grant had to say, he was annoyed and on his high horse again. But only for a minute or two when the reality of it all dawned on him, and he had to admit to himself that was it not for Simone's help, things would not have turned out as positive as they did.

He leaned back and said, "As far as I am concerned,

Simone Bouvier played a vital role in all of this, and I'm proud of her. No charges will be brought against her.

"I'm going to issue an order that her involvement be kept a secret. However, by my calculation, she should be very close to retirement, and I'm going to recommend she is placed on paid leave for the remainder of her time."

A very tired but relieved President Grant and Secretary of State thanked Robichaux, shook hands with him and his advisors, and were escorted back to Airforce One.

Chapter One Hundred Four
THE ONE YOU SHOULD WORRY ABOUT

The return home of each of the diplomatic missions and all the agents and operatives were not as coordinated as their departures had been. On a case-by-case basis, some were needed for ongoing investigations and round-up of the now leaderless Nabatean network. Several of the diplomats were invited to stay and be feted for their timely assistance with a terrorist threat. Others returned immediately with transcripts and recordings of the councilors' initial interrogations.

Now that the Nabateans were in custody, business could be discussed over the "old" secured phones again. So, Grant could talk to his counterparts at any time it was necessary. The world-wide joint operation gave him an opening to suggest more frequent and more open discussions, which he hoped would make for a more secure world.

In the aftermath of the raids across the globe, Carter and James continued to extract information from Sullivan. Now that they had more information gathered during the raids, there were a lot more questions.

Sullivan was cooperating voluntarily. He remained their best source of information in the short term, until they had time to study the information coming in from the captured Nabatean councilors and the quantum computers.

Sullivan's psyche was a paradox. On the one hand, he was recalling and producing information with the accuracy of a computer. His memory for detail seemed limitless, and the verifiable facts were accurate.

On the other hand, he was keeping up his delusion that he was the emissary of King Rabbel II Soter.

A psychiatrist who observed him assured them it was Sullivan's reality—as real as everything was real for Carter and the others.

Was he certifiably insane? Probably yes.

In his current state, he was not fit to stand trial. But that was not something anyone worried about for the time being. For the moment, he was a fountain of information, and that was what was important.

Shock after shock rolled over the interrogation team as Sullivan unpacked everything he knew about his bloodline, the people they controlled, the missions and assassinations. Perhaps worst of all was the deliberate creation of autistic savants. Carter had known the Nabateans had lost their humanity, but that part made him physically ill.

Everything was carefully recorded and videotaped. A few vetted CIA and FBI analysts were brought in to review those recordings, take notes, and launch operations to apprehend the remaining traitors, many of whom were high-ranking officials throughout most of the various government departments.

Sullivan never once even alluded to the fact that he was one of the bad guys— as much to blame for their actions as they were.

He showed no remorse at all for all the killings and lives ruined.

In fact, his account to Carter was that of an independent witness to all of it.

Over time, it came out that Sullivan had chosen Carter because most of the Council of the Nabateans, although they hated him with a passion, surreptitiously believed that he was somehow invincible.

Sullivan firmly believed there was only one person alive who could keep him safe from his bloodline members, a curious anomaly in his worldview, in which he was simultaneously a council member and an independent and omniscient observer with no ties to those evil people.

With the French President on board and the help of the UK government, the rest of the European governments were all briefed in detail about the Nabateans and their cooperation secured in the hunt for the missing group of savants and their equipment.

Every government who became privy to the Nabatean information immediately understood the urgency and instructed their law enforcement and security agencies to give the apprehension of the fugitives the highest priority.

In an unprecedented demonstration of collaboration and information exchange, the group was tracked down to a warehouse in Naples, Italy, within four days. They were taken from Graziella's house seven days before and transported with busses to the warehouse complex in Naples. For the fifty savants, it was the first time they saw the world outside. Reality was something very different from what they experienced by watching TV—it scared and upset most of them. The "normals" in charge of them had a very hard time controlling them, and in the end resorted to lacing their food and drinks with strong sedatives.

By day seven, the group was in tatters—hungry, penniless, cold, leaderless, and desperate when no one had turned up to take them to their next location. Two of the "normals" left the warehouse and went in search of help.

The two men, who had very little social skills and were not streetwise at all, were soon mugged and left bleeding on the street when their assailants found nothing of value on them. The police found them and questioned them and quickly realized what they had stumbled upon.

The message went up the chain of command to the Italian Chief of Police, who informed the Prime Minister. They had been warned not to approach the group under any circumstances. Bill made sure the message that went out to the law enforcement agencies of every country participating in the operation had put the fear of God into them. His message made it clear this group was extremely dangerous, they had advanced technology to protect themselves—no one but the CIA had the means to defeat it. Therefore, a US task force with proper equipment was flown in from the US and put on standby in one of US military bases in Germany to be deployed for the operation to apprehend the group when their location became known.

Within four hours of receiving the Italian Prime Minister's call, the operation was over. The group of fifty savants and five "normals" were in Italian police custody, and the equipment was on a US plane en route to a US military base in Germany, from where it would be flown to the US.

In D.C., President Grant and Bill let out a long sigh of relief when they got the report from the task force leader. There was only one lose end to tie up.

The Russians still didn't want to play ball—they didn't want to swap Mathieu Nabati for the nine Spetsnaz troops. The Russian President made it clear he had no use for them, and arrogantly, also indicated he had little use for a more open relationship with the US, or anyone else in the US orbit.

Grant wanted to tie up that remaining loose end. When he started hinting to the Russian President about important information he could share, President Kolenikov blew a gasket.

"You've been dishonest with me? Why are you hiding things? Why did you not give all information when we allowed your people to go on the raid to capture Nabati? Do you think I'm a fool?"

But Bill had before the video conference pointed out to Grant that the information Dylan swiped from Mathieu Nabati's electronic devices, plus the information in Graziella's head and the heads of the others alive and in custody in the other countries, along with the information gathered from all their computers and the IT center in Paris, and the equipment captured during the raid on the warehouse in Naples, would include everything Mathieu knew and more. So, it was not worth groveling to get him. "Let the Russian President shove Mathieu Nabati up his ass if he'd liked that," was Bill's advice.

Grant smiled into the camera, a big smile that must

have made Kolenikov wonder what he'd missed. "Do yourself a big favor, *Comrade*. Ask Mathieu Nabati to tell you the name of the twelfth councilor."

Kolenikov's smug expression turned to confusion. "But, there were only eleven and eleven are accounted for. What do you mean?"

"That's the thing. There were twelve. And number twelve is the one *you* should worry about." Grant smiled even bigger as he ended the call.

Chapter One Hundred Five

THREE MONTHS LATER

It was June 15 when the Devereuxs, with their family and a few other Freydís residents, boarded Carter's Desault Falcon 7X and headed home. It had been three months since the Ides of March, that fateful day, when Carter and Mackenzie landed in D.C. and were taken in by special agent Kelly White for questioning. As they all settled in for the flight, they couldn't help but reflect on the events of the past three months.

The quantum computers, captured during the raid on Graziella's house, contained not only the information about how the antimatter bombs were manufactured but also the exact location of the bombs in D.C. and New York. It was spine-chilling to learn what devastation those bombs would have caused were they to explode.

The information about the technology of how the bombs were constructed was one of those pieces of information the US had to share with France.

The global operations wrap up was going to take months, if not years. Carter's constant presence wasn't needed anymore. Sullivan had been wrung dry and afterward lapsed into a vegetative state. He was expected to remain in an institution the rest of his life. His wife had initiated divorce proceedings and left the D.C. area.

Others would handle the investigation in the US, and each country would handle their own to determine the fate of the prisoners they held.

Except for the council member in China, of whom they'd heard nothing before or since the second one was presumed dead, and the one in Saudi Arabia, it could literally take years for them to be fully investigated and brought to trial. Those in the know expected the Saudi investigation to take less than a month before the entire network was rooted out. A perfunctory trial would be held, and then public beheadings would begin.

In Russia, Igor Ustinov has disappeared, and no amount of speculation and questioning produced an answer—he was either dead or in prison. Very few people would ever know.

There was a lot of information to work through, and then some of it would require new policies and laws to be enacted. The savant program would be dismantled, of course. What to do with the souls involved, especially those who couldn't take care of themselves in even a minimal way, would have to be worked out. Numerous countries were involved, and negotiations to form a joint response were already underway.

Carter supposed that some benefit might come of it. The Nabateans had studied autism in deeper detail than anyone else to date. Maybe that information could help in preventing the worst forms of it. He still felt sick to his stomach whenever he thought of the lives ruined by Nabatean experiments on fetuses. Only brilliantly focused savants had been found in their facilities. What happened to the failures? So far, none of the detainees would say, but the implication was reprehensible.

Other revelations about medical science were as spine-chilling and as enraging. They'd had the cures for several types of cancer for decades. How many lives had been lost because they hoarded that knowledge for themselves? There was more. It would take more years to explore it all.

The QIT project, on the other hand, would be sped up now they had the Nabateans' own plans for quantum computing and communications devices. The scientists involved were already drunk with the abundance of new data.

Carter's role would again be to facilitate and optimize translations of the new library, as well as continuing and interpreting research on the A- and E-Codices. It could be the work of a lifetime, unless he decided to delegate his leadership and hunt down other archaeological mysteries. For now, he was content to stay home for a while, enjoy the kids and his friends, and be thankful he wasn't languishing in a federal prison.

With Sean's and Dylan's influence, McCormick was promised a deal for his testimony against the Nabateans who would be tried in the US. He could accept a sort of house arrest for five years on Jared's alpaca ranch—compensated by room and board only, or he could go to jail.

Jared was willing to cooperate, and McCormick admitted he couldn't expect anything better. Or as good, if the truth be known. He'd come to love the fresh Rocky Mountain air. He had just one question before he decided, though. Would Kelly White know where to find him? If so, he'd take his chances in prison.

Kelly, too, had a decision to make. Unbeknownst to her,

Carter and Mackenzie, accompanied by Sean and Dylan, intervened on her behalf with General Fleming. He was still teed off with her and wanted to throw the book at her.

But the pleas of the four swayed him to change his mind, and he agreed not to bring her up on charges, and that she could stay on as an investigator.

However, her service record would be notated—she would never again be entrusted with an investigation as the lead.

When Kelly heard the news, she decided to take a long leave and think about life. She'd been cured of the ambition to become the first woman in charge of INSCOM, and for her, it would never happen anyway. Maybe it was time to leave the Army and find a good man.

The Intelligence Committee hearings never reconvened. News of the world-wide roundup of an uber-conspiracy group outdid any questions about why Carter and Mackenzie, along with A-Echelon, were being let off the hook. Davis announced her retirement at the end of her current term.

President Grant, Bill, and James were also planning their retirement. Grant's would occur upon the inauguration of a new President. His party now had a substantial lead over the opposition. The three men discovered a mutual fascination with deep-sea fishing and were looking forward to a trip off the coast of Baja California the following spring.

Bill and Simone had it all worked out. They set a date for their wedding and agreed to live six months of the year in France and six months in the US.

Irene was tasked with determining the future direction of A-Echelon. Whether they could continue to be effective now that they no longer operated in the shadows, or a new organization with a similar goal would be formed was up to her. Either way, she was to lead it.

However, Carter and Mackenzie made it clear to her that they had, for now, seen enough operational duty. They'd be involved only behind a desk or in a lab, and preferably all of it from Freydís. At least that's what Carter said.

Mackenzie smiled fondly when she heard Carter saying that. Her husband was not the type to stay behind a desk for long. Not if there was still so much of the past to be unearthed.

Sean called Freydís home because Freydís was where Sam was. He had a serious question to ask her after their three-month separation.

Liu and Dylan couldn't get back to their Freydís cabin soon enough. They'd taken the back seats, so they could canoodle in relative privacy.

Mackenzie, in the co-pilot's seat, told Carter she'd probably be helping to plan a wedding, maybe two, by looks of it, on Freydís within the next few weeks. The kids and Mackenzie's parents all went to sleep as soon as they were in the air. It would be a peaceful and uneventful flight home.

"What will you do when you get home, Mackie? Now that all the excitement is over," Carter amended.

"Oh, it isn't over," she answered. "I've never stopped being excited about the respirocyte research. Just had to put it on the back burner. I think it's time to get back to it, especially now that I have access to even more research material. I owe it to the world, don't you agree?"

"Mackie, as long as we're together, you have my complete agreement on whatever you want to do. But yes, I think it's high time to get that project back on track and deliver."

Next in the Carter Devereux Mystery Thriller Series

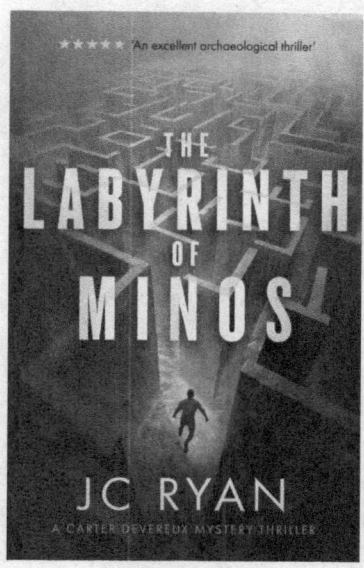

vinci-books.com/labyrinth-minos

A child-killing spree in London. Abducted children in Greece. Can Carter Devereux save his family before it's too late?

Carter Devereux, an expert on the Nabatean society, joins MI5 to investigate a child-killing spree in London. But when his own children are abducted in Greece, the case becomes personal. Suspecting a connection, Carter and his friends race to unravel the mystery and rescue his family. As they navigate a labyrinth of clues, an ancient and deadly threat emerges.

Turn the page for a free preview…

The Labyrinth of Minos: Chapter One

It was early on a crisp but sunny September morning. Carter and Mackenzie were out on the deck of their log home on their idyllic Quebecois ranch, Freydis, each with a mug of steaming coffee in hand. Their children, Liam, almost nine years old, and Beth, just turned five, together with the five other kids making up the scholars of the Freydis homeschool were out on a field trip. They were under the watchful eyes of Steve Anderson, Mackenzie's dad, an ex-science teacher, and Carter's old friend Ahote. It would be their last fishing expedition of the year before winter would arrive.

The children had begged to go and see the new wolf pups as part of the field trip. Keeva had given birth about two weeks ago but had finally come out of hiding and showed the small litter, only two pups, to Mackenzie. Loki, Keeva's mate, kept them close to the den, though. Mackenzie wanted the children to meet the pups as well, but Beth and one of the other children were a bit of a handful, and the pups too young to be manhandled.

Mackenzie would trust her life to the wolves, whose special connection to her had once given her the strength to carry on in the face of the darkest days of her life. To Carter and other observers, this relationship between Mackenzie and the majestic animals could only be described as mystifying, incomprehensible, something akin to telepathy.

Mackenzie, though, knew that wild animals could revert to their natural behavior in a fraction of a second if their instincts were triggered, especially when their young were threatened. The pups would have to be older, or Beth more settled, before it would be a good idea to introduce them. And then she hoped the wolf pups would develop as strong a connection with her own young as their parents had with her. Carter agreed with her reasoning.

"Let's wait for Keeva to bring the pups to us when she's ready," she'd suggested to them. Though disappointed, the children knew that tone of voice. It meant no arguing.

So, instead of accompanying the kids on their field trip, Carter and Mackenzie were taking the rare moment by themselves to discuss their projects. They'd moved from the kitchen, where the family breakfast had created a mess neither wanted to tackle right then, to the deck. Carter set his mug down and leaned across the table to hold his wife's hand. Her fiery hair shone in the golden morning sun, and he counted his blessings for the millionth time since he'd engineered their meeting on campus more than a decade ago.

It had been a few months since they'd wrapped up their last mission for A-Echelon, a top-secret arm of the CIA. They'd both been recruited to the agency, whose mission was to investigate ancient mysteries for any truth that could be exploited in the interest of national security for the US and her allies. Carter, an archaeologist of mixed but growing repute at the time, and Mackenzie, a molecular biologist, had met on the campus of the university where they both taught.

His involvement with A-Echelon came first, when he was recruited by his grandfather's handler, James Rhodes, now recently retired as head of the agency. Mackenzie's had come later, when her exploration of ancient medicine in search for modern applications caught the attention of James Rhodes during one of his visits to Freydis. At the time, James was the deputy director of A-Echelon, and when he saw what she had uncovered and the potential it held, immediately convinced his director, Hunter Patrick, that Mackenzie had to be recruited.

Carter's last two missions had involved both of them, which meant Mackenzie's research project had to go on the back burner. Now, with the Nabatean secret society defeated and all of them who were not dead in custody, Mackenzie and Carter needed to discuss what had to be done to get her research project back on track. Mackenzie every now and then said she was eager to get back to it, and she was also regularly prompted by the new Director of A-Echelon, James Rhodes's replacement, Irene O'Connell, to resume the work. But for some reason or another she seemed to be dragging her feet to make a start.

It was about three months since they had returned to Freydis after a harrowing experience with the malevolent members of the Council of the Covenant of Nabatea, as well as the shady character of Russell McCormick, Assistant Director of the Counterintelligence Division of the FBI, and Kelly White, a misguided Counterintelligence Special Agent in the US Army Intelligence and Security Command, INSCOM. The actions of those two succeeded not only in turning President Grant and Bill Griffin, Director of the

CIA, both of whom had always been very loyal and supportive, against them, but very nearly landed Carter and Mackenzie in jail. Fortunately, with the help of their trusted friends of Executive Advantage, Sean Walker and Dylan Mulligan, the charges leveled against the Devereuxs by McCormick and White were short-lived, and they could proceed to smoke out the Nabateans and stop them from a power-grab which would have had ghastly consequences.

The whole nightmare started on March 15 and ended only three months later. No wonder Carter and Mackenzie were taking their time to enjoy the peace and tranquility of Freydis and spend every moment they could with their children, family, and friends.

Upon their return to Freydis in June, Carter immediately got busy with reorganizing and managing the translation work on the Library of the Giants and starting work on the newly acquired Library of the Nabateans, which he and his team had unearthed in Matera, Italy. He had to hire more translators, procure more computer equipment, and oversee construction of more offices and accommodation for the ever-increasing number of people working and living on Freydis.

Freydis, the ranch Carter's late grandfather, Will Devereux had willed to him, had once been a rustic place with a single log cabin and Ahote and Bly's smaller cabin a mile or so away. Over the past two years, however, it had become a thriving little village with close to thirty people calling it home these days.

For some time, Carter had sensed that Mackenzie had settled back into the Freydis rhythm, and that she was back in the emotional space where he could broach the subject of restarting her research, yet he also sensed some hesitation on her part.

"Mackie," Carter said, "I have been getting the impression lately that you've been wanting to get back to your research, but something is holding you back. Right?"

She smiled and looked at him. "You know me too well, Carter. Not that it's a bad thing, though. I like it. And yes, I am sort of ready to take it up again."

"So, what is it that's holding you back?"

"The children on the one hand," she said. "I've been away from them so much. Someone needs to tame Beth, and even a boy Liam's age needs his mother. On the other hand, I have to admit, I'm a bit scared as well..." she paused for a moment.

Carter started to ask a question, but she held her hand up. "I'm the one who talked you out of leaving A-Echelon after you rescued us from that hell-hole in Saudi Arabia. I'm the one who told you we can't back down, but you know what scares me when I look back over the past few years? It's as if when you and I touch anything from ancient times, there is an evil force just waiting to destroy us."

Carter nodded in silence. Those were thoughts that had passed through his mind often. He didn't interrupt her.

"The children and I have fallen into the hands of bad people, our family was attacked and almost killed here on Freydis, you and I almost landed in jail not long ago, assassins were hired to kill us in Italy...

"How many more times will we escape the evil forces bent on terminating us? That's what's worrying me and holding me back. My respirocyte research has already gotten me and the children locked up, and it almost destroyed Liu's life as well. We also know the Nabateans wanted to get their hands on my research work, and they were more than happy to kill us in the process.

"I'm convinced I'll find what I've been looking for in

one of those libraries, or a lead to it. The question is, at what price?"

Carter took Mackenzie's hand again and said. "I know Mackie. It's as if we're tempting fate every time we set out to investigate – as if we stir up a hornets' nest – but as far as we know you're the most knowledgeable person in the world about the concept of respirocytes in ancient times. There is no one else with access to the information you have available in those ancient libraries."

Mackenzie nodded and started smiling. "Yep, I know all of that, and I'm not going to hand over my work to anyone. I have to maintain what control I can over it. I'm going to finish what I started. I just wanted to tell you what's been troubling me."

At first Carter was stumped by her response. Then he started laughing. "Now that's my Mackie. For a moment there I thought you were trying to tell me you wanted out. See, I don't know you as well as you alleged earlier."

She grinned. "Well, at least you know enough to see when something is bothering me. So, now that my psychoanalysis is complete, and you know what's going on in my mind, I guess we need to start planning how to get my project kickstarted again?"

Before they'd gone much further in their discussion, they were interrupted. Carter was needed at the translation building, where a team of translators worked around the clock to extract the information about ground-breaking science contained in the ancient libraries of the Giants.

Mackenzie gave in to the inevitable and went to clean the train wreck she'd made of the kitchen earlier. She didn't mind cooking every now and then, but it was definitely not one of her favorite activities. She did her part in the kitchen when she had to but made sure to keep her dishes quick and simple. If the recipe said it would take more than fifteen minutes to prepare, she'd usually start looking for another one.

After seeing to the needs of the translation team, instead of using one of the electric carts, Carter decided to walk the two miles to the Executive Advantage training facility, Camp Tala. He loved the exercise, and besides, he needed some time to think. The name Tala, the Sioux word for wolf, was James Rhodes's idea, passionately supported by Mackenzie, of course. Originally, the name had been selected because of the relationship Mackenzie and the people of Freydis had with the wolves on the ranch. However, the name took on a new meaning when, a few days after the construction of the camp started, the entire wolf pack turned up at the site as if they were reporting for duty.

It turned out that was exactly what they did, reported for duty. At least the six young ones did. They seemed to be all very keen to be enrolled in an Executive Advantage training program conducted by one of the members, John Ruschin, who was an experienced military dog handler. Soon, six of the young wolves were trained as military "dogs" and they certainly showed their mettle when they were instrumental in protecting the inhabitants of Freydis against a murderous attack by a group of ex-Russian Spetsnaz mercenaries, hired by the Council of the Covenant of Nabatea.

Carter used the time he was walking to think about how fast his son was growing up, and what he wanted to teach him. Liam already showed signs of intellectual brilliance. His time as a prisoner in Saudi Arabia with his mother had given him a sweet bond with her and his little sister, and as a result he was almost as protective of them as Mackie was of him.

Carter wasn't jealous of the connection, but he needed one of his own to develop, and his frequent absences from the ranch made it difficult to establish more than the normal father-son relationship. He knew that to guide a brilliant child in emotional intelligence would require more than that.

Grab your copy...
vinci-books.com/labyrinth-minos

About the Author

JC Ryan is a bestselling author renowned for his intricate espionage, archaeological thrillers, and conspiracy mysteries. With over 30 acclaimed novels, including the popular Rex Dalton K9 Thrillers, Rossler Foundation Mysteries, and Carter Devereux Mystery Thrillers, Ryan has captivated readers around the globe.

Drawing from his diverse professional background—as a military officer, lawyer, and IT manager—Ryan creates compelling narratives that skillfully blend historical accuracy with thrilling adventure. He is celebrated as a master storyteller, known for crafting riveting plots, meticulous historical details, and engaging, multidimensional characters. Ryan's meticulous research lends authenticity and depth to each story, immersing readers in richly constructed worlds filled with intrigue, suspense, and adventure.

Fans of David Baldacci, Lee Child's Jack Reacher, Tom Clancy's Jack Ryan, Nelson DeMille's John Corey, Vince Flynn's Mitch Rapp, Mark Greaney's Gray Man, Gregg Hurwitz's Orphan X, Robert Ludlum's Jason Bourne, Daniel Silva's Gabriel Allon, Brad Taylor's Pike Logan, Brad Thor's Scot Harvath, James Rollins' Sigma Force, Steve Berry's Cotton Malone, and Dan Brown's Robert Langdon will find JC Ryan's novels equally compelling and unforgettable.

When not writing, Ryan enjoys spending time with his college sweetheart, whom he married in 1978. They are proud parents of two daughters, have two sons-in-law, and are grandparents to two grandchildren.